DAUGHTERS OF THE LAKE

JANE RIDDELL

By Jane Riddell

Cover Art: Lisa Firth

Copyright © 2021 Jane Riddell

To my father, who encouraged me to write

1

Portia surveyed the playroom of her childhood home. Nothing had changed: the oak bookcases, the dressing up box that Dad had assembled one stormy afternoon. Even the whiteboard, where they wrote their "thought for the day", remained on the wall, several partially erased messages in red and purple pens bearing testimony to its regular use. How would her family would react if she wrote: *Bad idea coming to Switzerland. Should have stayed in London*?

She closed the door, leant against it briefly, then wandered into the private sitting room. There were more changes here. The green and wine striped sofa and matching armchairs were new. So was the rug. On the sideboard lay a tea tray with the customary crockery and a bundle of flimsy Japanese paper napkins. Beside it, two stands displayed cakes on silver doilies.

Her eye rested on the corner walnut bureau, focused on the visitor's book, and she made herself open it, read the names of attendees at Dad's funeral. The leather felt comforting, but its smell, not sufficiently cured to conceal its origins, evoked an involuntary swallow. It didn't seem like five years since they'd surrounded his chrysanthemum-bedecked coffin at the graveyard. Since she'd tolerated the incessant handshaking, mourners addressing her mother as "Frau Fontana" despite having known her for years. Bereavement was supposed to bond families. Not theirs. Was this why Mum had summoned them back?

She flicked through the pages of tributes to her father. On the last page were the immediate family's signatures. She read down the list – her siblings first: Annie's forward slanting, open writing, with a smudge beside it, as if a tear had landed on the page as she wrote; Lawrence's large, plain style and Vienne's smaller, tighter script. With a constricting of her chest, she then studied Elliot's calligraphic style – ironic that someone so scruffy as her ex could have sophisticated handwriting.

Everyone's signature was there except Lucy's.

It had felt inappropriate to be relieved about the funeral being a week after term began. To so easily justify Lucy's remaining at school, where the housemistress would keep an eye on her in case she became distressed by Papa's death. Inappropriate but understandable, certainly. With Lucy in Brunnen, Portia would constantly have been on tenterhooks.

Portia closed the book and wandered over to the window. Halfway down the lake, boats with candy striped sails whizzed across the water, turned and tacked back in the easterly breeze. Such freedom. In the garden, Herr Huber was flinging weeds into a bucket which pinged as stone hit metal. Beside him lay a basket of coral and red roses, probably destined for a table centre this evening.

She helped herself to tea from the sideboard, wishing

she could have the room to herself for longer. As the door opened, she stood to attention.

'Portia,' Vienne said, hesitating before hugging her and flopping into an armchair. 'I hate early starts.'

Vienne's habitual rosewater scent lingered on Portia's neck. I'm your sister, it said. *Remember?*

'How was your flight, Vienne?'

'You'd think with all my travelling I'd be relaxed about flying now. How long's it been since we saw each other?'

Portia tugged at a loose thread on her trouser seam. 'That charity concert.'

The evening when her past caught up with her.

Annie would be down soon, Mum too, hopefully. The walls of the spacious sitting room were closing in. Involuntarily she searched her bag for her Kalms, clutched the scuffed packet, ran her finger over the raised lettering: *relieves stress and irritability*. Apart from one tablet, hastily swallowed before a gruelling court session, the blister pack remained intact. Just carrying them round worked. Normally.

'Mum said you're playing in Prague.'

Vienne shuddered. 'Schumann. I'm frightfully nervous.'

'I read somewhere that if you lose your stage fright you don't perform so well,' Portia said.

This was what she needed to do: keep the conversation trundling along. Vienne's career was a safe topic, and they could compare notes: a barrister's work was often likened to a performance – a dramatic act requiring eloquence, clarity, supreme confidence.

What had happened to Mum? Had she become entangled with a guest? A problem in the kitchen? Hopefully someone else would turn up soon.

Vienne tugged at the fine gold chain which gleamed

against a flawless neck – she must use expensive creams. Portia ran a finger over her own neck, felt a fold of skin move.

'What a stupid row we had,' Vienne said. 'The number of times I picked up the phone to call you–'

'Have you heard from Lawrence?' Portia asked.

Vienne looked startled.

Portia softened her tone. 'Is he coming over or not?'

'Portia, why haven't we sorted things properly? We both live in London. Maybe this reunion of Mum's will give us time to talk. Then we can see each other more often at home.'

Reunion – the act of uniting again. An island in the Indian Ocean, east of Madagascar. Same word in French, with an accent on the "e". Portia fingered the hole in her trousers from the removed thread.

'And you must get lonely, with Elliot not around,' Vienne added.

Lonely. Not a word Portia normally associated with herself. Only with others – elderly widows and bachelors, those who spent hours gardening. Characters in Anita Brookner novels – middle-class, affluent protagonists (inherited wealth, of course) struggling to find enough activities to fill their days – they were particularly lonely. This was why she'd stopped reading Brookner. All this angst about solitude.... Portia wanted to make these spinsters – who invariably suffered from unrequited love – join a gym or do voluntary work or even find a job, instead of waiting for the phone to ring, with an indifferent invitation to dinner. Vienne loved Anita Brookner.

Was Mum lonely or did running a hotel fill her time? There was always something requiring attention. Always had been. As a child, Portia remembered the family settling to watch a film, then a member of staff would knock on the door. Her parents would exchange glances before one of them answered. Until Dad insisted on protected family time.

She stared out of the window. Herr Huber had now disappeared, but not before placing a couple of loungers on the grass. How blissful it would be to lie on one, sun on her face, a faint breeze preventing her from overheating. Even better to be on the lake. To take a paddle steamer to the southernmost point of the Urnersee, then the cable car into the Eggeberg mountains. She could smell the mountain air, its promise to whisk away her anxiety, obliterate her lethargy.

Vienne was speaking. 'Portia?' Her tone not actually pleading, more like a request.

'I'm sorry I lost my temper when we argued that day,' Portia said.

But this wouldn't satisfy Vienne. Compared to some, Portia didn't have a temper. No, her intimidating factor – apart from her height – was a whiplash tongue. Newly qualified lawyers were warned when they joined her Chambers. And however well they prepared, her pupils flinched when she appraised their court performances.

'I wish Mum had chosen the holidays for her reunion, then Lucy could be here,' Vienne said. 'Michael and I don't have plans for the summer yet. Let's all get together once term's finished.'

Portia opened her mouth to speak but her tongue stuck to her palate and a metallic taste lodged in her throat. This was ghastly. Perhaps she should play it safe, announce she'd been recalled to London because of the Zambian deportation or the Burmese case. Mum would be disappointed, but she wouldn't fuss.

Vienne's silence rebuked her as she awaited an answer;

the tick of the grandfather clock sounded menacing; the harbour horn suggested impatience.

Portia stared at her sister in her crisp white blouse and green skirt, glanced down at her own crushed linen trousers and unflattering blouse. So much heaving of weights at the gym, to no avail. She studied Vienne again: the heart-shaped face and large green eyes, her caramel brown hair loosely tied back with a velvet ribbon, concealing the scar on her temple – a legacy from falling when Dad taught her to skate.

'How is Lucy?' Vienne asked. 'She'll be in senior school now–'

'Senior two,' Portia said, more sharply than she'd intended. Lucy: thirteen, going on eighteen, going on eight.

'I often think of our time at school. I suppose it's changed a lot since then. More freedom. Is she happy there?'

Happy. Portia tried to remember whether she'd ever asked her daughter if she enjoyed school. Reports suggested Lucy did, certainly those relating to her first few years. Happy and doing well, they'd said. Last year's report, however, had been more critical: Lucy worked hard – most of the time – but was developing a temper; she was also more of a loner than the school would like. There'd been some loosely worded statement about monitoring the situation, though it wasn't clear if that referred to the temper problem or Lucy's social isolation. Both, probably.

Vienne retrieved her diary from her bag. 'Let's arrange for you to come to supper after Prague. Both of you. Michael will be down in a moment. We can check dates.'

Portia flushed and flicked a strand of hair behind her ear. Vienne was talking again. 'How is Annie keeping? When's the baby due?'

As Portia wondered how to reply, the door opened. Thank God, Annie. Vienne went over, then stood back to stare at her.

'Annie, I thought... I thought you were pregnant,' she said. Annie shook her head. 'Not as such.'

Vienne looked bemused, opened her mouth and closed it.

Portia glanced at Annie. Poor sweetheart, this was how everyone would react. Yet she could smile, tell Vienne she looked great. Perhaps she found it easier with Vienne who had no children. Sooner or later, Annie would probably explain that it was Ferne who was carrying their baby, that Ferne had left her.

Annie helped herself to coffee. 'Is Lawrence coming or not? Hilde doesn't know, Mum was vague.'

Portia shrugged. 'You know Lawrence.'

Vienne reached over to the coffee table, flicked through a newspaper and replaced it. 'I wish I'd worked harder to keep up my German.... You know, I haven't a clue what's going on with our family.'

She glided over to the window. Portia watched her, so petite, such flawless deportment, a petal drifting in the wind. If she'd been spared her adolescent bouts of labyrinthitis, Vienne would have completed ballet training and might well have become a famous dancer.

'I'm thinking of John Cleese's book – *Families and How to Survive Them*,' Annie said. 'First time I mentioned it to Ferne, I got the title wrong – *Families and How to Avoid Them*. We laughed ourselves stupid.' Annie was laughing now, and it didn't sound forced.

Vienne raised her neatly plucked eyebrows. 'Who's Ferne?'

'A friend of Annie's,' Portia said. Too quickly, she

realised, as Annie's expression conveyed she could answer for herself. Annie would survive. Her sweet façade was genuine enough but underneath she was deceptively resilient.

Vienne sighed. 'I haven't a clue what's going on.'

'So you keep reminding us,' Portia said.

She'd meant to be humorous, instead the comment sounded bitchy. Even her voice lacked control.

Portia turned to Annie. 'Are you okay?'

Annie wandered over to the sideboard. 'Have you tried the carrot cake? New recipe, Mum said.'

Portia could hear voices in the corridor, then Madalena opened the door. 'Ah, you're all here. It's so lovely to have you with me. Vienne, you look exhausted.'

'We were up at five,' Vienne said. 'We're not used to early starts, not having children to look after or hotels to run.'

Portia clicked her teeth at Vienne's comment: it wouldn't occur to her that Annie might be hurt by the casual remark about her childless state.

'What's happening with Lawrence?' Annie asked.

Portia stared at her younger sister. Although Annie's smile was fixed, her eyes now displayed a different emotion. It was the exaggerated upward thrust of her chin, however, which revealed how much she was struggling.

'He's arriving on Friday, I think,' Madalena said. 'Are your rooms okay?'

'Why so late?' Vienne asked.

As she noticed her mother's stoical expression, Portia shook her head. Her brother could have committed himself, this once.

'The conservatory looks wonderful, Mum,' Vienne said.

'Dad would have approved. Did you do all this all by yourself?'

'With help. Annie, is your room okay, dear?'

Annie nodded and gave the thumbs-up sign.

Madalena added sugar to her tea. 'Have you tried the cake?'

'It's delicious,' Vienne said. 'Thank God I never have to worry about my weight.'

Vienne seemed uncharacteristically chatty, obviously having looked forward to this get together for months, probably since the invitation arrived. Its formality had surprised Portia. *A Dinner to celebrate the 40th anniversary of the Hotel Zurbriggen. 1969 – 2009.* Thirty-six of these years with Dad. Her parents had worked hard, restoring the building to its Art Nouveau splendour, competing with other local hotels. Mum deserved to celebrate.

It wasn't unusual to arrange a special dinner but could there be more to the invitation? A chance for them all to be together? Something happening to the hotel? There were so many takeovers these days, big businesses devouring smaller ones. But the Zurbriggen wasn't small. Whatever was going on, she owed it to Madalena to be here in case she needed legal advice.

Vienne was quizzing Mum about the conservatory, insisting on a guided tour, which of course Madalena would be itching to give. Annie showed interest, too. Well, she would. Her garden mattered to her almost as much as her café.

Flowers were flowers, in Portia's opinion, necessitating a quick visit to the florist on the odd occasion she could summon the energy to invite friends for a meal. At least she'd been sensible enough to convert her small front garden to paving stones.

Her phone went. 'Portia Fontana.... What?!'

In her room, Portia adjusted the volume on her phone. 'I would have been mid-air then. What have you arranged?.... You never mentioned that.... What about your mother?.... Okay.... Yes, I'll call you back.'

She switched off her phone, sank into the soft, leather armchair by the bed and ran her hands through her hair. Five minutes in Brunnen and things were falling apart. It seemed unfair: she'd come here out of duty, making an effort, worrying about the hidden agenda in Mum's invitation. She'd been prepared to tolerate her discomfort with Vienne, in order to do the right thing. But this wasn't the real issue, she knew. This was yet another situation where, once more, she was paying a price for her past behaviour.

A knock on the door and Annie entered the room. 'You look like shit, Portia.'

Annie lay on the spare bed, put her hands behind her head. 'So, what's going on? Everyone's wondering why you didn't return after your call. Michael came down and Mum produced more cake and there's talk of a walk along the waterfront before dinner, if the rain holds off.... Who called you?'

'Elliot.'

'And? Lucy's okay, isn't she?'

'Depends whether or not you'd describe being expelled as okay.'

Annie sat up. 'Expelled? You're winding me up.... You're not. Why?'

'She set fire to someone's writing case.'

'Oh my God!'

Portia sighed. 'The school contacted Elliot this morning.'

'So, he's gone to collect her?'

'He drove to Harrogate this morning – to speak to the

school. He's taken Lucy to his mother's, but he's off to Boston. I can't believe this is happening. I know Lucy can be volatile – you've seen her in a strop, but to be e*xpelled*....'

And it was the first time Maureen wasn't able to help. Portia was lucky to have remained friends with her former mother-in-law. Of course, if she knew the true circumstances of the divorce, things would be different.

'Bring Lucy here. Madalena would love it, and Vienne's been banging on about seeing more of her.'

'Impossible,' Portia said.

'I don't understand. Just book her on a flight. I'll do it if you want.'

'It's complicated,' Portia said, standing, stretching. Already her shoulder muscles ached. If only she could flee. It would be lovely to be at home. Safe.

'It needn't be. I'll sort it out.'

Portia paced the room.

'Vienne's right,' Annie continued. 'You can't drop the barrister act.'

'Lucy's last report said she was developing a temper and becoming a bit of a loner. I should have spoken to the school then. But there was too much going on at work.'

Annie frowned. 'She seemed fine when I visited her in May. Bring her out here. She should be with you.'

'There are things you don't know.'

Annie's eyes opened in mock horror. 'What things?'

Portia sat down. 'I can't tell you. Don't look so anxious, it's nothing about Madalena.'

There was silence again, then, as if emerging from a trance, Annie glanced at her watch. 'I want to have a snooze before dinner.' She dropped a kiss on Portia's head. 'We'll talk again – soon. Boy oh boy – what a mess we're both in.'

Portia listened to Annie's canvas shoes padding along

the corridor, then she leant back in the armchair, raised her head to the ceiling and drummed her chin with her fingers. Outside she heard a lawn mower. She could smell cooking – something fishy. But she doubted she'd be able to eat.

She racked her brains for a solution, for someone to look after Lucy. Just until the Dinner. After that she'd fly back. She cast her mind over Lucy's friends, wondering if there were any parents she could ask. But, of course, this would involve complicated explanations, more lies. She was fed up with telling lies. There was only one person she could try, and she despised herself for what she was about to do.

She glanced at her watch. Elliot and Lucy would hopefully still be at his mother's. She dialled Maureen's number, praying she, not Elliot, would answer.

'Maureen? It's Portia. I'm sorry to bother you, and I know Elliot's already spoken to you, but there's a problem over who can look after Lucy while I'm in Brunnen. I was wondering if–'

She heard a muffled conversation in the background, the sound of Elliot's voice, then Lucy insisting, "I want to speak to Mummy", her voice higher pitched than usual, at the same time nasal, as if she'd been crying. Then came a knocking sound as if the receiver at the other end had fallen, a scuffling noise as someone lifted it.

'I'm sorry, Mummy,' Lucy said.

'How could you have done something so stupid, and so dangerous?'

There was a commotion. 'Lucy?' Portia asked.

Elliot was speaking now, his voice sharper than she'd ever heard it. She listened, knowing there was nothing she could say to change his mind. He would book a flight for Friday.

Lucy was coming to Brunnen.

2

_____

L ater that afternoon, Madalena gazed over the lake, at the reflection of the mountain peaks, the swans gliding past with regal dignity. At the time of issuing invitations to her family several months ago, it seemed a splendid idea, everyone gathering. Now that most of her children were here, she felt anxious. There'd been a palpable tension over tea and cake. Not to mention Portia's prolonged and unexplained absence.

She watched the boat depart for Luzern, its chugging competing with a digger: 4.25 pm, punctual as always. She leaned over the railing to be closer to the ripples of wash before they evaporated. Head down, deep in thought, she was startled by the bells of St Teresa's striking half past four. As she bent to remove a pebble from her sandal, she mentally ran through her list: check with Johann that the beef was delivered; make sure Hilde had ordered table place names; remind her not to accept last-minute bookings until the first week of July; view the accommodation she'd booked for Lawrence.

Madalena crossed the road and turned left, passing the

rows of plane and palm trees, the boxes of geraniums and red-brown canna lilies, as always, anticipating the first view of the Zurbriggen. There it was: its cream-washed exterior and traditional steep, grey-tiled roof; its red canopies on the ground floor windows; the red and white Swiss flag. Presiding over the lake with matriarchal pride. Her hotel....

As she took the path to the side door, she stopped to remove some overlooked weeds. She straightened and waved to the Misses Sowerby, comfortably installed on loungers under a cypress tree, Ruth reading a hardback, Alice peering through her binoculars.

It was hard to believe they'd been regular guests at the Zurbriggen for ten years now, their first visit being to celebrate their seventy-fifth birthday. Over the years, they'd seen changes in the hotel. But they themselves had barely changed, in her view at least, apart from Alice having had a hip replacement and now walking with a stick.

'Good afternoon,' Madalena said. 'I hope your room is comfortable?'

Ruth closed her book and sighed. 'Perfect as always. It was kind of you to arrange for flowers, and to have our favourite tartiflette for dinner last night.'

Alice adjusted the field glasses. 'There's another golden eagle, Ruth. This is the second one we've seen today, Frau Fontana.'

'You'll be busy now your children are here,' Ruth said. 'Someone told us your eldest is forty-one. You don't look old enough to have a child that age.'

Alice frowned at her sister. 'Ruth!'

Madalena laughed. 'I don't mind. It's true – Lawrence is forty-one. I was a young bride.'

'And the others?' Ruth asked.

Madalena retrieved Ruth's book that had fallen off the

lounger. 'Portia is forty, Vienne thirty-seven, and Annie thirty-five.'

Ruth squinted into the sun. 'And you are expecting a second grandchild, I mean your youngest daughter is. I mean, she's having a baby and you'll be a grandmother again.'

Alice lifted the binoculars. 'Ruth, dear, you're rambling.'

'How excited you must be about having them all here for your party,' Ruth said.

'Yes, I am. I will see you at dinner. Johann is making another of your favourites.'

Ruth beamed. 'Oh, what is it?'

Madalena patted Ruth's shoulder. 'You'll have to wait to find out.'

Hilde smiled when Madalena walked up to reception. 'Do you have last night's bar accounts, Hilde?'

The receptionist nodded and handed the bundle to Madalena. She scrutinised them. 'Remove two of the whiskies from Alice Sowerby's chit and note in the diary to replace their flowers on Friday.'

As Hilde looked questioningly at her, Madalena added, 'They economise all year to have their month here.'

'The piano tuner has arrived,' Hilde said. 'I showed him where the piano is.'

'Heavens, I forgot. Are Michael and Vienne up there?'

'They went for a walk.'

Madalena took the lift to the third floor. The piano tuner stood as she entered the room.

'*Guten tag*, Frau Fontana. I apologise for cancelling the appointment last week.'

'You couldn't help being unwell, Herr Kauffman,' she said. 'Don't let me interrupt you.'

She hovered, observing him at work on the Bechstein:

watching the keys connect to the hammers and dampers inside the piano; using tiny slivers of rubber to mute surrounding strings; tightening and loosening tuning pins. She listened as intently as he did to the changing pitch. The piano's polished rosewood casing gleamed in the sunlight – Vienne would be delighted.

'How refreshing to see the old-fashioned methods, rather than laptops,' Madalena said. How refreshing, too, to see such professionalism. If you did the small things properly, the big things took care of themselves. This was what she believed, but it hadn't always worked. She had mishandled one of the biggest things.

He smiled. 'Old techniques are always best. You have never requested my services before.'

'This is for my daughter, Vienne – she is performing in Prague in three weeks' time.'

'Vienne? Vienne Fotheringham is your daughter? I have all her recordings: Berlin, Milan, New York. You must be so proud of her.'

'I am proud of all my children.'

After the piano tuner finished, Madalena left the hotel. It would thunder tonight, she thought, as she walked along the path. The temperature had risen sharply during the last two days, a bank of clouds massing on the far side of the Urnersee.

Minutes later, rain bounced off the waterfront, waves rippled under the landing areas, the vista changing by the second. A moment ago, she could see three misty outlines of mountains – only one remained as the rain intensified. Now the water was a muted turquoise, contrasting with its earlier sparkling green. It had shimmered green when David brought her to this small Swiss town for their honeymoon. Shortly after, it turned to dull turquoise as they checked into the most impressive hotel she'd ever seen.

Now, as she walked along the lakeside to the Hotel Bergmann, her small frame almost obscured by a golfing umbrella, she could hardly believe over four decades had elapsed since she saw the hotel for the first time.

Little had changed at the Hotel Bergmann since then. On wet evenings, the same cluster of lights shone optimistically at the lakefront eating area. Pink geraniums, framing the garden, resigned themselves to the downpour; plane trees swayed gently. Accompanied by a subdued whishing of water, boats glided into the private landing area.

The dining room had retained its fifties aura, its frescoed walls and mature Kentish palms bestowing a timeless gaiety. Now, as chandeliers illuminated the room, she pictured waiters checking tables one more time: adjusting the angle of a heavy silver fork here; replacing a depleted salt cellar there.

The pianist, briefed to jolly up guests despondent over the sudden break in the weather, would begin with a light-hearted piece – *Moon River*, or something from *The Sound of Music* – as diners trooped in. Her first dinner there with David was accompanied by Gershwin songs, David humming *An American in Paris,* while they waited for their fish to be served.

Today, the wrought iron balconies overlooking the town were empty. Guests would be sipping pre-dinner drinks in the crimson carpeted drawing room. Discussing the villages the boat had visited on the Urnersee. Acknowledging their luck in seeing the lake and its towering mountains before the weather closed in. On such an evening, the chefs might make last minute changes to the menu, waiters serving thick *Gulaschesuppe*.

Sometimes Madalena believed she knew the Hotel Bergmann as well as her own hotel. In reflective moments, she realised she viewed the grand building as a parent hotel, her Zurbriggen as the child eager to learn. She liked to think her hotel, too, conveyed an ambience of past times.

Herr Adler awaited her in reception, bowing as she walked through the door. 'Madalena, *wie geht es Ihnen*?'

She smiled. '*Gut*, Christophe.'

'We are honoured to have one of your family staying with us,' he said when he showed her the room Lawrence would occupy. 'And, of course, I will give him a discount.'

'That won't be necessary.'

'You and I are old friends. It is my pleasure. Your son is a journalist, isn't he?'

Madalena nodded. 'This is lovely,' she said, noting the oak-framed double bed and wardrobe, the French windows giving onto a balcony, the splendid view of the Wald-stättersee.

Herr Adler smiled as she instinctively fingered the soft Egyptian cotton towels in the bathroom. Was he wondering why her son chose to stay at another hotel during his visit? She was. Lawrence's text, succinct and businesslike, had read: *Able to come to Brunnen. Please book a large room at the Hotel Bergmann, with lakeside view, if poss. Love Lawrence.* At least he would find nothing to complain of here.

Herr Adler was studying her. 'May I invite you to dinner this evening?'

'My children arrived today.'

'A quick drink, perhaps?' he suggested.

While they waited for their drinks, Madalena gazed round the drawing room. She turned to Herr Adler. 'Every time I come here, I remember my honeymoon. When I saw the building it seemed too intimidating. Then when we walked in, we heard piano music drifting out of here and I popped my head round the door. David and I had got the dates muddled and arrived a day early. Your father was so charming. He virtually apologised for not having antici-pated this might happen. When he learned it was our honeymoon, he upgraded us to a room with a view of the lake.... How is your father, Christophe?'

'He is well cared for in the nursing home. Bernhilde and I visit him every week.'

'He is a wise man,' she said. 'He taught me much about managing a hotel. He was always willing to advise, but he never intruded. David and I called him the Mahatma.'

As she left the Hotel Bergmann, tentacles of mist stretched down forested mountainsides and she shivered in the damp air. An insistent seven o'clock chorus of church bells directed her thoughts to her own hotel. By the water-front, the folk band packed away their long, wooden alphorns, abandoning the customary Wednesday evening practice. She let herself into the Zurbriggen as lightning zigzagged the sky, followed by a clap of thunder rebounding around the mountains. Rain now lashed down with renewed vigour, as if exhorted to do better. A pale blue sky merged seamlessly with the water. This feeling of wonder at being so close to the elements never palled.

During the train journey to Luzern the following morning, Lucy was the person uppermost in Madalena's thoughts. Portia had waited until the others finished left the dining room, before mentioning Lucy's expulsion and pending arrival, and requesting Madalena not to tell anyone else for the moment.

Twenty minutes after arriving in Luzern, Madalena was seated in a leather armchair. It faced a French window that gave onto a garden, dominated by a mature chestnut tree and a bed of white Belladonna lilies. In the distance, the lake sparkled and she wondered – as she so often did – how she would manage if ever she wasn't within easy reach of a stretch of water.

'Tell me about your marriage,' the man said.

She focused on the lilies, thinking of the pink variety she grew, the way the yellow centres blended into the pink. Everything should blend.

'How did you feel about your husband?'

She hesitated. 'We were happy.... We had our differences, but he treated me well.'

Madalena studied the man opposite her. Thirty-five perhaps, younger than Lawrence, but a gravitas conferring on him an additional ten years. How preoccupied people were with age, a way to pigeonhole, of knowing what to expect. This young man wore a navy suit and smart black shoes. Formality to compensate for tender years. In fifteen years' time, with receding hairline and more experience, would he have exchanged the suit for comfy cords and checked shirt?

Outside, the paddle steamer blasted its horn as it prepared once more to chug along the Vierwaldstättersee, a three-hour journey for passengers going to Flüelen. She pictured their content on such a fresh June morning: disembarking at the villages to gaze at verdant pastures, wooden chalets and pink and purple geranium window boxes; camcorders whirring, cameras clicking. The more energetic would walk from village to village, trekking poles tapping and scratching the ground. Some would climb. Others would opt for cable cars or cogwheel mountain trains. Forty years on, Madalena considered this her favourite day out. With or without company. As she grew older, her need to be in the countryside seemed to increase.

She straightened when she realised the young man was speaking.

'How did you meet?'

She must concentrate.

'In the Pyrenees. David was a walking guide. I had finished university.... When the holiday ended, I persuaded my parents to let me stay on. One day, David asked me if I wanted to join his group.'

She paused for a moment.

'We got on well from the start. He was passionate about mountains. Then his group finished and he asked me to travel with him in Switzerland. He was different... not just wanting to have sex.'

The man nodded. No hint of embarrassment. Of course not, he was a therapist, a professional.

'Please continue,' he said.

She thought for a moment. 'David was straightforward. I liked his smile, the way he threw his head back when he laughed. I wasn't madly in love. Not like some of my friends. It was more pragmatic. If we hadn't spotted the Zurbriggen Hotel, perhaps....'

Had he loved her? There were many kinds of love.

'He was consistent, steady,' Madalena said. 'Always affectionate.'

During the weeks after David's death, she'd escaped to the lake whenever possible. Walking from village to village. Realising, for the first time perhaps, how much she *had* loved him. Struggling to recall his voice, its special softness when he spoke to her, how his arm felt round her shoulder.

When the snows arrived, she'd walked even more,

relishing the combination of atmospheric pink wintry light of late afternoon and the ground crunching under her feet, in an otherwise silent space. Believed she was recovering, that she'd survive David's death. How wrong she'd been. She still recalled with horror what had happened next.

She looked at the therapist. 'I am wasting your time. I do feel better at the moment. Perhaps I could leave it just now while my children are visiting. I'll make another appointment when they have gone – if I may.'

She shook the young man's hand and left the room. Outside, she leant against the building, admitting to herself that she hadn't been honest with him, and that he would be perceptive enough to realise this. Rather than supporting her when her family were here, these meetings were an additional pressure.

It was one thirty. She had told her children she was visiting Luzern in search of fabrics for the public sitting room, and they would expect her to return with something. Perhaps she should nip into Casa Tessuti for samples.

When she stopped at the herbalist's shop off the Bundesstrasse, the assistant informed her that her prescription would be ready in ten minutes, and suggested she take a seat while waiting.

'We could arrange for this to be sent to Brunnen,' the herbalist said as she handed over the brown paper bag.

She smiled. 'I visit Luzern often.'

'The staff are discreet,' the assistant added, returning Madalena's card.

'Of course.' Madalena replaced the card in her purse, secured the eco-friendly bag in her daypack.

At the entrance to Casa Tessuti, she did an about turn. It was too lovely a day to be inside a moment longer than necessary: the blue of the water; the misty light on the mountains – *brumeuses* in French, so much softer, more evocative than the German *neblig* – glorious. On the far side of the lake, grand hotels beckoned the well-heeled for terraced lunches; closer by, pleasure boats touted for business. Instead of returning to Brunnen by train, she would take the paddle steamer, enjoy the breeze on her face, the motion of the paddles. By the time she reached the Zurbriggen, she could count on feeling relaxed and ready for Portia if she needed to talk about Lucy.

3

While Madalena was on the boat back to Brunnen, Vienne was standing by the window in her suite, rubbing cream into her fingers, working it over her skin, the ligaments, muscles and bones. She stretched her back and shoulders, then massaged her lower arms with a tennis ball. Her heart rate quickened as she thought ahead.

In eighteen days' time she would be in Prague, and by now would have practised on the concert piano and re-familiarised herself with the hall's acoustics. A rehearsal with the orchestra would follow, before a last-minute discussion with the conductor and first violinist. She would find time for a nap before the group dinner. The pre-concert day: the easy one.

If only Michael would be accompanying her this time. But at least for the moment he was safe, here in Brunnen with her family. For ten days she didn't have to worry.

She lifted the piano lid and spanned the keys, wishing she could be outside. It was a perfect afternoon, the mountain contours clearly defined under an azure sky, a mischievous breeze teasing the water.

She opened the window, sighed, then sat at the piano, spreading her fingers across the keys, automatically starting with the scales: C major, D minor, E major, F sharp minor. Her hands felt stiff and uncooperative, so she flicked her fingers up and down before deciding to skip the arpeggios. As she finished the scales, she became conscious of tightness in her chest. Had it been a mistake to travel so close to a concert? Should she be at home, living quietly in the run-up to a much-publicised event? One whose seats had sold within days of their release, one which would be reviewed in all the quality papers?

Aware of feeling dizzy, she placed the Schumann score on the piano rack. It must be stress. And tiredness. She opened the music at the first movement and arranged her fingers on the keys. Perhaps she should change her flight, return to London after the family dinner, allowing some extra days before Prague. But she wouldn't disappoint Madalena by leaving now.

As she applied more cream to her fingers, she made a mental note to arrange a physio treatment here, something to loosen her entire body. Her back ached, and as she stood to put the cream away, another wave of dizziness assailed her. She sat down, placed her fingers on the keys, but once more experienced the tingling sensation. And a blurring of the music. She rubbed her eyes, looked again – the notes were still out of focus. Maybe she should abandon the practice.

She went through to the bedroom, and as she sat down to remove her shoes, the room spun and her right leg felt numb. 'Michael,' she shouted, knowing he wasn't there. She phoned his mobile, only to receive its voicemail. 'It's me,' she said. 'Call me as soon as you can.'

Sliding under the bedclothes, she told herself to stay calm. The early flight had taken its toll and mountain air was tiring. Everyone knew this. Besides, the dizziness could be a recurrence of her residual labyrinthitis. Or another virus.

And she'd been so looking forward to this reunion, which was unlike her – maybe all those years of socialising with the orchestra had helped. As a girl, she'd often slipped away from family parties to her bedroom. And at school, she'd rejected the prep room in favour of the small, stuffy, off-limits laundry room, for mugging up on history and maths: how lovely it had been having her own space.

Perhaps this was why she'd never wanted children – the concept of a baby, totally dependent on her physically and emotionally, abhorrent. The idea of something attached to the breast, sleeping against her shoulder, made her feel claustrophobic. And the thought of a foetus growing and eventually moving inside her was more than she could have tolerated. Not that she'd ever be brave enough to admit this to people.

Slowly she turned over and closed her eyes, visualising a calm place: a green paned conservatory, overlooking a lawn surrounded by a high stone wall. She pictured herself on a bamboo lounger padded with thick, floral patterned cushions; sandals abandoned on a quarried floor. Gently drowsy from early evening sunshine reflected through the glass panes. Inhaling the scent of honeysuckle and warm earth, Rachmaninov's Third piano concerto playing from a cutting-edge sound system.

She woke to the sound of Michael opening the bedroom

door. He dropped his packages on the dressing table and came over.

'Recovering from the early start?'

'I texted you.'

'Battery's flat,' he said.

'What did you buy Madalena?'

'Candles and soap. We should have done this in London.... You look rough, are you all right?'

She hesitated, suddenly unwilling to tell him what had happened. As if by doing so, it would become real.

'Are they scented? The candles.'

'What's wrong, Vienne?'

She had to tell him sooner or later. This was too scary to keep to herself.

'Something happened.'

He stroked her face. 'What sort of something?'

Such untypical tenderness. He knew she was upset. How much gentler he was, when away from home.

'I felt strange,' she said. 'Tingling – in my hands.'

'The same as before? When we had the dinner party?'

Of course, she had told him. Not after everyone left, when they'd had such a frightful, alienating conversation. The next day, when they were closer.

'Similar,' she said. 'And dizzy. And things seem blurry. It's probably a bug.'

'Perhaps you should see a doctor in Brunnen,' Michael suggested.

Her mobile rang. 'I'm fine thanks, Trish.... No, it's not a problem. Yes, synthetic bedding.... Yes, fine. Okay. Yes. Thanks.'

Michael shook his head. 'I warned you you'd be hounded by calls here.'

Vienne shrugged. The phone calls were the least of her

worries if her health was deteriorating, if what she feared she might have, was the reality.

Vienne looked around the waiting room of the doctor's surgery. In the afternoon light, its health promoting posters gleamed with advice about eating enough fruit and vegetables, keeping up to date with immunisation and cervical smears. Bundles of leaflets advising on cheap ways to exercise and advertisements for stop-smoking services lay on a table by the window. There was a scary poster showing the different parts of the anatomy affected by excessive alcohol intake. The room smelled of freesia air freshener.

She sighed. She was already living healthily: cooking from basics, not smoking and not drinking much alcohol. Her weight was normal and she used her exercise bike. All this and she could still be ill. It didn't seem fair when there were chain smokers, couch potatoes and youngsters staggering out of pubs to vomit on the streets. And, what was worse, she'd read recently that almost half the men in the canton of Zurich were deemed unfit for military service due to being overweight. Switzerland was following in the UK's footsteps.

She didn't deserve to be ill.

She turned to study Michael. He didn't smoke and he kept to the recommended alcohol limit. Yet he'd developed a slight paunch, probably because he didn't take regular exercise now. And he'd been so fit during his rugby era. Perhaps they should buy bicycles, cycle in the countryside at weekends. Perhaps she should stop making puddings.

'Frau Fotheringham?' the doctor asked.

Vienne stood. 'Is it okay if my husband comes too?'

The doctor nodded. 'Of course. Please, come.'

He led the way into a large consulting room that overlooked a park.

'I am Doctor Nussbaum. Please, sit,' he said, indicating two chairs.

Vienne sat down and grabbed Michael's hand.

'I do not think this is anything serious.' Doctor Nussbaum said after noting her symptoms, checking her eyes and blood pressure.

'Should I see a neurologist?' she asked.

The doctor removed his spectacles and laid them on his desk. 'Is there something specific you are worried about?'

Vienne nodded. 'Multiple Sclerosis.'

There, the words were out. The first time she'd articulated them. Such horrid words, too. Such a horrid, frightening condition. And she didn't know if admitting her anxiety made her feel better or worse. Worse, because part of her believed if she didn't mention the condition, the doctor wouldn't consider it. Better, because if she did have MS, she needed to know. Needed to start treatment.

'My cousin had MS,' Michael intervened. 'And it's upset you, hasn't it, darling?'

'I've got a concert in two weeks' time,' Vienne said. 'I know I'm probably being stupid, but if I could rule out having the condition....'

She sat with her fingers crossed, willing the doctor to tell her there was nothing to indicate she had MS. That there was no need to refer her to a neurologist, to any specialist. More than anything, she wanted to leave the surgery knowing, for certain, nothing serious was wrong. It would be *such* a relief.

'I think that you have a virus. Post-fatigue stress disorder. Are you stressed?'

Vienne thought. Preparing for a concert always made her jittery. 'I'm a concert pianist. Stress goes with the job.'

'Have you been ill with any colds or other viruses recently?'

'I had a cough after Easter. For about six weeks.'

'This is probably the cause. But perhaps it would be wise to speak to a neurologist, to eliminate anything more serious. I can refer you to such a person or would you prefer to wait until you return to England?'

She forced herself to shake her head. 'I worry about my health. I'd rather get this sorted now.'

Sorted? A diagnosis of MS couldn't be sorted. People died from MS. She and Michael had read up on it when his cousin was diagnosed: the symptoms were frightful.

The doctor tapped a key on his computer, then dialled a number and spoke in German for a few moments, before removing the receiver from his ear. '*Das ist gut.* There is a cancellation at the Kantonsspital at eleven o'clock on the third of July. Is this possible?'

The day of Mum's party. Vienne looked at Michael who nodded.

'This is worse than I thought,' she said, as they left the health centre. 'I didn't expect to be referred to a neurologist. It's horrid.'

Michael squeezed her hand. 'He's being careful, Vienne, and he could see you were worried. I'm sure Madalena will lend us her car and I can drive you. Come on, let's get you back to the Zurbriggen. You look pooped.'

Vienne nodded, trying to breathe deeply. This was the only way to have peace of mind. Find out what was going on. She couldn't continue with this worry. Worrying about illness could be as debilitating as illness itself.

She slipped her hand into Michael's as they walked to

the tree-shaded hospital car park. Around her, birds chirped in the sunshine, further away she could hear a gentle hum of traffic, the more disruptive sound of a digger. She must try not to worry. She must also avoid upsetting Mum when she told her about the neurology appointment.

It was after four o'clock when Vienne made her way to the conservatory to find Madalena. As she arrived, she heard voices and saw a tall, fair haired man talking to Mum.

Madalena turned round. 'Vienne! Let me introduce you to Karl. Vienne, my daughter.'

Vienne shook hands with Karl.

'We were trying to decide how to arrange things for the Dinner,' Madalena said.

At a nod from Madalena, Karl lifted the garden hose to water the cheese plants.

Madalena took Vienne's arm. 'How did your appointment go, dear?'

Vienne hesitated. Now she was with Mum, she didn't want to talk about things. 'He doesn't think there's anything to worry about but... he's referred me to the neurologist at the Kantonsspital. Just to be sure.'

'Dr Nussbaum is very careful,' Madalena said. 'If he thinks it's nothing serious, that probably is the case.'

'I suppose you're right. Better to have peace of mind, especially before a concert.'

'You've always had a tendency to worry about your health, dear. Even as a child.'

Mum was right. Vienne could remember her angst, especially as a teenager, regarding every symptom as suggestive of a malignancy. It was silly to worry about having a serious condition at this stage. Besides, everything she was currently experiencing could be attributed to any number of minor things. She had to keep this in perspective or she *would* make herself ill.

'When is your consultation?' Madalena asked.

'Not great timing – the day of your Dinner. It was a cancellation.'

'Nevertheless, I think you were wise to take that appointment. Hopefully it will reassure you. Michael can drive you, that will be easier than going by train.'

Vienne nodded. 'Thanks, Mum. I'd better let you get on with your planning. I just wanted to tell you. Please don't mention it to the others.'

As she turned to leave, Karl smiled and waved his hand. Vienne went up to him and said, 'It was nice to meet you, if only briefly.'

His expression was one of admiration. 'I am a great fan of your music.'

They shook hands.

Vienne beamed as she left the conservatory. Strange how a compliment like that not only boosted her morale, but also made her feel safer, as if being a pianist was the reality in her life, whereas being an ill person was only an anxiety.

Seated by the open window of the dining room that evening, Vienne listened to the flapping Swiss flags as her family arrived, one by one, and hovered round the table for dinner.

'Portia, let's sit together,' she suggested.

Portia hesitated, exchanging glances with Annie. Portia always wanted to sit with Annie.

Vienne smiled at Michael. 'Where do you want to sit?'

'Anywhere.'

Not very helpful.

Vienne caught Madalena's eye, wondering if she'd suggest who sat where.

'I'll sit beside Vienne,' Annie said, moving to join her.

Johann had arrived to check some catering detail with Madalena, who was nodding, thanking him. As he left the dining room, his eye lingered on Annie. Lucky Annie, but in a pink and green floral dress, her unruly dark curls restrained by two pink combs, she did look pretty this evening.

Would Michael remember their anniversary next week? She must warn Mum not to mention it. It would mean nothing if he needed prodding. And she'd be adult about it if he did forget, not throw a wobbly as she'd done last year. Prompting him to trudge out to buy yellow roses past their best and Belgian chocolate truffles. How amazing she could think this far ahead, with the neurology appointment to get through.

Annie had reconsidered, and was now seated next to Portia, leaving Vienne sandwiched between Michael and Madalena. They needed another man.

Florian served a delicious-smelling soup, Annie circulated a basket of warm bread rolls. Anxiety had affected Vienne's appetite, and for more than food. She could smell Michael's aftershave – the *Bleu de Chanel*, her birthday present – and wanted to unbutton his shirt and press her face against his chest. They hadn't made love since before the awful dinner party. Still, that was less than two weeks ago. Not unusual for couples who'd been married fifteen years. Sixteen, almost. She sipped her wine, feeling her face flush as the fluid reached her throat, and scanned the table. Yes, Annie was this evening's star, her dark hair and eyes highlighted by the colours of her dress.

As for Portia – Vienne digested the eggshell blue blouse, the breasts straining against such flimsy fabric. You would think Portia was breastfeeding. From habit, she stared down at her own green dress. A flattering colour, but no compensation for her adolescent chest. Michael, talking to Portia, could hardly have failed to notice her tight blouse. His roving eye, his tendency to distract Vienne with some outrageous comment if he became aware of being observed, were deeply embedded traits. Nothing was more disgusting than a male eye devouring another woman's body. As if this was all that the woman amounted to. Portia had never appreciated Elliot, never known what a gem she'd married. Elliot concentrated on a woman's face, on what she had to say.

'This is yummy soup, Mum,' Annie said.

Madalena smiled. 'Johann's secret is fresh asparagus. I didn't know how lucky we were when we employed him. Your father guessed. He had a hunch for such things.'

Annie grasped Madalena's hand. She was so tactile, Vienne thought. Always ready with a hug, an arm round the shoulder. Meanwhile, Portia was fiddling with her gold bracelet. Involuntarily, Vienne shook her head – gold didn't go with blue. Her eyes slid again to Portia's blouse. Automatically, her hand fingered the right side of her bra, felt its shameful padding.

She looked at Madalena. Mum was top heavy too, but she never flaunted her body. The tailored aubergine blouse didn't cling to her, drawing attention to her breasts. Vienne now became aware of Annie watching her. She'd probably observed her staring at Portia's body, perceived her envy.

Vienne gulped as a horrible thought surfaced. What if Annie had noticed Michael ogling Portia? How humiliating. Horrid.

'How far did you walk today, Annie?' Madalena asked.

'Sisikon, then I took the boat back. It was lovely, so unchanged. No tacky touristy enterprises, only a sleepy village with the occasional outdoor restaurant selling drinks and ice cream. Local kids playing by the beach. It defines tranquillity.'

Madalena smiled. 'Nicely expressed, dear.'

Vienne sipped her wine. 'Let's all walk round the lake, sometime, see who gets furthest.' As soon as the words were out, she wondered if she'd have the strength to do such a thing with the neurology consultation awaiting her.

'It would be Lawrence,' Annie said.

Madalena retrieved the soup tureen from the sideboard. 'Second helping anyone? Portia? Michael?'

Nobody wanted more soup, so Madalena pressed the bell and Florian brought the raclette cheese and a selection of cold meats, closely followed by Gaston with plates of mushrooms, zucchini and onion. Annie placed the vegetables on the upper griddle of the raclette maker. A mock intensity of concentration followed as they carefully laid their raclette slices on the shovels – their childhood name – and roasted the cheese under the lower section of the machine. Laughs and little shrieks ricocheted around the room as they removed the dripping shovels and transferred the cheese to their plates. Madalena passed around the plate of beef, chicken and pork, and Annie served the vegetables. Michael refilled wine glasses.

Vienne could hear waves slapping against the shore in the strengthening wind. She visualised tambourines, the double cymbal Arabic ones with their delightful "shooshing" noise.

'Oh, I do so love the smell of raclette cheese,' Annie said. 'I wish I could find the right word to describe it.'

Portia raised her hand. 'Pungent.'

'Nutty,' Michael offered.

'Both of these,' Madalena said.

The conversation continued: the weather forecast, where Portia and Lucy might go riding, an expedition to the Rigi. If only she could participate in the lighthearted manner of her sisters, if only she didn't have this appointment hanging over her.

'Dad would have enjoyed this, our all being together,' Annie said. 'He had a thing about family meals, remember? They shouldn't be rushed. It was a time to catch up with what everyone had done during the day. Conversation time.'

'*Conversazione*,' Portia added.

Annie stood, fanned out her arms as if conducting an orchestra. '*CON–VER–SA–ZIONE*. If only I'd learned Italian at school.'

'We would brace ourselves when we heard a knock on the door,' Madalena explained to Michael. 'Sometimes toss a coin to see who should answer. Lawrence once volunteered to sort out the problem. He could hardly have been older than eleven.'

Michael seemed interested, Vienne noticed with relief. Still, he'd always been fond of Madalena. He liked her style, he'd told Vienne, when she first introduced him to her parents.

'Lawrence was always supremely confident,' Portia said.

Annie nodded. 'And resourceful. Do you remember that Christmas when the oven broke and the turkey didn't cook properly. Laurence suggested we went into Luzern for dinner. Phoned restaurants and hotels until he found one that would feed us.'

Portia laughed. 'You cried all the way until we reached the station and you saw the giant Christmas tree.'

'I can't have cried all that time – for an hour?' Annie asked.

'Ah, talking of Luzern, I thought we might go there on Thursday,' Madalena said. 'There's an exhibition at the Kunstmuseum. We could have lunch first.'

Vienne turned to Michael, 'That would be lovely, wouldn't it?'

'You know art isn't really my thing, darling,' he said.

'Do come with us, please....'

Madalena caught Michael's eye. 'Actually, I have a few jobs needing doing in the hotel – and I can't get someone until next week.'

'Better use of my time,' he said.

Vienne forced herself to smile. Michael was safe here, all that mattered. All they needed was more couple time. They should have a holiday after Prague. Somewhere romantic. Corsica, perhaps. He often talked about climbing Monte Cinto. Maybe she'd surprise him by booking a trip, present it as a *fait accompli*.

The Cinderella Complex. Liz shoving the book into her hand, demanding she read it. Skimming through it – something about women's unconscious desire to be taken care of by others, based on a fear of being independent. It was ridiculous, Vienne had thought. She earned more than Michael. The bit about choosing to stay in dysfunctional relationships was particularly irritating. There was nothing dysfunctional about her and Michael. Liz had got it wrong. Just because Vienne sometimes deferred to him, and let him deal with the practical stuff, didn't mean she'd lost her independence. This was the problem with such psychological twaddle: it made too much of things. But there definitely could be a problem with unmarried friends, she acknowledged – their need to find cracks in relationships. To stir.

'So, who's on the guest list for the celebration dinner?' Annie asked as Florian served apple pudding. 'I'm assuming you're inviting others.'

Madalena nodded thanks to Florian. 'The Lengaurs and the Rheins, and friends from my pottery and drama classes. My friend Karl will be there, and I wondered about including Ruth and Alice Sowerby – do you think this is a good idea?'

'They'd love it,' Annie said. 'They always stop to talk when you bump into them.'

'They have no close family left. They can always decline. I've also invited Johann and Hilde. There'll be about twenty. Oh, and Christophe and Bernhilde.'

'The rival hotel,' Portia said.

Madalena sniffed. 'You know it isn't like that.'

'I'm glad you've finally got some real Swiss friends,' Portia said. 'It wasn't like that when we were growing up.'

'There wasn't much time for friendships then,' Madalena said. 'It takes years to get to know the Swiss properly. They are so cautious. Once you become friends, though, that's it.'

'So, what's the format for the evening?' Annie asked.

'Drinks and savouries in the conservatory, dinner, then I wondered about hiring a boat and going out on the lake, if the weather's fine.'

'Brilliant,' Annie said.

Madalena looked at Portia and Vienne. 'Do you approve of my plans?'

Portia nodded. Vienne nodded too. There wouldn't be so many people, after all.

The wind had dropped, and through the open window she could hear the tinkle of cowbells from the hills above Brunnen. Such an evocative sound, reminding her of weekend walks when they were growing up, Dad always leading, until Lawrence was old enough to do so. She remembered the cowbells her parents had given her for her eighth birthday, the excitement of waking to six packages of increasing bulk, from the smallest one, barely thimble-sized, to one her tiny form could hardly lift. How she'd loved the different clunking sound of each bell, spending hours experimenting with spoons and knitting needles, and her hands, searching for different noises. Portia and Annie had been less interested, refusing to participate in her "orchestra". The cowbells were the origins of her love of music.

The scent of honeysuckle and rose drifted in from the garden as Gaston served coffee. What Vienne wanted most now was to sit outside with Michael, enjoy the night fragrance. She'd envisaged this happening when they bought their Hampstead house, and for the first month it had, a blisteringly hot August when they'd sat in a companionable silence, drinking beer, watching shadows stealing up the garden wall. This was another thing they didn't do so much these days, but they could while they were here, when they both had fewer claims on their time.

'You are lucky, having all this on your doorstep, Mum. I didn't appreciate it properly when I was a child,' Portia said.

Michael nodded. 'It is beautiful, and peaceful.'

'I thought about moving back, actually,' Portia was saying. 'Perhaps not to Brunnen, but somewhere in the canton.'

Madalena raised her eyebrows. 'I didn't know you'd considered this, dear.'

'When Elliot and I separated. However, I felt it was too much change for Lucy to deal with, to be honest. But this was four years ago.'

'Are you thinking about it now?' Madalena asked.

'You wouldn't want to move while Lucy is at school,' Vienne said, aware of an edge to her voice.

'There are excellent schools in Switzerland,' Madalena said.

Vienne pouted. 'There are excellent ones in London.'

She felt a kick on her ankle, glared at Michael.

'Be careful,' he told her.

No, you be careful, she wanted to warn him, conscious of her throbbing ankle. Her eyes pricked, reminding her it was approaching the bad time of the month. She had this to deal with as well as the pending appointment. Michael hadn't meant to be rough, she knew, but both the kick and comment were unnecessary, undermining her judgement.

She imagined she heard a boat's horn, but the last ferry for Luzern would have left over an hour ago. What she could hear were the alphorns from the local band practising by the waterfront, a sound she would expect to recognise from time immemorial. Now, if she had any sense, she would run through the first movement of the Schumann in her head – especially the crescendos – to see if this improved her mood. But before she could begin, Portia was talking again.

'We have an office in Zurich. It's not large, but sometimes you see part-time vacancies for barristers.'

'A friend of mine moved there last year,' Annie said. 'She loves it. Loads to do, and she's found a quaint old apartment near the river. I should visit her while I'm here.'

'How is the piano?' Madalena asked Vienne. 'The tuner came the day you arrived. He knows your work – I was so proud.'

Vienne nodded, and glanced at Portia. If she and Lucy moved to Switzerland, her hopes of becoming properly reacquainted with her niece, of playing a bigger role in her life, would amount to nothing. Portia couldn't be serious about uprooting them.

'Are you all right, dear?' Madalena was asking. 'Is the piano okay, a high enough standard for you?'

'The piano's great, Madalena,' Michael said. 'Vienne's been practising hard, haven't you darling? Vienne?'

'It's fine, Mum. Thanks for sorting it out.'

Vienne was trying to catch Portia's eye and failing. Could Portia be jealous of her? Of her handsome husband, her thriving career? But Portia had her own reputation. Had been written about in the Sunday broadsheets, interviewed on television after the verdict in a particularly emotive case. Her sister's eyes were dark, however, her expression flat, and it was hard at this moment to imagine her strutting around a courtroom, intimidating witnesses, impressing the jury with her sharpness.

'How about a drink at the Hotel Bergmann?' Annie suggested after they'd finished coffee.

'Good idea,' Portia said. 'Mum?'

'I'm meeting Karl.'

Vienne held her breath, aware of the pulse in her fingertips as she awaited Michael's reaction.

'I'm tired from the walk,' he said.

'What about you, Vienne?' Annie asked.

She hesitated. 'I should practise.'

Portia studied Madalena. 'This friend, Karl – are you close?'

Madalena hesitated. 'Yes. He's been good to me. He helped me build the conservatory. He's helped in other ways too.'

When her mother and sisters left, Vienne remained at the table. Michael was slumped in his seat, yawning. 'I'm pooped,' he said.

'It's nine o'clock. You can't go to bed yet.'

Her comment could have prompted a jokey response, or even a serious one about her joining him for an early night.

'I need to send a few emails first,' he said.

She knew his euphemisms by now: he was considerate enough to let her down gently. If she hurried, she could catch the others before they reached the grand hotel. It would be fun to have a sisterly chat, during which she might be able to ascertain whether or not Portia was seriously considering moving back. Besides, she wanted to find out if either Annie or Portia had met Karl, and what they thought about him and Mum.

4

After a rough night's sleep, Portia woke at nine the following morning. Having dressed quickly, she dialled Michael's room number, willing him to be the one to answer.

Five minutes later, there was a knock on her door, and she felt her forehead bead with sweat as Michael entered without bidding. She'd forgotten how attracted she was to his physical presence, his height, his rugby shoulders. The way shirts strained against his chest added to the allure.

'You look good, Portia.'

As he walked towards her, it could have been fourteen years earlier. 'What's so urgent?'

'Lucy's been expelled.'

'You're kidding me.'

'She set fire to another girl's writing case.'

'Well, you know my views on boarding school. I don't think it did much for Vienne's confidence and–'

'Lucy's coming here and Vienne's bound to work things out. It's a ghastly situation.'

Michael shook his head. 'Vienne's too preoccupied with

her concert and her health to notice much at all. I'm glad Lucy's left–'

'Expelled, Michael, not left.'

'Why can't she stay with Elliot?'

'He's off to Boston.'

Michael flopped down on the spare bed and ran his eyes over her. 'Nice blouse.'

Portia looked at her blouse. She didn't normally wear this sort of top, but she'd bought it to please Lucy who'd told her that she needed to be more trendy. Accordingly Portia had left the shop with a lime green crossover blouse which made her look as though she'd undergone breast augmentation.

'Can't you take anything seriously? If there hadn't been a sale in Debenhams....'

'Life is full of "ifs". You were hot.'

'Frustrated. Don't delude yourself it would have happened under any other circumstances.'

If Elliot hadn't been depressed, with barely enough energy to read, let alone make love; if she hadn't gone shopping that evening. Too many "ifs".

'Hey, I've already had my head bitten off by your sister,' he said. 'Cut me some slack.'

She smiled. 'You watch too many American movies. What you mean is, "Get off my back".'

He was staring at her blouse and she didn't find it unpleasant. She should, of course. She should be horrified that he was making his attraction plain, with Vienne only four doors away. And yet there was something clinical and dispassionate about him. Always had been: his curiosity about her – her views on things, her foibles – reminding her of a scientist with his microscope. Such detachment extended to the wider world – wars, political squabbles, dipping economies. Nothing seemed to touch him. But his lovemaking had been passionate.

Portia averted her eyes. 'There's no way you can get Vienne back to London? Can't you invent a work excuse? This is a disaster.' She heard the hysteria in her voice.

'Calm down, Portia. I don't think anyone will notice, let alone Vienne. Lucy's only twelve. If she were older—'

'Thirteen. Lucy's thirteen. What's Vienne doing here, anyway, just before a concert?'

'What does she look like now, Lucy?' Michael asked.

'Tallish. Her hair's the same colour and texture as yours.'

He grinned. 'Lots of people have dark, wavy hair. Elliot, for example.'

'Even so...'

'We've done well to keep Lucy and Vienne apart so much recently,' Michael said, leaning forward to light a cigarette.

Portia reached over to grab it. 'You can't smoke in here. It's a giveaway that you've been here. No one else smokes.'

As he bent forward to retrieve the cigarette, Portia could smell his aftershave. A gift from Vienne, of course. Not the type to buy himself perfume. But he'd buy it for Vienne. Portia had once asked Elliot why he never bought her perfume, or anything unpractical, and his reply that she wasn't that sort of woman, had hurt more than she would have imagined.

Michael made her feel more womanly than Elliot ever had. This was the appeal, of course: her craving for appreciation of more than her mind. Plus, tall men helped her feel more petite – his height was wasted on Vienne.

Portia raised her eyes to the heavens. 'What are we going to do?'

'Vienne won't recognise me in Lucy. She'll simply be glad to see her again.'

'And if she does?'

'If she does, I fob her off. Tell her she's tired or something.'

'And if she's not persuaded?'

'If she's not persuaded, Portia, we'll have to tell her the truth.' He sounded exasperated.

'That you and I were in bed together while she was performing Rachmaninov's Third piano concerto in Rome.'

Michael grinned. 'I thought barristers were strong on details. It was Venice, then Florence, and it was Rachmaninov's Second.'

He took her hand. His was warm but his fingers were bony. Bony and hairless. She hadn't noticed before.

They'd never pretended that what they had was more than ephemeral. It was sex, followed by matter-of-fact thanks, agreed time for the next rendezvous. A jibe, perhaps, about the soft mattress, the smell of pine floor polish. No disingenuous comments about guilt. He'd made a point of being home in time for Vienne's call, as if that legitimised their behaviour.

He kept hold of Portia's hand. 'I enjoyed our time together.'

She pulled her hand away. 'Don't you ever feel guilty about what we did?'

'Vienne told me Madalena drives to Zurich to get wine from Albert Reichmuth's shop because the building is made from recycled wine boxes. Do you think it's true?'

'For God's sake, take this seriously. Have you any idea how ghastly it would be if Vienne worked it out?'

Michael looked away then checked his watch. 'What's the point of guilt? It's done.... I have to go, she thinks I'm at reception. We're going to walk by the lake. Come along. She'd like that.'

'You simply don't get it, do you? I've lived a lie for fourteen years now. In Chambers, in court, everyone looks up to me. Then I go home, where I'm reminded in innumerable ways of what I've done. To Elliot, to Vienne, to Lucy.'

An expression of discomfort crossed Michael's face. 'I try to keep it in perspective. See you later, then.'

As the door closed, she clenched her fists. Then she turned the phone volume to "off" and flopped onto the armchair. Part of her wanted to believe that Michael's low-key reaction to the situation was a reasonable way to think, that she had lost her perspective. The more guarded side believed that what she'd worked hard to conceal for thirteen years, could be jeopardised by Lucy's visit.

At five minutes past three, Portia ran into the airport foyer, glancing at the arrivals board. The Manchester flight had landed thirty minutes ago, passengers already exiting from customs. And there, talking to an official-looking woman, was Lucy, taller, head high. Defiant, or just pretending? She wore a long Indian cotton skirt – new to Portia – and a sleeveless smock, also new. Elliot's mum had taken her shopping. Compensating, no doubt, for the bollocking she supposed Portia would give her daughter.

Lucy and her escort approached Portia, and the member of staff stood back as mother and daughter hugged.

'Thank you so much for looking after Lucy,' Portia said to the woman.

'No problem. Enjoy your holiday, Lucy.'

Portia turned to Lucy, who now slumped on a row of grey plastic chairs.

'What's the matter? Are you ill?' Portia asked.

She could think of advantages in her daughter being

unwell, not least a legitimate way to control access to her while they were in Brunnen.

Lucy shook her head. 'I'm exhausted. Grandma got a new mattress for the spare bedroom and it's bloody uncomfortable.'

'Language, darling. But I am pleased to see you, despite everything.'

And she was, in a way. Her flesh and blood, whatever the circumstances. Though of course the feeling would change the nearer they got to Brunnen. Her eyes strayed to the departures board, to the London flight scheduled for an hour's time. There was nothing to stop her from booking them on it. Escaping home. There were countless reasons why they might need to leave: Lucy experiencing panic attacks, needing to be in quiet and familiar surroundings; Elliot undergoing emergency surgery; an unexpected development with one of her clients.

Lucy blinked in the sunshine flooding the arrivals lounge.

'You are tired, you should wear your specs, rest your eyes,' Portia advised.

Lucy rummaged in her backpack. 'I don't need them.'

'The optician said—'

'That was a year ago. Lots of teenagers grow out of specs.... This is for you.' She thrust a grubby white envelope into Portia's damp hand.

'Maybe, but you don't know *you* have. They suit you.'

Lucy rummaged again in her backpack. 'I don't know where they are.'

'You didn't leave them at Grandma's?'

'Aren't you going to open the letter?'

Portia did and didn't want to know specifically what had happened with Lucy and school. Since the initial phone call two days ago, she'd speculated on the details, of course.

The one friend she'd confided in, and simply because she wanted to tell someone who wasn't family, had replied with a vague comment about hormones and boys. Not having children herself, Sarah tended to assume a "one size fits all" on the few occasions she ventured an opinion on teenagers. And she didn't know Lucy. Sarah was capable of spending hours with Portia in the bar next to Chambers, without mentioning Lucy, which sometimes suited and other times hurt.

'Shall we explore Zurich before we drive back to Brunnen?' Portia asked. 'It's such a lovely afternoon. We could walk round the Old Town, or by the river?'

'Won't they be waiting to see me – Granny, everyone?'

'You haven't been in Zurich for years.'

Lucy groaned. 'I can't be bothered.'

Portia lifted Lucy's grip bag – it felt light: she must have left stuff with Maureen, something else to sort out when they got back to London – and they made their way to the airport car park.

'A quick tour. I think it's late-night shopping too. You remember at Christmas, you wanted to dye your hair. We could have it done now.'

Lucy stopped walking, stared at her. 'Aren't you mad at me? Because of what happened?'

'We'll talk about that later. We need to decide about your hair.'

'Why now? Anyway, I've changed my mind. I don't have the right skin tone to go blonde.'

'If we choose the right shade–'

'You're always going on about tacky platinum blondes.'

Portia sighed. There was a new abrasiveness to her

daughter. Hopefully temporary. 'We'll phone Annie for advice. Then you could have it done this evening.'

'Has Uncle Lawrence arrived?'

As Lucy awaited a response, Portia stared at her. No one could fail to notice the resemblance, or was anxiety affecting her perceptions? Just because *she* thought Lucy looked like Michael, didn't mean everyone else would. After all, she'd had almost eight years of not worrying about her likeness to her father. And if she hadn't taken Lucy to that blasted charity concert, because Vienne was ill and there was a spare ticket, she would probably have continued not to worry too much. Years later, she could remember the tone of the woman who'd bounced up to them during the interval – when Lucy was at the Ladies – and said to Michael, 'You must be Lucy's father', his rapid response: 'Her uncle – by marriage', and the woman's protests, stopping just short of asking Michael if he was sure.

Relax, Portia now told herself. If she wanted her daughter to comply with her agenda, she needed to stay calm. Lucy never responded to pressure. It was like reeling in a fish. Slowly, gently.

'Mum, is Uncle Lawrence in Switzerland?'

'Why the sudden interest in him?'

'He said he'd take me to the transport museum in Luzern, the next time we were in Brunnen together.'

Portia's spirits rose. If Lawrence was prepared to spend time with Lucy, it could get her away from the hotel. She must encourage this relationship. She stared at the envelope poking out of her bag. Wondered whether to read it now, after all, or to quiz Lucy.

'It has to be said, your timing is dreadful, Lucy.'

'You mean if I'd been expelled a month ago it would be okay?'

'That's not what I mean.'

'I thought you'd be pleased I'm here – apart from, well.... When Granny's invitation arrived, you said you were sorry I'd miss it.'

Lucy was right. Portia smiled wryly. She was equally as capable of putting on a performance at home as she was in court.

'We could eat at Pizzeria Molino.'

'Mum, you hate pizza.'

'I want to do what you want. There'll be other things on the menu. Pasta, or something.'

'You hate pasta.'

'Come on, Lucy – large pepperoni pizza and a coke. All that salt and sugar. A teenager's dream.'

'I'd rather eat with everyone else.'

'Plenty of time for family meals. Come on.'

Lucy had stopped walking again. 'Are you all right, Mummy? You're acting kinda weird.'

'Don't be ridiculous.' She didn't mean to sound harsh but Lucy's expression revealed her hurt. Now she didn't look like a clone of Michael.

They reached the car, she put Lucy's grip bag into the boot and almost shoved her daughter into the passenger seat. Again, her attention was drawn to the envelope, but a glance at her daughter's face told her now was not the time to read the letter. Lucy was silent as Portia pulled out of the airport car park and headed southwest to the city.

As she waited for the traffic lights to turn green, she observed Lucy scratching her shoulder. Then she noticed the tattoo at the top of her arm, above a vaccination scar. The tattoo looked like a ferret. Dear God.

'Lucy, what's that on your shoulder?'

'What does it look like? A tattoo.'

'When was that done?'

'Yesterday.'

'When you were with Grandma? It's ghastly, so common. More importantly, it's illegal at your age, without the consent of a parent or guardian.'

Lucy rolled her eyes. 'It's cool. Everyone has them.'

'Grandma didn't give permission, surely?'

'Stay cool, Mum.' Lucy laughed.

'I really can't see what's so amusing.'

'It's a stick-on tattoo, duh.'

'Well... well, that's not so bad, I suppose. But don't let Granny see it.'

Lucy yawned. 'Whatever.'

In the centre of Zurich, Portia found an underground car park and chivvied Lucy out of the car, telling her she would enjoy herself and it wouldn't be for long. A quick walk in the Old Town: there might be a hairdressing shop open. Of course there wouldn't be time for Lucy to have her hair dyed.... Perhaps they could find an evening guided tour of the city. She was buying time, nothing more. Eventually they'd have to drive back to Brunnen, but by then everyone might have gone to bed.

Would there ever be an end to the price and fear extracted by guilt?

5

The morning after Lucy's arrival, Madalena woke at six as usual, a consequence of early starts during the years before they could afford to employ enough staff. Normally she would read, hoping to fall asleep again. But today, the freshness of the morning, the bells ringing out over the lake, summoned her, and she ignored her body's need for more sleep.

She opened the curtains, stepped onto the balcony and breathed deeply, inhaling the scent of roses framing her bedroom window. As she watched the mist flirt with the mountains, twisting and teasing in ever-changing ribbons, her heart experienced a frisson. The water below was a calm, clear jade, a perfect backdrop for her yoga.

She sat down on her mat, stretched out her legs and leaned forward to clasp her upright feet. Ah, better already.

After she'd finished, she made coffee and sat on the balcony. An hour before the digger would begin. Whenever the noise threatened to drive her crazy, she reminded herself that at least the new apartment block would not obscure the view from the Zurbriggen. As she looked around her, she counted four cranes. Did any other country have the same constant state of renovation as Switzerland? This obsession with perfection?

Now the cloud was lifting, the Urnersee changing to deep aquamarine, tentative patches of blue sky showing. Perhaps they should re-jig their plans, do something outdoors today instead of going into Luzern.

'So, lunch first or exhibition?' Annie asked as Madalena turned right into the Bahnhofplatz in Luzern.

Madalena glanced at her watch. 'If we visit the exhibition now, we'll be too late for most of the restaurants. Sometimes I despair of the Swiss rigidity. You can't do anything spontaneously.'

'France is equally bad if you want to eat out at odd times,' Vienne said. 'I suppose we're spoilt in England.... Portia, are you okay? You've hardly spoken since we left Brunnen.'

'Just tired,' Portia said. 'I sat up talking to Lucy until a ridiculous hour.'

'It's such a pity she didn't come with us today. I can't wait to catch up with her. It's time I became a proper aunt again,' Vienne said when they'd found a restaurant and ordered.

Proper aunt, Madalena registered. What on Earth did Vienne mean? She must find out what was going on between Portia and Vienne.

'Perhaps, given the circumstances, your enthusiasm is a tad inappropriate,' Portia remarked.

'I only meant.... Never mind. When does Lawrence's flight arrive, Mum?' Vienne asked.

Portia addressed her reply to the far side of the restaurant. 'Eleven o'clock.'

'Why don't we all go?' Vienne suggested.

Madalena said nothing.

Annie turned to Vienne. 'He'd be embarrassed, lovie.'

'I would be pleased,' Vienne said.

Portia shook her head. 'You're not Lawrence.'

Vienne looked perplexed. 'You don't know he wouldn't be pleased. We haven't seen each other for several years. When did you last see him, Portia?'

'That's got nothing to do with it. I'm sure he'd rather be met just by Mum.'

'I agree with Portia,' Annie said.

'What a surprise,' Vienne said.

Madalena looked up from adding pepper to her boeuf bourguignon. 'Let's concentrate on this afternoon, shall we?'

If this bickering continued, she would prefer to be back at the Zurbriggen, catching up on paperwork.

After lunch, they walked along the Bahnhofstrasse to the Kunstmuseum. It was such a beautiful afternoon, a waste to be inside. Would there be protests if she suggested they take a boat trip instead?

'So, how will we do this?' Annie asked as they entered the museum. 'In pairs or all together?'

'All together,' Vienne said.

'It's busy, it'll be easier in pairs,' Portia said. 'We can meet in the sculpture section, say in thirty minutes? Come on, Annie.'

Portia strolled off, Annie following, glancing back once.

Madalena took Vienne's arm. 'You can teach me all you know about art.'

'Have you and Portia argued?' she asked Vienne, several minutes later.

'I don't know what to do,' Vienne replied. 'We had an almighty row about three years ago – not long after Michael and I moved back from New York – it came from nowhere. I've hardly seen her since, and each time she's been distant with me.'

'For three years? What a waste. If I had a sister.... Do you want me to speak to Portia, find out what is going on?'

'I should be able to sort things out, at my age.'

Part of Madalena agreed; another part yearned to intervene. To do what mothers were conditioned to do: make things better for their children, even their adult ones. In her case, compensating for all those years when they were away at school and had to fend for themselves. The psychotherapist had helped her understand her desire to do this.

When they all met up again, the sculpture gallery was buzzing with a medley of languages. Sunlight poured through the floor to ceiling windows and Madalena wished she had brought her photochromic specs.

'If only I looked so great,' Annie said as they stared at a nude woman with perky breasts.

Portia flung an arm round Annie's shoulder. 'You do.'

'What do you think, Vienne?' Annie asked.

Vienne turned away. 'Not all women want to look as if they're breastfeeding.'

Annie exhaled deeply.

'I am sure Vienne didn't mean to be tactless,' Madalena said discreetly to Annie.

Maybe this was the opportunity she needed, the moment to draw Annie out, however briefly. Grief should be articulated. She had learned this the hard way: she didn't want Annie to.

'I'm fine.'

'If you want to talk.... Any time.'

'It's okay, Mum. I'm lucky enough to have inherited your coping gene.'

'Me, a coper?'

'Well, yeah. You cope with everything. I mean, nothing fazes you. Even when Dad died, you were back running the hotel within weeks. Not many women would have been able to. Every time something awful happens to me, I think of how you cope.'

How little Annie knew her. How little any of her children knew her. Her coping technique had been to walk, not to immerse herself in the hotel, and even the exercise had only worked for a while.... They knew nothing of this. Fleetingly she wrestled with the urge to unburden herself. Lighten the load. And if she were to choose a sympathetic ear, it would be Annie's.

'I wonder how Michael's getting on with the DIY,' Annie said.

'I am bothered about Vienne and Portia. Their relationship seems so strained.'

Annie shrugged. 'They're not wired the same way. Portia with her legal brain, Vienne and her music.'

'You are all so different,' Madalena said.

Just then, Vienne rushed over to them. 'Come and see this. There's some miniature sculptures of musicians in an orchestra. The detail is amazing.'

'I'll join you in a moment,' Madalena said, heading for the Ladies. She should know by now not to choose something heavy for lunch. Boeuf bourguignon was a dinner dish, one to be enjoyed when there was time afterwards for resting, not visiting an exhibition.

She splashed water on her face, ran a comb through her hair and stared at her reflection in the mirror, noticing the darkness of her eyes. Annie was obviously not on the verge of opening up to her about Ferne and the baby. Too stoical. She sighed – she couldn't force her daughter to confide in her.

When she returned to the sculpture room, Portia and Annie were gazing at another carving of a full-breasted woman, Portia cracking a joke, checking simultaneously that all her blouse buttons were done up. Annie laughed, then moved away, shook her head and turned back to Portia. Vienne stood some distance from them, studying a cast of Rodin's *Thinker*.

She turned to Madalena. 'See how the body is twisted in tension from the head down to the toes? This is to convey an intellectual struggle. Then you have his right arm supporting his head, but the left hand is open, as if ready for action. One of the casts is beside his and his wife's tomb in Paris, a lovely touch, don't you think? Perhaps I should arrange for a sculpture of a piano beside my coffin.'

Madalena placed her arm on Vienne's shoulder. 'Hopefully you won't have to be thinking about that for many years, dear. I'm sure your neurology consultation will show there's nothing wrong. Let's go and see the musicians.'

Vienne nodded, glanced at her sisters, then took Madalena to the adjoining room where she pointed out a group of inch high alabaster figurines, all with instruments. 'It's exquisite isn't it, such detail?'

Madalena nodded. 'Think of all the work which went into it, and I struggle to produce a symmetrical vase.'

'I like your work,' Vienne said, clutching Madalena's arm.

Madalena swallowed hard. As a child, Vienne constantly had reached for her arm, constantly needed reassurance. Was her daughter giving or seeking comfort now?

'We should join the others,' Madalena said and they left the room, Vienne's arm still on hers.

'They're probably joking over some vulgar sculpture,' Vienne said. 'Not that I'm a prude.... Let's find Tinguely's work. I even persuaded Michael to look at his sculptures when we were in New York. If anything can interest my uncultured husband, it's kinetic art. We spent over three hours in the Museum of Modern Art.'

'It's been a lovely trip,' Portia said, over coffee and cake. 'I might bring Lucy to the exhibition. She's developing an interest in art.'

As they wove their way in and out of the pedestrians, en route to the car park, Luzern was now rolling towards a busy evening. Pavement café drinks; strolls by the river to gaze at the medieval Chapel Bridge; immersion in the city's squares of ancient churches and government buildings with their frescoed façades and sense of history; huddles of busking violinists so absorbed in their music they barely noticed the francs chucked into their dusty hats. No matter how often Madalena visited this city, its vibrancy, the hazy mountain light, provoked a sharp intake of breath, a fluttering.

Overall, the day had gone okay, she felt, as she rummaged in her purse for coins for the parking ticket. The rift between Portia and Vienne was worrying, nevertheless. She *would* have a word with Portia, see if she could glean the nature of the problem.

At the airport the next day, Madalena trembled when she saw the flight arrival announcement. She glanced at her smart linen suit and silk blouse. Why had she got so dressed up? It was Lawrence arriving, not the hotel inspectorate.

She opened a newspaper and gazed unseeingly at it for some moments, before closing the paper. Surrounding her were advertisements for banks and Rolex watches. Would the Swiss love of money and all things material, ever change? Would Switzerland always be a tax haven for people who were already too wealthy? Mind you, it hadn't always been a prosperous country.

Nearby, a woman cleaned the floor with an electric mop. The rhythmic noise of the machine, its meticulous, circular movements, were strangely soothing, and as Madalena's eyes met those of the cleaner, they exchanged smiles. This commonplace encounter lifted her spirits. Some people would continue worshipping the Swiss franc. Others would continue taking pride in cleaning floors.

For the umpteenth time, she wondered why Lawrence needed to stay somewhere else. He loved her yet had rejected her Zurbriggen for the Hotel Bergmann. This issue of what was going on would hang between them until she had an answer. Like a mist lingering over the Urnersee. This was the worst thing – one of the worst things – about being a mother. You could not control the power your children had to hurt you.

As she thought of Lawrence's favourite *wiener schnitzel* which Johann was cooking for this evening, a horrible thought occurred. What if her son planned to eat at the Hotel Bergmann, only intended to drop in at the Zurbriggen from time to time?

A trickle of people emerged from Customs, looking around to be claimed. She smoothed back her hair, adjusted her jacket collar. There he was: fit looking, tanned, his wavy light brown hair showing no signs of receding – a clone of David, even his average height. Lawrence spotted her and waved, and momentarily she saw the child she had met at the airport for the school holidays, aware already of the preciousness of time before he would return again to the UK for another term. Now she saw the adult, noting with relief the decent sized suitcase clutched in his left hand.

'I am glad you're here,' Madalena said after hugging him.

'Sorry I took so long to make up my mind whether or not to come,' he said sheepishly.

'You're here and that's what matters.'

The Butzenbüelring, heading south towards Hangstrasse, was heaving, the air through the open window of the Renault, warm. Madalena glanced at her son – he looked drowsy.

'Did you manage to get a room with a balcony?' Lawrence asked.

She nodded. 'I hope you think it's worth the additional seventy francs per night.' She refrained from pointing out that she could have given him a room with an equally beautiful view, for no cost.

'That's great, thanks for organising it.'

'We should be in Brunnen in an hour,' Madalena said. 'I expect you're tired. Flying exhausts me.'

'I had an early start. The drive to Inverness is hard to predict. But I'm glad to be away. Winter was terrible – I nearly went crazy with the gales and horizontal rain, the lack of daylight. It doesn't usually bother me, but for some reason it did this year.'

'How are the home improvements coming along? You never mention them.'

He sighed. 'Things about the cottage are starting to bug me, too, things I can't easily change: the creaks and groans of the floorboards and the noisy pipes. It needs so much work doing but... I don't know.'

Madalena changed gear, glanced at him. 'How's Rebecca?'

'Fine.'

'You didn't think about bringing her here? You know, you've never introduced me to her when I've stayed with you.'

'She couldn't have come over during term time.'

Madalena frowned. 'I thought she did supply teaching. That she could please herself.'

'She's got a full-time job now. Everyone else here?'

'They arrived on Monday.'

'How's Annie?'

'She's not going to be a mother, after all. She seems to be coping, nevertheless.'

There was a silence, then Lawrence said. 'She's tough as old boots.'

'Strong, dear. Not tough. Tough has negative connotations. Yes, all my children are strong.'

He smiled. 'Strong parents, strong children.'

They exited the A14, headed towards Weggis and Gersau. Not long to go. What should she do when they arrived at the Hotel Bergmann? Go in with Lawrence, check his reservation was okay, that he was happy with his room? Might Herr Adler be expecting to see her? Was it possible to avoid being seen with her son? Sooner or later she would have to ask him what was going on. Whatever was responsible for Lawrence's decision, it wasn't just Herr Adler who'd know. With a surname like Fontana, other members of staff would make the connection. People would speculate.

∾

That afternoon, Madalena could smell the mix of compost and scent from her roses, indicating imminent rain. With luck, it would remain dry for her tea party. For some inexplicable reason, it felt important that this first meeting of Karl with her children should take place outside. She spotted Karl before he saw her.

'Punctual, as always,' she said, as he kissed her cheek.

'Especially when food is included.' He looked round the patio. 'You did invite us for afternoon tea?'

Madalena laughed. 'I'll bring out the cakes once the others have arrived.'

'Your hands are trembling,' he remarked.

She sighed. 'I was remembering when David met my parents. We had only known each other for eight months.'

And she'd been pregnant, something her parents wouldn't let her forget – throughout the planning of their wedding, and the event itself: the impersonal registry office ceremony; the hotel reception where the subjects of oil paintings gazed disdainfully at her, swaddled as she was in green taffeta, an additional layer of material concealing her expanding abdomen - her mother's insistence.

'I passed two elderly ladies in the garden,' Karl was saying. 'They were most interested in me, although one of them was trying not to show it.'

'Ruth and Alice Sowerby. They'll be wondering who you are. They are hopelessly romantic.'

'I see. Did I mention I missed lunch today?'

Madalena smiled. 'Be patient.'

For the third time, she checked the table: cups, saucers, sugar bowl, side plates, the Japanese paper napkins.

'Relax,' Karl said. 'It's you I am marrying, not one of your daughters.'

At least she and Karl would have control over their

wedding. Fleetingly, she considered getting married secretly. Returning to the Zurbriggen to announce the deed already done. The requisite official paperwork, however, prevented spontaneous eloping. Perhaps this was just as well. The tiny part questioning whether she was ready to remarry, refused to be silenced.

'They should be here soon. Ah, I can see Portia and Lucy.' Portia was striding towards the patio, Lucy several paces behind.

She smoothed back her hair.

'You look lovely, *liebling*,' Karl said.

Madalena introduced them.

Portia and Karl shook hands, Lucy raised her arm, said, 'Hi Karl', and turned to Madalena. 'I'm starving, Granny.'

'You can help me with the cakes,' Madalena said.

Lucy helped her fetch the cakes and lay them on the patio table. Vienne and Michael arrived, then shortly after, Lawrence and Annie.

'So, how did you two meet?' Annie asked, as Madalena introduced her to Karl.

Madalena hesitated. Even although she and Karl had discussed this occasion, they hadn't actually agreed how they would explain their getting to know each other.

'At a garden centre,' Karl said.

She suppressed a smile. Ingenious, furthermore, consistent with her telling Vienne and Annie of his involvement with her conservatory, which *was* true.

'The conservatory is lovely. I wish we had one, not that I'd be much use with it,' Vienne said.

As Vienne chatted to Karl, Madalena recalled her parents' reaction when she announced that she and David were buying the Zurbriggen. Their bombardment of questions about how they could afford this, how they would manage a hotel when they were so young and had a child on the way. David's restraint in the face of thinly veiled hostility had been admirable. Fortunately, his parents had been more positive.

'Do you have a family, Karl?' Portia asked, once Vienne had slipped away to talk to Michael.

He nodded. 'A son. My wife died when Thobias was five, so it was only the two of us.'

'Does he live in Brunnen?'

Karl shook his head. 'He is a professor of philosophy at the University of Heidelberg.'

'And do you see each other often?'

Madalena sniffed. 'You aren't in court now, Portia. More tea anyone?'

Lawrence refilled his own cup. 'Heidelberg is beautiful. I spent a weekend there after a walking holiday in the Bavarian Alps.'

How strange it was to observe her son talking with Karl. Almost like watching one husband appraise the other. Nevertheless, their conversation seemed to be going well. What a relief. Lawrence wasn't the easiest person to relate to.

She helped herself to more tea. Karl and Portia were now chatting again. Although Madalena couldn't hear what they were saying, Portia's solemn expression and head nodding indicated she was assessing him.

Lawrence was sitting beside Lucy, who was stroking a tabby cat that had wandered into the garden. Madalena overheard something about a visit to a museum. She liked to think of Lawrence spending time with his niece, whom she presumably rarely saw. How often did Lucy see her father? Probably not enough for someone her age. At least here, in the absence of Elliot, she had two uncles, one of whom was making an effort.

As she observed Vienne talking to Michael, she detected dissension: something in the hunch of Vienne's shoulders, Michael's standing at right angles to her. Perhaps Vienne had noticed Lawrence with Lucy, was trying to persuade Michael to become more involved. Perhaps she was ruminating over her health and had exhausted Michael's patience.

While circulating with plates of cake, Madalena became aware that Portia and Lucy weren't there. Annie was talking to Karl, smiling, laughing.

As Annie went to refill her coffee cup, Karl was suddenly by Madalena's side. 'How am I doing?'

She reached up to kiss his cheek.

'Am I to take that as a positive response?' he asked.

'You may, yes.'

As she'd expect, given his profession, he understood the importance of this tea party. Furthermore, he was letting her children take the initiative to engage him in conversation, rather than imposing his company on them. It might be sensible to invite him to the picnic she planned for two days' time. Another opportunity for her children to get to know him before the Dinner. No doubt they would be speculating with each other about what he meant to her.

To her relief, Portia had returned with Lucy, and Lawrence was heading in their direction.

Annie was seated by the patio table, nibbling chocolate cake. She looked much better than when she'd arrived five days before. Occasionally, when she believed she wasn't under scrutiny, her chin tilted upwards and she blinked hard, but this wasn't happening so frequently now. Also, the fact that she was spending so much time with her camera suggested she was deriving some pleasure from her visit.

How lovely it had been when Annie came to her apartment last night, to show her the latest batch of photos she'd downloaded onto her laptop. It whisked Madalena back decades, to when her youngest would seek her out on her own for "mother and daughter" time. Moreover, the photos were excellent. She hadn't been aware of Annie's gift for interpreting light conditions and choosing unusual compositions. Perhaps such creativity was part of the healing process.

Now, as she studied the sky, she wondered how long it would be before the rain arrived. Hopefully it would hold off for a while longer. Karl was due back at the *Psychiatriezen− trum Luzern-Stadt* at six, but after he left it could pour all evening. They'd be inside, enjoying a family dinner.

6

A nnie halted in front of her friend's apartment block in Zurich. During the train journey, she'd thought about yesterday's tea party. Despite warming to Karl, she'd felt even lonelier afterwards, and now visiting Claire didn't seem like such a wise idea. Talking to her would only heighten the memories of her time with Ferne. As she turned to retrace her steps, however, she heard a voice from an upper balcony.

'Buzzer ten. Name's on it.'

She forced a smile and waved to Claire, jumping as the nearby clock struck eleven-thirty.

Minutes later, she was seated in Claire's kitchen, sipping an apple and mango smoothie. Sunshine streamed through the large window, highlighting the strong green walls, as Claire's hands moved feverishly around the table, gathering together tiny tubes of paint and brushes and scraps of cloth.

'You suit your hair longer,' Annie said.

Claire smiled. 'I thought with Michelle having such short hair....'

'It's a cool apartment.'

'Ticks most of the boxes. It can be noisy at the weekends – people congregate outside the bar, especially during the summer. But we got it for a reduced rent if we agreed to do it up.... Fortunately, the landlady approves of my taste. *And* she's bought one of my paintings.'

'That's brilliant! I keep meaning to paint my cottage.'

'Annie, I'm sorry it didn't work out with Ferne.'

'Sometimes I feel I'm getting over it. Other times–'

Claire peered at her. 'In just over a week?'

'It was the way it happened, the way I found out, I mean.... I know I'm being self-indulgent, going over it. I suppose....'

'Have you talked to anyone?'

Annie shook her head. 'I phoned Portia when it happened. But it's not so easy face to face with her.'

'The high-flying human rights barrister, yeah? What happened?'

Annie took a deep breath. 'I'd been shopping. I'd bought a carry tot and lovely soft baby towels and then I spotted the mobiles of jungle animals to hang above the baby's cot....'

She paused, remembering the way the mobile spun had round, tigers, monkeys and giraffes blending into each other. She could recall the freshness of the new towels; the plastic of the baby carrier handles; her longing to show Ferne her purchases, anticipating a jokey comment, followed by a hug, a compliment on her taste.

Claire refilled Annie's glass, sipped at her own.

'It was a dreary Monday,' Annie continued. 'It was raining when I arrived at the café. I remember looking around the room and thinking it was worth all the effort I'd spent on the interior, because it was so cosy and welcoming – especially on a crap morning: the oilskin tablecloths, the terracotta tiles which I actually laid myself. Jazz was playing,

I could smell lentil soup and coffee, and I looked round for Ferne....'

She stopped, remembering the tingling sensation she'd experienced, the quickness of breath.

'Ferne wasn't by the counter. I went into the kitchen. There was a scuffle as I entered. She was with Stephen... in his arms, and.... Anyway, I had to get through the next four hours at the café before we could talk. Talk properly. It was hell. I kept telling myself I'd misunderstood. Stephen had simply been giving her a friendly hug, maybe reassuring her about the baby being healthy. But deep down, I knew I hadn't got it wrong. Ferne looked so uncomfortable. After we closed for the day, she told me everything.'

There was silence. Claire reached out an arm. Annie could smell her perfume – the *Christian Dior* one that Ferne wore.

'Have you seen her again?' Claire asked eventually.

Annie shook her head. 'Apart from her moving her stuff out.... She's looking after the café while I'm here, I didn't have any choice.... But I'll find someone else when I return.... Anyway, that's more than enough about me.'

'You need to talk, Annie.'

'The worst... the worst thing is the betrayal of trust. I always thought if I couldn't trust Ferne then I couldn't trust anyone.... It leaves you feeling so cynical. I never believed a woman would treat me in such a way. Stupid of me, I suppose.'

'Women are no different to men when it comes to behaving badly. Everyone feels this way when life drops a pile of crap on them.'

Despite herself, Annie smiled. 'How are things with you and Michelle?'

She tried to recall what Michelle looked like. Tall with

short fair hair. Athletic. And a boring job – something in accounting.

'I was worried she wouldn't join me here, but she did,' Claire said, 'and she loves Zurich as much as I do. The best city in the world, she says. I told her that before I left, but she had to find out for herself.... We could meet her for lunch, if you like.'

'Claire, do you ever find yourself attracted to men?' Annie asked. 'I mean, at the same time as being with Michelle?'

Claire raised an eyebrow. 'Have you met someone?'

'Sort of. Not really. The chef in Mum's hotel – nothing's happened, I just sense he might be interested. When he looks at me sometimes.... I just wonder, I mean I think I react to him. It's nothing....'

Claire finished her smoothie. 'Nothing's ever one hundred per cent. There was an artist – a guy – I fancied. It was more of an emotional thing, about art.... You've had relationships with men in the past. You might again – when you're ready. Now, how about a walk by the river?'

Annie looked out of the window. 'It's raining.' As the church bells struck midday, she stood. 'Let's meet Michelle for lunch.'

Having lunch with people other than family could be therapeutic. Even if she found herself knee-deep in envy of Claire and Michelle's settled relationship.

'You grew up in Switzerland, didn't you?' Michelle asked at lunch.

Annie nodded.

'Brunnen,' Claire said.

Michelle poured herself a glass of water. 'Ever considered moving back? Especially now, with what's happened?'

Annie shrugged. The smell of the raclette cheese

melting under the mini grill on the nearby table made her feel queasy. Too many things were making her squeamish at the moment.

'The gay scene's thriving in Zurich,' Michelle said.

'Well, yeah, but meeting another woman is the last thing on my mind,' Annie said, thanking the waitress who brought her salad.

Michelle's eyes opened wide. 'You're not considering a relationship with a man, surely?'

'Ease up, Michelle,' Claire said.

Annie arranged a forkful of lettuce and tomato. 'I've had relationships with men before. Quite a few.'

In fact, she'd been on the verge of another one when she met Ferne. An invitation to a party, after which the guy had been sent abroad on business, and by the time he returned, she was embroiled with Ferne.

'You must be tolerant,' Michelle said. 'Constant mess, loo seat always up, dirty dishes. Not to mention an inability to discuss emotions.'

Claire yawned. 'How stereotyped. There are women with disgusting habits, too, you know.' She gave Michelle a pointed look.

Michelle smiled, softening her face. Her eyes were strikingly blue.

Around them conversation hummed, orders were called to the kitchen. Outside, the rain had halted, and the grey of the river changed to a muted blue. A pleasure boat made its way past, and through the open window Annie could hear the commentary in French then Spanish.

'I wouldn't want to give up the café,' Annie said. 'I worked so hard at renovating it, building up my clientèle.'

'You could start a business here, specialising in British cuisine,' Claire suggested.

And yet, Annie thought, as well as the cottage, the café was so closely connected with Ferne. Then there was the village. Everything, it seemed, linked with her ex. And with Stephen living nearby, there'd constantly be the risk of running into the three of them. She'd had no time to accustom herself to living alone again before coming over to Brunnen.

'If there was a business looking for a new management.... The thing is, I like being my own boss.'

And she'd want the business to have ethical aspects, like Madalena's hotel. And her ropey German would be a hindrance. She'd thought being bilingual was a permanent state. Evidently not.

Michelle added more pepper to her lasagne. 'How did Ferne conceive the baby?'

Before Annie could answer, Claire intervened, 'Michelle, for God's sake. They've only just split up.'

'It's okay,' Annie said. 'Ferne and Stephen slept together. It was a natural conception.'

'And it didn't bother you?' Michelle asked.

Annie shook her head. 'Ferne and I discussed it, everything. We wanted one of us to be the biological mother.... And we didn't like the idea of using some stranger's defrosted sperm – it didn't seem right.'

'Didn't you worry when they were ... together?' Michelle persisted.

'Not really. I mean, I felt quite detached. Like it was a lab experiment, mixing two chemicals together, seeing what happened.'

Now, while explaining her thinking, it did seem naïve. And for the first time, she wondered if Ferne had felt attracted to Stephen even then. If she'd always considered Annie as expedient rather than a long-term partner.

Back in Brunnen again, Annie popped into Madalena's office.

'How was Zurich?' Madalena asked.

Annie shrugged. 'It was good seeing Claire.... Mum, I'm so confused...'

Madalena closed her computer. 'Sit down, dear.'

Annie sat down, then immediately stood. 'Later, perhaps? I need to get out on the lake. The light's perfect. Could I take a snack from the kitchen?'

In the kitchen, Annie found a cake tin. As she was deciding what to take, Johann emerged from the storage room.

'Mum said I could take some food,' she told him.

He smiled. 'I baked a gingerbread this morning. Do you like gingerbread?'

He was standing close to her. As she looked at her shirt, she noticed an undone button. Before she could react, however, he reached out, did up the button, one hand resting briefly on her stomach, its warmth searing through the thin cheesecloth.

'I'll take these,' she said, clasping two cinnamon buns.

She left the kitchen, making an effort to walk slowly. In her bedroom, she sank onto the bed. She looked down at her blouse again, still feeling the imprint of his lingering hand.

Time was pushing on, Annie told herself as she packed her rucksack and headed for the lake. When she found the right spot, she set up the tripod, extending one of its legs to ensure it was stable on the sand. As she took a reading of the light, the tripod wobbled, so she adjusted it further and looked through the camera lens. The late afternoon light was perfect, but she needed a steady camera.

Exasperated, she flopped onto a bench and stared out over the lake, appreciating the smell of wood smoke from a nearby chalet. A toddler in blue and red striped dungarees gripped its mother's hand as they walked along the shore a few yards from her. She watched as the infant stumbled and the mother lifted him and smothered his flushed cheek with kisses.

Annie bowed her head. How could she have believed Brunnen would be a refuge? It was only now she recognised how much she'd included her childhood home in her future landscape. Taking the child out on the lake in the water steamer, explaining how the engine worked. Or up to Rigi on the cogged wheel railway. Reinstating – with Madalena's blessing – their childhood Christmas festivities, the traditional Swiss meal, which she and Ferne would cook. When it was cold enough for the Urnersee to freeze over, teaching the child to skate, using a kitchen chair as support, as Dad had done with Vienne.

Loneliness was a malignant condition. Her siblings had someone to share things with. She needed someone.

Should she phone Ferne, gauge whether anything had changed over the last few days? A week was a long time for someone with Ferne's fickleness. No, she wouldn't contact her. There was no point in putting herself through the misery of hearing that soft Dublin voice. Anyway, what would they say to each other? Ferne would get in touch if she wanted to.

Annie fervently now wished that she'd missed the ladies' session at her local swimming pool one blustery March morning four years earlier. That she hadn't got talking to Ferne, seduced by the lazy brogue which could lull her to sleep. Ferne would have discovered a better swimming pool a month later or decided she couldn't be bothered swimming.

Annie glanced at her watch – four o'clock in the UK. Ferne would be unloading the dishwasher in the café kitchen, making a last-minute order to the wholesaler, writing the following day's specials on the blackboard. Then she'd close up, perhaps pop into JoJo Maman Bébé, although she already had too many baby clothes. Annie pictured the chestnut tree in her garden which wouldn't now have a swing attached to it, or energetic limbs scrambling along its branches.

Claire was right. It did take time to absorb such loss.

Annie's thoughts turned to Johann, to their encounter in the kitchen. If she was so gutted by losing Ferne, why was she reacting to a man's touch? Was she as changeable as Ferne? Or just desperate for someone to want her?

As she raised her head, she noticed a familiar figure walking along the lakeside path. The figure was small, but she recognised the gait despite the hazy sun. She willed him to turn around and retrace his steps, conscious of being ill-prepared for this encounter with Lawrence. The last meeting on their own – slightly over two years ago in York – had been horrible, criticisms bandied back and forwards like a ping-pong ball on speed.

She half rose, intending once more to stabilise the tripod. Pools of light on the Urnersee changed every minute as if undecided about how they wanted to be. Mountains and sailing boats were mirrored in the calm water. Such loveliness. Not that she'd be able to concentrate on photography, though. Not with her brother in attendance.

No, better to remain seated, muster as much dignity as she could. She'd nothing to rebuke herself with, where

Lawrence was concerned. He drew closer, reached her and stopped, seemingly as awkward as she was.

'Settled into your grand hotel?' Annie asked.

She'd meant to be lighthearted, but hit the wrong tone, the words sounding snide.

'How are you?' he asked.

Annie shrugged. Too easy to say "fine", too risky to tell him the truth.

He placed a tentative arm on her shoulder. 'Mum told me about the baby.'

'It happens,' she said.

He looked over the lake, squinting in the sunlight. 'Is Ferne—?'

'How's work? Getting enough commissions?'

Lawrence groaned. 'I'll have to work while I'm here. Deadline looming.'

'I'm surprised you were lured away,' Annie said. 'No doubt the glamorous environment of the Hotel Bergmann will lend itself to the creative process.'

'You don't understand.... Am I permitted to sit beside you?'

She nodded, suddenly exhausted, as if the release from this morning's conversation had been transient. Grief was draining. And she had the walk back to the Zurbriggen. She thought of her comfy bed, how restorative it would be to lie on it, listening to Celtus on her iPod.

'I *am* sorry about the baby, Annie.'

Yeah, right. Did he know it was Ferne who was pregnant? Annie could barely remember what she'd told Madalena. Their conversation was a blur, something she'd had to get through at the time because she couldn't shut her mother out, not completely.

'Any idea what's going on with Mum?' Lawrence asked. 'There's more than an anniversary celebration.'

Annie lacked the energy to reply.

His tone changed, becoming quieter, less confident. 'I have to talk to her about something – something unpleasant. I've been putting it off for too long.'

Annie scrutinised him before replying, 'You mustn't upset her, especially not before the Dinner.'

'Don't worry, I'll wait until it's over. And it wouldn't be right to tell you before her. Please don't mention this to anyone.'

Annie nodded, relieved he hadn't confided in her. She was in no mood for revelations, especially from him. In the past, before the whole café/Ferne debacle, she'd have wheedled it out of him, justifying her curiosity by knowing it would help him to unburden.

'How's the café?' Lawrence asked.

'The clientèle are loyal. You didn't scare them all away.'

'Look, I didn't come and find you to argue.'

She gave a squawky laugh. 'You must have changed then.'

He shook his head. 'I doubt it.'

'So do I.... How's Rebecca?'

Lawrence didn't reply.

'Didn't she want to come, too? Mum would have made her welcome.'

'Our relationship isn't going anywhere. I really should end it.'

'Is it difficult because of her daughter?'

'No, I love Tammy – Tamsin. She's cool. Actually, I've got a crush on someone else.'

'Who?'

'A journalist I met at one of those dinners.'

'So why don't you finish with Rebecca and pursue this journalist?'

Lawrence hesitated. 'She might be married.'

Annie sighed. 'You know your problem – one of them, anyway? You have a thing about unavailable women. I bet if Rebecca was married or with someone, you'd be keener on her. You should be in therapy.'

'God, you sound like her. Self-styled psychologist. What would you know about heterosexual relationships?'

'Sod off.'

Annie collapsed the tripod and placed it in her camera bag, hoping Lawrence would leave. When she'd finished packing up, he had walked away in the direction of Flüelen. Long strides, if less confident ones. She considered going after him, but more memories were pursuing her of that bleak day when she'd discovered the truth about Ferne and Stephen: sitting with Ferne's bag of yarn, the muted blues and pinks, rusts and grass greens, all those beautiful colours. Picking out strands and sniffing them, pressing their softness against her cheek.

Later, taking the bag into the garden and placing it by the horse chestnut tree, between the two branches where the hammock would have been. Gathering twigs, scrunching newspaper, emptying the yarn onto the fire, the acrid smell of burning wool stinging her eyes.

She'd pictured the empty evenings and Sundays ahead of her, while Stephen and Ferne raised their baby. On hearing the poignant sound of an oboe from a neighbour's house piercing the silent evening, she'd been unable to hold back the tears any longer.

She now interrupted her return walk to Brunnen, set up the tripod again, more successfully this time. After experimenting with various lenses, she selected the right one, set the shutter speed and fixed the aperture for a long focal length. Her sadness receded as she concentrated on photographing the lake, the boats with their stripey sails, the sharp contours of Gitschen. As she packed away her equipment once more, she felt restored to peace. This feeling wouldn't last, but experiencing it, even for a short while, helped.

In the distance, the Hotel Bergmann, her brother's temporary home, gleamed in the evening light.

7

On the balcony of their suite next morning, Vienne gazed at her white arms. Hopefully, after some sunshine, she'd return to London with a tan. Then the sleeveless black dress might work for the concert, provided she could find a new padded bra, which of course would necessitate a demoralising visit to Oxford Street. She should never have bought the dress. Its lack of detail around the bustline gave her figure an even more boyish appearance.

The ever-increasing fixation with women's bodies was sickening. She thought of the website she'd recently stumbled upon which denounced the Australian Bratz padded bra for six-year-olds; a newspaper, in defence of such practices, claiming something about supporting fashionable items which gave girls modesty as they went through developmental changes. Developmental changes at six? It was despicable, loathsome. No wonder eating disorders continued to rise. The desperation for a perfect body.

She blamed school for most of her feelings of inadequacy, unable as she was to shake off the memories of cruel comments. Countless times she'd turned to Portia for comfort after taunting about her small boobs, after being mocked for not participating in her classmates' nightly ritual of standing by the communal wash-hand basins, naked to the waist, pulling back their shoulders and arms, chanting the mantra, "I must, I must increase my bust". Portia, already well-endowed, would simply hug her, assure her she had a "neat" figure and was much prettier than the other girls her age.

But Vienne wouldn't dwell on this now, with it being such a beautiful day. She stepped back into the room, went over to Michael who was on his laptop.

'You're very quiet, are you okay?'.

'Just trying to finish this report,' he said.

'I'm determined to spend time with Lucy today. Portia can't hog her indefinitely.... are you listening, Michael?'

'She *is* her daughter.'

'I know, let's take her to Vitznau with us.'

'You're not thinking, darling. We haven't spent time with Lucy since she was about ten.'

'Michael, I know you're fed up hearing this, but I'm baffled about Portia and me. I thought being together here would make a difference, but she obviously doesn't want to sort things out. And I'll never be able to understand why we had that horrid row after we moved back from the States. None of this makes sense.'

'Life seldom makes sense.'

'What do you think will happen to Lucy now? Do you think Portia will find another boarding school for her?'

'Your family are so hung up on boarding schools. Do you really think such places are the best environment for a child? It's not as if you were particularly happy there.'

'At least I had Portia for part of the time. Annie too. But

it's different for Lucy, being an only child. What do you think?'

Michael sighed. 'I think you should let me finish my report.'

'I don't know why you couldn't have done that before we left London. It's depressing you working on holiday.'

'You practise.'

'That's different.'

He could at least be prepared to have a general conversation about Lucy.

'Well, I'd like an opinion.'

Michael sounded weary with indifference. 'About what?'

'Schools for Lucy. I think it would be better for her to be at home, have stability. If she went to a day school then I'd have a chance to become a proper aunt again. Besides, I've had an idea. This is all based on Lucy going to a day school and being at home with Portia–'

'Christ, you've only just heard the girl's been expelled.'

'It's important to think ahead. My idea is this: Lucy can stay with us when Portia's travels coincide with Elliot's. Portia's bound to realise the benefits of having us around, and I'll bet you anything she'll regret the years when we didn't see each other much.'

'Next you'll be saying we should have had children after all.'

'No, we agreed not to, and I haven't changed my mind. Having Lucy to stay would be different. It would probably only be for short periods, a few days perhaps. I think, given time and some effort, you'd make a lovely uncle.'

Yes, this reunion was the ideal opportunity to compensate for lost time. Once he got used to having a young person around, Michael wouldn't object to Lucy's visits. And the main guest bedroom would be ideal for converting – a desk for Lucy's homework, perhaps a new bed. A cabin bed, with the desk underneath.

She visualised her niece sitting at the island worktop in their kitchen, hands clasped round a hot chocolate – in her special mug – as she rambled on about her day at school. Lucy would look forward to seeing Portia again, but would feel sad about leaving them.

Michael stretched, rose from his chair and walked over to the balcony. 'The light is stunning. Wish I'd brought my camera. Did you remember yours?'

Vienne followed him onto the balcony. 'Michael, don't you think you'd enjoy being an uncle again?'

'We don't know Lucy. And it sounds like she'd be difficult to have around. Schools don't expel pupils lightly. What if she wrecked our home?'

'Don't be ridiculous. She's not a vandal.'

'We don't know *what* she is, Vienne.'

'Well, at least we should have them over to dinner. Make an effort. It would be horrid and completely unjustifiable to cut her off just because she's going through a difficult phase. Perhaps more family around is what she needs, not that I know anything about teenagers.'

'This doesn't make sense, your sudden burning desire to become an aunt. Why now?'

'It's not new, you know I saw her a bit when she was little, although Portia never made it easy.... Thanks for your understanding.'

She wanted to walk away from Michael's nasty mood, his tactless comments and negativity. But leaving wouldn't achieve anything. They had to reach some agreement on their approach with Lucy. It was as if he'd accepted that Lucy wouldn't be a part of their lives.

Michael approached her now, gathered her to him. 'I

remember not long after we first met, you told me you'd rather have a Fazioli grand piano than a child.'

Had she really made such a comment? He must have thought her spoilt as well as uncaring. Most women hankered after having children. Most of her friends had at least one, though fortunately they refrained from dominating their lunches with stories of Brownies and exorbitant school fees.

'Did you think I was heartless?'

Michael laughed. 'Expensive. You were talking upwards of £240,000.'

'You must have thought I was cold.'

'Actually, I was quite relieved. It was difficult deciding when to tell you I wasn't paternal.'

'I'll mention my idea to Portia as soon as possible. I won't push her, just suggest that you and I could help out at times. It might make the difference between Lucy going to another boarding school and staying at home.'

Michael took her arm. 'A word of advice, darling: hold fire. Portia's had a shock. You don't want to look as if you're taking advantage of Lucy's expulsion by rushing in with your plans, do you?'

Vienne pulled her arm away.

He muttered something about checking at reception if a fax had arrived. When he'd gone, she felt relieved. His lack of enthusiasm was depressing. Still, given time, he might change, especially when he realised her pleasure from having a bigger role in Lucy's life. Family was family. And Lucy staying with them would only be for a few years. She was growing up fast. Did Portia feel sad about this?

Vienne was mulling this over when she heard the sound of a piano from a nearby chalet. Sibelius's Romance Op 24 No. 9, played by a child, one with talent. She moved over to the window. Yes, whoever it was could have a future in music. There was both feeling and control in the rendition. Did Lucy play the piano?

The Sibelius raised her spirits, turned her thoughts to the spare bedroom, what she could do with it to make it more teenager-friendly. A cabin bed with the desk and chair underneath was a great idea. And a comfy armchair where Lucy could listen to music. Her own TV, except that might mean they'd never see her.... Vienne almost wished the concert was over so that she could focus on the next phase of her life. Perhaps she should invite Portia and Lucy for the weekend. Aunt Vienne – it had a strong ring to it, gravitas. But she'd try to be a fun aunt as well.

Michael didn't know what he was talking about. Once again, he was trying to influence her and here was a chance to assert herself. Besides, if Portia knew that they'd be around for Lucy, this might be exactly the kind of support she needed. Right now.

After breakfast, Vienne felt better. It was an ideal day for taking the steamer to Vitznau, and, despite their unpleasant conversation earlier, Michael hadn't changed his mind about going on the *Hotel du Lac* tour. Amazing, considering his caustic comments throughout the film: Anna Massey made a poor heroine – which was just the point, Vienne had argued; Denholm Elliot was too slimy as Philip Neville.

'Morning,' Madalena called from reception. 'Coffee, cold drink? There's some of Johann's homemade *apfelsaft.*'

'*Apfelsaft,* please. I was going to lie in the garden until Michael's finished his wretched report,' she said.

'I'll bring a glass to you. Lucy's there. "Chilling out" as she puts it.'

'Lucy? Great. I'll be company for her.'

'Take a short cut through the French windows in the sitting room,' Madalena suggested.

Vienne quickened her pace. Such an opportunity. Time on her own with her niece.

'Isn't it a lovely morning, Mrs Fotheringham?' came a voice as she entered the sitting room. She looked round. Ruth and Alice Sowerby were drinking tea in the far corner. She hesitated before approaching them.

'Are you enjoying your holiday?' she asked.

'Oh yes, yes we are, aren't we Ruth?' Alice said. 'How is the preparation going for your concert?'

Ruth's eyes sparkled. 'It must be so exciting, being up there on the platform, all eyes on you.'

'Quite nerve-racking, actually.'

She sat down in a chair facing the French windows, relieved to see Lucy stretched out on a lounger, clasping a magazine. Five minutes would cost nothing. It would be a kindness. 'Do call me Vienne.... Having a routine helps to minimise nerves.'

'Yes?' Ruth said, leaning forward.

'I always practise on the morning of the concert. In the afternoon I go for a walk – if it's Prague, I usually cross over one of the bridges to the other side of the city.'

'What happens after your walk?' Ruth asked.

'I do some relaxation techniques. Around five o'clock, I have a back and shoulder massage from the orchestra phys-iotherapist. Then a bath – not too hot – and a light supper in my room and–'

'I suppose a car comes to collect you,' Alice said.

Vienne glanced through the French windows. Lucy was adjusting her headphones. 'No, I like to walk to the venue – unless it's really cold or wet. My gown – usually black–'

Ruth sighed. 'Black....'

'My dress is always there, waiting for me in my changing room.'

'You must be so nervous just before the concert starts,' Ruth said.

Vienne smiled. 'I have a technique for my nerves.'

Ruth clasped her hands. 'What is it? Do tell us...'

'People tend to laugh when I describe it.'

'We won't laugh,' Alice said. 'Will we Ruth?'

Ruth giggled nervously, then composed herself.

'Well, it's really quite simple. I shake my hands back and forth, then I make my whole body shiver. I imagine the orchestra tuning, focussing on correcting a flat note. I visualise them looking at the score one last time.'

Vienne looked out of the French windows again. The lounger Lucy had occupied was now empty, with none of her possessions beside it. Maybe she should try to catch her in the corridor. About to stand up, she saw Lucy strolling across the lawn, watched her lie down on the lounger again, fiddle with her iPod.

'Just before the concert, the conductor – and this happens offstage – presents me with a bouquet of orange lilies, and he bows and kisses my hand.'

'*So* romantic,' Ruth said. 'Then? What happens then?'

'My personal assistant – Trish – puts the flowers in water, and hovers, just in case I need something at the last minute.'

'Such as?' Ruth asked. 'Whisky? Gin?'

'I never drink alcohol before a performance. I might want an aspirin, or a glass of water – always *Highland Spring,* the sparkling one. And the physio is there again, too, just in case...'

'To deal with any little twinges,' Alice suggested.

'Exactly.'

'You have such smooth hands?' Ruth said. 'What do you use on them?'

'Japanese cherry blossom moisturiser.'

Ruth frowned at her own mottled hands. 'I used to have lovely skin, didn't I, Alice? The ravages of age....'

'And when you walk on stage, finally,' Alice said, 'it must be such a wonderful moment.'

'It is quite something,' Vienne admitted. 'Now, if you'll both excuse me, I need to speak to my niece.'

'It's been wonderful talking to you, Mrs Fotheringham,' Ruth said. 'Hasn't it, Alice?'

'Indeed it has. Thank you, Vienne.'

Vienne paused at the rose arch entrance to the garden. She mustn't rush in, overwhelm Lucy. She needed to have her report back to Portia about their nice chat.

She'd keep the conversation light, no quick *crescendos*. *Pianissimo*, at least initially. See how it went. She was accustomed to having conversations with children, generally those younger than Lucy – before agreeing to teach them, and normally the first question she'd ask would be about school. Not appropriate with Lucy, though, given the circumstances.

She could ask what sports she enjoyed, enquire about summer holidays. With luck, she might learn more than she had from Portia, about how they planned to spend July and August. And she would enquire about Elliot – it would be appropriate to acknowledge his role in Lucy's life.

Elliot was okay, more than okay, the kind of man you felt safe with – comfortable and comforting. Like wearing a woolly hat on a snowy afternoon. His lived-in face and warm Northern accent, his unruly hair and floppy walk. Not that she fancied him. He was too scruffy in his baggy trousers and oversized jumpers. It *was* possible to find clothes that fitted, if one tried hard enough.

No, Elliot wouldn't have suited her, not when his idea of opera was Gilbert and Sullivan. He was a carry-out and DVD man, not a dinner party companion, although he knew a lot about many things and was always interested in what people had to say. And there was his reassuring cosiness.... He must have been devastated about the divorce, prone as he was to depression. There was a hardness to Portia, kicking someone who was already vulnerable. Portia should have stuck by him then Lucy wouldn't have been sent away to school. Lucy needed all the love she could get, from aunts and uncles, too.

Her niece lay under the shade of a cypress tree. She wore a sleeveless t-shirt, pedal pushers and trainers and her short, dark hair was heavily gelled. She was reading a magazine, headphones on. Vienne ignored the inner voice warning her that Lucy would probably prefer to be on her own, halted behind her, stomach fluttering. This was silly. Everything didn't rest on this conversation. She must regard it as a beginning. An *intermezzo*. Only a few instruments, quiet and understated.

She tapped Lucy on the shoulder, wincing at the thud from the headphones.

'Hi,' Lucy said.

'Not wanting to get a tan?' Vienne asked.

'Skin cancer's on the increase. I saw a programme about it on TV.'

Vienne pointed at the *New Scientist* Lucy held. 'You're interested in science?'

'I like physics,' Lucy said, squinting into the sun. 'And articles about buildings.'

An easy way in and so soon. Slowly now. 'I suppose you've learned a lot from your father about architecture.'

Lucy shrugged. 'I've been doing graph com at school – graphic communication.'

'Do you mean technical drawing?'

'Yeah.' Lucy was turning the page of her magazine.

Against her better judgement, Vienne ignored the obvious message. 'Do you see your father much?'

'I used to,' Lucy mumbled. 'But it might change.'

Vienne tried not to smile. Elliot had been headhunted by an offer from China or maybe Dubai. Or perhaps a prestigious firm in Louisiana or Chicago. This was her chance, but she mustn't rush in. 'I'm sure you'll be able to visit, wherever he goes.'

'Dad's not going away.'

'Then what do you mean you might not be seeing him so much in the future?'

Lucy fiddled with her iPod, 'I don't want to talk about it.'

'I didn't mean to upset you, I'm sorry. I'm just *so* pleased to talk to you, after–'

'Well, I don't want to talk about my father, whoever he is,' Lucy said, gathering her things and clambering off the lounger.

Vienne stared after her, cursing her clumsiness. She'd bungled the opportunity and Portia would find out. And, what was worse, there was no one to confide in, not properly: Michael overcome with indifference; Annie in cahoots with Portia. She remembered Mum's offer at the museum, to speak to Portia about what was going on. Had she done so? If Vienne now relayed her conversation with Lucy, doubtless Mum would agree Vienne had been insensitive. It was rather sad, she thought, three siblings and she was close to none of them.

A minute later, while she was deciding what to do, Annie strolled over, glass in hand. Barefooted and so youthful looking.

'Mum asked me to bring you this.... I thought Lucy was here....'

Vienne tugged at her neck chain. 'I've upset her.'

Annie laid the glass on an upturned tree stump doubling as a drinks table. 'What happened?'

'I only mentioned that if Elliot moved abroad, she could visit him, and she rushed off. I was trying to reassure her, not upset her. Not that I know about teenagers, apart from the few I teach, and they're probably at their best then.... I was only trying to be supportive.'

And pave the way for Lucy staying with them. She felt ashamed. The correct thing to do was sort things with Portia, not approach Lucy on the sly.

Annie blew out her cheeks. 'Elliot's not moving, as far as I know.'

'She said something strange,' Vienne added. 'She said she didn't want to talk about her father, whoever he is. Do you think she's having a breakdown?'

'I'll talk to her,' Annie said.

Vienne sank onto Lucy's lounger, lifted the glass of *apfelsaft,* replacing it quickly as the garden spun in front of her. Stress, these frightful symptoms must be caused by stress. When the spinning stopped, she rose from the chair and made her way to the hotel, via the French windows of the sitting room.

Ruth and Alice remained seated where she'd left them. Alice looked sleepy but Ruth's eye was roving the room and she beckoned to her. Vienne went over.

'We've rung for coffee,' Ruth said. 'Do tell us more about

Prague, if you have time. Father took us there when we were girls. I've never forgotten it.'

Vienne hesitated. She'd blown it with Lucy; she might as well give a bit more time to Alice and Ruth. She checked her watch. Michael would have to finish his blasted report soon or they'd miss the boat.

'I spent my honeymoon there,' she said.

'Oh, so rom*antic*,' Ruth remarked, with such fervour that Alice, who had nodded off, woke up.

Vienne smiled. 'It *was* romantic. We stayed in a lovely hotel.'

'Near the river?' Alice asked.

'Yes, in fact. Near the famous Charles Bridge. On the first Sunday, minutes after a waiter had wheeled in our breakfast table–'

'You had a breakfast table brought to your room?' Ruth said. 'Fancy that, Alice.'

'Just after we started eating, the church bells of St Nicholas rang out. It was a magnificent sound – I couldn't help it, I slipped on my boots and winter coat over my nightdress and rushed out into the snowy morning, like a Pied Piper rat.'

'The Pied Piper...' Alice said.

Ruth looked wistful. 'I wanted to study in Prague. But Father wouldn't hear of it. He believed–'

'Shush, Ruth. Let Vienne continue.'

'Well, I followed the sound until it led to a square where I listened to the bells. I was spellbound. Later, I couldn't find my way back to the hotel so I returned to the square. There was Michael – he'd come to find me.'

'You must have been *so* in love,' Ruth said, fingering her handkerchief.

Vienne smiled. 'It's a beautiful city.... I should go now.

We're off to Vitznau this afternoon – a tour of the hotel where *Hotel du Lac* was filmed.'

'*Hotel du Lac* is my favourite Anita Brookner book,' Ruth said.

Vienne pondered. The correct thing to do, the caring thing, would be to invite the sisters to join them on the tour. Give them a day out. But it would be so much nicer to have Michael to herself. Besides, how would he react to having two elderly women with them?

'If you would like to join us on the trip....'

Ruth's face lit up, but Alice replied first. 'It's most kind of you, but we wouldn't dream of imposing, would we Ruth?'

'I suppose not. We could go ourselves, another day,' Ruth said.

Vienne nodded. 'If you'll excuse me.... The boat leaves at twelve.'

A few tardy passengers brandished their tickets for inspection and bumbled onto the gangway as the horn sounded for the midday boat to Luzern. Engines chuntered and the boat pulled away from the shore, Brunnen gradually shrinking as they breezed through the water towards Vitznau. Vienne watched passengers beckon and call to each other, pointing to landmarks. Parents gripped the hands of small children while walking on deck. Binoculars and cameras were deployed.

'It won't be too blowy, for you, will it?' Michael asked, when they found a seat on the top deck.

'If only I hadn't bungled the conversation with Lucy.'

'Well, you don't have much experience of teenagers, do you, darling?'

Vienne turned to him. 'Michael, do you think it's normal for people of Lucy's age to question who their parents are, when they've split up?'

She hadn't intended to ask him this. He wasn't the analytical sort, never probing beneath the surface. This had become apparent to her soon after they'd met. And the expression he now wore reminded her of her first impression of him. Self-contained. Detached. She'd been playing the piano to patients from the long-stay care of the elderly wards at the local hospital. As she finished a Chopin piece, she'd looked up to see a visitor wheeling in an elderly man, slumped to one side. This had happened the next week and the one after. The following week the visitor wasn't there, and on enquiring, she was informed that the patient was very ill.

Something had propelled her to the ward, where she'd found Michael sitting by the bedside in a side room, clasping the man's hand. On this occasion, his grief showed. She'd been about to slip away when he spotted her and came to the door. He explained that his uncle had suffered a massive stroke.

Michael had turned up at the end of her performance two weeks later, informed her of his uncle's death. They'd had a cup of tea at the WRVS café, where he'd talked about Geoffrey having brought him up after the death of his parents, until the volunteer gently reminded them the café was closing. Michael had immediately stood, thanked Vienne for listening, and, as an afterthought, invited her for a drive in the country.

He was now tugging her arm. 'What are you on about?'

Vienne spoke slowly, deliberately. 'I misunderstood something Lucy said – I thought Elliot was moving abroad. Then she said something about not wanting to talk about her father, whoever he was and–'

'Are you sure that's what she said?'

'Certain. I told Annie – she was going to talk to her. Perhaps I should mention it to Portia, in case Annie forgets.'

Michael stood. 'I'm going inside.'

'I thought you'd taken a Traveleeze. I'll come with you.'

'No, stay, enjoy the journey. I'll come back up if I feel better.'

Vienne watched her husband make his way down the stairs, clutching the rail. Ten minutes later, she wondered if she should go and see how he was. The views of meadows, green and lush from the recent rain, were lovely – it was a shame for him to be missing this.

Suddenly, Michael was by her side.

'Are you okay?' she asked.

'I've been thinking,' he said, and something in his tone made her heart sink. He wasn't well enough for the trip. He wanted to return to Brunnen by bus.

'Perhaps we should fly home now and you can see a specialist there.'

'I couldn't do this to Mum. Besides, the appointment is only a few days away.... Michael, don't you want to be here? I thought you'd been looking forward to Brunnen.'

Michael was scanning the water, his eyes dark. 'I didn't know things would turn out like this.'

'It probably *is* nothing. The symptoms come and go – you usually tell me I worry too much.'

Vienne waited for him to reassure her again.

'Perhaps you...' he began.

'Perhaps I what?'

'I don't know.'

'Michael, forget about me for the moment. Are you up to visiting the hotel?'

He nodded, expression inscrutable. Was he concerned that her upsetting Lucy could worsen the situation with

Portia? It was out of character for him to become involved, but she couldn't attribute his mood dip to anything else. It was more than motion sickness. They were silent for the remainder of the journey.

As they joined the others who'd signed up for the tour round the Bellevue Hotel, she forced herself to switch off her ruminations about Michael. There was nothing to be done at the moment and she was loath to spoil the afternoon. She smiled at the other Anita Brookner fans as the guide, a jolly Swiss woman in a grey suit with *Hotel du Lac* embossed on its jacket lapel, began the itinerary with a summary of the film. Succinct but unnecessary.

Vienne experienced a surge of excitement when they were shown the room that the heroine, Edith, had been given, when they were allowed to step onto the small balcony with the wonderful view of the Waldstättersee. She laughed – though she wasn't quite sure why – when they were taken to the suite that the vulgar Mrs Pusey had occupied with her spoiled daughter. If Vienne had been on holiday with Mum, they would both have been content with rooms similar to Edith's, the one dismissed by Mrs Pusey as "little".

'I did feel enormously sorry for the countess being turfed out of her chateau by her son,' one of the participants remarked later, as they ate coffee and cake at the patisserie.

'Me too,' Vienne said. 'Especially the scene where he drops her off after their afternoon out on the boat, and she cries into a lace handkerchief, before hobbling back to the hotel.'

How easy it was to identify with characters in films. Not that Mum would ever be lonely in the way the countess was. But all Edith had wanted was for the man she loved to come home to her every evening. That continuity, reassurance.

That emotional security, yearned for, Vienne reckoned, by most women. Most men, too, probably, if they'd dare admit it.

'Thank you so much, it's been wonderful,' Vienne told the guide when the tour finished. 'I can't wait to read the book again when I return to London.'

The woman smiled, acknowledging the generous tip.

While Vienne waited for Michael to return from the loo, she noticed a poster advertising reduced price rooms for the next month. It would be lovely to stay here overnight. Perhaps she should book them in, surprise him. She visualised eating on the terrace overlooking the lake, walking along the shore at sunset. Sleeping in the following morning then breakfasting on their own. Concert practice could be abandoned for one day.

It might be an idea to have a break from the family. Things with Portia were no better. Michael seemed preoccupied. And as for her longing to get to know Lucy again, to become more than a notional aunt, today had demonstrated how far they were from developing a close relationship. No doubt her niece would now regard her as insensitive.

'There you are,' Michael was saying, as if Vienne had been the one to disappear.

'Are you okay? You've been away for ages.'

'Did you enjoy the tour, darling?'

'It was wonderful. Such a lovely thing to do. I'm *so* glad you told me about it. It makes me want to read the book again.'

'For the fifth time.'

Vienne clasped his arm. 'Michael, I've had a great idea. Let's stay overnight. They've got reduced rates at the moment, while they finish refurbishing. Wouldn't it be lovely?'

His reaction would have been imperceptible to anyone else. A minuscule pulling back, a twitching of his left cheek muscle. He loved her, she knew, but his need for space was disconcerting. She was fed up having to be careful when discussing their long-term future. Fed up with renewing their marriage vows every year. Far from being a positive thing to do, what no one understood was that this annual reaffirmation was actually his way of *not* committing to permanence. It had taken her years to come to terms with this, to accept he wasn't the type to pin down.

He was looking over the lake to Mount Pilatus, where cloud slowly descended, obscuring its top.

'You don't want to, do you?'

'It would be antisocial, darling, don't you think? You told me Madalena's already upset by Lawrence staying at the Hotel Bergmann.'

Michael was right and she chided herself for being selfish: they were on their own most of the time, after all. Except that it didn't seem like this. He was there but he was also absent. Not that she could fathom out how this "absence" manifested itself, because in many ways he was attentive.

According to an article Vienne had read, Anita Brookner suffered from loneliness. Unmarried, no children. No doubt this partly explained her skill in depicting her heroines' solitude. Reading her books made Vienne aware of the fullness of her own life. She couldn't remember ever having woken up wondering how to fill the day.

'You're right,' she said. 'We should go back, now. Mum would prefer it.'

Michael looked relieved.

Nearby, a young couple were checking in and Vienne heard mention of a honeymoon suite. She studied them. He couldn't have been older than twenty-two, the woman looked about nineteen. They displayed none of the clichéd behaviours of newlyweds: a clutching of hands, doe-eyed looks, frequent kisses. But there was something about their shared demeanour, their togetherness, despite their tender years, that produced an ache in her: she sensed the understated but quiet confidence that they were meant to be with each other; she loved the woman-girl's timeless floral dress, and the man-boy's beige suit. She could imagine them dining at expensive hotels in Luzern or Zurich, going on private boat trips, just the two of them, for there was an air of wealth about them, although not ostentatious or remotely vulgar. No flashy jewellery or designer luggage.

Vienne watched them as they thanked the receptionist before following the porter to the lift – exchanging smiles with each other but not touching. When she turned round, Michael was staring at her, an uncharacteristically tender expression on his face.

8

Minutes after talking to Vienne in the garden, Annie knocked on Portia and Lucy's door and waited. She knocked again. At least thirty seconds passed before she heard footsteps and the door opened. Her niece was wearing a pale blue towelling dressing gown and had a towel wrapped around her hair.

Annie remembered herself aged thirteen and even younger, because, despite the sophisticated way she'd tied the towel, like a turban, Lucy looked more like ten, with her short, dark hair off her face. Annie had planned to tread carefully, gauge Lucy's demeanour. Instead she flung her arms round her, unsure which of them was more in need of the hug.

'I suppose Vienne told you I was upset,' Lucy muttered, pulling free.

'Would it help to talk?' Annie said, stepping into the room.

The twin-bedded room resembled a before and after scene. One bed was made, the chair beside it empty except for a linen blouse draped over its back. The other bed remained unmade, its pillows on the floor, a heap of t-shirts, magazines, trainers and a diary on top of the scrunched-up duvet.

Annie lifted the diary. 'I kept a five-year diary when I was your age.... It's okay, I'm not going to read it.'

'Daddy gave me it for my twelfth birthday,' Lucy said, her eyes welling with tears.

Annie replaced the diary. 'So, what's going on, lovie? This whole school thing – why did you set fire to someone's writing case?'

Lucy sniffed and wiped her nose on her sleeve. 'You won't tell Mummy?'

Annie shook her head. 'No, but *you* must. She's worried about you.'

Lucy shook her head. 'She only worries about her clients. Otherwise she wouldn't have sent me away.'

'You're the most important person to her, Lucy.'

Annie felt a wave of irritation. She shouldn't have to be reassuring Lucy like this. It was up to Portia to make it clear to her daughter that she was far more important than her bloody job. Especially as Elliot didn't live with them anymore.

Lucy's face crumpled, and a tear edged its way out of her right eye and slithered down her face. 'Whatever. Anyway, I'd had enough....'

'Enough of what, exactly?'

'Everything.'

'Such as?'

'They were teasing me about my sticky out ears. Calling me Mr Spock.'

Annie plonked herself on the bed beside Lucy. 'Girls can be cruel. Was this going on when I last took you out from school?'

'Maybe. I think it had just started. Why?'

'If you'd told me, I could have spoken to the housemistress.'

'Then I'd be in trouble for telling tales.... I wish I hadn't got my hair cut so short. Nobody noticed my ears before then.'

'Some film stars have sticky out ears. Kate Hudson, for one,' Annie said. 'And she was named one of the fifty Most Beautiful People in the World. Really, lovie, you look great. Your colouring, your beautiful eyes.'

'Sticky out ears are genetic. Neither of my parents have them.'

'Genetics doesn't account for everything.'

'Daddy and I have never been close.'

Lucy slid off the bed, retrieved a bag from the wardrobe and thrust a framed photo into Annie's hands. 'This is Daddy and me when I was six. Do you think I look like him?'

Annie studied the photo. Elliot was sitting in a garden or a park, with Lucy on his knee. He had one arm round her waist, the other dangled by his side. She was smiling at the camera, a young "no holds barred" smile; he seemed to be staring at some distant object. There had to be a helpful answer to Lucy's question, if she thought hard enough. But she mustn't resort to platitudes – her niece would see through them.

'I remember even as a little girl knowing something wasn't right,' Lucy continued, her voice muffled. 'When he hugged me, it never felt like a real hug. And then he left....'

Annie waited while Lucy scratched her shoulder and examined it.

She was talking again, her voice flat as if this was a story she'd told before and been forced to retell. 'Zoë – she's the one who started the teasing – and Cassie waited until "lights out" and then they'd come to my dorm and sit on the bed and ask me how it felt having Mr Spock ears, if they were real.'

Lucy bent her head, and tears fell on her dressing gown.

'Oh, how nasty,' Annie said.

There was silence. Lucy seemed to be on the verge of confessing something. Again, Annie waited.

Lucy's voice was low. 'I heard a conversation once. Shortly before Daddy left. It was late, they thought I was asleep. He told Mummy he'd tried everything but couldn't pretend anymore. It was too painful.'

'What do you think he meant?' Annie asked. She was out of her depth.

She lifted a discarded towel from the floor, ran her fingers over it. If only Portia were here. She would know what to say – at least she should do.

'I thought he'd stopped loving me and Mummy. I crept back to bed – they'd have been upset if they knew I heard. When I asked Mummy why they'd divorced, she wouldn't say much. And then when the girls at school teased me about my ears....'

'You set fire to the writing case?'

Lucy sniffed hard, wiped her nose on her sleeve. 'It was Zoë's birthday and her parents gave her a leather writing case. She kept telling me it was from both of them – you know, emphasising the "both" and telling me what they planned to do when her parents visited. And then one night... one night she asked when Daddy had last visited... I had to think hard. I lied, I said it had only been five weeks before.... it wasn't true – and she knew. Then she said that he was probably embarrassed to be seen with a freak like me. The look she gave me was horrible. Like she despised me.'

Annie gasped. 'Oh Lucy, that's vicious. You poor pet. Give me a cuddle.'

Lucy melted into Annie's arms. How slim she was. But she often left the dining room early and never accepted second helpings. It was then Annie noticed the two large bars of chocolate and box of jellybeans on Lucy's bedside table. She must be filling up with junk food.

'When Zoë went out with her parents, Cassie went too, so I sneaked into her cubicle and found the writing case.... You would tell me the truth, wouldn't you?'

'About what, lovie?'

'About my father.'

Annie hesitated. 'I'm sure Elliot *is* your father. But you need to talk to Mum, tell her everything you've told me.'

She swallowed hard under Lucy's scrutiny. Her niece seemed so young, so vulnerable. Perhaps the expulsion *was* for the best. Not everyone could deal with the cruelty girls dished out and Lucy had no anchor. In Annie's time she, Vienne and Portia often talked in the evenings about what had happened that day. There'd been the occasional episode of nasty behaviour, but she'd got off more lightly than most. If she'd been aware earlier that Lucy was being bullied, instead of breezing up to school and whisking her off to a film or to go shopping, she'd have allowed more time for actually talking. Then, perhaps, she could have helped.

Instead of relishing her role as the "fun" aunt.

'Mum should be back soon,' she told Lucy. 'Or you could come for a swim at the new pool. You could leave a note.'

'I want to stay here,' Lucy said.

Annie glanced at her watch. 'Are you sure you'll be okay?' Lucy reached for the opened bar of chocolate, broke off some squares. 'I'm not going to top myself, if that's what you mean.... Promise you won't say anything to Mum.'

Without thinking, Annie nodded.

She returned to her room to collect her swimming stuff, wondering if she should have cajoled Lucy into coming swimming, or at least stayed with her until Portia returned.

In reception, Hilde and Johann were talking, and he smiled at her when she walked past. As she strolled along the road to the swimming pool, momentarily forgetting about Lucy, she remembered Johann's smile, the feel of his hand on her stomach. She liked his wavy fair hair and blue eyes. But it was the thin framed glasses which gave him a sexy look. She quickened her pace along the Gersauerstrasse.

Later, as she ran her pre-dinner bath, Annie thought again that if she'd been more switched on, she would have picked up on how bad things were with Lucy. And then she could have spoken to the housemistress. But perhaps not. At one level, her niece seemed to be open, at another, she was private, deeper perhaps than most people realised. However, despite having promised Lucy not to mention their conversation to Portia, Annie knew she'd have to do something, warn Portia somehow.

Annie retrieved a sachet of bubble bath from the basket of complimentary toiletries and ripped open the corner with her teeth. She poured the champagne coloured liquid into the bath, stirring the water to encourage the bubbles.

How was she managing to cope this well, such a short time after the break-up? Or had Ferne's revelation yet to fully sink in? Perhaps Brunnen was a temporary escape and she'd plummet when she returned to her empty cottage and lonely Sundays.

As she undressed, she cast her mind back over the day's events – the snatched conversation with Vienne, the longer one with Lucy followed by a swim; lunch with Mum, Portia and Lawrence which had gone surprisingly well, although Lucy had been quiet until Johann brought a large chocolate cake. Afterwards, to Portia's apparent relief, Lucy had agreed to help Madalena in the conservatory. When Annie joined them later for a cup of tea, Lucy had been smiling and was obviously pleased at Madalena's mention of how helpful she'd been. A different child to the one who'd been in tears earlier. But this wasn't necessarily cause for reassurance. Would it be a breach of confidence to speak to Mum, without going into the details?

She dressed again and made her way to Madalena's apartment. When she knocked on the door, there was no reply. Mum's office was also empty and Hilde wasn't in reception. As she was about to give up, she remembered the conservatory. Again, there was no sign of Madalena. When she walked back past reception, she saw Hilde putting on her jacket.

'Do you know where my mother is?'

'She has gone to the Hotel Bergmann.'

Annie considered skipping her bath and going to meet Mum on her way back. But she might be with Lawrence. Passing the kitchen, she popped her head round the door. Gaston was counting plates. Johann was checking something in the oven.

'What's for dinner?' she asked Gaston.

Johann turned round. 'Frau Fontana has told us not to say anything about the meal.'

'Really?' Annie said playfully.

Johann's gaze lingered on her.

'Not even a hint?'

He shook his head in attempted severity. 'You will have to be patient.'

She gave him a mock salute as she left the kitchen.

Back in her room, Annie undressed for the second time and stepped into the bath, adding more hot water, and bubble bath to obliterate the smell of chlorine from the swimming pool. Ignoring her mobile phone ringing, she slid under the frangipani-scented bubbles.

The bath was soothing, the bubbles, the steam, and her thoughts turned to Johann. She knew he was single, that his fiancée had been killed in a riding accident eight years ago. She also knew Mum considered him indispensable and would have appointed him manager had he not been wedded to the kitchen. According to Madalena, Johann represented the best qualities of the Swiss: responsible, hard-working, punctual, courteous – the list continued. Sometimes Annie wondered if he was more like a son than an employee to Mum. She could understand why.

Ferne, Johann, Ferne. Her mind leaped from one to the other, conjuring up images, with nothing coherent: no structured thoughts, no logic. She was stuck in "feeling" mode. A dangerous place to be. Or was it?

The church bells striking seven roused her from her muddled thinking. She scrambled out of the bath, dried herself and dressed quickly. Black trousers, fuschia pink strappy top and – pièce de résistance – her "clickety" shoes, the only unpractical footwear she possessed. A four-inch heel which knackered her back but made her feel feminine. After combing her hair, she applied lipstick, a smidgeon of mascara, and studied herself. Then she dipped her thumb into a pot of gel, warmed the sticky cream between her palms and ran her fingers through her hair. That was better. More texture. Having checked the mirror again, she peeled off the pink strappy top and replaced it with a green lacy one. Now she could smile at her reflection.

Spraying herself with *Romance*, she remembered, with a

pang, its last use – on Ferne's thirty-second birthday. A group of them had gone to a Moroccan restaurant for lamb tajine, and rice pudding with pistachios and rose petals. Ferne, twelve weeks pregnant, refused alcohol so they'd all drunk water. Stephen wasn't with them.

As Annie left the room, her mobile announced a text. Again, she ignored it, assuming it was yet another advertisement from Tesco. Halfway along the corridor, she turned to retrace her steps and check her phone, heart flipping at the message from Ferne: *Stephen left. Come home please. I need you.*

Her mind flooded. Did this mean Ferne's relationship with Stephen was permanently over? That she wanted Annie back for more than just support? She waited for some emotion to bubble up: happiness, if not elation. No bubbling. Perhaps she was more of a survivor than she realised. Even so, her hands were shaking.

She replaced her phone on the bedside table and cautiously navigated her way downstairs in her high heels. What she needed was camomile tea to relax her, and Mum would have some. The kitchen was empty as she put the kettle on, listened to the increasing *foof* as the water heated. Then another sound made her turn.

Johann stood in front of her in a freshly laundered chef's uniform. Without his glasses, the blue of his eyes caused her stomach to flutter. He reached out and lifted her chin. In her high heels, she was only a couple of inches smaller than him. Her pulse raced as he moved closer. While holding his gaze, miniscule fragments of time stretched into seconds.

'Annie,' he said. '*Schön* Annie. *Weiblich* Annie.'

Her heart soared. He considered her beautiful. Beautiful and feminine.

He moved his mouth towards hers. He kissed her, gently

at first, then more frenziedly. He enveloped her in his arms and continued to kiss her. Then he stopped, pulled away and left the kitchen. She stood for a moment, conscious of her hands trembling even more now.

Her lips felt swollen and tingly as she reheated the water. She found a mug, added water and a sachet of camomile tea. She put a finger to her lips, ran it round them. The tingly sensation remained, her body one giant pulse.

9

As the boat raced away from the Brunnen pier in evening light, Karl smiled at Madalena, before focusing on the engine. She sat back and tried to relax. More and more she was regretting the invitation to her children: this was not the way to announce things. She had felt particularly conscious of this at dinner, when she studied her family around the table, wondering why the conversation was so subdued. Even Annie, normally chatty despite her current circumstances, had seemed flushed and preoccupied, and hadn't joined them for coffee afterwards.

As Madalena fiddled with her bracelet, a whistle now grabbed her attention and she saw Karl waving to her. Seated on the thwart, tiller in hand, body twisted round with his long legs bent at the knees, he resembled an over-grown schoolboy, not a 58-year-old. Carefully she made her way to the bow of the boat, grateful for the grip on her new canvas shoes.

'You look unhappy,' he remarked.

'Despite this splendid evening?'

'Would you rather return to the Zurbriggen and be with your children?'

'No, I wanted to see you.'

This was true but approaching Lawrence's hotel was triggering a resurgence of hurt. They were sailing by the Hotel Bergmann now, past its lakeside restaurant where patrons sipped drinks under orange and white striped sun umbrellas. Where waiters were securing flapping table-cloths to the tables, and a smell of fish and garlic wafted over the water. She had always felt attached to this hotel because of the wonderful honeymoon she'd spent there. From now on, however, she would associate it with her son's rejection. Childish, she knew.

'I don't feel close to my children,' she said. 'I've been looking forward to their visit for months, but now they are here, they could belong to someone else. Except Annie.'

Karl stroked her hand with his free one, while steering with the other. 'When you returned from visiting Portia and Lawrence in February, you were happy with how the visits had gone. What's changed?'

'Hard to say exactly.... At least they've come over.'

But what were their real motives? Did they suspect something, agree to be here in order to protect their own interests? Annie was unlikely to have a hidden agenda, or Vienne. Portia and Lawrence might have.

'Try not to worry so much,' Karl said, changing direction. 'You might be reading too much into things... I think we should go to Flüelen this evening.'

She gazed over the lake, at the fading light, the mountains now in deep shadow. 'You are meant to listen, not reassure me.'

'You don't say enough for me to listen to, and this isn't a professional relationship.'

'Perhaps this is not the way to do things, Karl – at the Dinner. I am a simple creature. I always underestimate how complicated everything can be.'

She trailed her hand in the water. Sooner or later, being out on the lake must soothe her. Water had always provided comfort: the river near her childhood apartment block in Copenhagen, where, as a young girl, she would lean against a hawthorn tree, peeling off its smooth bark, humming a lullaby, *Den Lille Ole*. When her family moved to London, a Victorian swimming pool with its vaulted, glass ceiling and striped curtained cubicles, had become her refuge.

At Flüelen, Karl secured the boat, took Madalena's arm and guided her onto the landing.

'I think you should meet the family again before the celebration,' Madalena said when the waiter had brought their beer. 'They need time to get to know you.'

'I agree. But there is something else bothering you.'

She kissed his cheek. 'Sometimes I think you know me better than anyone. It's just that.... you haven't said what you thought of them when you met.'

'Are you asking me as your future husband or as a psychologist?'

Madalena shoved back her hair. 'What a question.'

'I'm sorry. That wasn't fair. I liked them all, in different ways. Annie appears to be the most straightforward. She is suffering, of course, but in a healthy way, if this makes sense. Portia was obviously assessing me for unscrupulous intentions but–'

'I apologise for that,' Madalena said. 'She is a barrister through and through. She wouldn't mean to cause offence.'

'None taken. I imagine she is brilliant in court. If I had some human rights issue, I'd feel privileged and hopeful if she were fighting my case.'

Madalena squeezed his hand.

He was frowning now. 'She has her own struggles, I sense. She is anxious.'

'Hardly surprising,' Madalena said. 'With Lucy being expelled.'

'Mmm. Perhaps there's also something else.... Would you like something to eat?'

Madalena laughed. 'Not after the splendid dinner Johann prepared this evening.'

She studied Karl. Despite his huge appetite he remained slim.

He was trying to catch the waiter's attention.

'What did you think of Vienne?' Madalena asked.

The waiter appeared.

'*Rösti* with cheese and ham, please,' Karl requested, 'and another beer. Another one for you, *liebling*?'

She shook her head.

'Vienne was different to how I expected her to be, from knowing her music. She is very sweet, but–'

'I wonder about her marriage, Karl.'

'She doesn't seem secure with Michael. I imagine he is not an easy husband but I liked him. Lawrence, I sense, is a little lost, though he appears to be strong and self-contained.'

A perceptive assessment of her son, Madalena thought, respecting Karl for not allowing her hurt over his behaviour, to influence his own judgement of Lawrence. Karl was a decent man, as well as a wise and reliable one and perhaps her reservation about marrying him was receding.

If only she could bring closure to David's death.

'And Lucy?'

'Your granddaughter is complex,' Karl said. 'I detect lots

of potential in her, but at the moment she is confused and lost.... Does she see her father often?'

'I hope you don't think I'm being disloyal by discussing them with you,' Madalena said.

Karl shook his head. 'This was one of the things I missed most about not having my wife there when Thobias was growing up. We never went through any real crises but so often I would have liked to have someone to share my concerns with. Sometimes I would–'

He broke off as a man halted by their table and greeted him.

'Thomas, this is Madalena. *Liebling,* this is Thomas, we studied together in the United States.' Karl hesitated, glancing at her before inviting Thomas to join them.

Madalena drifted into her own thoughts, as she occasionally still did during a German conversation involving more than one other person.

'Madalena?' Karl summoned her back to the present. She forced herself to pay attention. 'Thomas has invited us to dinner before he and his wife leave.'

'How lovely,' her voice said. Automatic pilot. Swiss courtesy, valued above anything else.

Karl had never seemed strikingly Swiss, either Swiss German or Swiss French. Perhaps because he'd studied in California, where, no doubt, any caution, woodenness, had been laughed out of him. Ironically, David, despite possessing no German blood, had seemed more Germanic. A pragmatic, scrupulous planning approach to everything.

As the men chatted, she thought of the work Karl had done on her house in Bauen, how difficult she had been to help. Mentally comparing his work unfavourably to David's, which, unsurprisingly, Karl picked up on, explaining why he was performing a task a certain way. She blushed now, recalling her initial petty reluctance to lend him David's tools. Nevertheless, having convinced her there was no breach of ethics in their having a relationship, as she hadn't been his patient, Karl had quietly pursued her. On the odd occasion when she doubted the wisdom of having bought the house at Bauen, she reminded herself that it had brought them together.

As it began to rain, church bells rang out over the lake, reviving her spirits. Such a glorious sound, and more poignant with the rain – the subdued colours of mountain and water, the rousing noise of something timeless.

How strange the dichotomy, the fact that she could be two people. Efficient hotel owner and loving mother – solid, always there, except of course the children weren't always there. And the other side: fragile woman succumbing to grief.

The conversation between Karl and Thomas continued. She drank her Feldschlösschen. Then Thomas was leaving and the men embraced.

'Aren't you inviting me in for coffee?' Karl asked when they returned to Brunnen.

Madalena hesitated. 'I'm too tired.'

He nodded. He never applied pressure on her to do anything, something else she loved about him.

'I asked for your opinion of my children,' she said. 'What I didn't tell you was that I was proud of you. And your response to the question about how we met was inspired.'

'Are you planning to tell them the truth?' Karl asked.

She shook her head. 'I don't think I'm brave enough. It would completely change how they think of me.'

Karl said nothing. Madalena knew he believed she'd feel lighter if her children knew the circumstances of their meeting.

A room of white walls giving onto pastures and mountains. Madalena can see the lake: without the view she would shrivel up. Already she feels shrivelled up and dead. Because David is dead.

Meals from grey-coated men and women who mop floors and clean locker tops, who return to remove her untouched tray, with barely a flicker of an eyelid. This surprises her. Eating is important, keeps you well, but no one makes her eat.

Nurses who bathe and dress her. Who brush her hair as if she were a child. Who talk to her as an adult.

Medication dispensed in tiny plastic containers. Now it is different. People watch her, make sure she swallows the pills: the green ones, colour of grass; the red ones like blood; deep blue ones like the Urnersee in mid-summer.

Catatonic is their verdict. She is aware of their assessment, their criteria: her immobility, the refusal to talk, her staring and grimacing. Catatonic. She likes the word, the two "t"s giving it force, the four syllables lending it weight, the label legitimising her grief.

Stronger medication. Pressure to talk, to stop holding it in. But if she lets it go, lets it out, there will be nothing left. She will be nothing. Perhaps she never was anything.

Disconnectedness. They have abducted her mind, locked it away.

In a group of people with wild hair and strange expressions. One woman wears a suit and ankle boots. 'This is a Gucci suit. I was a model,' the woman explains. She looks corpulent and hirsute.

One man has knee-length hair. 'I am Jesus,' he insists. 'Son of Satan.'

Johann, the chef employed by the Zurbriggen shortly before

David died, visits. He brings her snowdrops, a chocolate cake, ideas for a menu design. He updates her on what is happening in the hotel. How Hilde, the new receptionist, is coping well. How Florian is becoming a skilled waiter. Although Johann is young enough to be her son, Madalena responds to him, to his reports, his gifts. Not with words, but with nods, changes in expression. She cannot respond to anyone else. Once she speaks, addressing him as "David", and there are looks of concern from staff commandeered to observe his visits.

Then finally, the thing she has dreaded is suggested: electro-convulsive therapy. The prospect of electric currents passed through her brain to trigger a seizure is barbaric, she thinks; it jolts her out of silence and she agrees to talk to the therapist.

And the story of her grief emerges, in bits, like the squeezing of a tube.

But the first thing she says is that her family – her children, all safely far away in the UK – must not be contacted. Must not know what has happened. They believe she is strong, and this must never change. Johann colludes in her deception, fielding phone calls, letting her know when the children have emailed her. Fortunately, her illness has coincided with busy periods in their lives.

And so, the reason for her grief emerges: David, her constant husband, never told her he loved her and, for this reason alone, she can't heal.

Madalena now replaced the photograph of David on the dressing table, changed into her nightgown and stepped onto the balcony of her apartment. The lake, a glassy black in the moonlight, held her in awe so she lingered. Eventually she went inside and in her kitchenette, made a mug of hot chocolate to help her sleep. Perhaps she should have gone back to Karl's home. Although he hadn't invited her, his expression conveyed that he would like to be with her overnight.

As she sipped her hot chocolate, she was conscious of her sore head and realised the wind had warmed up. It was the *Föhn* causing the headache. Just as well she was safely in her apartment, not driving. She'd read awful stories about car drivers having accidents during those winds, about normally tranquil people experiencing crazy spells. The wind wouldn't last long. Tomorrow, when she woke, her headache would have disappeared.

10

As Portia brushed her teeth the following morning, a niggle surfaced. It contained no substance, simply a feeling that something significant – negatively so – would happen today. Like the hunches people got before they missed a plane that subsequently crashed.

She rinsed her mouth, combed her hair, and returned to the bedroom, determined to win Lucy round.

Lucy lay on her bed, one knee crossing the other. Her denim shorts looked ridiculous over the black tights. What had happened to pretty frocks, or even flouncy skirts?

'I wish you'd come with me, Lucy. You could look at the shops until I'm finished.'

'I'm thirteen, not three. Stop fussing! I'll be fine. Anyway, it's not as if I'm on my own here. There's Annie and Granny.'

'What will you do while I'm having my hair done?'

'The garden, I guess. The new loungers are comfy.'

Portia hesitated. 'Make sure you use sun cream and–'

'Yeah, yeah,' Lucy said, flicking through a copy of Vogue. 'You should go, Mum, you'll be late. You're always late.'

'To be truthful, I'm worried about you, darling... After all that's happened.'

Immediately she regretted her words. There wasn't time at the moment to talk about things properly, and, of course, if Lucy responded in a way that suggested she wanted to, Portia would have to postpone the conversation and then she'd feel bad.

Lucy yawned. 'I'll probably have a nap. Go on, you'll be late.'

Portia sighed. Lucy had slept ten hours last night, almost eleven, in fact. She couldn't be tired.

As she left, Portia turned to glance at her daughter. Perhaps she should find Annie. Ask her to keep an eye on Lucy until she returned. She tried to remember what Vienne and Michael were doing.

'You'll be laaate,' Lucy said.

'I'll be back by eleven, sooner perhaps. I thought we might...'

But her words were lost. Lucy's new rainbow coloured headphones now gripped her ears, emitting a sinister, unrelenting beat.

Reluctantly, Portia shut the door. In the heat, her back already felt damp under its linen shirt. Passing Annie's room she halted, but her sister might still be asleep. She'd looked so preoccupied after dinner last night. As if she needed a cry, in fact. Lawrence's tone with her over coffee had been inexcusable. He wouldn't have been like that in Mum's presence.

At reception, Madalena called out. 'You and Lucy will be here for lunch, won't you?'

'Yes. Full house?'

Madalena removed her specs. 'Michael mentioned

taking the boat to Flüelen.... Perhaps Lucy could go with them. Vienne would be thrilled.'

'Lucy's tired.... I won't be long.'

'I'll keep an eye on her. And Portia?'

'Yes?'

'I *would* like to talk to you about Lucy sometime.'

Portia nodded in exasperation. 'I'll be late for my appointment.'

'I can give you a lift, dear.'

'I'll walk, but thanks.'

'As you wish.'

When she reached the hairdressers, Portia texted Lucy and waited for her reply. After five minutes she dialled the number, heard her daughter's voice. 'You've reached Lucy Wallman. Leave a message if you want. Cool.' How cavalier. Her original message had contained none of this overly assertive tone, such studied disinterest. She'd have to speak to Lucy about this, too.

At the far end of the salon, Portia's hairdresser was blow-drying a customer's hair, lifting section after section of long red locks. Portia raised her head to the ceiling, drummed her chin with her fingers. As she was about to tell the receptionist she felt ill and needed to cancel, a girl, no older than fifteen, invited her over to the wash-hand basins. Portia hesitated before following her. The girl's short top revealed a pierced navel. At least Lucy wasn't into body piercing. Yet. As far as she knew.

While the girl ran the tap, Portia tried Lucy's mobile again. Once more it rang and rang, then came the brusque message. She shifted position in her chair, leaned back to slot her head into the neck support and assured the girl the water temperature was okay.

The radio switched from music to a news bulletin: the

Swiss Government's concern about the franc's high value and its impact on exports; a problem with safety in Geneva. From her chair, Portia could see the Urnersee, above it, green pastures. The weather was perfect, clouds whirling across a blue sky, enough of a breeze now to keep the temperature manageable. She would make sure she and Lucy had some fun today.

While crossing the street after her hair appointment, Portia spotted Annie and quickened her pace.

'Where are you off to?' Portia asked when she reached her sister.

'Swimming.'

'You look flushed, is everything all right? What is it?' Something had happened to Annie. Something to do with Ferne?

'Do you want coffee?' Annie asked.

Portia glanced at her watch, frowned. 'I should get back – Lucy.'

'The thing is, I need to talk to you... soon.'

Portia's stomach turned. 'Is Lucy okay? What's she done?'

'Sorry, I didn't mean to scare you,' Annie said. 'She's fine, I mean she's safe – she's with Mum. But it would be easier to talk away from the Zurbriggen. Could we go for coffee? Cake?'

Portia checked her watch again. Another half hour wouldn't make much difference. Especially if Lucy was with Madalena.

They continued along the road, past several hotels, a boutique, a shop selling water sports equipment, until they came to a bar. There they found a quiet table, ordered coffee.

'Has there been a development with Ferne?' Portia asked.

Annie nodded. 'Stephen's left her.... I think she wants us to get back together.'

Portia studied her sister. 'That's great, isn't it? It's what you wanted.'

Annie was silent.

Portia peeked at her watch. 'What is it?'

'I had... I had an encounter with Johann last night.'

'What sort of encounter?'

'He kissed me,' Annie said.

Portia's eyes widened. 'Where?'

'On the mouth.'

'I meant where in the hotel?'

'Does it matter? The kitchen. I didn't expect it but suddenly he was there and ... we were kissing.'

'Does this mean you're now "batting for the other side" again?'

How could people switch from relationships with men, to those with woman? It was one thing knowing from the start. Another going backwards and forwards. Annie was all over the place.

Annie stabbed her chocolate cake with the fork. 'I hate that expression. Nothing's cut and dried. Lots of people go from men to women and vice versa.'

Portia flicked a strand of hair behind her ear. 'I couldn't.'

'But I *am* confused,' Annie said. 'If a kiss from a man can mean so much, then how can I go back to Ferne? I don't know if I ever felt that kind of reaction with her. Perhaps women getting together is more about, well, being similar emotionally. Especially if they've been badly treated by guys. Perhaps the physical side isn't so important in a lesbian relationship.... What do you think?'

'I've no idea. It's just not something I could ever contemplate,' Portia said. 'Aagh – the very thought of it.'

Annie reached back to remove her hair clips, freeing her dark curls. 'I'll feel so guilty, though, if I don't go back to her. She'll be distraught. No Stephen. And no me.'

'She ditched *you*, remember?'

'Yeah, I remember. Anyway, this wasn't what I wanted to talk to you about.'

'Let me guess,' Portia said. 'You're worried about Madalena and Karl. Naturally I've been wondering how close they are. Though he seems pleasant enough and–'

'It's Lucy.'

'You said she was okay – I knew I shouldn't have left her on her own this morning, but she absolutely refused to come with me–'

'Stay cool, Portia. I told you: nothing's happened. Not today, anyway.'

Annie relayed her conversations with Vienne and Lucy the previous day. Portia listened in silence, feeling as if she was slipping into a nightmare that she'd dreaded happening.

'I feel bad about not picking up on how things were for her when I last took her out from school,' Annie continued. 'If I'd been more tuned in, perhaps I could have done something and she wouldn't have been expelled.'

Portia shook her head. There was a nauseous feeling in her stomach. 'Everything's starting to unravel. I'd a hunch something ghastly would happen.'

'Sounds like things have been unravelling with Lucy for a while,' Annie said.

The door opened and a Japanese couple entered. The man spoke fluent German to the waiter, smiled at his heavily pregnant partner. Portia glanced at Annie, but she didn't seem to have noticed the woman.

Portia clasped her hands together, bit her thumbs. 'How did Vienne seem?'

'Concerned she'd upset Lucy.'

Portia nodded, continued nodding. 'You mustn't tell anyone what I'm about to tell you. Do you promise?'

Annie looked hurt. 'We've always trusted each other.' Portia hesitated. Was this the right thing to do? Thirteen years of concealing the truth, and now sharing it. But Annie always confided in her. Last week had been a classic example, phoning when the Ferne situation blew up, blasting Annie's future to rubble. An hour of tears and bewildered ranting, while several sheets of paper on which Portia would write her closing summary for court the next day, lay on the kitchen table, the papers' whiteness, their blankness, taunting her with their reminder of what she had still to do.

Portia leaned forward. 'Lucy isn't Elliot's daughter.'

'Yeah, right.... *Not* funny, Portia.'

'Elliot is not Lucy's father.'

Annie stared at her. 'I don't understand.'

'It was when he was depressed, after his father died. I had an affair...'

'An affair!'

'With Michael.'

Annie gasped. 'Vienne's Michael?'

Portia nodded.

'Oh my God.'

Portia pulled back. Where was the relief she'd expected?

Annie wasn't looking at her sympathetically: her face had blanched, her mouth was open. But her sister didn't understand how it had happened. How could she?

Portia stared out of the window. The street was busier

now, people going about their errands, quietly but efficiently. People with normal lives. Not ones on the verge of disintegrating. Should she explain, try to justify her actions to Annie?

'Lucy doesn't know anything. And she mustn't. Not ever.'

'For fuck's sake, Portia.... How could you do this? To Vienne? To your sister? And to Elliot?'

'How could you understand how difficult it was with him then?'

She should explain more. Say something to remove that horrid expression on Annie's face. But she hadn't prepared for this. Hadn't expected to need to.

Would a description of events help her case? Result in a verdict of a crime committed under mitigating circumstances? The windy autumn evening, a sale at Debenhams. The revolving door sticking, her brother-in-law on the opposite side, gesticulating at her. Then, on the street, struggling to hear each other, a car horn sabotaging their efforts.

Michael's suggestion they go for a drink. Vienne away on tour.

An alpha male irritated by a traffic jam, a baby born ten months later. Cause and effect. Portia saw it all the time at work.

Of course, the primate in the Audi couldn't be blamed. But Portia often wondered what would have happened if the car hadn't honked for so long, if she and Michael would simply have exchanged a few words – perhaps making tentative plans for the four of them to meet for dinner – and then gone their separate ways.

Even if she relayed the events like this, though, it would be unlikely to exonerate her in Annie's eyes. Vienne might continue to remain ignorant of what had happened, but that didn't excuse Portia's betrayal. And there was Elliot who'd suffered so much, probably continued to suffer.

'Does Elliot know he's not Lucy's father?'

Portia sighed. 'He worked it out. We hadn't been... you know.'

'Does he know it was Michael?'

'Dear God, no. He must never know. The whole thing would... he'd... well, he wouldn't be violent, but he'd confront Michael... The thought of it...'

Annie was shaking her head, like someone with a nervous tic. 'Vienne asked me once what I thought the problem was with you and her.'

It felt like Annie was siding with Vienne. This was silly. Annie simply needed time to absorb this. Portia needed time to adjust to someone else knowing.

'Vienne's only met Lucy several times since she was about ten. That's when I got worried about the resemblance – someone mistook Michael for Lucy's father. It was ghastly. It's the easiest way, the only way, in fact, to deal with things, keeping Vienne and Lucy apart.'

'And you believed you could continue like this for ever?' Annie said.

'I keep hoping Lucy's looks change, so she resembles me more.'

'So, this is why you and Elliot split? Nothing to do with his depression.'

'Well, if he hadn't been depressed then.... Please don't judge me.... Annie, do you think Lucy looks like me... at all?'

Annie was shaking her head as if she couldn't stop. 'This is such a lot to take in...'

'Remember, no one else must know.'

Annie ran her finger along her lips to indicate they were zipped. Again, Portia waited for relief to sink in; instead she felt worse. As if, somehow, the confession made things more real. How could they become more real, though? She'd been living with this secret, this weight, for almost fourteen years. And she trusted Annie. However great her revulsion, she'd keep quiet.

'I keep thinking Lucy and I should return to London now, play it safe. Every time I see an expression on her face that I see on Michael's, I want to escape. Especially the one they both give when they think you've said something stupid. Believe me, I get that one enough from Lucy.... Do you think they look alike?'

Annie thought for a moment. 'No, I don't.'

Portia sipped her coffee. The nausea had intensified. Perhaps she should order a croissant. 'You were right to tell Lucy to talk to me, but what in heaven's name will I say?'

Annie glanced at her watch. 'You'll think of something.... I'd better go if I'm to have time to swim.'

'No doubt Vienne will be wondering why Lucy was so odd.'

'She's probably attributing it to PMT or something, I don't know. But she might have told Michael.'

'She'll certainly think about it. About Lucy questioning who her father is. It'll be the beginning of doubt, certainly. Perhaps Michael will be able to distract her.'

'I must go, Portia. We'll talk again soon.'

Portia watched as Annie left the café, bumping against a table, her bag catching on the door handle. She waited to see if Annie would wave through the window to her. There was no wave. The situation was like a ball of wool whose wrapper had torn. With no constraints, it was unravelling and the scary thing was she had no idea how much it would unwind.

Portia laid down her biography of Tony Benn. 'Lucy, are you nearly finished?' she called to the closed bathroom door.

She was exhausted and chiding herself for procrastination. She'd had all afternoon to raise the subject of her daughter's conversation with Vienne, and she'd found excuse after excuse to postpone: as they'd driven to the stables, selected their horses, and headed off along the well-worn paths. Time after time, she'd let opportunities slip by. Even when they stopped riding, tied up the horses and rested by the picnic spot overlooking the lake, Portia had shied away from broaching the subject, reluctant to spoil their afternoon. Lucy had been cheerful, relaxed and jokey, as if nothing had happened with Vienne or Annie.

'You've been in there nearly an hour. Hurry up, please.'

The door opened and Lucy appeared, wet hair dripping over the floor, her dressing gown half soaked.

'For God's sake, use a towel,' Portia said, grabbing one from the back of a chair, draping it round her daughter's head.

Lucy flicked the remote control and flopped down on the bed. 'You shouldn't swear in front of me. You're a poor role model.'

'Don't switch on the TV. You must get ready. Madalena's expecting us at seven.'

'Why do you all call her Madalena?' Lucy asked, swapping from a chat show to a news programme.

'I don't always,' Portia said, 'But I like the name.... Come on, Lucy, get dressed. You know that in Switzerland it's unforgivable to be late.'

'Granny's Danish.'

'But she's picked up a lot of Swiss habits over the years.'

'I might start calling you "Portia", Mummy. Would you like that?'

'I certainly wouldn't,' Portia said, without understanding why the idea was so unappealing.

'Mummy, come and see – isn't that the judge you said is horrible?'

As Lucy looked at her, Portia's heart raced. It could have been Michael.

'Come and see, Mummy.'

Portia stared at the screen. It *was* Lord Swanston.

'He's in trouble again,' Lucy said, laughing. 'I might be a lawyer when I grow up. What d'you think? Would I be good?'

Portia switched off the television. 'You need to get ready.'

'I'm tired,' Lucy said, climbing under the bedcover. '*Do* you think I'd make a good lawyer?'

'I could bring you something to eat here, if you'd rather,' Portia offered. 'You could watch TV, have an early night.'

She'd try and grab Michael on his own this evening, discuss what ways they could devise to keep Vienne and Lucy apart. Already her heart rate was decreasing.

In the shower, she thought hard. Madalena had suggested a picnic in Bauen tomorrow. But perhaps she and Lucy could do something on their own again, maybe shop in Luzern. This would take care of another day. And they'd booked a second riding afternoon. As soon as possible, though, and hopefully this evening, she must find out from Michael if Vienne had relayed her conversation with Lucy. What he thought his wife inferred from it.

When she returned to the bedroom, Lucy was putting on her long skirt and nibbling on a piece of chocolate.

'I thought you were tired,' Portia said.

'I want to see Granny.'

'Okay, darling, but perhaps you should wear your specs tonight. Rest your eyes a bit.... It's so important. Your eyes.'

'I told you, I haven't got my specs here.... Jeez, can't you remember anything apart from work?'

Lucy was delving around in a drawer for a top, shaking her head as if her mother was an idiot, and Portia felt a surge of anger. 'Don't *talk* to me like this. I won't, will not have you being rude.'

'Whatever.'

Lucy shuffled over to the dressing table, rummaged in Portia's makeup bag. 'Can I use your lipstick?'

'You're too young.'

'The other girls are allowed to,' Lucy said. 'Anyway, I'm almost fourteen.'

'We're in June. October isn't almost.'

'Please. Just this evening.'

Portia nodded abstractedly, as she stepped into her dress and frowned at her reflection in the mirror. The grey dress minimised her breasts and was comfortable, but it made her seem so matronly, compared with her nubile daughter. Her hair was lank, too, and her skin looked pale despite days of sunshine. Even her eyes – her selling point, if she had one – lacked lustre.

'I'll do your eyes,' Lucy said, unscrewing the lid of the eye cream before Portia could reply. 'Sit down, don't move.'

Portia sat with her eyes shut whilst her daughter applied eyeliner, eye shadow and mascara. All the things she carried around in her cosmetics bag and usually ignored.

'You can open now,' Lucy said.

Portia glanced in the mirror. Her eyes seemed larger, brighter. But how she looked this evening was the least of her worries.

'Thanks, sweetheart.'

'You can do your own lipstick. Now you do my eyes,' Lucy said, nudging her mother out of the seat.

Portia wrestled with feigning illness and asking Lucy to look after her this evening. She thought frantically for some way of making up her daughter to change Lucy's face. If she was heavy-handed with the eye pencil, could she somehow alter the appearance of Lucy's eyes? Make them seem closer together?

'Not like that,' Lucy said, grabbing the eye pencil, deftly outlining her eyes.

She had beautiful eyes, but although they were the same indigo colour as Portia's, their expressions were her father's. No amount of fiddling with eye pencil would change this. Nor would hair dye affect her appearance significantly.

'You could use my reading glasses, tonight,' Portia tried again, as Lucy yawned. 'It's a common prescription. You might have to look at a menu.'

Lucy applied mascara. 'Then how will *you* manage?... There, d'you like what I've done?'

'*Very* professional. Where did you learn all this?'

'During free time on Sunday afternoons,' Lucy said. 'Can I use your perfume?'

Before Portia had a chance to say no, Lucy had sprayed herself with Calvin Klein.

Portia sneezed as she inhaled the rich fragrance. 'That's enough, Lucy.'

'Someone might as well use it.'

From the garden, Portia heard a conversation in German. Two male voices and a female one. If only she could go and join whoever it was. If only she could be anywhere but here. No doubt this evening's conversation would be dominated by plans for tomorrow's picnic, which she was unlikely to relax enough to enjoy if Vienne was there. But she couldn't do something else with Lucy. Not on this occasion, one which seemingly meant a lot to her mother.

She picked up her bag. 'Time to go down for supper.'

'I'll teach you how to use makeup properly,' Lucy offered. 'You're not too old to learn. If you make an effort.'

As Portia searched for a withering reply, Lucy flung her arms round her. 'Love you, Mummy.'

'I love you, too, darling,' Portia said, suddenly feeling old.

11

M adalena opened the door of the cold room and surveyed its shelves. Whenever she thought ahead to the picnic at Bauen her mind went blank: she couldn't actually picture her family seated at the oak table Karl had built for the garden. Nor could she imagine them in her sitting room – on the sofa and armchairs, or at the table. Furthermore, the selection of cheeses, breads and cold meats now facing her, seemed to mock her indecision. Plain loaves or the twisted Wurzel-brot? Cold pork and chicken? Or just beef? For the umpteenth time, she wondered why she'd firmly rejected Annie and Vienne's offers of help the previous evening.

While she wrapped cold chicken and beef in foil, she thought about her chalet in Bauen. About the lingering guilt because she already had an apartment in the hotel, because the chalet was unconnected with David, and lastly, because none of her children had any input into her decision to buy it. Would they consider this a betrayal of their father? Could she continue to enjoy her "days off" home, if they failed to understand its significance, considered her extravagant?

As she finished packing the chilly bins, an image came to her of young Portia and Vienne running into the kitchen, pleading with Gunther to give them cakes fresh from the oven, or a jug of hot chocolate to brighten up homework time. The box of Scrabble, now illogically housed under the vegetable rack, reminded her of cherished holiday Saturday evenings: she partnering Annie, Portia helping Vienne think of impressive words; twelve-year-old Lawrence checking the dictionary, triumphantly proving a spelling mistake. David appearing later with bedtime cereal, reluctantly pointing to the clock, failing to conceal his yawns. So many happy times. The pleasure of such occasions heightened by the knowledge that in several weeks' time, often sooner, the children would be travelling back to their respective schools in the UK.

Her mood dropped. Try as she might, and she'd been trying for years, she couldn't deny it – boarding school had exacted its toll on her children. How spineless she had been, complying with David's wishes. With more help in the hotel, with tactical re-jigging, they could have managed. The children could then have attended day schools here. And things might have been different: Portia more compassionate over Elliot's depression, Vienne more maternal, Lawrence less selfish. As for Annie – she seemed to have suffered least and to Madalena's thinking, it now showed. A beautiful person, inside as well as out.

The kitchen door opened, revealing her youngest, flustered, as if she had run all the way from her bedroom. Annie scanned the room and smiled when she spotted her mother locking the cold room door. Madalena's heart melted as she stared at her daughter who looked eighteen again, leaving school and eager to study at Leith's School of Food and Wine in London. Was she recovering from the break-up with Ferne? Madalena wondered, as she embraced Annie for as long as she would permit.

As Annie checked the picnic hamper for plates, glasses and cutlery, humming to herself, Madalena's worry receded: her daughter would survive the breakup, even though she'd be losing being a mother as well as having a partner. When they carried the chilly bins and picnic basket to the foyer, Annie smiled at Hilde, joking about wishing for an orderly admin workspace like hers, requesting advice.

Threatening clouds were drifting east over the Urnersee, followed by frisky white ones and patches of blue sky – they might be lucky after all.

'The weather should be okay,' Madalena said as she ushered Annie into her office.

'A rival eaterie opened in January,' Annie said. 'And I've had to raise my prices because of increased rent. And here I was, thinking that the interview with *Great British Food* would mean more security but that's not the case at all. You can never afford to be complacent. So, I'm thinking about getting some marketing help.'

'Good plan, dear. Just be careful not to overdo it. What with all you're going through. Apparently, our immune systems don't function so well when we're grieving.'

She waited, hoping Annie might open up about Ferne, but her daughter was now looking around the office impatiently. Wanting to be outside, probably.

As Madalena glanced out of her interior office window, she saw Portia and Michael at reception. A button on Portia's blouse had strained free and her pale skin and shadows under the eyes contributed to her worn look. Something to do with Lucy, no doubt.

She rose to meet Portia, took her arm and led her to the

family sitting room, Annie and Michael following, shutting the door behind them.

Madalena sat on the sofa beside Portia while Annie mentioned something about changing into cooler trousers.

Michael hovered by the bookcase, fingering a well-thumbed travel guide to Barcelona. There was silence while Madalena waited for Portia to explain what was bothering her.

'Fetch some coffee from the kitchen, would you, please?' Madalena asked Michael.

He nodded. 'Madalena, I'm afraid that Vienne doesn't feel up to the trip today, and I think I should stay with her. I'm sorry, I know you'll be disappointed....'

'I understand.'

When Michael left, Portia stood, clenching her hands together, thumbs pressed between her teeth, sighed then freed her thumbs. 'Mum, sorry but Lucy doesn't want to come on the picnic. I know this is hard on you, especially with....'

Madalena frowned. 'I hoped she would be keen to see my pied à terre.'

Portia was studying her. 'To be honest, I've never really understood why you need a second home.'

She'd been right – she *was* being judged. With effort, she forced herself to look at Portia.

Her daughter was staring at some distant point. 'I know this is a big day – you want us all to be together, and there's always someone doing something else and not being at dinner, or whatever, but–'

'This is *family* time,' Madalena said. 'I don't see you for most of the year.'

Portia sighed and grimaced at her cotton trousers. 'I've been here less than a week and already these are too tight.'

Michael appeared with a jug of coffee and two cups. Madalena indicated the coffee table, thanked him and told him to make sure Vienne rested. As he left the room, she returned her attention to Portia.

'I know you think I am being selfish, dear. Nevertheless, it is important to me Lucy is there today. Is she unwell?'

'What do we mean by "unwell"? How does one define "wellness"? When I was her age, sometimes I didn't want to do things, I needed space,' Portia said.

Madalena watched her daughter pace the room, as if delivering an eloquent address to the jury. As she continued pacing, Madalena felt a growing irritation. Was Portia actually here in Brunnen, or rehearsing a closing argument in London? Moreover, was that rain rapping against the window? She turned round and stared through the double glazing at a cloudless sky, an azure lake.

Facing her daughter again, she leant forward – this might not influence the outcome but was worth a try: her drama classes had not been wasted. 'Portia, I can see you are upset and thinking I'm only considering *my* needs. And I know mothers are supposed to put their children's needs first, and no doubt their grandchildren's also. And I *am* grateful you made the effort to come to Brunnen. Especially at a busy time. But please persuade Lucy to come along today. I will make it up to her.'

At a knock on the door, she frowned, shook her head at Portia, putting a finger to her lips. As the gardener trundled past the open window, Madalena turned to Portia, who was seated again. 'The boat leaves at twelve thirty.'

'I'll see what I can do but I have to put her needs first, Mum. You've brought up four children, you, of all people, should understand.'

Madalena experienced the all too familiar hollow

feeling in the pit of her stomach, her guilt about having been a part-time mother. Portia was slumped in her chair, staring at her knees as if trying to decide. Motionless, Madalena watched her stand, smile resignedly and leave the room, her expression unreadable.

'Isn't it amazing?' Portia remarked, as cars stopped to let them cross the road to the waterfront. 'This wouldn't happen in England, except at traffic lights, of course.'

'It would in Skye,' Lawrence said.

Portia shrugged. 'Perhaps. It's so Swiss, their old-fashioned courtesy.'

Lawrence held up his arm. 'They aren't always polite. Take queuing, for example. A few days ago I almost thumped a man who barged in front of me most blatantly. It was obvious I'd been waiting longer.'

'Well, I think there are more good things about the Swiss than bad,' Annie said.

They arrived in time to watch the boat from Luzern glide into the harbour. Above them, clouds frolicked across a pale blue sky crisscrossed with evaporating vapour trails. Ahead of them came a hum of conversation from passengers, a searching for boat tickets and cameras.

Madalena smiled. A perfect day for the lake. She and Portia had weathered their storm and now she felt as if several decades had rolled back and she was thirty again, on a family outing with a large picnic and kites and frisbees. Anticipating her children running around barefoot, fishing for rainbow trout.

She turned to speak to Portia but her daughter was now remonstrating with Lucy.

'For God's sake, try to look more enthusiastic,' Portia said.

Lucy glared at her. 'Make me.'

'But you normally love boat trips, darling.'

'I want to go *back*.'

Portia lowered her voice. 'I explained that Granny's keen for you to be here. It's important to her, especially as she doesn't see you very often.'

'You can't make me go.'

Madalena moved away.

'Come on, you stragglers,' Lawrence called. 'We're about to board.'

There were whipping noises as the crew flung ropes round landing posts. The sound of metal against concrete as they positioned the gangplank. As the staff stood aside to let passengers disembark, Madalena watched Lucy slouching off in the direction of the hotel, scuffing her feet, kicking the odd loose stone. She'd probably watch TV or sit in the garden. For a moment, Madalena wrestled with her disappointment. Portia had undoubtedly done her best, however, and there'd still be the four of them to enjoy the picnic... Perhaps when she showed her house to Vienne and Michael, Lucy would come too. In the meantime, Hilde should be informed that Lucy would need lunch.

Soon the boat was approaching Bauen, its cluster of white houses with their sloping roofs, drawing nearer. The forest-framed meadows beckoned to her, above, the bare rock face like a gaping wound. Madalena sighed with pleasure. Nevertheless, when the lakefront church bells rang out their midday welcome and she noticed Portia's tense expression, she experienced a surge of resentment towards her granddaughter. This could have been a splendid day. Even though Vienne and Michael weren't here. Portia would obviously spend the time worrying.

As the bells sounded more insistent, Portia tapped her on the arm. 'Mum, I'm sorry but I'm going back to Brunnen. I need to check Lucy's okay. The next boat's in ten minutes – I can see it.'

'Vienne and Michael will be there. They can keep an eye on her, at least Michael can, if Vienne is resting. I'll phone him and–'

'Mum, please don't interfere.'

'As you wish.'

'Do you want me to come with you, lovie?' Annie asked.

Portia nodded.

Annie hugged Madalena. 'I'm sorry. Another time?'

'It's just you and me, then,' Lawrence said, as he and Madalena watched the boat pull away from Bauen.

'So it would seem. Karl's been delayed at the hospital.'

She despised the bitter note in her voice. However, despite having summoned up all her understanding, she couldn't stretch it to justifying Annie going back to Brunnen with Portia.

Madalena straightened: she would enjoy being with Lawrence, make the most of their time together.

He grabbed her hand. 'I'm keen to see your *pied à terre*.'

'I hope you are hungry. I prepared a picnic for eight people.'

The path led them past palm and chestnut trees, the air silent apart from chirping birds. High above, a golden eagle soared; nearby a humming saw broke through the stillness. Five minutes later, they reached a small, wooden, sloping roofed house, surrounded by palms and a banana tree.

'I'm always surprised to see palms here,' Lawrence remarked. 'It's so tranquil.'

Madalena nodded. 'No one expects such a microclimate in one small part of the lake. I appreciate the change in vegetation.'

She unlocked the door. 'I can hardly believe I have owned this place for three years and none of you has seen it.'

Lawrence edged his way in.

'Come on,' she called laughingly. 'Coffee?'

She watched as he looked around him, his expression startled.

'Not what you anticipated, Lawrence?'

He had the grace to look embarrassed. 'I expected functional but with a feeling of being unused. This is cool.'

Madalena now saw the house through his eyes: an open-planned room with streaky yellow walls and a terracotta tiled floor littered with cotton scatter rugs in reds and greens. An oak table and matching chairs by the window; a sofa which doubled as a bed, dominating one wall. A small oak corner wardrobe, a bookcase and several comfy chairs. She was glad of the fragrance of incense, mixed with wild flowers. Her son had admitted to often working on an article under scented candlelight. Regardless of their age, the desire to please, to impress one's children, never lessened.

As he sniffed the flowers, Madalena took his arm. 'I always make sure there are flowers here, even if I am not.'

'You must miss Dad a lot.'

'I tried to give this place a different stamp to the hotel. To help me separate from him. I would come here to construct another me.'

'I always liked who you were,' Lawrence said.

She smiled. 'I started yoga. And I joined a pottery class. Let me show you my crockery.'

She produced some thick china plates and a jug. 'Karl

has talked about building an extension for a pottery workshop.'

'I didn't know you were so artistic, Mum.'

High praise indeed, from Lawrence, she thought as she retreated into the tiny kitchen to make coffee. Through the window she could hear birdsong, see a squirrel darting about in the garden.

When she appeared with coffee mugs, he was ensconced on the sofa, studying a family photograph. She leaned over his shoulder. There was Portia with her long, straight, fair hair and a train tracks brace on her upper teeth, Vienne next to her in jodhpurs and tight-fitting jacket. Annie wore jeans and a polo neck sweater and clutched something made from Lego. There was Lawrence, his light brown hair recently cut, his anorak short on the sleeves, hand gripping Annie's.

'This must have been taken not long before I left for boarding school,' he said.

Madalena nodded. 'I would bring your panda into my room and have a cry. For a few days I'd restrict myself to food you hated.... I'd stare at your row of shoes in your bedroom: your slippers, your walking shoes – do you remember we called them "clumpers"? And the green wellies with yellow frogs. Your father teased me.'

Lawrence stared out of the window. 'At school they teased me for wetting myself.'

Madalena joined him on the sofa. 'I never knew.'

'I'd knock on matron's door at night. I could see the glow of light from the corridor. She'd make me hot milk and give me a chocolate biscuit.'

'Oh Lawrence....'

'Sometimes she'd give me a cuddle and tell me I'd soon settle. It was why I went to her – she was the only woman you ever saw. I used to pretend I was hugging you.... It was the one place you could cry which was safe.'

Madalena touched his shoulder.

He pulled away. 'You think I'm spoiled and cold. That I'm not one of the family, because I'm staying at another hotel.'

'It did hurt me.'

'It wasn't about the Zurbriggen not being grand enough.... I needed space. I suppose the idea of us all being together made me twitchy. Everyone wondering about everyone else.'

Lawrence was paraphrasing her own thoughts and she found it inexplicably comforting. Family reunions *were* risky. You couldn't always know where your children were in their lives, how they regarded you. How often had she observed this in her guests? Tension in the public dining room. Family members occasionally checking out earlier than planned. Why, then, had she considered her family situation so rock solid? Especially when she had her own issues. Things she'd concealed.

'And now you are here?'

Lawrence thought for a moment. 'It's easier than I'd anticipated. But I have my temporary bolthole in the Bergmann.'

Madalena went through to the kitchen, returning with the coffee jug and milk. 'How is Rebecca? Will I ever meet her? I was surprised not to, last time I visited you.'

'We're just friends.'

'You've been friends for a long time.'

'Yeah, well... I'm a mess. She's got me sussed out, but I can't seem to change. She told me I'll never commit to someone and she's probably right.... Were you ever unsure about Dad?'

Madalena considered. 'There are a multitude of reasons for marrying. Your father and I were happy. We were different in many ways – certainly emotionally – but the relationship worked.'

Economical with the truth. Who penned this phrase? A cabinet secretary – ah yes, Robert Armstrong.

Lawrence might be forty-one, but when she looked at him, she saw the child, the young man. The vulnerability beneath a frequently brash manner. She was glad now that the others weren't here, that she had this opportunity to talk to him on his own.

'Rebecca may be correct. However, it may be that she is simply not right for you.'

'I love Tammy, Tamsin.'

'You would be living with Rebecca, as well as Tamsin.'

He grinned. 'Actually, I'm most taken with Benji.'

'Benji?'

'Tamsin's tortoise. It's got a lot of personality – for a tortoise.'

He unpacked the picnic lunch. 'It must have taken a lot of work, doing up this place.'

Madalena nodded, remembering her first view of it. It was a month after discharge from hospital. One day, needing open spaces, to escape her guests' demands, she had taken the first boat to Bauen, planning to walk to Fluëlen. In Bauen, she had noticed a chalet with a *verkäuflich* sign.

'When I first saw the house, there was a vast hole in the roof and termite damage on the lower walls, and the window frames were rotten – I thought I must be mad even to give it a second thought. The garden was wild – six-foot weeds, dying bushes. But the view over the Urnersee was splendid.'

She stopped and glanced at Lawrence. He wasn't looking at her, but she knew by his quietness that she had his full attention.

'I sat for ages on a tree stump, just staring at the building, visualising myself there. Wondering if it would work as a retreat. Wondering if I could afford it. Wondering... what your father would have thought.'

'Dad would have wanted you to do what you needed to, to be happy,' he said, spreading cheese onto a chunk of bread.

At this comment, Madalena's heart swelled with love. For both David and her son.

She drifted into further memories of that visit to Bauen: the familiar looking man fishing nearby; their exchange of pleasantries; her emboldened asking for his opinion of the house; Karl's inspection of its exterior.

She now accepted the sandwich Lawrence had made. 'Karl helped a lot. I don't think I could have managed without him.'

She waited, anticipating his reaction. He was smiling.

'I'm glad you had... have him, Mum. I like him.'

Her relief must have been evident when she replied, 'I'm so pleased, dear.'

She poured them both a mug of fruit juice. 'Once a professional engineer had seen the house, Karl offered to fix the roof and do other structural work.'

Lawrence bit into his sandwich, chewed for a moment, then asked. 'Did you start feeling better then, I mean, more resigned to Dad not being around?'

Madalena thought. Purchasing the house was far from being a panacea. Fifteen months on from David's death, she had experienced moments of paralysing grief. Like a rogue wave, it would creep up and topple her when least expected. She learned to recognise some triggers. Not all.

'In some ways. The first time *apfelstrudel* appeared on the dinner menu, I had to leave the kitchen. Sorting through his climbing equipment was hard. The walking boots, all his ropes and karabiners and ice crampons. I remember picking up his favourite woolly hat which smelt strongly of his hair.... Enough about me – this is pure self-indulgence. I would rather talk about you.'

'Not a lot to say, really. I work, I walk... I read a lot. Sometimes I help Tammy with her maths homework. Or do repairs for Rebecca.'

'Have a slice of Johann's apricot flan.'

Madalena opened the second picnic hamper, removed the pastry and cut two slices, passing one to him.

He bit into it with obvious relish. 'It's such an achievement, staying with the one person for all those years. Thirty-five....'

'Perhaps the act of getting married means you work harder at the relationship. Perhaps that seems old-fashioned.'

He finished his flan, took a drink of fruit juice then stood.

'I need exercise. Fancy a walk? Or do you have things to do here?'

Did he want her to accompany him? Hard to know with her son.

'A few things to sort out. I'll see you this evening.'

Lawrence's revelation about school occupied her thoughts as she watched him set off on the path to Baumgarten. She'd read about the damage boarding schools could do, especially boys' prep schools. Young boys forced into dissociating themselves from their parents, particularly their mothers, as the only way to survive such massive emotional deprivation; harrowing tales about parents and children not recognising each other on visits, or at the end of term. One statement had stayed with her, a quote from a staff member: *We want to make soldiers of them.*

It was one thing knowing about it second-hand, another hearing of the distressing experience of one of her children. Equally, if not more disturbing, however, was the connection she'd recently made between those schools' attitudes towards their pupils, and her husband's attitude towards Lawrence. Despite her ongoing and frequently expressed concern, David had taken him to mountains which Madalena considered too advanced for him to climb. Frequently quoting Chris Bonnington, some nonsense about the importance of being master of a danger.

To her horror, David had insisted on taking twelve-year-old Lawrence to climb the northeast face of *Piz Badile*. Ignoring her rant (which she seldomly allowed herself to do), about finding it difficult enough when he went climbing, let alone took their son, whom, she convinced herself, was frightened but didn't want to admit to. Reluctant to let Dad down. To be viewed as weak. On that occasion, Madalena had even threatened to leave Switzerland. Deeply imprinted on her memory, too, was the protracted row they'd had when David announced his intention to climb the north face of the Eiger – the *Mordwand*, the Murder Wall. Annie had been barely four, at the time.

Ironic, she thought now, that David had died whilst climbing. Ironic, too, that Lawrence, she suspected, now confined himself to lower peaks. There was nothing very large on Skye.

Her children's plights continued to occupy her thoughts as she sorted through the remains – remains? They had barely made a dent in it – of the picnic, storing the perishable items in her fridge.

After she finished, she contacted Hilde. 'Just phoning to check that the meat's been delivered for tomorrow.... Splendid.... What?.... Tell them not to worry about what to wear, and they certainly don't need to waste money having their hair done.'

Madalena frowned as she rang off. Perhaps her invitation to Alice and Ruth Sowerby had caused more anxiety than anticipatory pleasure. She must reassure them when she saw them this evening.

She checked her watch: forty minutes until the next boat to Brunnen. At the bookcase, she perused the books she and David had gathered over their married life. Looked through the hardbacks, sniffing their old, thin paper. The smell of roses drifted in from the garden – she would cut some before leaving.

She pulled out a red, hardbacked volume of Shakespeare. David had loved Shakespeare, reading and rereading *Hamlet* and *Othello*. He had also loved poetry. Something she'd found a refreshing trait, offsetting, as it did, what she'd describe as essentially a pragmatic personality.

As she opened a volume of Keats at *Ode to Autumn – Season of mists and mellow fruitfulness....* she could hear his voice reading it to her. While skipping to a later part of the book, an unaddressed envelope fluttered out. She bent to retrieve it – it contained one flimsy sheet of paper. With trembling hands, she clutched it: had David kept a secret? Something accounting for the parts of him she had been unable to reach?

Having laid the envelope on the bookcase, she went outside and sat at Karl's table, smoothing back her hair, trying to think coherently. It was up to her – she could destroy the envelope without knowing its contents, or she could read them. She paced the garden. Then she returned to the chalet and sat on the sofa, staring at the envelope. Eventually, she removed the single sheet of paper from it, aware it still wasn't too late to change her mind. She laid it down, took a few deep breaths and picked it up again. She read:

Madalena,

I am so sorry about what happened last night. I was tired and demoralised and it seemed we would never get the problems with the kitchen sorted out. I shouldn't have said what I did. Please forgive me. You are my rock. Without you I wouldn't have the motivation or courage to do any of this.

I love you, Madalena. I love you deeply.

David.

She read the letter again. Then she read out loud the final line: *I love you, Madalena. I love you deeply*, like an actor learning a script.

Now she waded through memories, in search of the incident. Ah yes.... the stress caused by staffing problems, a freezer which didn't freeze, and an intermittently faulty boiler, eventually triggering a huge row – off the Richter scale for them. David must have written the note, shoved it into the book, unable, somehow, to give it to her.

Twice her phone rang and she ignored it.

The third time, she answered.

'We thought you'd be back by now,' Annie said.

'I had something important to do.'

There was silence at the other end of the line. Then, 'You sound strange, Mum. Muffled.'

'I'm fine, dear. I'll see you at dinner.'

When she finished her call, Madalena retrieved the

book of Keats, lay down on the sofa and read the poems from cover to cover. Here and there, David had marked in pencil the letter "M" against sections of poetry. What stirred her most was an excerpt from a poem he had written at the end of the book:

Love is my religion.
And I could die for that.
I could die for you.

David had loved her.... Of course she knew that. But she couldn't recall him ever actually telling her. Not even on their wedding day. Or in response to her telling him she loved him.

There were people who loved but were unable to state that love. They might show it in infinite ways but articulating the words proved impossible. What caused this? Did it mean there was some caveat to the love? Or could it be that they didn't feel the need to mention it? That they assumed the person knew? With David, she suspected it might be connected to his upbringing. A distant father and a mother who'd spent much of her adult life as a semi-invalid. An older brother who'd left the family home as soon as possible....

Why was it so important to hear the words rather than know the feeling existed?

She rose stiffly, and, despite the daylight, lit the lanterns on either side of the fireplace. In a kitchen drawer, she found candles and frangipani-scented joss sticks and placed them around the sitting room. Then she made lemon balm tea.

In the flickering light, she went through ten albums of photographs: all the stages of her children's development. It was David who'd glued in the photos – spurning the modern plastic-pocket albums. By each photo, in his painstaking writing, he'd added a comment about the event. It was years since she'd looked at the albums – his systematic record of their family life.

Before leaving, she put the poetry book in her bag, intending to read again the poems marked with "M". Perhaps doing so would finally bring the closure she so much needed.

12

Vienne gripped Michael's hand as they entered the dining room for dinner, wishing she could filter some of his strength into her own body. The nap she'd taken after their short walk had done little to refresh her. Instead she felt headachy. Something *was* wrong. And tomorrow she would find out what.

She studied her family as they hovered around the table, drinks in hand: Lawrence in short-sleeved shirt and beige trousers was tapping his foot. Annie's knee-length flouncy skirt and black top suited her, and her dark curly hair seemed thicker than ever, prompting Vienne to put her hand to her own hair, secured in a French roll.

Madalena, in mushroom brown, with a beautiful scarf of autumnal colours, defined understated elegance, and as Vienne noticed the gleaming gold watch, a present from her father on their thirtieth wedding anniversary, she felt a rush of love for her mother. And curiosity. There was something different about her this evening. Something indefinable.

Lucy looked okay, if somewhat Bohemian, in her Indian cotton skirt and gypsy-style blouse. She would be a beauty when she was older, those purple-blue eyes, the high cheek-bones. As her eyes met Lucy's, she remembered their conversation two days ago and felt her neck redden. Still, perhaps there'd be an opportunity to apologise after dinner.

Portia in her blue-grey dress with its high mandarin collar looked remarkably prim. She was now talking to Lawrence, their expressions suggesting disagreement.

As they sat down, Vienne glanced at her own printed blouse and repositioned the demeaning padded bra. She must change the way she perceived her body: those repetitive thoughts swimming round her head every day were exhausting. What purpose did they serve? Nothing. Exactly. She lifted her spoon and tasted the soup. Delicious: broccoli and something else she couldn't identify.

'What did you do today?' Lawrence asked Lucy.

'Me? I went riding this afternoon. This morning I thought about who my father is.'

There was silence.

'How philosophical,' Lawrence said. 'I don't think many of us know who we really are. Are you interested in philosophy?'

'I don't really understand what philosophy is.'

Lawrence chuckled. 'Not sure I do, either.... Have you seen your father recently?'

There was a clinking noise as Lucy laid her spoon on her plate. 'Interesting question. I don't know. Have I, Mummy?'

Portia interrupted her conversation with Madalena. 'Have you what?'

'Have I seen my father recently?'

'Surely you remember when you last saw him?' Lawrence said. 'You're far too young to be forgetful.'

Vienne felt her neck redden again as she tugged at her wedding ring. Had she unleashed something horrid in Lucy during their conversation? Would an apology make any difference?

'So, have you allocated tasks for us tomorrow?' Annie asked Madalena.

Madalena laughed. 'You're forgetting this is a hotel, dear. I have staff to do that. Gaston and Florian will be serving drinks and nibbles, and then the meal. What you *could* do is make sure Ruth and Alice Sowerby mingle.'

'I'll keep an eye on them,' Lawrence said, and everyone stared at him.

'What?' he asked. 'Does no one value my interpersonal skills?'

'A bit rusty, I expect,' Annie said.

'Hilaire.... I do get invited to journalists' dinners, from time to time. I attended one in London fairly recently, as it happens.'

Portia guffawed. 'Oh, the time when you wanted to stay with me and I was away.... Hardly the same thing. I imagine these events are very cut-throat. Big dog eat little dog.'

'Perhaps you're confusing them with the poncy dinners held by the legal fraternity. I expect you're one of the big dogs.'

As Portia opened her mouth to respond, Annie laid a hand on her arm. 'Walk away.'

Vienne waited to see what would happen. Mum, too, was watching Portia. This was one of their family characteristics: conversations suddenly spiralling downwards.

'More soup, anyone?' Madalena asked.

The discussion reverted to tomorrow's celebration and remained on the topic throughout the veal casserole and the pudding. Lucy hardly spoke and seemed to be avoiding eye contact with Portia who frowned at her from time to time. Vienne struggled to participate. In fifteen hours' time, her neurology consultation would be over. Unless, of course, they kept her in hospital for more tests.

The room darkened, forked lightening zigzagged the sky and they all jumped when this was followed by a bellow of thunder. Vienne took a mouthful of *mousse au chocolat*. Perfect, exactly as it should be: smooth consistency, good quality chocolate, not too rich. Nevertheless, her appetite had waned. The candles were flickering and the room felt too warm. The now familiar tingling sensation in her back had returned, accompanied by an outbreak of perspiration on her brow. Could this be a hot flush or a symptom of MS?

Later, Vienne noticed Michael talking to Portia over coffee in the private sitting room, and her heart went out to him. He'd be reassuring her that she hadn't meant to upset Lucy, perhaps relaying their wish to have Lucy to stay when Portia and Elliot were out of London at the same time. She considered joining their conversation, decided against. Better to let him smooth things over.

She glanced around for Lucy, hoping for a quick word, but there was no sign of her.

Vienne sat down beside Annie. 'I didn't get the chance to tell you about the *Hotel du Lac* tour.'

Annie smiled. 'Madalena said you'd enjoyed it.'

'You're not really an Anita Brookner fan, are you?'

'Bit too introspective for me, lovie. I'm more a Clare Francis devotee.'

Vienne described the tour. Anything to distract her from the neurology appointment. When she looked up again, Michael and Portia had disappeared. Perhaps they'd opted for the privacy of the garden, but this was unlikely: it was raining heavily, rumbles of thunder still sounding sporadically.

Vienne concentrated on breathing deeply while waiting to be called by the neurologist. Nearby, she could smell wet paint. Was horrified to hear a laugh – this was a hospital, full of ill people. A phone rang and rang, stopped, then rang again. Then a Tannoy summoned a doctor. The tingling of her right hand seemed worse and her head throbbed.

'Do you have any paracetamol?' she asked Michael, who was thumbing through a newspaper, despite understanding no German.

'Steady on, you took some two hours ago.'

Her phone went and she sighed as she answered. 'Yes, Charlie.... Okay, tell them I can do it the day after the concert.... Yes, I'd prefer it to be pre-recorded.... I've already agreed to – we discussed this before I left, don't you remember? I have to go now. Phone me tomorrow if you need to. But not too early.'

As she rang off, she was amazed at herself. Had she really just conducted such a call while waiting to find out she might have a debilitating condition? What did radio interviews and hotel rooms matter at a time like this? It was hard to imagine being well enough to perform in Prague.

'My head's awful,' she said to Michael. 'You do love me, don't you?'

He turned to stare at her.

'You would look after me, wouldn't you? If I was ill, I mean, really ill, not likely to get better, I mean, if I have MS or something else neurological?'

Michael pecked her cheek. 'You're not ill, darling. Not seriously.'

'Dr. Nussbaum referred me.'

'He's being careful and he knows you're worried. He wants you to be reassured.'

'I don't think he would have, if he thought it wasn't necessary.'

Michael turned the page. 'He's looking after your emotional health.'

'And what would *you* know about emotional health?'

Her phone went again. 'Hallo for the second time, Charlie! .... Okay, okay.... Yes, I know.'

She switched off her phone and shoved it into her bag. 'Frau Fotheringham,' came the sound over the PA.

It was happening, Vienne thought, stumbling against Michael as she stood.

'You really think I'll be okay?'

'Yes, Vienne, I do.'

Vienne looked at her watch. Perhaps in half an hour she'd have the reassurance she craved. Or maybe an hour. Maybe she wouldn't know today – if they had to take blood or do some horrid form of X-ray. As she walked along the corridor to the open door, she glanced at the other waiting patients. A couple were joking, someone was knitting. Perhaps she *had* got everything out of perspective, as Michael kept telling her.

'*Ich bin Doctor Fruehauf,*' a young man introduced himself.

Vienne was conscious of her rapid breathing as she eyed him. Was this shrimp of a lad really a doctor? How could someone so young make an important diagnosis? Especially in such an attractive room, with its golden poppy yellow walls and those tasteful double windows giving onto the garden. She wanted to flee, to be outside where she'd feel calmer.

Then she noticed an older man in the corner, drying his

hands. The man approached her and shook her hand. 'I am Doctor Kauffman. Doctor Fruehauf is a medical student. Do you mind if he is present during your consultation?'

Vienne nodded her assent. Thank God, her health issues *would* be dealt with by an adult.

Dr Kauffman skimmed through what she assumed to be a referral letter, before saying, 'Please describe the symptoms you have been experiencing.'

She stared at the medical student who was scribbling furiously.

'He's writing very fast,' she said to Michael.

Michael tutted. 'Of course he is. You're a patient.'

'My wife is very anxious,' he told the doctor and medical student. Unnecessarily, Vienne thought, as she relayed her symptoms.

'We will begin by testing your mental state,' Dr. Kauffman said, when she'd finished. 'Please tell me your full name.'

'Vienne Almira Fotheringham.'

'Can you tell me what the date is?'

'The third of July 2011.'

'Can you tell me where you are?'

'I'm at the Kantosspital in Luzern, in Switzerland.'

The doctor spoke to the medical student who jotted something down. Vienne looked at Michael, but he was gazing out of the window. Still, this was a positive sign. He wouldn't be doing so if he was anxious, if he'd only been pretending that he thought she wasn't seriously ill.

Dr. Kauffman showed her a card with a word written on it. 'Please spell the word.'

She did.

'Now please spell the word backwards.'

She did.

'Now, I will tell you a short story,' the doctor said.

Vienne suppressed a laugh. This was like nursery. She listened to the story about a cat which escaped from its owner and was found in a neighbouring village. She allowed herself a smile when the doctor finished.

'Now, Frau Fotheringham, I would like you to tell me everything you can remember about the story. Please.'

Vienne told the doctor about the escaped cat.

He gave her sums to do. Asked her to mimic combing her hair, pretend to strike a match and blow it out. He placed a sheet of paper in front of her and she had to draw triangles and squares alternately. He tested her grasp reflex and questioned her about delusions and hallucinations. If she experienced depression or anxiety. If her eating or sleep patterns had changed recently. He asked about her concentration and self-esteem. She had to pat her nose with her finger, then touch the heel of one foot to the opposite knee. The questions and the tests continued.

Finally, Dr Kauffman told her they were finished. Her heart pounded so hard she thought it would give out. This was the worst stage. When she waited to learn if she was likely to be alive in five years. Or even one. The doctor and medical student were conferring, the doctor studying what the young man had written, nodding. Pointing out things.

She opened her mouth to ask a question but only a croaking sound emerged. The student handed her a glass of water, his eye contact fleeting. This was bad. He couldn't even look at her properly because of what she was about to hear. Her hand shook as she raised the glass to her dry lips.

Just tell me, she thought, as she sipped the water, splashing some on her trousers. No prelude to a concert was this frightful, this debilitating. Her legs felt weak, she doubted she could stand. She looked at Michael, trying to ascertain from his face what her future held, but his expression was inscrutable. Maybe he knew something she didn't. Maybe this German doctor had already communicated a diagnosis to him, her husband. Knowing he was the stronger of the two of them.

'Frau Fotheringham...' the doctor began and paused.

Vienne felt herself sway. Her vision blurred and the room span.

'We have completed basic tests for indications of a lesion in the brain.'

A lesion? A lesion! Oh God, nothing had been mentioned about a lesion. What was a lesion, anyway? A tumour?

'I am pleased to tell you we have found nothing of concern. I think Doctor Nussbaum is correct in his diagnosis. I think you have a virus which is making you tired and giving you some tingling sensations. My advice is to rest, and to become less anxious. This will assist your recovery.'

Michael squeezed her hand and momentarily she panicked. Maybe she had imagined the doctor's reassuring words. Because she needed to. She turned to her husband, but he was looking at the doctor.

'Do either of you have some questions?' Doctor Kauffman asked.

'I'm okay, then? I'm not seriously ill?' Vienne asked.

Michael shook his head. 'He's just told you that, numpty.'

'This is correct,' the doctor said. 'All you must do is to rest and to learn to relax. I will prescribe also a medication for relaxation.'

He wrote a prescription, handed it to her. She dropped it and Michael picked it up, shoved it in his wallet.

Doctor Kauffman stood now, followed by Michael and

the medical student. Vienne hesitated, then, aware that the three men were staring at her, she stood too. Doctor Kauffman shook hands with her, then with Michael, and showed them out of his room. Vienne caught the student's eye as she left. His expression was serious.

She was aware of walking slowly behind Michael as they made their way to the lift. So slowly it was as if they weren't together. She studied his walk – a slight roll of the shoulders, a long stride, his slip-on shoes squeaking on the highly polished vinyl floor. A confident walk, that of someone who rarely worried about anything. Contrastingly, her steps were tiny, tiny and shuffling, like those of a despairing Japanese woman in a tragic drama.

'Shall we have lunch in Luzern or would you prefer to drive back to Brunnen now?' Michael asked as they walked to the car park.

'You decide,' Vienne said.

'Here, I think. I'm in the mood for Italian.'

'What a surprise.'

He grabbed her hand, 'Come on then. It's a gorgeous day. We should find somewhere with outside tables.'

It was so easy for men. Too easily reassured, taking everything at face value. Sometimes they simply didn't want to know the truth. Still, she let him lead her along the busy streets until they found a restaurant that met with his approval.

'You're quiet,' Michael remarked as she picked at her food. 'Can't you perk up? I suppose you're tired from all those tests.'

'I didn't mention my headaches.'

He sighed. 'Darling, you did.'

'And I'm sure I didn't emphasise *adequately* how tired I've been over the past few months.'

'You don't have MS, Vienne. You don't have anything serious. The examinations were thorough. D'you know how long we were there for?'

She thought. '30 minutes, no, 40?'

'Over an hour.'

An hour and a half of basic tests that a child could have passed. No X-rays, no MRIs or CT scans. Not even a blood test. The whole process was too simple, too crude. And, because of this, what she'd have to do now – she wouldn't be at peace otherwise – was to have the process repeated after she returned to London. Despite the looming concert. Was she strong enough to cope?

'A scan would rule things out, definitely.'

'If Dr. Kauffman thought you needed a scan, Vienne, he'd have arranged for one. Are we going to talk about this throughout the meal?'

'I suppose you're right about the scan. But the tests they got me to do could have been for nursery children and they didn't even take a blood sample. Not that I know much about medicine, but–'

'They were testing for motor control. Dr. Kauffman explained. There's nothing wrong with you, except for a lingering virus. Why can't you let yourself believe it?'

Why couldn't she, indeed? Perhaps she needed more time. After all, she'd spent weeks worrying. It might be a few days before she felt reassured. Perhaps longer. She should explain this to Michael. She needed him to understand.

'When I looked at the medical student, as we left–' she began.

'The six-year-old?'

'His expression was too serious, Michael. I'd have thought he'd be smiling.'

'It's almost as if you want something to be wrong.'

She sipped her water. 'What a horrid thing to suggest.'

'Well, then, accept you're healthy. Enjoy your lunch, it's expensive enough.'

He signalled to the waiter, ordered another glass of wine and scanned the restaurant. 'We were lucky to arrive here when we did. They're turning people away now.'

'You're sure, absolutely sure I don't have anything to worry about?'

Michael reached for her hand, knocking a spoon to the floor. He bent down to retrieve it. His expression was one of studied patience. 'I can't speak for the future. None of us can. But for the moment, yes, you are well. Accept it, please?'

Vienne inhaled deeply. Her husband was right. Besides, the Swiss healthcare system was reputed to be one of the best in the world and the physician probably did know what he was doing. Suddenly, like something clicking into focus, she felt lighter. She became aware of the rays of light on the river, the colourful canopies of surrounding restaurants, the vibrant banter around her.

An ambulance whizzed past on the other side of the river, siren blaring. Some poor person was in a bad way but *she* was well.

She didn't need to arrange for a walking frame, or for bath aids. There was no need to check out support groups for people with MS, or complete the list of music for her funeral service. She could continue her career. And, more immediately, she could enjoy the build-up to this evening's Dinner, the event itself.

Vienne giggled as she stepped out of the bath and into the towelling dressing gown. Maybe Madalena would let her take it home. Its softness and warmth were exquisite. Better than a hug.

'Get a move on, darling, it's after seven,' Michael said, appearing in the bathroom. 'Christ, have you drunk all that this evening?'

'Three small glasses.'

'Three large ones. A lot on an empty stomach for someone who hardly drinks.'

She gave a twirl. 'I haven't got MS or some other ghastly progressive disease. All I need to do is relax and get more sleep. And ... I'll be back to normal. It's wonderful, isn't it?'

'What is?' he asked as he rummaged in the cabinet.

'That I'm not ill,' she said, peering at him.

He looked strained. Maybe today had taken its toll and was only showing now. Now that there was nothing to be concerned about. This often happened, she knew. People kept going while they had to. Then after whatever it was had passed, when there was no need to worry anymore, a reaction kicked in. With her it was tiredness, mixed with exhilaration. Her husband was prone to headaches.

'Which suit are you wearing?'

He swallowed two tablets and rinsed them down with tap water. 'What?'

'Michael, are you all right? I asked what you were wearing tonight.'

He shook his head. 'Haven't decided. The blue suit, I suppose.'

'Let's visit some of the galleries together, while we're here,' Vienne said. 'Now I know there's nothing wrong with me. Mum told me there's a Dada exhibition in Zurich, and a Bourbaki – perhaps that's more your thing. Did you know that Dadaism originated in Switzerland? Around 1910. Let's go for dinner afterwards, just you and me.'

'Perhaps.'

She gave another twirl. 'You don't seem keen.'

Silence.

'You are glad everything went okay today? That there's nothing wrong with me?'

'Jesus Christ, Vienne! You're the definition of neurotic. This is doing my head in.'

She scrutinised him. 'You seem distant, that's all.'

'We're running out of time, I've still to have a bath.'

She grabbed him round the waist. 'Shall I scrub your back? I am well, I am healthy.'

'You are drunk. Make a coffee. A strong one.'

'But I don't want a coffee,' she said, waltzing round the bedroom, staggering as she reached their bed. Perhaps Michael was right, the wine had taken effect more than she realised. But she was *well*.

He caught her, then reached over to switch on the electric kettle. 'What you need, Vienne, is a black coffee – *before* we join the others.'

'I don't need coffee,' she said. 'I don't need anything, now I know I'm not ill.'

She cavorted through to the sitting room, ran her fingers up and down the piano.

'There, better already,' she called to her husband, before skipping back to the bedroom.

Michael undid his trouser belt. 'Make a coffee, for Christ's sake.... Did you hear me? You can't go down to dinner like this.'

He added two teaspoons of coffee to a china mug and glared at her as she lay down on the bed, pulling the dressing gown more closely round her. Why was he in such a state? He sometimes got tipsy. Tiddily tipsy.

As he wandered over to the chair, she watched him

remove his shirt, trousers and underpants, giggled as he padded into the bathroom, wearing only his navy socks. Such a ridiculous sight, men naked apart from their socks.

Closing her eyes, she replayed again the final conversation with the neurologist, his diagnosis that she only had a virus. That all she required was rest and relaxation. Rest and relaxation. The words themselves soothed her.

After lunch, Michael had spotted a shop advertising English books. There might be something on relaxation, he told her. She'd laughed, high on the diagnosis of a post-viral condition. To her pleasure and his evident relief, such a CD, moreover, in English, nestled between books on mindfulness and becoming friends with oneself. Back at the Zurbriggen, she'd slipped off her shoes and lain down, listened to the CD, feeling her eyes becoming heavy by the time she visualised her heartbeat being regular and calm. Happy to be under a cosy duvet. Aware that she should give Madalena the reassuring news, but reluctant to move.

She'd woken again at six and spent such a luxurious hour in the bath, soaping herself over and over. Sipping her wine.

How lovely it would be to lie here all evening, simply enjoying the knowledge she wasn't ill. Michael could bring her a sandwich from the kitchen; soup and a sandwich, would be enough after their lunch out. Perhaps she'd read for a while. Maybe even practise for the concert... The concert! Now she could work towards it, without being weighed down by health anxieties....

If only the celebratory dinner was tomorrow. By then she'd be more in the mood for it, even more relaxed and able to socialise. She raised her head off the pillow, sipped her coffee. Time to get up and get dressed.

Swaying slightly as she stood, she giggled. This was

nothing to worry about, just a combination of exhaustion and alcohol. She wasn't swaying because she was ill, because she wasn't ill – not the teensiest, weensiest bit. She was well. Vienne Almira Fotheringham, concert pianist. About to give another stunning performance which would bring stunning reviews and more stunning CDs, and further her reputation as one of Europe's top stunning pianists.

Her spirits dipped – but only a bit – as she opened a drawer to lift out a cream-coloured bra. Even its pretty lace trim and red rose motif couldn't compensate for the lack of contents that would shortly fill it. Still, she was well, HEALTHY! Tumpty tum. Pumpty pum.

Suddenly she needed to have Michael touch her breasts. Reassure her he liked them. She put on clean knickers, floated through to the bathroom, and, ignoring his surprised look, plonked herself on the rim of the bath. Then she bent over, allowing her dressing gown to fall open. As she glanced down at her right breast, its nipple erect, like a tightly closed rosebud, she experienced a fillip of desire. A desire which spread wavelike over her body as she waited for him to touch her.

He gripped the chrome handles, stood awkwardly and reached for a towel. He'd left the bathroom before she had time to formulate a question.

13

Portia was not enjoying the lead up to the evening.

'For heaven's sake, keep still,' Annie said, as she gripped the curling tongs, twisted them, then stopped.

Portia reached round to scratch her shoulder. 'Why are we making so much effort to look glamorous? It's not a Hollywood première.... I haven't seen you wear nail varnish for years. Don't you think the colour's a bit vampish?'

Annie handed her sister the hairdryer. 'It's not dry enough.'

'Does it matter?'

'Dry it properly, then I'll rub in some mousse.'

Portia sighed as she looked at Lucy, lying on her bed, writing her diary. 'I don't have mousse. Lucy, please go and have your bath or shower.'

Lucy glanced up. 'There's loads of time.'

'I'll get mine,' Annie said. 'Keep drying.... Oh, and I saw Ruth and Alice Sowerby in the lounge. They were already changed half an hour ago. They've had their hair done and they were chatting about what they might be getting to eat this evening.'

'What were they wearing?'

'Alice is in a deep green velvet dress and Ruth is wearing an ankle length crimson velvet skirt and a white blouse with a pie crust collar. Both of them have little – not exactly fascinators – but bits of black netting in their hair with a row of pearls. They looked so sweet.'

Portia wiped an eye. 'Don't tell me anything more about them or else I'll cry...'

'D'you know what *would* be nice?' Annie said. 'We should take a photograph of them – just the two of them – in the conservatory.'

'And we could have it framed and present it to them when they leave.... I wonder if they bring over these outfits every year, you know, hoping there might be an occasion to wear them.'

'Lovely idea, the frame, I mean.... I'll get the mousse, dry your hair.'

Portia switched on the hair dryer and glanced at Lucy again, at the pen tottering across the pages of her diary. 'Lucy, please,' she shouted over the noise.

No response.

Fifty minutes to go. She pictured the guests getting ready, their speculative conversations. What would be going on in Vienne's bedroom, as she and Michael changed? Had her sister been given good news by the neurologist, or was she in limbo, awaiting test results?

The dressing table mirror reflected Portia's guilt, her blue eyes dark and accusing. 'It's not that I want Vienne to be ill,' she murmured to herself, confident her words couldn't be heard over the hairdryer, 'but I need her to be preoccupied.' She studied her expression again but she still looked shamefaced.

Would having friends and other hotel guests make Madalena's Dinner easier? Their attendance would add a formality, certainly, but it would also reduce the intensity. She must remind Lucy to be sociable, especially with the Sowerby sisters. Mum's invitation, no doubt, had been well-intentioned, but the prospect must be daunting – in some ways. For Alice, in particular. Ruth would probably enjoy the occasion more.

As a delicious smell wafted up, Portia prayed for a miracle to relax her enough to enjoy the evening. Perhaps she should take one of her Kalms.

Annie returned with a tube of mousse, felt Portia's hair and pointed to a damp bit at the back.

'Aren't you getting ready, lovie?' she asked her niece.

Lucy shrugged and Annie turned away. Portia breathed puffs of air onto the mirror, half-heartedly pointing her hairdryer at the back of her head.

'Shower, Lucy!' she said.

'I had a bath last night.'

'And wash your hair.'

'I want to finish what I'm doing.'

Annie squeezed out a blob of foamy mousse, rubbed it between her palms and applied it to Portia's head. 'This'll give more volume. And make it wavier.'

She took a section of hair, rolled it round the hot tong, held it for ten seconds, opened the tong and let the wave slide off.

'You're something of a pro at this,' Portia said.

Doubtless this was what millions of women did every day before going to work.

'I waved Ferne's hair sometimes. It's the same texture....

Stop fidgeting.'

'Have you heard any more from her?' Portia asked, watching her daughter roll off the bed and slouch into the bathroom, returning to get her headphones, then to fetch the towel hanging over her chair, each time the scowl on her face more intimidating, if a mother could be intimidated by a thirteen-year-old daughter.

Annie shook her head, as she lifted another section of hair. 'Keep still!'

'You always seem so unruffled,' Portia said, listening for the sound of the bath filling or the shower.

Annie grimaced. 'You know I'm not a crier. Usually. Sorry about last week... Keep *still*, Portia.'

Hearing the noise of water from the bathroom, Portia relaxed her shoulders. As Annie selected sections of hair, rolled them round the tongs, held and released, Portia's thoughts circled back to Vienne. It would be a difficult evening for her if she hadn't received reassurance. If she awaited results. She was bound to be distracted, in fact.

She turned to Annie. 'You haven't heard how Vienne got on, have you?'

'Portia, if you move once more, I'm abandoning this.'

'I keep postponing talking to Lucy about what she said to Vienne. I suppose I'll have to, after this evening. Although, I've still no idea what to say.... Aren't you finished yet?'

Annie rested the tongs on a newspaper, shook the waves out and sprayed Portia's hair. 'So, what do you think? You can't put off talking to her forever. It must be buzzing round her head.'

'You're right, I know, about talking to Lucy.' Portia looked in the mirror. 'Actually, I look rather nice.'

'Nice?' Annie squawked. 'You look brilliant, it softens

your features.'

'Even my long nose? I suppose I should make an effort with my face this evening.'

'Your skin looks dry. What moisturiser do you use?'

'Anything that comes free... Forty isn't a kind age,' Portia said. 'It heralds a decade of gradual disintegration. And, according to Lucy, who already considers herself a sage on skincare, two camps exist.'

Annie yawned. 'Really? And what might these be?'

'I'm *so* glad you're interested. The first type, apparently, rush to a René Guinot salon for exotic-sounding facial treatments like cathiodermy, reducing other expenses in order to afford pricey creams with seductive promises. Of course, such descriptions tend to include the phrase "reduce the appearance" of fine lines. A great get-out clause, in case of litigation – far more prevalent in the States, as you know.'

'And the other camp?'

'The other group resign themselves to the hackneyed "growing old with dignity" philosophy: the earth mothers who don't mind if their skins resemble prunes provided their allotment potatoes are grown organically. Actually, Lucy's theory is incomplete. There must be three camps, as I don't fit either. Personally, I can think of better ways to spend my salary. And you don't fit either category, do you? In fact, you disprove the theory. I'm sure you don't add pesticides to your vegetables, and you look as if you use face creams.'

Annie nodded. 'Yes, but not the rip-off ones. Just shows that most theories can be disproved.... Portia, when you got Mum's invitation, did you want to come over?'

Portia hesitated. 'Yes, and no. No, because I was twitchy about seeing Vienne – even before all this erupted,' and she pointed at the closed bathroom door. 'At first, I took it at face value – an invitation to a celebratory dinner. Then I wondered if Mum planned to sell the hotel, and I thought I should be here, make sure she got a decent amount for it. That's the "yes" part. You?'

Annie unplugged the tongs. 'I hadn't considered she might sell. I thought it would be fun, and I needed a break from the café.'

'I suppose the Ferne thing changed how you felt,' Portia said.

'Just a bit.'

'Do you think Mum will announce something this evening? It's marvellous how she's managed to continue running the hotel without Dad.... Do you think she and Karl are close?'

Annie yawned again. 'Dunno. Did you like him?'

'I'm always wary of new people. Shame really – to be so cynical, I mean.'

As Annie nodded, the bathroom door opened and Lucy emerged in a lemon towelling robe, her hair dripping wet. A cloud of steam drifted behind her. Portia grabbed a towel and rubbed it over her daughter's head, while Lucy stood there, shoulders slumped.

'That's better, darling,' Portia said. 'What do you think of my hair?'

Lucy turned away. 'It's all right, I guess.' She lay down on the bed, crossed her legs and flicked through a copy of *Elle*.

Portia stared at her daughter. 'You must get dressed. It's after seven.'

Lucy continued scrutinising the magazine, jerking her upper leg from side to side.

'Answer me when I'm talking to you, Lucy. You need to get dressed.'

'In a minute,' she said, without looking up.

Annie glanced at Lucy, shrugged her shoulders at Portia, and left the room.

Portia opened the wardrobe door and sighed as she inspected her clothes. How much easier it was to dress for Chambers. All she needed to do was select one of three trouser suits – worth every penny for their forgiving cut and their relative crush-resistance – and a white, grey or pale blue blouse. One simply tailored saffron yellow cocktail dress was more than adequate for the occasional mandatory work function, and would have been ideal for this evening, had she not spilt wine over it and forgotten to have it dry-cleaned.

'I wish I had a bigger choice of clothes.'

'If I said that, you'd tell me I have loads of things,' Lucy muttered.

'What?' Portia asked.

The choice facing her was the drab grey dress she'd worn last night, or a crimson sleeveless georgette which was clingy and had a dodgy neckline. What in heaven's name had induced her to buy it? she wondered, as she slipped it on, adjusted the shoulders and rearranged it again in an effort to conceal a centimetre of bra.

'Lucy, will you *please* get dressed. We'll be late,' she said.

Her daughter dropped the magazine, removed her headphones and sat up. 'I've nothing to wear.'

'What about your new trousers, with the purple top, which, if you remember, we spent hours choosing?'

Lucy mumbled something, lifted her notebook and started scribbling again.

Portia fiddled once more with her dress. 'What's wrong with my suggestion? And what are you writing? I do wish you'd let me see.'

'It's private... Anyway, I'm not hungry.'

Portia stopped fiddling. 'But you are coming down? Granny will be so disappointed if you aren't there. She was very upset about the boat trip.'

Portia slid the dress off her shoulders, reached into a drawer for another bra and swapped it for the one she was wearing. This was better. Or was she showing too much cleavage? No gown to hide under now.

She checked again on Lucy, who'd got as far as putting on tights, before lying down on the bed once more.

'Any time this evening, Lucy....'

Portia re-zipped her dress and sat at the dressing table to examine the contents of her cosmetics bag. She removed the top from a mascara, dabbed the brush on her hand to check the colour, and sighed at the dried-up blue mark before chucking the mascara into the wastepaper basket. After rubbing some grey eye cream on her eyelids, she scrutinised herself in the mirror. Now she looked like a blonde panda. She found a tissue and removed the cream.

As she lingered there, the evening light streaming through the open window portrayed her in a gentle, romantic way, like the heroine in some Harlequin romance. She smiled at her reflection. Annie had done a surprising job with her hair.

Then her pulse quickened as she became conscious of the silence. Here she was, being girly and fluffy, when her daughter was making little effort to get ready.

She went over to Lucy. 'What is it, sweetheart? You've been acting strangely all day. Is it about school?'

'Finally, you've noticed not everything's perfect in my world,' Lucy said.

Portia flinched. 'I'm sorry we haven't had time to talk properly. And we can't talk, just now, not properly. But tomorrow we will, I promise.'

'Whatever.'

Portia retrieved her shoes from the wardrobe, smiling in satisfaction as she looked at their low front, the slim heel higher than she normally wore. Annie was right. They were elegant and would look good against the sheen of her black tights.

The words cracked across the room. 'Elliot isn't my father, is he?'

Portia dropped a shoe as she spun round. 'What?'

'You heard. I'm illegitimate, aren't I? That's why Da... he left, isn't it?'

Slowly Portia sank onto the chair by the dressing table. 'What *are* you talking about?'

Her mouth was dry, she needed to pee. Surely Lucy hadn't overheard her discussing the situation with Annie? They'd been careful, talking only when the shower was on.

'Who *is* my father, then? I have a right to know.'

Portia went to sit by her daughter. Took her hand. It felt cold, and the scallop-edged ring on Lucy's middle finger dug into her skin. 'Girls can be horrid, especially at boarding school.'

Lucy jerked her hand away. 'You haven't answered my question.'

A glimmer of a smile edged across Portia's face. 'I see you've inherited my interrogation skills.'

'Don't patronise me,' Lucy said, pushing her away, standing. 'Who is he? Who is my father? My proper one?'

'I don't know why you're asking me this now,' Portia said, playing for time. Lucy wouldn't be fobbed off, reassured, by woolly answers.

'I bet you shagged lots of men. Look at you in that dress. It's disgusting at your age.'

In horror, Portia watched Lucy dash into the bathroom, slamming the door.

She waited a moment, clasping her hands together, biting both thumbs. She tugged at the wine georgette, knowing her sweaty palms would leave a stain. Then she went to the door and turned the handle. It was locked. She knocked, gently at first, then more insistently.

'Come out. Please.'

'Make me.'

'We can talk. Lucy, please.' She knocked again, horrified by the wobble in her voice.

She waited. One minute? Five? Then she heard the click of a turning lock. Saw the door edge open, jamming on a damp towel. Lucy stood there in her dressing gown and black tights, ten feet away, miles away.

As Portia tried to embrace her, Lucy raised her arms. 'You know what you are, don't you? You're a *SLAG*!'

It was involuntary. Like the blinking of an eye, a shiver. Portia reached out and slapped her daughter's face.

'That's abuse. I can report you, you know that, don't you, Mother?' Lucy said coldly. 'Where would *you* be then? The defendant not the barrister.'

Portia gaped at her daughter. Lucy's eyes weren't filling with tears. Nor was she rubbing her face, the red part, where Portia's hand had struck.

'I'm sorry, I'm so sorry. I didn't mean to hit you. Please forgive me.'

'Yes, Mother,' Lucy said, returning to the bed, opening her magazine.

Portia sank into the armchair, put her head in her hands. Her heart was thudding, and tears weren't far away. She looked round, hoping Lucy might have abandoned her magazine, would give her a hug.

With effort, she walked to the dressing table, removed the top from her lipstick and applied it. Registered the darkness of her eyes, her pale skin. In the silence of the room, she heard a page being turned, then another, as she waited for a sign of Lucy softening.

She had a flashback to her last case, the burst of applause when the jury found her defendant not guilty, the frenzy outside the court building – the press, the client's friends and relatives crowding round her. And this was her other side: her private life, one continuous effort to conceal the truth, an ongoing inability to forgive her actions and the suffering they had caused. Lucy's anger was driven by hurt and bewilderment.

'Lucy, I really am sorry. Don't shut me out. Please, darling....'

Silence.

As Portia made herself look round, she wanted to grab those expensive headphones from Lucy, and snap them in two. Anything to provoke a reaction. The tears were now flowing freely. She grabbed a tissue and wiped her face.

Out on the lake a horn blared. Reproaching her. If only she could undo the last five minutes, rewrite the behaviour which no amount of rationalising, citing provocation, could justify. She stared at her hair, at Annie's efforts. Wondered if Lucy was right. If her affair with Michael meant she *was* a slag.

Wearily, she opened a tube of "concealer" cream which promised to give an even skin tone, squeezed a blob of separated oil and grubby beige lotion onto her finger, scraped it off and dumped the tube in the wastepaper basket. After another disastrous attempt with the grey eye cream, she gave up.

Staring through the mirror at her daughter's upright,

unforgiving back, she realised that Lucy's unexpected reaction to her slap disturbed her as much as the hitting. Anything else would have been better: crying, returning the slap, or engaging in a verbal tussle which ended in tears and hugs and mutual declarations of love and regret, Lucy's words, Portia's actions. Anything other than these icy, coherent remarks, that contemptuous "mother".

A conversation below the window reached her, nudging her into action. She must go downstairs and do and say the expected things. As she struggled to slip on her shoes, she wondered if they, too, portrayed her in the wrong way.

She gathered up her court papers, shoved them in her briefcase and laid it in the bottom of the wardrobe. At the door she hesitated. 'I'm going down to the conservatory now. But if you'd rather we talked... but I think you want to be on your own for the moment. So, I'm leaving. I hope you'll come down soon.'

She waited for a response from Lucy.

Silence.

Quietly, she shut the door, rearranged the top of her dress and walked along the corridor.

At the conservatory entrance, Portia stopped. The glasshouse had been transformed: its broken glass pane replaced, its frames cleaned. The green tiled floor gleamed and new floral-patterned cushions adorned the bamboo sofas. Plants had been shuffled around to create more space, lemon trees, palms, avocado plants and bamboo trees placed to either side of the walls, like a reception committee; orchids and other plants tucked away in safe places. Portia registered all these details with the precision and detachment of someone assigned to prepare a report.

Guests had already assembled. Alice and Ruth Sowerby were seated on one of the sofas, Herr Adler from the Hotel

Bergmann standing beside them attentively, Ruth giggling at something he said. Both sisters clutched wine glasses. The scene reminded Portia of an episode from *Poirot*: the yuccas and palms, the Sowerby sisters formally dressed, their newly waved white hair sporting black fascinators, their lipstick a tad too red.

Madalena was discussing something with Johann at the far end of the conservatory, and nearby, Hilde was talking to a woman Portia vaguely recognised – Herr Adler's wife, perhaps. Karl was offering Vienne a tray of nibbles. A sound from behind made Portia turn round, some fantasy flooding her mind – Lucy appearing in a pretty frock, remorseful, ready to apologise and be angelic.

'Hi,' Lawrence said. 'Lucy not here yet?'

'Any minute now,' Portia said brightly. If she kept willing her daughter to join them and behave well, this might happen.

'I'll mention the museum visit to her this evening. Now I must say hallo to Mum.'

As Portia looked round the room again, deciding who to talk to, Vienne approached her.

'Where's Lucy?'

'She'll be here any minute.... How did your appointment go?'

'The neurologist thinks it's only a virus which–'

Michael joined them. 'Evening, Portia. Vienne, Madalena wants to speak to you.'

Portia rushed over to Annie as she stood in the doorway. 'I need to talk,' Portia said.

'Lucy?'

'She knows. We had a frightful row. It was ghastly, simply ghastly. I hit her.'

Annie gasped. 'Oh Portia.'

'She called me a slag. A slag! I slapped her. I've never done that before. I always told myself no matter how provocative she might be, I wouldn't, would never, resort to violence.'

Annie put her arm round her sister. 'It was a foul thing to say. D'you want me to have a word?'

Portia considered. Annie and Lucy had always been close but tonight any intervening might aggravate things.

Gaston appeared with a tray of wine. Annie took two glasses, handed one to Portia.

'To be honest, I've no idea what to do,' Portia said. 'If I go back to our room, it might make things worse, in fact.'

A memory of another family occasion surfaced. Easter with Elliot's parents in Yorkshire. Seven-year-old Lucy demanding to wear her new dress on a country walk, not the jeans and wellies Portia advised. Lucy's temper had suddenly flared and she'd slammed the bedroom door so hard that a small picture fell to the ground, the glass splintering. Grandma Carmichael had been upset. Elliot had been furious, calling Lucy a spoiled brat and glaring at Portia as if it was all her fault.

'I'll give her ten minutes, then go up,' Portia told Annie. 'You should mingle.'

As Annie left, Portia's eye roamed the conservatory. Several more guests had arrived in the last few minutes and were circulating, shaking hands. She watched as a couple approached the Sowerby sisters and introduced themselves. Then she saw a couple of women greet Madalena, kissing her three times. They'd be the pottery crowd.

Everyone must be here now, surely? As she did a head count, her eye rested on Vienne, who was grasping a wine glass and gazing into space. Perhaps the neurology appointment had failed to reassure her. Her sister had always been a hypochondriac.

Evening light shone brightly through the glass panes, but in the next half hour it would start to dim. They would probably eat dinner by candlelight. Candles were forgiving, would help to conceal Lucy's facial features.

As Karl approached with a tray of food, Madalena behind him, Lucy arrived.

Portia gaped at her daughter hovering by the conservatory entrance in a low-necked camisole top, short clingy skirt and Doc Martin boots.

She went up to Lucy. 'You need to change.'

Lucy smirked. 'Make me, Mother. Yes, I'd love a glass of wine, thank you.'

'Lucy, *please*...'

Madalena came over to them. 'Evening, Lucy. You are looking very grown-up.'

'Mum, I'm sorry. I'll sort this,' Portia said.

Gaston brought another tray, offered Lucy a vol au vent. Michael was circulating with a bottle of wine in each hand. More guests had arrived and were being greeted by Karl. Alice and Ruth Sowerby remained seated, heads turned in Lucy's direction. Alice's mouth was wide open, Ruth looked intrigued.

'Lucy–' Portia began.

'It's okay,' Madalena said.

'You're not embarrassed by me, Mummy, I hope. Children shouldn't embarrass their parents. And parents should certainly *never* embarrass their children.'

Michael approached them, refilled Portia's glass. Madalena shook her head when he made to refill hers.

'Is no one going to offer me some wine, then?' Lucy asked.

'Not this evening, dear,' Madalena said, smoothing back her hair. 'You can help me in the kitchen.'

Portia watched as Madalena and Lucy left the conservatory. Shortly after, she laid down her glass and made her way to the kitchen, pausing at the door. Both Mum and Lucy had their backs to her.

'Lucy, I know you're growing up, but do you really think your outfit is suitable for this occasion?' Madalena asked.

Lucy bowed her head. Portia couldn't hear what she said, but it must have been a satisfactory response, because Mum was nodding.

'Please go and change, then we'll forget all about it, as long as you behave appropriately for the rest of the evening.'

Lucy nodded and scuttled out of the kitchen.

Unseen, Portia made her way back to the conservatory. Michael approached her, and, relieved by the result of the conversation in the kitchen, she found the energy to talk to him.

'I hear Vienne's had the all clear from the neurologist.'

'Hopefully she'll let it reassure her, not get into a flap again.'

Portia took a deep breath. 'Lucy's worked out that Elliot isn't her father. We've just had a ghastly row.... Has Vienne said anything more about their conversation?'

'Not since I spoke to you last night.'

'I need to know what you think she thinks.'

'Vienne's been preoccupied with her health worries, and she's still got the concert.... As I've told you, she's keen to play a bigger role in Lucy's life. She–'

'Dear God,' Portia said, looking up at the conservatory roof. The volume of surrounding conversations increased and she felt dizzy.

This wasn't going to simply fade away. It would only get worse, in fact.

Michael was talking again. 'She's got all those ideas, she's racing ahead as if we can play happy families. I don't know how we're going to deal with the situation.'

'Finally, you're taking it seriously. You and I'll have to meet up, of course, when we return to London. Discuss how we can avoid ...'

Avoid what? All contact? Sooner or later, Vienne would confront her. Underneath her quiet and seemingly passive façade, there was a determined streak, a fighting one. No one could become a concert pianist without being strong. It was amazing, quite frankly, that Vienne hadn't challenged her before about seeing Lucy so infrequently.

'I'd better circulate,' Michael said. 'Chin up. Perhaps Madalena will sort Lucy out.'

He squeezed her shoulder and wandered off.

Involuntarily, Portia glanced down at her dress. It had slipped again and all she could see was cleavage. Lucy was right – she looked ghastly. Fleshy and cheap, like the subject of a Blackpool postcard. They were both fleshy and cheap this evening.

Her wine tasted sour. What she wanted was cocoa. What she wanted was to watch something cosy on television with her daughter, hugging their mugs. Smiling at each other. Feeling safe.

Maybe Madalena would sort Lucy out, Michael had remarked, as if all that was required was an Elastoplast or paracetamol. Lucy changing into something more modest would help, certainly. But it wouldn't make her less of a loose cannon.

She tugged her dress again, catching Vienne's eye as she did so.

s Madalena finished a conversation with her friends from the pottery class, she noticed Gaston hovering.

'I will give my speech when Lucy's here,' she told him. 'You can then serve the champagne.'

She glanced at the entrance to the conservatory. Still no sign of her granddaughter. Scanning the room didn't lift her mood. Portia looked miserable as she talked to Annie. Michael was discussing something with Lawrence, but his eyes kept shifting to Vienne who had allowed Karl to refill her wine glass again. Vienne's behaviour was an enigma. Having received good news from the neurologist, she would have expected her daughter to be happy this evening. Not drinking her way through it.

Ten minutes to eight. Lucy should have returned by now. What must Ruth and Alice Sowerby be thinking about her granddaughter's outfit? Were they worldly enough to dismiss it as a "growing up" thing? Feel for Portia, whom they would have noticed not only didn't have a husband with her but wore no wedding ring?

Had it been a mistake inviting the elderly sisters to join her celebratory dinner? An unconscious self-satisfaction? A patronising gesture? Like families who always asked People-On-Their-Own for Christmas lunch before the actual day. Inviting the same "poor souls", year after year, for the same meal; presiding in regal fashion over the serving of turkey and bread sauce, a rich plum pudding stuffed with trinkets, the fresh fruit salad, its rosewater replaced by Grand Marnier to aid the Christmas cheer. Deluding themselves that their invitation made a significant difference, was The-Right-Thing-To-Do. The gifts – Marks and Spencer's leather gloves, a silk tie or scarf – meaning that their guests had at least one Yuletide present. Was she any different to those she criticised?

If David were here, he would tease her out of questioning mode. But of course, if he were alive, this occasion would be taking place for different reasons.

She caught Christophe Adler's eye, and as they exchanged smiles, she wondered how he interpreted what had happened. As a father, himself, though, he'd have experienced the challenges of adolescent behaviour. She scanned the conservatory again. Her drama group friends were examining her Alpine plants, obviously impressed. The Lengaurs were studying her lemon tree, also apparently admiring. She must focus on the positive aspects of this evening, not on her escalating concern about Lucy.

Suddenly she wanted to get her speech over, whether or not her granddaughter was present. She retrieved her notes from her evening bag, tinkled the nearby cowbell, and silence descended.

'*Willkommen, Familie unt Freundeskreis*, welcome, family and friends. Now is the time to explain more fully why I invited you here,' she said, signalling to Gaston. Glass clanged against metal as the waiter opened champagne and circulated amongst the guests.

'As you know, this is the fortieth anniversary of the Zurbriggen,' she continued. 'David and I opened our hotel with ten rooms and within five years had expanded to twenty-five. We then expanded to forty rooms and began offering facilities for business meetings. It was hard work for many years, and often difficult to compete with other bigger hotels. Nevertheless, we managed to earn and maintain a reputation for providing a friendly service and keeping our prices reasonable....'

Madalena paused as a series of fireworks exploded by the lake, the noise ricocheting around the mountains.

'If David were alive today, he would be proud of what the Zurbriggen offers: we have resisted pressure for a late-opening bar, jacuzzis in the en suite bathrooms, and evenings of international cuisine. We always agreed to specialise in Swiss cooking. And this has worked. Many of our clientele are regulars, and one of the things they appreciate is being served traditional Swiss food.

'But if you think I take all the credit for this, you are mistaken. I might own the hotel, but much of its success is due to my splendid team. Being Swiss-German – as all of them are – I would expect them to work harder than the Swiss-French! I believe everyone here this evening – apart from my British guests – is Swiss-German, so I can get away with these comments. Seriously, my staff work hard, they take a pride in everything they do. Furthermore, they often display effort beyond the call of duty. Of course they do! They embrace the Swiss ethic. Can we think of any other country that would vote against reducing the working week? I think not.

'All my staff are treasures. In particular, Johann and

Hilde. Time and time again, Hilde has gently encouraged me to be more organised, and, even more challenging, has displayed an impressive resilience in teaching me about the benefits of computers for office management.

'Johann has unlimited energy and extraordinary creativity when it comes to devising and perfecting new recipes. Whatever the situation, he is always calm in the kitchen, and manages his staff well. Both he and Hilde have taught me much, and without them I would be lost.... I can see from their faces that I've said more than enough, so I won't embarrass them anymore, apart from giving them particular thanks.

'I have asked you here to help me celebrate what I believe is an achievement. There is, however, another reason and this may come as a surprise.' She paused and caught the eye of all her children. 'I am getting married again – to Karl.'

Karl took her hand.

'We have known each other for several years and he was there for me after David died. Lastly, and I promise you no more revelations after this, at least not this evening: I am retiring, so am looking for someone – perhaps even one of my children – to take over the running of the hotel. I believe–'

As Madalena peered at her postcard notes, a piercing noise rang out. There was a general cry of surprise. Lawrence was the first to shout: 'Smoke detector.'

Florian ran into the conservatory. 'The fire is in room 202, Frau Fontana.'

'202!' Portia cried out. That's my room!'

'Have you phoned the fire service?' Madalena demanded.

'*Ja, ja*,' Florian said.

Lawrence, Michael and Annie were already tearing along the corridor, Portia not far behind them.

Madalena took Karl's arm. 'Please make sure everyone leaves by the conservatory door and assembles in the garden. Ask Hilde to stay with them.'

She turned to Johann. 'Evacuate the other guests to the garden. Check the public dining room and sitting room first, then the rooms on the first floor. Florian, you and Gaston check the second and third floors.'

Madalena followed her children, calling after them: 'The fire extinguishers are halfway along the corridor.'

When she reached the second floor, Madalena paused for breath. At the end of the corridor she could see the open bedroom door and Lucy flapping at something with a towel. She kicked off her shoes and ran along to the room. Lucy was by the wardrobe, beating a bag on the ground, around her a charred mass of paper. The flames had spread to the carpet and the dressing gown and towel lying on it.

'Get back, get back, it's dangerous,' Portia shouted, pulling her daughter away.

'It was only meant to be your briefcase,' Lucy cried. 'I couldn't stop it.'

Portia gawped. '*You* did this? It was deliberate?'

Lawrence charged into the room with a fire extinguisher and began dousing the carpet and curtains with water. Annie and Michael ran in with more fire extinguishers and sprayed foam across the beds and the floor.

Madalena stood, rooted to the ground, her head trembling.

Michael called over to her. 'It doesn't look too bad.'

'Aren't there sprinklers?' Lawrence asked as Annie and Michael now shoved the beds and chairs back.

'Probably not hot enough for them to be activated,' Michael said. 'The smoke alone won't trigger them.'

Portia stood with her arms round a whimpering Lucy.

By the time the fire service arrived, the fire was out: the carpet scorched, the walls smoke-stained. Portia's briefcase was covered with treacly bits and black smudges, some damaged papers poking out. The room smelled of smoke and roast pork.

'I'm sorry, I'm sorry,' Lucy cried.

Portia remained with her arms around her daughter. 'It's okay.'

It was far from okay, Madalena thought. If the smoke detector had failed, or even been slow to react, the building could have gone on fire.

'You should leave the room,' the fireman in charge told her.

She nodded. 'Please go outside,' she told the others.

'Don't send me away again, Mummy,' Lucy begged.

Portia shook her head. 'I won't. I won't. Come on, Lucy. We must go outside.'

Madalena slumped against a wall, body shaking. Lucy's actions were unbelievable. When they talked in the kitchen, she'd seemed contrite, not angry or vengeful.

'Mum, I'm so, so sorry,' Portia said. 'About this, about the Dinner. I'll pay for the damage, of course. And–'

Madalena stared at Lucy. 'Why would you do this? The hotel could have burned down. Do you have *any* idea how hard your grandfather and I worked to...?'

'I'm sorry, Granny,' Lucy managed between sobs.

'I'll check the rooms nearby,' Lawrence said.

'That's our job, sir,' a fireman said. 'You must all leave, now.' There was the sound of muffled conversation on walkie-talkies. Madalena wanted to linger to see if the other bedrooms on the corridors were safe, if the fire really had been extinguished. She felt weak and tearful, half expecting a further outburst of flames.

Michael took her arm. 'You need a stiff drink, Madalena. Come down to the private sitting room. Lawrence can report back what the firemen think, or they can come and find you.'

She nodded. 'I must check on my guests.'

'Karl is with them. Give yourself some time. You've had a shock.'

'Would you prefer a camomile tea, rather than a drink? I could make you one.' Annie asked.

'Thanks, dear, later perhaps. Please go and check everyone is all right outside. They will be wondering what is going on.'

Shaking her head, she followed Michael downstairs and into the family sitting room. Shortly after, Karl and Annie appeared. Madalena was pleased to see Karl, yet appreciative of his sensitivity in not rushing to her, claiming her attention.

Ten minutes later, Lawrence arrived with the firemen. 'The other rooms are okay, Mum.'

Madalena nodded her thanks and addressed the fireman in charge. 'I am hosting a Dinner this evening. My guests were in the conservatory – can they return there now?'

'Yes, they can. We are satisfied that the building is safe, Frau Fontana. We will leave the papers with you for insurance purposes.'

As she staggered slightly, Karl took her arm.

She turned to Lawrence and Annie. 'Please look after our guests. They can have the dessert – the cakes are in the kitchen. And coffee, offer them coffee. Annie, organise this, please. Karl, you go too. I will join you shortly.'

As Annie and the men went to round up the guests, Madalena resisted the urge to go and lie down. She had to sort out this mess but she had no idea where to begin. There were her guests, too.... And after all her planning.... It was too bad of Lucy. She must talk to her now.... Where were Lucy and Portia? And where was Vienne?

At that moment, the door opened and Portia entered the room, followed by a cowed looking Lucy. Madalena gave them a moment while Portia helped herself to coffee and gave Lucy a glass of water.

Despite her wish to sound calm, Madalena was aware of the barely concealed anger in her voice. 'Can you help me understand how this happened?'

Portia shook her head. 'It's me Lucy's angry with, Mum. No one else. And certainly not you.'

At this, Lucy shot out of the room.

As Portia made to follow her, Madalena held up her hand. 'Have you considered professional help for Lucy? This is far from normal behaviour.'

'Lucy doesn't need a shrink, just.... I must go and find her.'

Madalena followed Portia upstairs, calling to her, 'Surely she won't have gone back to your room. You can't sleep there now.'

'I had important papers in my briefcase,' Portia said. 'Original copies of documents.'

Madalena gasped. How could Portia be thinking about her clients now? This was history repeating itself. All her children had been sent to boarding school, to enable their parents to run the hotel. Portia was showing a similar lack of judgement.

'If you have *any* sense, Portia,' she said, 'you will learn from my mistakes.'

When they reached the bedroom, it was empty. Portia knocked on the bathroom door. 'Lucy?'

Silence. She turned the handle. The room was locked. Madalena tried. 'Lucy, it's Granny. Please come out.'

Still nothing.

'Go, Mum,' Portia urged. 'You should be with your guests.'

'I expect they will leave soon,' Madalena said. 'It would be impossible to continue now.'

Immediately, she regretted her words, knowing it was unfair to lash out at Portia. The Zurbriggen was far from being ruined. Furthermore, even the bedroom could be repaired. She would have to replace the carpet and wallpaper, and organise professional cleaning, but as far as she knew, this was the extent of the damage. Portia and Lucy would need to move to another room, of course, but this could be done later.

Poor Karl, their engagement barely announced before things went haywire. He must be wondering what sort of family he had become entangled with.

'I really am sorry,' Portia said. 'I'll get this sorted out. Get Lucy sorted out. She's not a bad person... she's just confused and lost at the moment.'

'Don't let this get any worse, dear.'

'Please go. I need to talk to her on my own.'

Wearily, Madalena patted Portia on the shoulder and left the room. As she reached the end of the corridor, she saw Annie sprinting up the stairs.

'Shouldn't you lie down?' Annie asked. 'You look very white.'

'I have guests to look after.'

'People are leaving. I think they feel awkward. Perhaps you could invite them again in a few days' time. Take two... Sorry, terrible joke.'

'This took months of planning,' Madalena said.

Again, she was spiralling down into self-pity mode instead of keeping things in perspective. It might have been so much worse – people could have been injured. She would return to the conservatory and see what could be salvaged of the evening. Maintain some dignity. As David's face flashed before her, she saw him nod, heard his voice telling her this was the right way to handle things. She managed to smile at Annie, gripped the banisters and walked downstairs.

The conservatory was much quieter than when she'd left it. There was no sign of Karl.

'He's giving the Lengaurs a lift home,' Annie informed her when she came back down.

'Ah. Did he say if he'd be returning?'

Annie shrugged. 'There was so much going on.'

'Of course. Would you help Portia and Lucy move into room 24? You'll find the keys in reception. The beds, everything, should be ready for use.'

Madalena then circulated, making sure the remaining guests had coffee and cake. Conversation was subdued, people conveyed their condolences about the fire. Part of her longed to get to bed. Another part yearned to be with Karl.

An hour later, there was still no sign of Karl. Madalena had insisted the staff go home, and only the family now remained, except for Portia and Lucy, neither of whom she had seen since Lucy locked herself in the bathroom. Michael and Vienne said goodnight, then Lawrence, having checked there was nothing more he could do, left for his hotel. After instructing Annie to stop clearing up, Madalena locked the main doors, checked the ground floor windows were locked and made her way to her apartment. There, she paced its rooms, knowing she should make herself a camomile tea, have a bath.

Instead, she changed into casual clothes, grabbed her jacket and left the apartment. She got into her car and drove round the west side of the lake to Karl's home.

The road was quiet and well lit, but everything felt strange under a cloudy, starless sky. It occurred to her that if the car broke down, she'd be vulnerable on this lonely stretch of road. At this time of night. Especially, as in her haste, she'd forgotten to bring her phone.

When she arrived, she parked outside the grounds of Karl's house, and searched for signs he was at home. There were no chinks of light behind the closed shutters. Nor was the car in the driveway, although it might be in the garage. She could, of course, ring the doorbell.

Automatically she reached into her pocket for her phone, before remembering it was sitting on her dressing table. She was trembling all over. More than anything, she wanted to feel Karl's arms around her, to be safe. Calm and safe.

She checked her watch. Eleven o'clock. The sensible thing would be to head back to the hotel. Tomorrow she'd have things to do in the aftermath of the fire.

She turned on the ignition, then switched it off again, got out of the car, and walked round Karl's house, trying to detect any lights. There was only darkness. She returned to her car and sat there for another half hour, wondering why she was behaving like a lovesick maiden. On the point of returning to the Zurbriggen, something prompted her to get out of the car again, and take the public path running along-side Karl's garden.

What was a pleasant enough path in broad daylight felt different in the shadowy darkness. Several times she jumped when a cat ran past her. There were rustles from bushes, to her left, a bird flew into a tree. Then an owl hooted, nearly causing her to cry out in surprise. She wished now she'd brought the torch from the car boot. Ahead of her, the lake was pitch black, but from the lantern by the nearby pier, she spotted a figure, looking over the water. Heart thudding, she stared, unsure if it was Karl. The figure shifted and she recognised his profile. He still hadn't seen her.

Wondering if this was the right thing to do, if it wouldn't be fairer to respect his space, she approached him. At the sound of her steps, he turned. He stretched out his arms, and she ran to him.

'*Liebling,*' he said. 'I am glad you have come to me.'

15

While Madalena was driving to Karl's house, Vienne had returned to the conservatory and was now slumped in a chair. As she refilled her wine glass, she heard muffled footsteps approaching. She listened as they drew nearer, praying it wasn't Portia, eventually forcing herself to look up in the darkening light. It was Annie.

'Portia isn't here,' Vienne said.

'I needed to unwind. If I go to bed now, I won't sleep.'

Vienne reached for her wine glass. 'Me neither.'

'Some evening, huh?' Annie said, reaching for the coffee pot, pouring herself a large cup, adding two cubes of brown sugar. 'Poor Mum – all her work…. Hard on Karl, too. I mean, we'd hardly had time to react to their news before…. Oh, I do hope they'll be happy.'

'Happy!' Vienne said, refilling her glass.

Mum had been happy with Dad and would be happy with Karl. Some women, it seemed, could keep their men. You probably had to be very special to live with someone who never cheated on you and she simply wasn't special enough.

Maybe she was making too much of the shoulder squeeze Michael had given Portia. But it had been more than a brotherly action. Definitely. The combination of Portia's low necked dress and Michael's body language.... And he'd ignored her, when she came to him in the bathroom. She topped up her glass once more.

'I think you've had enough to drink, Vienne,' Annie said.

'I'm not drunk.'

'You're in a bad place though, aren't you, lovie?'

Vienne hesitated. Maybe she should ask Annie if she knew anything. But Michael wouldn't betray her. Surely not. And not with her sister.... It was one thing, his flirting, quite another actually doing anything. It was the alcohol affecting her, distorting her thinking, her perceptions. Driving her into – what was it? There was a name for this. Something Shakespearean – the Othello Syndrome. Erotic jealousy, alcoholic paranoia, delusions of spousal infidelity. Jealousy that Michael fancied Portia.

Michael and Portia, bodies entwined. Michael drowning in flesh. Drowning in flesh. Who'd used this expression? Some writer... D.H. Lawrence in *Women in love*. Ursula – or was it Gudrun? No, it was Ursula, played by Glenda Jackson, with her hallmark mocking smile. Ursula, who'd uttered the powerful line, "I want to drown in flesh." Referring to her lover's thighs.... Portia and Michael drowning in each other's flesh....

Annie and Vienne looked round at the sound of footsteps.

'I am so sorry to disturb you, but I dropped my handkerchief,' Ruth Sowerby said. 'It's got my initials on it: RS.'

Annie got to her feet and helped the elderly woman

search, scrambling under the palms and cheese plants, under the bamboo sofas and chairs.

'Is this it?' Annie asked, holding up a piece of worn white cotton with a ragged lace trim.

Ruth grabbed it. 'Oh, thank goodness. Thank you, dear.' She sank onto a chair. 'What a relief.'

'Would you like some coffee?' Annie asked. 'It's still hot enough.'

Ruth leant forward. 'It was given to me by a young man. I suppose you'd call him a "lover" nowadays. It was all very hush, hush...' She paused, her gaze distant.

Vienne caught Annie's eye.

'I hope I'm not embarrassing you. But, you see, I've never told anyone about this before, and you seem such *nice* young ladies.' Ruth clasped her hands on her lap, the hanky pressed between them. 'It was during the war when Alice and I were land girls. Alice was ill with flu, you see, and the stable boy – the other girls said he was sweet on me. He had such a gentle manner and a sweet smile, and one day we went into the barn and we.... It only happened once but I never forgot him. After the war he wrote to me and sent me this.'

Vienne stared at the elderly woman. Her chest sagged as it did with people that age. Nevertheless, she must have had a good figure once. Michael would have drowned in those voluptuous breasts of Portia. *I want to drown in flesh.* Glenda Jackson's tone, unashamedly, brutally, single-mindedly focused on Rupert's body. That was what people were like when they wanted something. Unrelenting. Instant gratification. That's all it was.

When could the affair have happened? She cast her mind back over recent tours. There'd been so many. Michael drowning in flesh. Portia's flesh.

'No one knows about my little tryst. Not even Alice,' Ruth Sowerby was saying. 'She would be horrified – she likes to think of us as *virgos intactae*. You won't say anything?'

'Of course not,' Annie said.

Ruth sighed. 'It *was* rather pleasant, the experience. Oh, forgive me for prattling on. Alice is always telling me I talk too much.... I must be off to bed. We're not used to these late nights. And all the excitement of the fire.... I do hope your poor mother isn't too distressed. Please tell her, if there's anything we can do to help.... Good night.'

She stood, put the handkerchief in her pocket, patting it. 'I always wash it by hand... the lace trim.... Everything is so fragile.'

'Let me walk you back to your room,' Annie said.

'Thank you, dear, but I shall be fine. Your kind mother always gives us the lovely room on the first floor, the one with the special view, *so* easy to get to. I expect you and Vienne will be wanting to talk about the fire. Good night.'

'So, one should never make assumptions,' Annie said, once Ruth was out of earshot. 'I *am* glad for her – at least once is better than never.... Coffee?'

Vienne shook her head.

Annie laid her hand on Vienne's arm. 'Life can be shit, can't it? You're pretty soused, aren't you? I'd better escort *you* to your room.'

Vienne shook her head again. 'Not yet.'

Annie hesitated, then kissed her cheek. 'Don't stay too long, lovie. Night, night.'

Vienne managed a fleeting smile before a shadow crossed her face. A memory was returning, as she listened to her sister's bare feet padding across the tiled floor. New York, five years ago. Michael upstate on business, allowing herself to be dragged along to a girlie evening with his colleague's wife; the hostess producing a box of goodies. Finding herself with a cleavage cream, which someone laughingly grabbed from her. The voice telling her about this awesome clinic in Manhattan. Adding the word "augmentation" as Vienne looked blank. Leaving the gathering in the middle of a conversation about the importance of making an effort, to stop your husband straying.

A woman was more than just her body. Perhaps Michael appreciated Portia's legal mind, her sharpness. Perhaps he found her more stimulating to talk to. Perhaps it wasn't just physical. What had they been discussing this evening, before he gripped Portia's shoulder?

She gulped her wine, spilling some on the table. And only hours ago she'd felt so much better. She didn't have multiple sclerosis or anything warranting investigation. She could continue her career. Would be around for Michael when he turned forty. She had her music and she had him. Or so she'd believed.

How could Portia betray her? White spots danced in front of her closed eyes. Her phone vibrated in her pocket; she ignored it.

"Look after yourself," Annie had advised. Yes, but how? She'd never been able to control Michael. This was the trouble with good-looking men: women regarded them as available, despite the man's domestic circumstances, despite their own. It was exhausting, such constant worry about what her husband was doing. Too exhausting. Still, she had a choice, she had to believe that. Perhaps this evening she should choose to stop loving him. Let him go.

She broke off a leaf from the cheese plant, crumpled it in her hand. "Everything is so fragile," Ruth Sowerby had said. Perhaps "destructible" was more accurate. People were destructive. Relationships were destructible, often destructive. She broke off another leaf.

Sooner or later, she'd have to return to her bedroom. To Michael. First, she should eat something. She took a slice of banana loaf, but it was too rich and she could hardly swallow it. She forced herself to drink half a cup of coffee. What she wanted was more wine. Drowning in wine. Drowning in flesh....

Vienne found Michael on the balcony, looking over the lake. The water was exceptionally calm. He stood when she came out to join him.

'What an evening,' he said. 'I felt so sorry for Madalena. And I'd planned to tell you about the surprise I've organised, unless, of course, you'd rather I cancel it, given what's happened.... Do sit down, darling.'

Vienne stepped back into their room. He followed her.

'Is something wrong?' he asked. 'Apart from the obvious.'

Vienne reached out and slapped his face.

'What the fuck...?'

She ripped open her blouse, tore off her loathsome padded bra.

'Am I so repugnant you had to go looking for your ton of flesh?'

Michael bent, attempted to redo the buttons of her blouse. 'You're drunk.'

Vienne shoved his hands away. 'Portia – my sister – and you.'

He pulled back, lost his balance, clattering to the floor.

She despised him. He was a nothing. Portia was a nothing. The two of them together amounted to nothing. Nobodies.

'Go on, touch me, if you can bring yourself to.'

He pushed himself up, reached for her hand. 'Your skin is so smooth, so young.'

Vienne leant forward. 'Michael, how could you?'

She could smell the alcohol on her breath, the coffee on his. She noticed one of his bottom row teeth overlapping with another and wondered why he'd never received ortho-dontic treatment.

'How could I what?'

'Sleep with Portia.'

He tugged at his tie. 'What on Earth makes you think I'd do that?'

Vienne laughed bitterly. 'Intuition. It doesn't matter how much you deny it, I know you did.'

He paced the floor.

'Admit it,' she said.

Her phone went, she ignored it. It went again, this time she answered. 'Trish .... No, we're an hour ahead here, not an hour behind. What is it? .... No, leave it as it is.'

She hung up.

Michael bent, took her hand, flinching as she jerked it away. 'I've never slept with Portia. I love you.'

'I don't believe you. I saw how you were with her this evening, in the conservatory. I might have been at the other side of the room, but I noticed.'

Michael brought a chair over to where she was sitting. She stared at his legs, at the thigh muscles still toned from his rugby days. Thighs he would have wrapped around Portia. She thought of his hairy chest, the smell of him.

She pictured them sipping wine, its effect heightening the sexual act. Michael would have thought only of Portia.

Not of her. Because he wouldn't have been able to see it through if he had thought of her.

'Portia was simply asking about how you got on at the neurologist.'

'How often? Where?'

Silence.

'When did it happen?' Vienne asked.

Not that his answer would change anything. She was heading nowhere with this conversation. There was no reply he could give which would make her feel better. What was that film where the husband had an affair with his wife's sister, and years later, after he'd died, the wife managed to forgive her sister? Helena Bonham Carter had played the adulterous sister. Paul Bettany, the husband. Vienne had watched the film with Michael and he'd been able to sit through it. Had he felt even the slightest bit guilty?

Michael shook his head. 'I've never slept with Portia. You must believe me.'

'It's so easy for you, Michael. When I'm away on tour.'

'It's easy for you, too.'

'Don't drag me down to your level. I've never been unfaithful.'

'I'm sure you'll had opportunities, an attractive woman like you.'

'What matters is that I've never betrayed you.'

She felt a roaring in her ears. He would have held Portia afterwards, might still have felt desire. Confused it with love. Believed he could be in love with two sisters. She didn't think she could bear it, if he'd thought it even momentarily. And she wasn't brave enough to ask him if he'd ever felt – however fleetingly – he *was* in love with Portia.

'You're drunk, Vienne. This is alcohol talking. Plus, you're tired after the neurology appointment.'

She laughed. A horrid shrieking laugh, like someone deranged. She *was* deranged.

Michael stood, stretched his back, his arm muscles revealed through the thin fabric of his shirt. He walked over to the window and looked out, as if he wanted to escape. Then he glanced at his watch. Her heart was racing, he couldn't leave her alone, not at the moment, not with such dark thoughts, such hopelessness. She could smell cigar smoke drifting in from outside. The scent of roses. She felt desperate, but someone was smoking, and roses continued to grow, their fragrance filling the air.

She struggled to stand. 'I'm going to be sick.'

Michael guided her through to the bathroom, put his hand on her forehead as she threw up. Then he took her back to the bedroom, helped her undress and get into bed, brought her a glass of water. He pulled a chair nearer to her and sat down.

'You have nothing to worry about,' he said, as she lay back on the pillow and groaned. 'I've never slept with Portia. I promise you.'

Her mouth tasted of regurgitated acid. She sipped the water.

'You were so happy earlier, darling. You are well and you will give a great performance in Prague.'

Vienne stared at the ceiling. Prague! Could she really go through with that, give of her best when she felt so wretched?

A heavy silence hung between them.

'I don't know.... The way you were with her this evening. It seemed so....'

Shallow breathing prevented her from continuing. She forced herself to take a deeper inhalation of air, then another. It was working. Her chest was loosening.

Michael leant forward, took her hands in his. His were warm, radiating heat. Like a healer called in to mend her. Not the man who'd abused her trust, shattered her belief in him. In them.

She got out of bed. 'I'm having this out with Portia. I need to know.'

He reached out, pulled her back. 'You can't do that.'

'Watch me.'

'Lucy will be there. You can't make a scene. We don't even know what room they're in now.... You have to believe me when I tell you nothing's ever happened between Portia and me.'

She wanted to believe him. She wanted to enjoy their marriage without constantly wondering what he was up to. She wanted to enjoy not having to worry about her health.

There was no choice. She would believe him because the alternative was unbearable.

16

P ortia paced the room. It had been fifteen minutes since Madalena left to return to her guests in the conservatory. Nearly twenty, since Lucy locked herself in the bathroom.

Part of her wanted to rejoin the guests, help Mum salvage what she could from the evening. Another part needed to know if the look Vienne had given her after her conversation with Michael, was as insightful as it seemed at the time. Her overriding need, however, was to stay here. Hope that Lucy emerged soon. Then they could talk, despite the fact she still had no idea what to tell her about Elliot.

She jumped as more fireworks exploded by the lake.

Perhaps Mum was right and Lucy did need professional help. Setting fire to things, even once, was worrying; twice, significantly more so. But was this simply a cry for help, Lucy desperate for Portia's attention? If she hadn't read through her clients' notes this afternoon, would Lucy have been less incensed, demonstrated her rage less dramatically? Maybe they should do family therapy. Not something she relished, but if it helped Lucy....

She went to the bathroom door. 'Lucy, what are you doing? Please come out. I won't be angry, I promise.'

Silence.

She tried the door, knowing it was locked. Dear God, what was going on in there?

'Lucy, please tell me what you're doing. I won't be angry, darling, honestly I won't.'

Could Lucy be depressed? According to recent reports, eighty thousand children and young people in the UK suffered from depression. And there was a high suicide rate in teenagers.... For the nth time, she tried to remember what her toilet bag contained. Paracetamol? Razors? Any other medication?

The cognitive side of her knew that anger often protected people from depression, and Lucy certainly was angry. But this didn't mean that she wouldn't self-harm.... Did it?

From behind the door came the sound of water: perhaps her daughter was having a bath. An ordinary bath. She put her nose to the keyhole, hoping to smell the passionfruit scented shower gel, indicating there was nothing to worry about. But all she could smell were burned curtains and carpet, and the stench from her briefcase. She lifted the briefcase, Elliot's last present, fingered the scorched leather. Racked her brains again trying to remember if she had painkillers in the bathroom. She checked the top drawer of the dressing table to see if she'd put her heavy-duty co-codamol there. The tablets weren't there, neither were they in her makeup bag. Or her handbag. They must be in the bathroom.

She had to act, find someone strong to kick the door in. Lawrence or Michael – what a choice.

As she was about to leave the room, the bathroom door

opened and Lucy stumbled out, still in her camisole top and mini-skirt. She looked ghastly, her face so pale and streaked with mascara, eyes dull, hair wild and punky, as if she'd been running her hands through it.

Portia flung her arms round her. 'I was worried....'

Lucy's face contorted. 'I'm terribly sorry, Mummy.'

'Let's get into our pjs and make ourselves comfy,' Portia said, leading Lucy over to the bed. 'I'll find more sheets and duvets. We can't sleep in these. They reek of smoke and they're damp.'

Minutes later, she returned with clean linen, and made up the beds. She then used the discarded sheets to mop the floor. The room still smelled horrible, so she opened the windows as wide as they'd go. Staying here wasn't ideal, but Lucy looked exhausted.

When they'd changed, she got Lucy into bed and covered her with the duvet. She sat stroking her daughter's forehead, as she had done when she was little and feverish. How smooth her skin was. Like a child's. She was still a child. A confused child. Never had Portia felt so guilty about her past behaviour as she did now. She would give a limb if it could undo the damage she and Michael had caused to people they loved.

Now she was aware of a headache. They should really move to another room this evening, but she couldn't disturb Madalena again.

'I s'pose Granny hates me,' Lucy said.

'She got a fright, certainly. But she's concerned about you, as I am.'

Lucy's face crumpled. 'I'm concerned about me, too.'

Portia took a deep breath, conscious of observing herself from a distance as she embarked on the conversation she'd never anticipated. 'Earlier, before the dinner, what you said about.... about Elliot, about your father....'

She stopped. There was still time to pull back. Perhaps Lucy hadn't meant what she said this evening, had only been in a strop. As she stared at her daughter, however, she knew this wasn't the case. Lucy was waiting, with a gravitas to her waiting. This wouldn't go away.

'You want to know about your father, and you have a right to.'

She glanced at her daughter, lying so still in bed.

Portia inhaled deeply again. Once the statement was out, she couldn't retract it. Like a witness. 'This is difficult to tell you, sweetheart, but you're right, I'm afraid. Elliot is *not* your biological father. I am *so* sorry. I wish with all my heart he was.'

Lucy was silent for a moment. 'What happened?' she asked, her voice small, gravelly.

'Your father – Elliot – wasn't well. He'd been diagnosed with clinical depression. It wasn't long after his own father died.'

She studied her daughter, so still and quiet, as if this was how she must remain, in order to learn the truth. Aware of her voice, low and deliberate, Portia continued.

'Things were difficult, and I met someone.... And it shouldn't have happened – I shouldn't have behaved as I did. And then I found out I was pregnant and....'

Memories inundated her: missing a period, wondering if she might be pregnant by Michael, suggesting to Elliot they try making love in the morning when he had more energy. Elliot, ever keen to please, acquiescing, pumping away to no avail, Portia wondering how to communicate to him that she needed to be in court in an hour and it was okay if they just stopped.

She now wandered over to the open window, to the cool, refreshing night air. Amidst explaining to Lucy what had happened, she was briefly overcome with emotion. Poor Elliot. She swallowed hard and returned to Lucy's bedside.

Lucy averted her head. Portia waited. Eventually, her daughter turned to face her.

'Did you think about... about going to a clinic and...?'

Portia gulped. 'Getting rid of you? No, never.'

'Not even once, even for a second?'

Portia gripped Lucy's clammy hand. 'No! Not even at my worst moment – when.... Never. And I've never regretted it.'

Lucy attempted a smile. 'Even when I've been horrible?'

'Never, sweetheart. And I never will. This is the thing about being a parent. The love is so deep, so primitive. You might despair of your child's behaviour at times, but you never stop loving them. Not people like me.'

'You mean people from our background? Well-off.'

'It's got nothing to do with money or privilege,' Portia said. 'The poorest people, the ones struggling from day to day, can make equally good parents, better ones some-times... if they've received love themselves. Maybe even when they haven't. That's what I think, certainly.'

She got up to close the windows, then wandered back to Lucy's bed again. It was Elliot's face she saw, though, his struggles.

When Elliot twigged she was pregnant and the baby was unlikely to be his, he'd agreed to raise the child. Because he was gradually recovering from his depression, she'd convinced herself he would be a good father. Throughout labour, he held her hand and kissed her forehead, reas-suring her she *could* deliver the baby. That she had to push harder. Simply go for it. When a tiny, baffled Lucy emerged, he cut the umbilical cord. Cradled her while the midwife stitched Portia. He bought red carnations and celebratory balloons, and a musical card which played *Happy Birthday to You* incessantly until Portia had flung it out of the window.

Lucy was now tugging her arm. 'Who is he? My real father.'

'I can't tell you.'

'Was he married?'

'Yes, he was. He is.'

'Has he ever seen me?'

Portia hesitated. 'Yes.' She clenched her hands, hoping Lucy wouldn't ask any more questions. The fewer lies required, the better.

'You did love him, didn't you, Mummy?'

Some lies were necessary. 'Yes, darling, I did.'

She stared at Lucy's face. It was hard to fathom what she was thinking. She was now picking at the bedspread, looking up then down.

'What is it, sweetheart?'

'Did Daddy leave because of you or because of me?'

Portia hesitated again. She'd only have one chance to respond to this: if she got it wrong, she wouldn't be able to backpedal.

'I want the truth,' Lucy said, the firmness to her voice contrasting with the fear her eyes conveyed.

'I know, I know. Daddy left for two reasons. The first one was because I... I'd had an affair.'

She glanced at Lucy's face. Its expression tore at her.

'And the second?'

Portia took Lucy's hands. 'The second is that I think he found it too hard being around you and knowing he wasn't your biological father. It was almost as if–'

'As if he didn't dare love me?'

'Exactly.'

In the early days, when Lucy was new to them both, Elliot had stared at the baby on his lap, as if trying to work out what he needed to do to make things okay. To make Lucy his. He prepared healthy meals, shopped for nappies and dummies, and a ghastly contraption for Portia to express milk. He took Lucy to infant swimming classes and became proficient at massaging away her tummy aches. In the park with mums, he debated the pros and cons of nurseries and the best approach to weaning, relieved to be accepted by the women, once he'd demonstrated an understanding of the debilitating effects of sore nipples and perineal pain.

Once, Portia had woken from a deep sleep to hear him crying.

'As if he loved you too much and that frightened him because you weren't his,' she now told Lucy, hoping this might help her daughter.

Portia hadn't understood Elliot's situation at first. She knew from friends that fathers sometimes had a bit of catching up to do when bonding with their baby. It was natural. They hadn't carried the baby for nine months; they didn't have the same amount of "flesh" time as they couldn't breastfeed. She'd therefore been prepared for Elliot feeling slightly detached and assumed he'd soon be doting on Lucy as much as she did. So, it took time before she realised what was happening. It wasn't that he couldn't feel the right way about Lucy. It was because he was scared to. In case her real father might claim her. And no amount of reassuring from Portia could persuade him that this wouldn't happen. Could never happen.

'I suppose he worried that my real father might

suddenly decide he wanted to become my dad,' Lucy said slowly.

'Oh, darling....'

Portia couldn't continue. She looked at Lucy: at the young face now cleaned of heavy eye makeup; the blue and green polka dot pyjamas, a Christmas present from Grandma Carmichael three years ago, fraying at the wrists, the legs, originally too long, now three-quarter length. The pyjamas Lucy insisted on keeping.

'Did he know who my real... the other man was?'

'No, and there was never any risk of him claiming you. Some men simply aren't paternal.'

There was a glimmer of a smile on Lucy's face. 'So, Daddy really did love me?'

'Does love you. It's easier for him, perhaps, not being with you full-time. And of course when he's with me, he's reminded... he remembers what happened.'

'As long as he loves me,' Lucy said. 'But my real father obviously doesn't.'

'Listen to me, Lucy. If I could go back and change the past, then I would – but then I wouldn't have you. But if it could have worked out another way.... Elliot does love you, I swear on my life.'

There was a new gravitas in her daughter's expression. 'Then this will have to be enough.'

Staring at her, Portia saw both the hurt child and the emerging woman.

There was a knock on the door. Wearily Portia rose from the bed. If this was Madalena here to give Lucy a roasting....

'I came to help you move,' Annie said, jangling some keys.

'We've been talking,' Portia said. 'Lucy's in bed and I'm loath to disturb her. I've changed the sheets.'

'You're not seriously planning to sleep here?'

Portia reconsidered. 'I suppose not.'

Annie entered the room. 'I'll help you.... Where *is* Lucy?'

Portia looked at the empty bed. 'Brushing her teeth, probably.'

Annie lowered her voice. 'I've just had a rather heavy session with Vienne in the conservatory. She's in that scary mode of being drunk but insightful. I think she suspects something, and for all we know, she's having it out with Michael right now.'

Portia flopped onto the bed, cradled her head in her hands. 'God, you didn't tell her anything, did you?'

'What do *you* think?'

'I wish I could crawl into a hole.... I'll have to talk to him tomorrow.'

She opened drawers and lifted out clothes. Everything felt heavy. Annie had retrieved the suitcase and grip bag from the top of the wardrobe, and was packing the bundles Portia handed to her, when Lucy emerged from the bathroom.

'Do we have to move tonight?'

'You can help,' Annie said. 'Get your toiletries from the bathroom, Mum's stuff too.'

Portia finished emptying the drawers and wardrobe. Lucy stood by the bathroom door, clutching her toothbrush and toothpaste.

Twenty minutes later, they were settled in their new room and Lucy had fallen asleep. Annie hugged Portia and left.

Portia sank into her armchair, retrieved a notebook from her bag and noted what she needed to do:

1. Find out what Vienne knows.

2. If she knows Michael is Lucy's father, persuade her not

to tell Lucy (arguments for persuasion: nothing to gain, will hurt and confuse Lucy, won't reverse history).

3. If she doesn't, then nothing to be done with her.

4. Contact Elliot and explain situation.

5. Arrange for him to visit asap – reassure Lucy he loves her.

6. Persuade him to be a bigger part of her life: family holidays, birthdays, Christmas.

7. Find day school in London.

She returned the notebook to her bag, zipped it up.

When she glanced over, Lucy was awake again, was lying there, clutching a pillow. Portia sat on the end of the bed thinking how vulnerable she looked.

'I almost wish you were young enough for me to read you a story. Do you remember *The Baby Blue Cat and the Whole Batch of Cookies* and *Henry Babysits*? I got them at a car boot sale for twenty pence. They were American.'

'When I was nine, I invented a "wish" box,' Lucy said. 'Every evening in bed, I'd open my box and add another wish.'

'What sort of wishes?' Portia asked, wanting to know, yet dreading Lucy's response. This was the horrid thing about knowledge, the fact you could never "unknow" it. You could bury it, but it would always be there, always threatening to surface.

Lucy hesitated. 'Promise you won't be angry? The biggest one was that Daddy would miss me so much he had to come home. Then when I went away to school, I would daydream about him kidnapping me because he couldn't bear not to live with me.'

'Oh, sweetheart,' Portia said.

'By the time I was twelve, I accepted he wouldn't come back to live with us. Then when Zoë and Cassie started taunting me about my sticky out ears and I knew that neither you or Daddy had them, I began to wonder if he was my father, after all.... Mummy, don't be annoyed, please, but do you ever miss living here? I mean, do you ever think of moving back? I've got to have a change of school, anyway....'

'Whatever happens, Lucy, you must promise me you won't start any more fires. You could have set the whole place alight tonight. Will you promise?'

Lucy nodded sleepily. Portia slid further along the bed, took her hand. She had to request this of Lucy, even if it wasn't fair, putting another burden on her.

'Another thing, darling. No one else knows that Elliot isn't your natural father. I'd rather it stayed like this.'

As she waited for Lucy to reply, she wondered if this was a fair request to make. What if her daughter really needed to talk to someone about this? Perhaps she *should* arrange counselling.

'Does Annie know?'

Portia hesitated. If Lucy knew Annie had withheld such information, this might damage their relationship. But Annie had only known for several days.

'It's okay, Mummy, I won't tell anyone. I don't want people to know.'

'Granny would be very upset. Grandma also.'

'But she isn't my Grandma.'

'She b*elieves* she is and she certainly loves you like a grandchild. And you're her only grandchild.'

'If Da... Elliot has never told her the truth, that must mean something,' Lucy said.

Portia swallowed hard.

Later, now in bed herself, she wondered again about moving back to Switzerland. Running the Zurbriggen wasn't an option. What she could do, though, was relocate to the

Zurich office, commutable from Brunnen. She could also negotiate part-time work and enroll Lucy in the local school. Or they could live in Zurich and visit Brunnen regularly. Lucy already spoke some German and would quickly become fluent if immersed in the language at school. Or she could go to one of the international schools in Zurich and be taught in English.

Counteracting the positives of returning to Switzerland, was a voice reminding Portia that living here wasn't simply about enjoying lakes and mountains. It meant tolerating its tax haven status and other despicable practices. And yet, by working here as a human rights lawyer, perhaps she could concentrate on war crimes. This way she could justify her return, especially if it would be good for Lucy.

Portia didn't wake until after ten o'clock the following morning. Lucy's bed was empty and briefly she panicked, before hearing voices outside. She wandered over to the window and looked out. Lucy, in jeans and checked shirt, hands clad in yellow gardening gloves, was snipping roses, passing them to Madalena, who carefully removed the thorns before laying the flowers in a basket. Mum seemed to be pointing out something in the roses, Lucy nodding. Lingering by the window, Portia heard them laugh, felt a lump in her throat, partly about Lucy, partly about Mum's magnanimity in doing something with her granddaughter so soon after the fire.

When they were growing up, Mum had explained how to differentiate between a flower and a weed, demonstrated the best way to prune honeysuckle and japonica. She'd always conducted difficult conversations with them in the garden, relying on its peaceful atmosphere to soothe them as much as it did her.

What would happen today? Portia wondered. Before last night's shenanigans, there'd been talk of taking the mountain train to Staffelhöbe. But the sky was dark and already spats of rain were rapping against the window. She heard Lucy exclaiming in disappointment, then asking if she could arrange the flowers.

The uncertainty of what was going on with Vienne and Michael now gained momentum. Like a constant threat, as if her sister might burst into the bedroom any minute, launching a thousand accusations. But Vienne wouldn't burst in anywhere.

There were three possibilities: Vienne's wild imaginings after the aborted dinner were paranoia, fuelled by alcohol, and she hadn't cottoned onto the truth. (A remote, if wonderful, hope.) She had noticed the resemblance between Lucy and Michael and extracted the truth from him. Or she'd recognised the likeness and he had denied it.

Portia dialled Vienne and Michael's room number.

'It's Portia,' she said, when Michael answered.

He muttered something before saying, 'Are you mad, phoning the room?'

'Is she there?'

'She's sleeping. She took something.'

'What happened last night. Did she say anything? Does she know?'

'I can't talk now.'

Michael sounded exasperated, frightened even. And it *was* risky phoning their bedroom. Anyone could have worked this out.

'I suppose that means "yes".'

He lowered his voice. 'For Christ's sake, she might surface.'

'Meet me in the sitting room.'

There was an edge to his voice, 'I can't,' then a change of tone as he said, 'It's all right, darling, go back to sleep.'

Portia took a deep breath. 'Does she or doesn't she know?'

But he'd replaced the phone, leaving her with the lonely sound of the dialling tone. She pulled on yesterday's crushed skirt and blouse and left the room.

Outside Vienne and Michael's door, she hovered, listening for sounds of conversation. She thought she heard the shower but couldn't be sure. Fleetingly, she considered knocking, then she moved on, rebuking herself. Last night's events had impaired her judgement. She should go downstairs, find some coffee, see what Lucy wanted to do.

At the sound of footsteps behind her, she turned round, heart racing.

'In here,' Michael said, shoving her into a storeroom full of floor mops and buckets, shutting the door behind them.

'What does she know?' Portia asked, pressed against a container which smelled of bleach, and something digging into her shoulder blade.

Michael considered. 'She asked about you and me but I denied it.'

'Dear God.... Did she believe you?'

'I can't be certain.'

'What happens now?'

'Nothing happens now, Portia. We just pray Vienne doesn't work out anything else. The more you and Lucy keep out of her way, the better.'

'Lucy knows,' Portia said.

'Knows what?'

'That Elliot isn't her father.'

'You told me that at the Dinner.'

'Correction – what I said was that she'd worked it out. But I've now actually admitted it's true and we've talked.'

'Christ, you haven't told her it's me, have you?'

She'd never heard Michael sound so anxious before.

Typical, though, that his concern was solely for himself. They could be stuck in this broom cupboard for hours and he still wouldn't show any interest in how Lucy had reacted to the revelation about Elliot. Her brother-in-law had the emotional integrity of a peanut.

'Don't worry, your secret's safe where she's concerned.'

Portia retraced her steps to her room, undressed and crawled under the duvet, wondering if Michael had ever experienced an iota of paternal feeling for their daughter. She turned from side to side, willing her eyes to feel heavy, but she was too strung up by their conversation. Lucy would be back soon, and then there was the remainder of the day to navigate. Would her daughter raise the issue of her father's identity again? Seek further assurance that Elliot loved her? It was naïve to think that one conversation would be enough.... A day of unknown quantity lay ahead. Left to her own devices, Portia would stay in bed and read.

Her phone went.

Madalena's voice sounded cheery. 'I wanted to let you know that Lucy is in the office helping me with paperwork. Regard it as work experience.'

'Send her up here, whenever you want. You must have loads to do after... last night.'

'I'll let her stay for half an hour or so, then I need to get on with other things.'

Ten minutes later, Portia abandoned her attempt to fall asleep. She got out of bed and sat down in the armchair, rubbing her chin. If she was going to do this at all, now was the best time. She lifted the phone and found the number of the one person who could help.

'Elliot?' she whispered into the phone, even though Lucy was in reception.

'Portia?' came a sleepy voice.

'I thought you'd be awake.'

'I just got back. Can I speak to you tomorrow?'

She transferred the phone to her other ear. 'Back?'

'Boston.'

Of course. He'd been away. 'This is urgent. I'm phoning from Brunnen.'

She heard a noise which sounded like a bedhead knocking against the wall, as if Elliot was struggling to sit. 'What's wrong?'

'Everything. It's all a frightful mess. Lucy has...'

She couldn't find the words.

She heard his sigh. 'I'm sorry, pet, but I'm too jet-lagged to discuss her at the moment, unless she's ill or something. I'll talk to you tomorrow, or even later today.'

'She found out you're not her father and... She's lost, Elliot. She needs you. We had a frightful row before Mum's Dinner. She said – well, she was ghastly and I hit her and then–'

'Slow down, Porsh.'

'She might turn up any minute. She's with Mum but... Could you come over and then we can talk properly? Just for a few days. Long enough to make her feel loved. She's so fragile.'

'There are meetings, site visits. I can't just drop everything.'

From the end of the phone, Portia could now detect the radio, a skittish voice, a jingle. Radio Two.'

'Please, Elliot. So much has happened.... I know you're busy but I wouldn't ask if it weren't urgent.'

She heard the sound of a finger tapping on wood, and finally his voice once more. 'I need to go. We'll speak again tomorrow.'

The phone clicked.

Portia sank back into the armchair and closed her eyes. Elliot would be justified in refusing her request – he had his own life now. Michael's one concern was not to distress Vienne. Portia's one concern, her one responsibility, was to make sure Lucy was okay, as okay as she could be, given the circumstances. And spending time with Elliot would help her.

Again, Portia wondered about moving back to Switzerland. A fresh start. Especially as Lucy had implied this was what she'd like. At the moment, their life in London seemed far away.

17

On the night of the fire, Annie dreamed she was at the helm of a sailing boat, skilfully navigating a choppy sea. At the stern, a figure, securely tied in braided rope, issued orders, which she laughingly ignored. When she awoke to a scuffling noise, she thought her prisoner had escaped, but on opening her eyes, noticed something white on the floor by the door, an envelope. At first, she assumed it had drifted off the dressing table in the breeze from the window, but something prompted her to wander over.

She lifted it, read her name, scrutinised the unfamiliar script. The note inside it said: *I am inviting you to lunch today, if you are free. Johann. P.S. Look outside your door.* Outside her room lay a bunch of pink and purple geraniums. She sniffed their fragrance, then took them into the bathroom, where, as if in readiness, one of Madalena's pottery jugs sat on the cabinet. She filled the jug with water and arranged the flowers.

Johann was rolling out dough when she entered the kitchen twenty minutes later. Something with a delicious smell – soup, perhaps – bubbled away in a nearby boiler, and she realised she was ravenous.

'Thanks for the beautiful flowers.'

He bowed his head. 'Are you accepting my invitation?'

Annie nodded.

He stopped rolling, washed his hands, and lifted a spatula to flip over some slabs of meat marinating in wine. 'If you like Italian food, we can go to a restaurant in Brunnen. Twelve o'clock?'

She nodded again and rushed out of the kitchen, bumping against a crate of oranges.

Outside, she leaned against the wall. Whooped with pleasure. Then she made her way to the private dining room for breakfast, catching a glimpse of her flushed face in a wall mirror.

In the dining room, she was pleased to find herself on her own. Free to revel in delicious anticipation.

'Just cereal and toast, please,' she requested when Gaston took her order.

As Annie waited, her phone rang. 'Hang on a moment,' she said, making her way to reception, where Ruth and Alice Sowerby were discussing the fire with Hilde.

Madalena's office looked empty. Annie signalled to Hilde that she wanted to use the room and the receptionist gave her the thumbs up.

'Ferne?... Yes, I got your text, but it was Mum's Dinner and.... When?.... What happened?.... I'm so *sorry*. Are *you* alright?.... I don't know.... Well, yeah.... Okay.... I'm so sorry, lovie.'

She hung up, clasped her arms tightly around her waist, shaking her head. She remained there, in Madalena's comfy leather chair, visualising how it must have been. An unstoppable bleed.... Ferne rushed to hospital by wailing ambulance, prepared for theatre. Awaking from the anaesthetic to the sombre expressions of doctors and midwives.

She imagined Ferne in a side room, face drained of colour, eyes puffy from crying. The room's absence of equipment accentuating the atmosphere of finality. She could still feel the baby's kick against Ferne's stomach. Ferne would be tormented by infants whimpering for milk, aware of her own redundant supply; tormented by overhearing other people's celebrations: elated if drained fathers, proud grandparents and curious siblings, bubbly friends and boisterous colleagues.

Annie pictured her pushing away her breakfast tray: a standardised meal, regardless of whether or not the patient needed extra milk to aid breastfeeding, of whether or not her baby was alive. At least she'd have her own room – in former days it might have been different.

So, having lost both Stephen and the baby, Ferne wanted her back. Despite it only being ten days since they separated, Annie was fully aware of the constant shifting of her own feelings. It had started the first time she became conscious of Johann's attractiveness, and leaped backwards and forwards since then. Even if she and Ferne did resume their relationship, she would feel like a consolation prize. Always wonder if Ferne might leave her again.

Of course, she couldn't have comunicated this on the phone, not to someone so exhausted and raw with grief. Nor had it been the right moment to remind Ferne that she'd done the ditching. She would phone her tomorrow, or the next day, gently explain why they couldn't get back together again.

Wearily she rose and left Madalena's office, nodding a greeting to Alice and Ruth, the latter, she noticed, clutching her lace hanky. To her relief, the dining room was still quiet.

As she ate a slice of toast, she chided herself for not having phoned Ferne when she received her text. It almost certainly wouldn't have affected the outcome, but she would feel less negligent.

Annie cast her mind back to the early stages of their relationship. Struggling to come to terms with her father's death, she'd received much-needed comfort from Ferne who'd listened and avoided platitudes; somehow knowing when action was required, when her presence was all Annie wanted. Ferne had moved into the cottage with the ease of a gate slipping into its catch, and within weeks it seemed as if she'd always lived there. Grief had bonded them. But it wouldn't now. Perhaps because she sensed that her present pain might be less to do with losing Ferne, and more with losing the chance of motherhood.

After breakfast, she bought a card at reception – a photo of the Waldstättersee in subdued light – addressed the envelope and wrote: *Thinking of you. Love from Annie.*

'I have stamps for England,' Hilde told her, as Annie rummaged in her purse.

'Thanks, but I need exercise. I'll walk to the post office. Please tell my mother that I won't be here for lunch.'

The walk to the post office in Brunnen normally lasted ten minutes. Today it took longer as Annie's thoughts switched from Ferne's distress to what she'd wear for lunch with Johann. Sabotaging her decision-making process, though, was a niggle – an insistent, inner voice telling her she should feel guilty about embarking on a date within hours of hearing that Ferne had lost the baby. Condemning her behaviour as callous.

Counteracting this, her more compassionate and self-loving side assured her that, given the circumstances, she could justify moving on. A tug-of-war continued between the opposing views, as she entered the post office to request stamps and airmail stickers for the UK.

She visualised the pregnancy calendar in the kitchen, its last few months of dates virtually obliterated by scrawly green inked notes. In addition to GP and hospital appointments, and NCT antenatal courses, Ferne had documented symptoms, fluctuating emotions, her birth plans. Circling the calendar taped on the fridge, were sepia photos of her in profile, her naked abdomen at various stages of pregnancy. Incongruously secured by grinning Teletubby magnets.

Annie now realised she didn't even know if the baby had been a boy or girl. Perhaps it was better this way.

Initially, Johann and Annie didn't talk much. He seemed comfortable with the silence. She wasn't. It had been years since she dated, making her feel she ought to be displaying an "L" sign, as she wondered what to talk about, if Johann liked her outfit, if he might be regretting his invitation. She scanned the restaurant, absorbing its paintings of St Mark's Square and the Doge's palace, its Venetian masks and gondola oars, aware of opera playing in the background.

She remembered the evening gondola ride she and Ferne had taken, clutching each other in the eerie light and sinister shadows. And here she was, in an Italian restaurant, with a man, on a date. Sending soundless messages to her hands to stop quivering.

When the waiter brought their food, Johann was appraising her. Did he like what he saw? She liked what she saw: his pale blue shirt, the leather neckband bearing an amber stone. Today she noticed his watch. Expensive looking, but not ostentatious. She studied his hands – smallish, hairy, nails carefully trimmed.

Thankful for her own hands to have a task at last, she lifted her fork and knife.

'Do you approve of the changes Madalena has made in the hotel?' Johann asked.

'Knocking down the wall between the public sitting room and smaller room has made a huge difference. It's so much brighter. And I love the conservatory.'

'I think your mother is most at peace when she's surrounded by plants,' Johann said. 'It was the same for my mother.'

Past tense, Anne noted. Mum had mentioned something about Johann's mother? What was it?

'My mother has Pick's Disease – a form of Alzheimer's,' he said.

'I'm sorry…. Do you see her often?'

'She is in a home in Neuchatel. I visit her when I can.'

'She must appreciate you making the journey.'

He sipped his water. 'She does not recognise me now but sometimes she knows my sister. Perhaps it is because Freda looked after Mother in the beginning.'

Annie studied his passive face. Watched as he finished his glass of water, poured another one and drank again.

'How painful for you. I mean, I can't imagine my mother not knowing me.'

'I always take flowers. She responds to those. She smiles when I give them to her. Sometimes she holds them throughout my visit.'

'Is she able to appreciate the scent? I thought that was one of the first senses people lose with Alzheimer's.'

Johann nodded. 'She was a perfumier, this was why she

knew first that she was not well.... They encourage sensory activities at the nursing home.'

There was silence, then the conversation moved on to Annie's café – a typical day, the magazine interview.

'And your friend?' he asked. 'Ferne.'

'Finished,' she said. 'I'm dealing with it, but it's harder for her because...'

She stopped – it seemed inappropriate to be telling him before any of her family knew.

'I know what you are thinking,' he said. 'That it is very un-Swiss to discuss such personal things with someone you don't know well. But Madalena has talked about you so often, I feel I do know you.'

'Ferne lost the baby. I found out this morning.'

Johann's expression and tone were neutral. 'How sad for her... Do you think you will be together again?'

It was only now that Annie knew for certain that she and Ferne couldn't resume their relationship. Suddenly she felt lighter. It was important to be clear, really clear, about what she wanted. And what she wanted was to support Ferne through her bereavement and keep in touch. As friends.

It was also only now that she realised she'd have to find someone else to look after the café until she returned to Yorkshire. It could survive being closed for a few days, but any longer than that, she'd be in danger of losing regular customers.

'Things change, feelings change. Mum told me you'd been engaged,' she said.

Johann sipped his wine. 'Gerta was thrown from her horse. She broke her neck. She didn't die immediately, but I knew she was unlikely to recover.'

'Has there been anyone else since?'

He shook his head.

Annie switched her attention to her food. Such a dance, this conversation. A series of precise steps, each of them sounding out the other's personal status; acquiring the information they needed, careful to respond with detachment – Johann better at this than she.

When they'd finished their fish, Johann leant forward and took her hand. 'You know that Madalena hopes you will return to Switzerland to look after the Zurbriggen when she retires.'

'Did she actually tell you that?'

He shook his head. 'Not exactly. She wondered if you would be willing to do so. She mentioned Lawrence, also.'

Yeah, right. Herself and Lawrence....

'I couldn't work with him,' she said.

'Madalena seemed less sure about him than you,' Johann added.

She was being disloyal, Annie knew, revealing more family stuff, as if enough hadn't already been chucked into the public domain. The idea of working with Lawrence, of sharing decisions, and most importantly, of being able to trust him, was unthinkable, however. Moreover, she didn't feel up to discussing the Zurbriggen's future at the moment. She took another sip of wine. Soon its effect would kick in and she'd relax.

'Would you consider together we manage it?' Johann asked.

She blinked. 'The hotel?'

'Yes. The Zurbriggen.... When Madalena retires.'

Annie's spirits plummeted. This wasn't a date, it was a business meeting, an opportunity for Johann to ascertain her views. So, he viewed her as a possible colleague. Not a girlfriend. She sat back, inhaled shallow gulps of air. How could she have misjudged the occasion?

'Do you know where the Ladies is?' she asked.

He pointed straight ahead.

As she rose, her thigh caught the corner of the table and she winced in pain.

In the Ladies, Annie sank onto the loo seat and covered her face with her hands. How could she have mistaken this invitation? Misinterpreted the vibe? Minutes earlier, Johann had been asking her about Ferne. She'd asked him about his fiancée. Not a prelude to a business conversation. And he'd given her flowers. But even if the flower giving was simply part of Swiss culture, she couldn't explain away the kiss.

While glancing at herself in the mirror, she blushed when remembering her preparations: the time it took to decide on the deep pink lacy top and rose quartz pendant earrings; her efforts to achieve the right amount of texture in her hair; the scrupulous making up. How stupid could she get? And now she'd have to return to Johann, dredge up enthusiasm for the artichoke risotto that the waiter would shortly bring – if he hadn't already. And, more difficult, switch into potential colleague mode.

She remembered the conflicting voices as she'd made her way to the post office. Oh dear. She continued to stare into the mirror, working to convert her expression into one of gritty determination.

'Are you all right?' Johann asked when she returned to their table.

She studied his face. 'So, you think we could work together?'

As he returned her gaze, his expression changed, and she knew he had cottoned onto her misunderstanding. Then, while she wondered if she was reading him correctly, his expression changed again. Tenderness or pity?

She appraised him, trying to see past the physical – his wavy fair hair, the light blue, hazel-flecked eyes, the horn-rimmed spectacles. Trying to dumb down her response to the subtle, citrus fragrance she now associated with him, not to remember the feel of his lips, unexpectedly voluptuous from the inside. Then, as he raised his wine glass, she spotted it, a slight trembling of his hand. She sat back, now able to breathe more deeply as she realised he also was nervous.

Johann nodded. 'I can cook and I am practical. You have experience of managing a business. Madalena says you are good with people and that you work hard.'

Annie looked around the restaurant again, at its wood-panelled walls and bracket lamps. Pavarotti's heartache had been replaced by jazz. Dixieland jazz. The kind she'd normally be itching to dance to. Outside, the darkening sky made the interior even cosier, but the ambience and music meant little now that she knew Johann's interest in her was professional. And yet, there'd been the kiss.

'Well, yeah, but... I mean, the hotel's much bigger than it was when my parents took it on.'

Johann dabbed his mouth with the napkin. 'But with modern technology.... There is also Hilde. She wishes to have more responsibility. She has business knowledge and also experience with people. Perhaps the three of us can work together.'

Annie hesitated. Did he have a personal interest in Hilde? Could she work with him if he and Hilde became an item?

She fingered the candles, digging into the molten wax. 'Have you discussed this with her?'

'I wanted to speak with you first. Also, Hilde will be married soon and she is preoccupied.'

'Oh,' Annie said, trying to conceal her relief. 'I didn't know.'

'No one else at the hotel knows. It is not the Swiss way to talk about our personal lives at work. Hilde will inform Madalena once the family visit is over.'

'I need to think about this, Johann. I did wonder about it when Mum announced she wanted to retire. I mean, it would be fun to live here again, but the thing is, it's a huge commitment. And I've loved managing the café.'

'We could make it work,' he said warmly. 'But I am interested to know your opinion. Do you have the same belief that I do?'

What confidence he had. In her. In himself. Could he be thinking of more than a working relationship? It all seemed to rest on the kiss: how much, if anything, this had meant to him. She stared out at the rain.

'The other night, in the kitchen–' she started.

The waiter brought their main course, and by the time they'd been offered parmesan cheese and black pepper, asked if they'd like another bottle of wine or more mineral water, Annie's courage to ask her question had deserted her. It occurred to her that this was the price she paid for moving on too quickly. As if someone – friend or foe – decreed she slow down.

She added vinaigrette to the salad, looked at Johann and moved her mouth into a smile.

18

Madalena was pondering the Zurbriggen's future, as she placed her yoga mat on the balcony, extended her legs and bent her head. Since the trauma of the fire two days ago, none of her children had mentioned taking over the management. Perhaps it was unrealistic to expect any of them to uproot themselves. More likely, that they hadn't yet had enough time to consider such an upheaval.

The sound of knocking on her apartment door broke into her thoughts. She glanced at her watch: nine thirty. Reluctantly, she left the balcony and went to answer.

'Lawrence!'

'I need to talk to you. Could we go to Bauen?'

She stood aside to let him into her apartment. 'Have you had breakfast?'

'I had something at the Hotel Bergmann. I can come back later, if you'd rather.... I'm sorry if I disturbed you.'

'We can talk now, if it's here. I have to go into Luzern later.'

He was staring at her and she suddenly felt uncomfortable.

'You look beautiful,' he said. 'The green of your kimono.... I'm not interrupting anything, am I?'

Madalena laughed. 'Karl isn't here. You can check if you like.'

Lawrence lingered, hands resting on the top of the sofa. He looked rough.

'I'll make coffee,' she said.

He followed her into the kitchenette. 'How are you? After the fire, I mean. I'm sorry – I should have come round yesterday.'

'I think we all needed space after what happened,' she said. 'I'm all right. Nevertheless, it was a shock. Portia and Lucy have had a long talk. Hopefully, Lucy is in a better place now.'

Madalena brought the coffee through to the sitting room, bracing herself for Lawrence to announce he was leaving Switzerland early. That he'd been put off by all this family stuff.

She sat down on the sofa. 'You know, when you left me in Bauen, the day you talked about school, I wished we'd had longer together. What you told me was so awful, it was hard to stop thinking about it and–'

'I didn't mean to dump it on you,' he said. 'Consider it a moment of weakness and forget about it.'

'You weren't weak.'

'At my age...'

'Lawrence, don't you think we all retain an element of the child in us? A fragile part that remembers hurtful things years later.' It was so easy to project one's own vulnerabilities onto others. 'Matron sounded kind. At least she was there for you. These schools you know, I read books about them, after you had all finished–'

'Mrs Dobson left,' Lawrence said. 'At the beginning of my second year I went to see her. There was no answer from her door. I kept knocking...'

'Sit down, dear,' Madalena said.

He chose a chair by the window. 'Finally, I opened the door, the room was empty. No sheets on the windowsill, waiting to be darned. No bags of socks. I realised she was gone and I was on my own.... Years later, I heard one of the masters tell another that Mrs Dobson had been too motherly with us.'

Madalena waited, an all too familiar feeling of wretchedness flaring. A memory was materialising: stitching name tags on Lawrence's socks, ensuring her stitches were neat, as if it made any real difference.

She stared at her son's dead expression. 'Oh Lawrence, I am so sorry, sorry we sent you – all of you – away. If we had known...' The words sounded trite. Trite and overused. Sometimes language was inadequate.

Lawrence walked over to a chest of drawers, lifted a crimson and green Cloisonné vase and examined it. He ran his finger round its neck, peered inside it, and replaced it.

'What would you have done?'

She sighed. 'Worked something out. Re-jigged things, somehow.... But now, how are things now? Are you happy in Skye?'

He considered. 'I was. I'm not sure if I'm the sort who can live in one place for too long.'

'And Rebecca?'

'We talked about this before, Mum. In Bauen. History...' He raised his arm to discourage questions.

So, footloose again. Was he destined to remain single,

and did it bother him? *We want to make soldiers of them.* Such
a dreadful aim for young children away from home.

'Mum?'

Madalena surveyed him. 'Do you remember my speech,
before the fire? Since I decided to retire, I've been
wondering who might take over the hotel. It would mean a
lot if it was one of my children. Portia isn't the least bit practical and—'

Lawrence shot her a quizzical look. 'You're not considering me, surely?'

Was she letting emotion interfere with business sense?

'Have you considered it?'

He laughed. 'You're joking! Managing things, being
polite to people.... It would kill me. I'd find it easier over-
seeing a space mission.'

Finally, he was sitting again, his expression now bewildered, with a glimmer of a smile. At least this conveyed
some energy.

'Not on your own, dear. Perhaps with Annie? You
worked together at her café. If you are looking for something new, if you haven't any ties with Skye...'

'She obviously hasn't told you what happened, how it all
ended.'

'Obviously not,' Madalena said. 'What did happen,
Lawrence?'

'That's a story for another time.'

'Well, do think about my suggestion. I have yet to
mention it to Annie, but I will soon. I'm just giving her
time... with Ferne losing the baby.'

He looked away. 'It was Ferne who was pregnant?'

'I thought you knew.'

He shook his head. Madalena added more milk to her
coffee, sipped it and waited.

Lawrence inhaled deeply. 'I'm flattered you'd trust me to run your hotel, but there's something you should know.'

'You're leaving early.'

She would remain calm if he was. After all, he *had* made the effort to come over. Even if he'd stayed in another hotel.

'I have to tell you something which might... might change your mind... about everything.'

Madalena straightened. 'What *are* you talking about?'

'It's about... Dad.'

'Lawrence?'

As he stood again, turned away from her, she was filled with dread. Now that she had found closure with David, she couldn't bear to hear anything that threatened this. At the same time, if Lawrence needed to talk to her, she couldn't let him down by refusing to listen. Not when she hadn't always been there for him during his school years.

'Do you remember I came over to see you before moving to Skye?' Lawrence said. 'It wasn't just a holiday. It was to ask Dad for a loan. For a mortgage for the cottage.'

'I didn't know.'

'Well, he refused; he told me it would be better for me to be independent.'

'Your father avoided asking for help if at all possible,' Madalena said.

Lawrence paced the room, twisting his hands. 'I was angry. I'd been so sure he'd agree, I'd counted on it.... Then I found a bank card for an account he'd told me he hardly ever used... and I found his PIN number. I withdrew money every day for ten days. Ten thousand francs. You see, I only regarded it as a loan. When I was back in the UK again, during the move, the packing, everything, I was able to justify what I'd done. Convince myself I was... entitled to help from my father. I would repay him with interest, then he'd benefit too.'

Lawrence stopped pacing and looked at her. She sat there, hands clasped in her lap, hoping her expression was neutral.

'A month later, Dad wrote to me. He told me he'd seen his bank statement – I'd forgotten about these. He'd contacted the bank in Luzern and they'd identified me on their CCTV recordings.... When they showed him the tapes, he told them I was his nephew, and that he didn't want to take the matter any further. He'd been too upset to phone me, and he didn't want you to know.'

Madalena reached out her arm. Lawrence ignored it.

'Then you phoned to say he'd had a climbing accident. He was dead. And I knew deep down it was my fault. I'd put him under too much stress.'

She went to the bookcase, lifted a photo of David, which she'd taken secretly, catching him in reflective mood. She studied the photo, then faced Lawrence. 'When we bought the Zurbriggen, your father – extremely reluctantly – accepted a loan from your grandfather and he couldn't pay it back quickly enough.'

She replaced the photo. 'I remember the day the final payment was made – he looked different, at peace. At last we were independent. It meant so much. He would never have wanted you to go through the same thing.'

Stepping onto the balcony, Madalena studied her surroundings. This morning the lake was slate grey, the cloud low lying. Mercifully, the digger had yet to begin. Her hand – resting on her chest – registered her quickened heartbeat. She took several deep breaths and returned to the sitting room.

'Your father had a family history of heart disease. The

heart attack could have happened at any time, regardless of how fit he was, how stress-free a life he led. His fall was caused by heart failure, not stress.'

'Even so...' Lawrence began.

She sat down beside him, took his arm. 'You were not responsible for his death. You *must* believe that.'

Lawrence's face relaxed. 'Yeah, well, I should have told you before.'

'Let it go, dear. Move on.'

He went over to the bookcase and stared at the picture of his father. 'It's a lovely photo,' he said, his back turned. He swivelled round. 'Could we go for a walk now, you and me? It feels wrong, somehow, breaking off at this point.'

'I have an appointment in Zurich.' She glanced at her watch. 'We will talk again soon. Tomorrow, perhaps? I thought you were going to say you were leaving early. I'm so glad you're not.'

'Even after what I've told you?'

She nodded. 'I must get ready.'

After he left, Madalena sank onto the sofa, her mind engulfed with memories: the hospital phone call informing her of David's admission; Johann driving her to Luzern, waiting in the relatives' room, while she sat with David, hoping he might recognise her. The nurses checking his beeping machines. The doctor who eventually laid his arm on hers, saying, 'Your husband is slipping away.'

David's last few breaths, taken with no indication he was aware of her presence.

Doctor Fischer's hair was shorter, making him look older. On the coffee table next to him, a vase of roses nestled between his diary and notebook. Since the previous week, his shelves had been taken to task: no doubling up of books, no journal bundles on the floor. The room smelled of flowers and cinnamon.

Today Madalena was aware of the effort taken over her surroundings: its comfortable armchairs; the gentle light from bracket lamps although it was only three o'clock; the calming prints of sunlit forests and rolling hills.

Today she was also aware of valuing Doctor Fischer more. Karl had been supportive when she took refuge at his house after the disastrous evening, but there were some things she couldn't share with him.

'I appreciate you seeing me at short notice,' she said. 'I know I wanted to put this "on hold" while my family was here, but too much has happened.'

'Where would you like to start?'

Where indeed? It had been less than three hours since Lawrence's revelation and she could still feel the sudden lurch her stomach had taken when he admitted what he'd done.

Doctor Fischer smiled at her. 'We don't have to cover everything today. Life can be overwhelming.'

This was the word. She was overwhelmed.

'Shall I tell you everything that has happened since I last saw you. Is that all right?'

He smiled again. A smile conveying empathy and competence. 'It doesn't have to be a report,' he said. His tone wasn't a rebuke.

'I am interested in knowing your feelings,' he continued. 'When things are difficult, we sometimes distance ourselves by focusing on the facts. It's how we react to a situation that is relevant.'

Madalena relayed the week's events: her shock over

Lucy's fire and subsequent anxiety about her hotelier's reputation; her longer-term concern about her granddaughter. Her desire to discuss the situation with Portia without damaging their relationship. She talked about Vienne drinking too much at the Dinner, and her worry over the state of her daughter's marriage. She threw in her concern that, because of her family, Karl might reconsider marrying her. Lastly, she mentioned Lawrence's revelation.

'What is troubling you most at the moment?'

'Lawrence. What he told me today. I was shocked – I *am* shocked, but my instinct was to protect him from any more suffering. This meant lying.'

She raised her hand and fingered the throbbing area above her right ear.

Doctor Fischer was leaning forward now, his head tilted to one side. His expression was gentle. Gentleness in men was so beguiling, whatever their age.

'I lied about David having a family history of heart disease. If I had been prepared for what Lawrence told me, I might have responded differently. David concealed what Lawrence did to protect me. I wanted to protect Lawrence. David did go through an anxious period.'

'Can you describe your husband's anxiety?'

She considered. She had not discussed this with anyone. Nevertheless, there was no point in being here if she was unwilling to divulge her real concerns.

'Once or twice, I found him lying on the sofa in our sitting room in the middle of the day. This was so out of character. He told me he was tired. I let myself believe him. I never suggested he see his doctor, although I thought he should. He also made several trips into Luzern at the time and he was evasive about the reason. At one point I worried he might be.... Again, I refrained from asking too many questions.'

'What were you worried about?'

'It is impossible to be completely secure in one's relationship. Perhaps David's heart attack *was* caused by the stress of what Lawrence did. Perhaps his death was premature. However, I will never know, and I have forgiven Lawrence.'

Doctor Fischer spoke slowly. 'You only learned about this today. Perhaps it is early to forgive such behaviour.'

'He has carried this burden around for years now. Bearing a grudge will not bring my husband back.'

The therapist asked more questions about Lawrence, enabling her to realise that she did, in fact, have mixed feelings about her son, that it was less straightforward than immediate forgiveness. It was important to be aware of her ambivalence, Doctor Fischer told her. Denying one's deepest feelings never worked. They had a habit of manifesting themselves in various ways, at unexpected times.

'I am worried I might have a delayed reaction to all this,' Madalena admitted.

'As you did when your husband died.'

'I don't want to end up in hospital again. Especially while my children are here. They think I'm strong.'

'This is a great pressure for you, always to be considered strong,' he said.

Madalena shrugged. 'I have been like this for so long.... Goodness, I'd no idea of the time.'

'Perhaps we could start our next session by exploring why you need to be considered strong,' Doctor Fischer suggested.

Madalena nodded, conscious that the pain above her ear had gone.

'How are you feeling?'

'Calmer,' she said, standing. 'Thank you.'

As she left the hospital, she felt lighter, despite her fatigue, despite the muggy weather. She was now looking forward to her evening with Portia and Lucy.

About to cross the road, her heart sank when she saw a familiar figure on the other side. It was Portia. She waited for the lights to change to green and made her way over.

Portia rushed up to her. 'Mum? What were you doing at the hospital?'

'I thought you and Lucy weren't coming into Luzern until this evening.'

'She wanted some music. What's going on? Are you ill?'

Madalena hesitated. 'I was seeing Karl.'

'During working hours?'

'Where's Lucy?'

Portia pointed to the Musik Hug. 'I can't stand the sound of grunge, and it's too crowded. I need a drink.'

Lucy emerged from the shop, sauntered towards them. She looked more like her normal self; hgone was the cowering, unhappy child after the fire.

'I don't know why you can't download songs from YouTube,' Portia told her.

Lucy tutted. 'Because it's illegal. Hi Granny. Where have you sprung from?'

'Lucy! That's no way to talk to Granny.'

Madalena laughed. With any luck, Lucy's presence would distract Portia from further interrogation.

'I suppose you're thinking of iTunes, and you have to pay for those,' Lucy said to Portia. 'You are so out of touch. I suppose in your day they didn't have all this stuff. Just dreary old gramophone records.'

'Steady on, I'm not *that* old.'

'Why don't you get a drink, and I'll stay with Lucy,' Madalena offered.

Portia thought for a moment. 'If you can stand it. Three CDs, this is your limit, Lucy.'

'Come on,' Lucy said, grabbing Madalena's hand.

Madalena hung around the store, as customers came and went, listening to music in booths, calling friends over to show them what they'd found. Lucy wandered aimlessly from aisle to aisle. At least the air conditioning was on.

Now the constant thudding beat seemed unbearable. She looked around for Lucy, spotting her in a booth, head-phones on. She approached her, causing her to jump.

'Haven't you decided yet, darling?'

'There's two more things I need to listen to.'

To Madalena's relief, Portia had returned.

The earlier mugginess had lessened as Madalena, Portia and Lucy were shown to a table in the Indian restaurant. At six-thirty, it was early to be eating, but already several tables were occupied, and there was a pleasing atmosphere of busyness.

'I can't remember when the three of us last ate together,' Portia said as she studied the menu. 'I think I'll have the lamb jalfrezi with pilau rice. Mum, do you know what you want? Lucy?'

Lucy scowled and replaced the menu. 'I don't like Indian food.'

'Nonsense,' Portia said. 'You've always managed to eat your way through our takeaways at home. What about a chicken dish? Chicken korma or Kashmiri chicken? Lots of fruit. Not too spicy.'

'I want to go back to Brunnen. I didn't want to have dinner in Luzern.'

Portia looked puzzled. 'You were fine about it last night, when we went to the Chinese restaurant.'

Lucy scrunched up her face. 'That was different.'

As Madalena stared at her granddaughter, she found herself tensing. Lucy's demeanour reminded her of how she had been on the evening of the fire. Despite the heat of the restaurant, Madalena shivered.

'I don't like your tone, Lucy,' Portia said.

'I don't like your tone,' Lucy mimicked.

'Dear God, what's got into you? I won't let you talk to me in such a way, I really won't.'

'Yes, Mother.'

Portia and Madalena stared at each other.

'Leave it,' Madalena mouthed.

'I saw what you mouthed to Mummy,' Lucy said.

During the silence, Madalena let her eye slide around the room. She wanted to enjoy the escapist aspect of her surroundings, to imagine herself in the vibrancy and intensity of India. The restaurant was filling, next to them a table of men drinking beer, joking, their high spirits infectious. She, too, wanted to feel jolly.

The waiter took their order, Portia deciding for Lucy.

'When does Elliot return from Boston?' Madalena asked.

'He's back,' Portia said.

Madalena sipped her wine. 'Have you plans to do anything, the three of you?'

'Well, have we, Mum?' Lucy asked.

'Lucy, your tone is totally unacceptable. You will show me some respect.'

'Make me,' Lucy said, nostrils flaring. She rose from the table and strode out of the restaurant.

Portia stood, too, but as she made to leave the table, Madalena grabbed her hand. 'Give her space.'

Portia sat down heavily. 'I won't have her behaving like this.'

In the corner of her eye, Madalena saw a waiter approach them then retreat. As the men at the next table plonked a tip in the ashtray and left, a young couple took their place, joined minutes later by another couple. The women were dressed in black, their lips tastefully painted, diamond engagement rings flashing in the lights above the table.

They looked so happy, so carefree. One of the men was waving a knife from side to side as if conducting an orchestra. The women laughed.

Madalena now realised Portia was talking to her.

'What did you say?'

Portia sighed. 'You really think counselling might help Lucy? Personally, I've never really believed in all that therapy stuff. Perhaps I'm wrong, though.... I should go and find her.'

'Give her a few more minutes.'

'Mum, I know you're trying to help, of course. But who knows what she'll do, in this mood?'

'She is probably hanging around outside the restaurant. She'll be back soon, saying she's starving.'

'But she might wander off. I know it's Switzerland, but she isn't a local and she's only thirteen. And in her current frame of mind she's both vulnerable and a liability.'

'I am sure she'll be back soon.'

The scent of coriander and cloves, of garlic and cumin, was even stronger, as if someone had left the swinging doors of the kitchen open. Madalena became aware of how hungry she was.

Portia stood again. 'I need to find her.'

Madalena sniffed. 'As you wish, dear.'

'Sorry.'

She sighed as she observed Portia speaking briefly to the waiter. She was probably right to go after Lucy – she could get lost in the labyrinth of narrow, cobbled streets.

The waiter approached their table and looked enquiringly at her.

'My daughter and granddaughter will be back soon,' she told him.

She glanced over to the entrance of the restaurant, where Portia stood, as if wondering in which direction to go.

Then she heard the screech of car tyres, a scream.

19

Something was hindering Portia from moving and she twisted her head round to find the culprit. Nothing. No restraining arm, no leash attaching her to the lamppost. Only a light rain. Amidst exclamations and agitated comments, a thick German voice issued instructions to call an ambulance.

This was it. Retribution. Her affair with Michael punished by the death of her beloved daughter. Images flashed before her: Elliot, crushed when he'd learned of her betrayal; Lucy, bewildered and lost; and Vienne – if she discovered the truth – distraught. *Revenge, a dish best served cold*. Fourteen years later was certainly cold enough. She wondered why she wasn't crying. Why she was standing here, accepting her fate.

As three men lifted Lucy from the car, a protest lodged in Portia's mind – you didn't move a patient with a head injury. Or a spinal one. People were moving Lucy, however, without knowing the state of her head or her back. But she couldn't be left on a car bonnet. Now they were laying her on a bench outside a florist's, and she could see a trickle of blood from Lucy's waist.

Already a crowd had gathered, watching as a woman listened to Lucy's heart, nodded, examined her neck and nodded again. The nodding was a positive sign. It meant Lucy was alive. On television, if the person was dead, people shook their heads and covered the victim's face with a jacket.

Portia stared at all those strangers. Helpful strangers. Someone put a coat over Lucy, but only her body. Not her beautiful face, with its indigo eyes and soft, childlike skin, yet to succumb to teenage woes. Another unknown cradled Lucy's head. The woman explained something, pulled back the coat and applied a scarf to the wound by Lucy's waist. Dear God.... All those strange people ministering to her daughter, while she remained standing here.

'What happened?'

Someone was holding her arm, saying her name. It was Mum, her wedding ring pressing into Portia's arm.

'Portia, what happened?' Madalena asked again.

'She just ran out.'

Around her, pedestrians opened umbrellas, an ambulance siren blared. Nearby, an elderly dark-skinned woman peddled roses. A thud of music blasted from a passing car, a roar erupted from the football stadium. While Lucy lay there motionless, people shopped and queued for the cinema. Portia tried again to move towards her daughter, but her feet wouldn't cooperate.

Maybe it was best to stay away. She'd damaged Lucy enough already.

As the ambulance arrived, people stood back to make room. Two uniformed men hopped out, requested more space, and onlookers dispersed to resume their Friday evening. One paramedic checked Lucy's heart and spoke to the woman who seemed to know something about Lucy's condition. The other produced a packet with a bottle attached to a tube. They examined Lucy's arm, installed a needle and attached a drip. They fitted a support round her neck and slipped an oxygen mask over her face. All this was encouraging.

The older ambulance man brought a stretcher and they lifted Lucy onto it. They covered her with a blanket that looked thick and comforting, and nodded thanks to the woman whom Portia had decided must be a doctor. They attached two straps round Lucy's unresisting body and carried the stretcher to the ambulance where they secured it with more straps.

Portia now felt the rain soaking her forehead, her blouse.

A police car arrived, followed by a fire engine, and shortly after, she became conscious of a nearby argument concerning the car Lucy had collided with, and the one which slammed into it when it screeched to a halt. A policeman was interviewing someone, making notes. Witnesses chipping in. The argument escalated and there was a mess of smashed headlights and bumpers to be dealt with. These were only cars.

Meanwhile, she felt nauseous from the smell of curry wafting from the Indian restaurant, where they were meant to have had a lovely evening and Madalena was to have seen Lucy's good side. Mum returned from talking to a paramedic.

'They are taking Lucy to the Kinderspital. We'll go by taxi.... Portia, do you understand?'

'Can't we go in the ambulance?'

'No, dear. A taxi will get us there quickly, please try not

to worry.'

'Not worry?' Portia repeated, and laughed.

Madalena hailed a taxi and guided Portia into it.

The taxi reeked of air freshener and she retched. She could hear the ambulance siren ahead. Someone was holding her hand – Madalena, her grip firm, but not strong enough to stop the trembling.

Portia halted as she reached the waiting area of the accident and emergency department. A few parents were reading to children, holding infants. One little girl had a homemade bandage on her hand, another an ugly looking bruise on her forehead. The atmosphere was quiet, however, no one howling in pain, no child even looking particularly unwell.

In one corner, several ambulance men huddled together, sipping coffee, then, at the sound of their walkie-talkies, they dumped the plastic cups and rushed out of the building. Madalena and Annie were seated by the window. Both had their hands clasped in their laps, as if attending church.

Portia stepped closer into the room, at which point Annie noticed her, rushed over and flung her arms round her. 'How's Lucy?'

Portia took Annie's outstretched hand, allowed herself to be led to where Madalena remained seated, and slumped onto a chair, her face crumpling before she straightened and composed herself. Lucy was still alive. Lucy would be okay. If she thought about it clearly enough and for long enough, she would believe this. She shoved some strands of hair behind her ears.

'She's broken her right arm and two ribs are cracked and she's lost a lot of blood from a ruptured spleen. She needs a transfusion but I can't give blood because I visited Madagascar recently. And it's complicated because her blood group is AB negative which is very uncommon, in fact. Normally they'd have stocks of it but there was a bad accident last week and–'

'Have you contacted Elliot?' Madalena asked.

Portia hesitated. 'They can give her some O type group, to start with.'

'I've no idea what blood group I am,' Annie said. 'Mum, do you know?'

Portia hugged Madalena. 'I need to get back. I wanted to let you know....'

Annie stood. 'Shall I come, too?'

'I'm the only one allowed there at the moment.'

'Is she conscious?' Annie asked.

Portia nodded. 'But drowsy from the morphine. I must go.'

The doctor assessing Lucy's injuries decided against strapping her cracked ribs in case she required a splenectomy. As he explained this to Portia, a commotion could be heard, followed by a Tannoy announcement.

'I have to go – there's an emergency,' he said. 'I'll send someone to put a splint on your daughter's arm.'

Portia could hear a child screaming, people crying, the scuffle of feet and squeaking trolley wheels. Someone calling out instructions. Something metal crashing to the ground. She shivered, clutching Lucy's hand. All those Saturday evenings of watching *Casualty* with Lucy.

The pandemonium died down or moved away. In the next cubicle, however, an infant was uttering bark-like coughs, a mother half crying, half talking in rapid Italian, a calmer voice responding, also in Italian. Then all went quiet and Portia froze.

A nurse rushed in, apologised for keeping them waiting. 'What's happened?' Portia asked.

The nurse lowered her voice. 'A stabbing.'

'Oh God!' Portia clutched Lucy's hand more tightly. 'And next door – it's gone silent. Do you know what's going on?'

'I can't discuss other patients,' the nurse said.

Portia flinched. 'Of course not, sorry. Such a horrid cough and then... nothing. I hope the baby's okay.'

The nurse glanced at the cubicle curtains. Portia assessed her age. Twenty-four? Twenty-six?

The nurse applied a splint to Lucy's broken arm. Lucy seemed to be only semi-conscious. It must be the morphine.

'Will she need to have her spleen removed?' Portia asked.

'The doctors will let you know when they've decided.'

When the nurse had finished, Portia returned to the reception area and updated Madalena and Annie, answering their questions.

'You look exhausted, you should get back to Brunnen,' she urged. 'I'll walk you to the car park. I could do with some fresh air.'

'Are you sure you'll be okay?' Annie asked, when they reached the car.

Portia nodded. 'You drive.'

Portia hugged her mother and Annie, lingering until the car was out of sight, before returning to the waiting area. She should stay here, then she wouldn't be tempted to prod Lucy regularly to check she was okay.

Only now did she become aware of her surroundings: the green vinyl-covered chairs and grainy prints of alpine flowers; the water fountain and cone-shaped plastic cups; the cracked bottom pane in one of the high windows. A flatscreen television broadcast a documentary about the nuclear disaster in Fukushima. Overhead, the whirling ceiling fan made little impact.

Two men were now standing by the water fountain. One of them was filling cups with water, the other seemed out of it.

His right trouser leg was torn at the knee and he reeked of alcohol. What were they doing in a children's hospital? A middle-aged woman was knitting socks with garish yellow wool.

Portia had never knitted for Elliot. Had he minded? Would she have been a better wife if she'd presented him every year with a chunky fisherman's jumper, laboured over while they watched *Newsnight* or *Question Time*? If she'd ironed his shirts and made jolly puddings?

The click of the needles irritated her more than the quivering light. If she shut her eyes, she could escape the flicker. Not so the needles. Vienne would have found music in the clicking needles, a rhythm to their movement. Vienne....

Portia stood now as the doctor returned.

'I am sorry I was called away. Frau Fontana, it is necessary to remove your daughter's spleen if you are in agreement. She must also have a blood transfusion. We are giving her O type blood now, then we'd like to test her father's blood–'

'She will be alright, Doctor....?'

'Doctor Meissner. Yes, it is possible to live a normal life without a spleen. We will discuss the implications with you after the operation.'

'You're going to operate now? Can I see Lucy first?'

'Of course. Please follow me.'

Lucy lay quietly in the treatment cubicle, eyes closed. On one side, a plastic bag of blood now dripped into her wrist. On the other, a clear bag of fluid.

Portia pointed to the transparent bag. 'What's in there?'

'Saline,' Doctor Meissner said. 'To prevent dehydration.'

Lucy opened her eyes. 'Mummy?'

'It's all right, darling, you're going to be fine.' How often had she heard this said on TV dramas? Derided the writers for hackneyed comments. Such lack of imagination. But they weren't empty words: Doctor Meissner had assured her Lucy would be okay.

'You were hit by a car, do you remember?'

Lucy nodded. 'I'm sorry, Mummy.'

Portia bent to kiss her daughter's damp forehead, smoothed back her wispy dark hair, which she'd exhorted her to dye blonde. 'It's all right, sweetheart. You're going to be okay, and this is all that matters. I love you *so* much.'

'Love you, Mummy,' Lucy said drowsily.

A woman – nurse? doctor? Portia couldn't read the name badge without her specs – handed her some papers, requested she read them, and indicated where she should sign her consent to the operation. She skimmed the document and signed her name. Panic was bubbling. It was the darkness outside disorientating her, distorting her perception of time, exaggerating Lucy's vulnerability.

Two gowned theatre attendants were checking the name on Lucy's wristband.

'How long will she be in surgery?' Portia asked.

'It depends,' one of them said. 'An hour perhaps. If everything goes to plan.'

'Goes to plan? Could... could there be problems?'

The other attendant took her arm. 'Your daughter will be fine. It's a straightforward operation.'

After watching them wheel Lucy away, Portia returned to the waiting area, presently empty. She clasped her hands together and bit her thumbs, wishing now she hadn't persuaded Annie to return to Brunnen with Madalena.

Someone had switched off the fan and the room smelled of alcohol. From above, she could hear a floor polisher. She opened her bag, located the Kalms and swallowed a couple of tablets.

Moments later, a nurse came into the room. 'Frau Fontana?'

Portia jumped up. 'Has something happened to Lucy?'

'No, please relax. I thought you would prefer to wait in the ward where your daughter will be, after her surgery.'

Portia sighed. 'Thanks. I'm just a bit... Thanks.'

The nurse escorted her along a shiny corridor, up a flight of stairs and along another shiny corridor to the ward and showed her the day room.

'The chairs are more comfortable in here. I'll bring you a blanket.'

At two o'clock, Portia awoke from a troubled sleep, pushing aside the blanket. She glanced at her watch, wondering if Lucy was out of theatre yet. Doctor Meissner had promised he would let her know. Perhaps there *had* been complications – Lucy's heart stopping, finding something horrid inside her body. She took two more *Kalms* and closed her eyes.

When she awoke again, dawn was breaking. As a wailing ambulance stopped outside the hospital, she visualised paramedics transferring the patient onto a trolley, wheeling it in. Like they would have done with Lucy. She stretched and went out into the empty corridor, glanced out of the window at a chugging helicopter circling the building.

Then she heard the pad of feet. It was Doctor Meissner, in theatre scrubs.

'I am sorry – I was called to an emergency,' he said. 'Your daughter's surgery was successful. There were no complications.'

'Thank God. Thank you so much.' She noticed the shadows beneath his eyes, the unshaved face. How long had he been working for? Twelve hours, eighteen?

'We would like to have some of her own blood type to transfuse. I understand her father is not in Switzerland. Can you contact him to see if he is a match?'

Portia nodded.

'I'll take you to her.'

Lucy lay sleeping in a side room. There was no dressing over her wound, but she was still attached to the two drips. A heart monitor showed zigzag patterns, beeped intermittently. In the corner was an oxygen cylinder. Standard procedure, she assumed. She stared at Lucy, at the tube going into her nose.

'Why has she got one of these?'

'The nasogastric tube will prevent the build-up of stomach acid and minimise nausea and vomiting. It will be removed after one or two days,' Doctor Meissner said. 'Lucy is doing well. In several weeks' time you will be scolding her for being rude or being on her computer too much.'

Portia smiled. 'Can I sit with her?'

As Doctor Meissner left, a nurse entered the room. She took Lucy's temperature and blood pressure and wrote on the chart at the end of the bed. She smiled at Portia. 'She's doing really well.'

On her own again with Lucy, Portia wrestled the urge to wake her, to check for herself she was all right, but she looked too peaceful. Her colour was better now, more pink and natural. Letting her sleep was the right thing to do, of course. She bent to kiss her cheek, sat down beside her bed and stroked her hand.

20

D espite a poor night's sleep, her thoughts focused on Lucy, Annie rose early the following morning, looked out of the window and sighed with relief when she saw the blue sky. If she was going to do this, it should be today. First, though, she must phone Portia. As she was about to do so, a text arrived from her sister: Lucy was fine, the operation had gone well. Annie replied: *Phew, so relieved. Speak soon. Hugs*.

Heartened by the good news, she dressed quickly, made a sandwich from the breakfast items in the private dining room, left a note for Madalena in her office, and was on the road by eight.

As she climbed the path to Morschach, she could hear the contents of her backpack rattling about. She put her hand round, felt the package – its smoothness palpable even through the canvas – and reassured herself it was intact.

When she reached the village, she found a grassy spot and ate her sandwich, even though it was barely eleven o'clock. Then she retrieved the trowel from her backpack, knelt down and dug a hole. The grass and earth smelled sweet and innocent after recent rain. She placed the small box in the hole and began covering it with earth. Then she stopped, reached in and removed the box. Opening it, she gazed again at the tiny lemon coloured bootees, the velour black and white striped zebra, and the card, on which she'd written: *Sorry you didn't make it. I would have loved you.*

As Annie closed the box and resealed it, a tear slid down her face. Then more. She reburied the box, covered the hole with earth, replaced the tufts of grass and stamped on them. Then she found some stones and made a cairn.

For a while she sat on the grass, wondering what had happened to Ferne when she came round from the anaesthetic. If she'd held the baby, spent any time with it. Ferne had once mentioned a friend who'd given birth to a stillborn baby and had bathed and dressed him, sung to him, before finally saying goodbye. On hearing this, Annie had been unconvinced this could bring any comfort. Now she realised it was about enabling closure, in the way people needed to have a body to bury, in order to believe in the person's death and be able to grieve.

She stood, aware of feeling lighter, and resolved to move on. When she returned to Yorkshire, she might suggest she and Ferne drive into the Danby moors to make a shrine.

After photographing the cairn, she repacked her backpack and retraced her steps. Minutes later, she noticed she wasn't alone. About a hundred yards away, a familiar figure leant against a boulder, clutching a metal flask. Perhaps he might not notice her. She continued walking until she stumbled on a piece of loose rock. When she looked round, the figure spotted her, waved. She sighed and limped over to him.

'Have a drink,' Lawrence said, proffering the flask. His breath stank of whisky.

She shook her head. Lawrence raised the flask to his lips.

She grabbed it from him. 'You've had enough. Have you eaten today?'

'Just this,' he said, brandishing his flask. 'The good...the food of life. The good food of life. The good *mood* food of life.'

She helped him stand upright. 'You can get something in the village. Come on.'

'The last time I was here was with Dad,' Lawrence said, clutching her arm. 'I miss him, Annie, I really miss him.'

'I miss him too.'

She'd have to stay with her brother while he ate. Or did she? She glanced at her watch. Perhaps if she got him settled with a meal, she could leave him.

In Morschach, Annie found a café, guided Lawrence into a chair at a corner table and ordered veal escalope and rösti potatoes. While they waited for their food, she confiscated his flask and insisted he drank a large glass of water.

'Do you ever feel bored with life?' he asked. Before she could answer, he continued. 'I'm fed up with Skye. Although I like the climbing. I'd like to live in France. Had a great weekend in Paris last autumn. The ambience there, boy.... 'Specially Montparnasse. And the women, *les femmes*.... Yeah. Went to all these literary cafés. Planned to write but too many distractions. Jeez. The way they dress, these biker jackets and their short skirts and ankle boots. They're an invitation–'

'Lawrence! I'm not one of your drinking buddies.'

'They all smoke, of course, Gauloise – so sexy.... Yeah, could visualise myself there, in a studio overlooking the Seine. Clichéd, I know, but, hey ho.... Done the sums.

Enough for a year, more if I rent out the cottage. Even with no income. But I'd find something in journalism. Got ideas.'

'I hope your veal comes soon,' Annie said.

'What's the hurry?'

'Mum and I are visiting Lucy.'

'I could come too,' he suggested.

She stared at him. 'That would go down well.'

The waitress brought his food.

Lawrence inspected his plate. 'I'll never eat all this – didn't you order anything?'

The combination of tiredness and the smell of alcohol from his breath made her queasy, so she took a dollop of potatoes. He shoved a chunk of veal into his mouth and chewed, took another forkful. She helped herself to more potatoes, dunking them in the sauce. The nausea receded.

'I could write a weekly column for a British newspaper, a 21st century Alistair Cooke, but more interesting: *Une lettre de Paris*. Has a distinctive ring to it,' he said.

'And Rebecca?'

'Met someone else. Got a letter. S'okay, I'm cool with it. Don't have to end it now myself. No more sodding hand-knitted jerseys and sodium bicarbonate toothpaste.... What do you think of my idea?'

'Paris? Isn't this the alcohol talking?'

'Loads of people uproot themselves at my age.'

As he finished his meal, Annie ordered them both a double espresso. At least the stench of whisky had gone – for the moment – and he was more sober for having eaten, but she would need to make sure he got back to Brunnen safely.

'Don't you have an opinion?' Lawrence asked.

'It is a bit clichéd. And expensive. I mean, you'd pay

more to rent somewhere in Paris than you'd get for your cottage.'

'I'd find regular freelance work. *Une lettre de Paris.* Clever, eh?'

She shrugged. 'If it hasn't already been done to death. You'd need an original angle. I mean, everyone writes about the romance of living in a garret overlooking the Seine and spending time in chic cafés. At least they used to.'

'Yeah, yeah. I've also got an idea for a crime novel,' he said. 'I've already created the main character. DI Rebus.... er, Wallace.'

He continued talking while Annie asked for the bill, paid it and calculated a tip.

She couldn't visualise Lawrence in Paris. Although he looked athletic and younger in his climbing gear today, he normally seemed middle-aged and bland in chinos and checked shirt. No doubt when he glanced in the mirror, he saw something different. But maybe she was being harsh. Perhaps he *would* blend in at his literary cafés. Perhaps he *would* write a crime novel full of tension, rival DI Rebus and other contemporary sleuths. What did she know, after all? A café owner, a mediocrity, and, she now realised, not so content with being so.

'Thanks for the encouragement and your confidence,' Lawrence said as they left the café.

'There's no point in coming out with the usual "what a great idea".'

'Why shouldn't I go for it?'

'We need to head back now,' she said. 'Best to take the train.'

He stopped. 'I want to walk.'

'Not enough time.'

'I'm in no rush.'

'Lawrence, we're taking the train, don't argue.'

To Annie's frustration, Lawrence talked for most of the return journey, his ramblings sabotaging every thought entering her mind. Even when she peered out at the wonderful view over the Urnersee, today a pale blue mirror, his monologue continued: gripes about how boring Rebecca had been, about his freelance assignments being too parochial. She challenged nothing. Sooner or later, he'd run dry. Hopefully.

When they reached Brunnen, she accompanied him to the Hotel Bergmann, managing to sneak him past reception where, thankfully, the clerk was embroiled with an anxious guest. In Lawrence's room, she half shoved him onto the bed, removed his walking boots and ordered him to sleep off the alcohol. By the time she'd washed her hands of the dirt from his boots, he was snoring. As she made her way along the waterfront to the Zurbriggen, she reminded herself she'd done this for Madalena.

Annie felt twitchy as Madalena drove them to Luzern. It was always the same after being with Lawrence. As if his restlessness, his general dissatisfaction, transferred itself to her by osmosis. She was fed up being so easily affected by other people's moods. When Ferne had enthused about a tapestry exhibition, where there'd be people from New York who might be interested in her work, Annie had absorbed her high. When Ferne had bemoaned her favourite yarn supplier going bankrupt, complaining that it would now be much harder to find the muted colours she loved, Annie had experienced a headache lasting well into the evening.

'Have you spoken to Portia today, Mum?' she asked.

Madalena nodded, as she changed lanes. 'Lucy's doing well. Complaining about her restricted diet and how she's bored with everything on her iPod.'

Annie grinned. Early days, however. 'I hope it continues.'

'She will recover. You mustn't worry.'

'You're so strong,' Annie said. 'I mean, you never go to pieces. To be honest, I don't know how you manage.'

Madalena switched on the air conditioning. 'How was your walk?'

'Not exactly what I'd expected.'

Would Lawrence still be sleeping? Should she have lingered longer, to check he didn't roam around the hotel, behaving inappropriately? There was Mum's relationship with Herr Adler to consider.

'And lunch with Johann? How did that go?'

'The meal was fine. I like him. He's straightforward, the kind you could trust.'

'He is solid, dear. I know that sounds stuffy, but it can be useful. He is calm, resourceful. Like your father.'

'We discussed running the hotel together,' Annie said. 'With Hilde's help, possibly.'

'I see. You would consider this? Until now, Johann has turned down the chance of additional responsibility. He would be a good manager. You see, I have a vision for how I would like the Zurbriggen to continue. I would want my female staff to continue being paid the same as male staff for equivalent work – not in keeping with Swiss traditions, I know. And I'd want the staff still to be involved in decision-making.'

'I'm thinking about it. It may be time for a change, if you believe I could handle it. And I can't imagine any of the others wanting to take it on.'

'I also wondered about Lawrence.'

Annie laughed. If Madalena knew of his current state, she would rule him out. If he could get drunk once, he could again. Mum was staring at her, so she allowed herself a silence, as if considering her response.

'Johann mentioned this. The thing is, it didn't work out at the café, Lawrence and me. It would be even less likely to work out with a hotel – you haven't spoken to him, I hope.'

'I did raise it with him, but he indicated there had been issues with you in the past. It was a while ago, nevertheless.'

'It doesn't matter how long ago it was.' Annie leant back in her seat, stretched her arms. 'Anyway, I've arranged to see Johann again tomorrow, to talk more. And Hilde. Perhaps you should join us, Mum. Providing Lucy's still okay.'

'I would remain in charge for a while, to give you a transition phase.... As for you and Johann...?'

'It was a business meeting.'

'Ah.... Another of the Swiss personality traits is caution.'

Annie remembered the kiss. Not much caution displayed there.

'I do think he cares for you,' Madalena was saying. 'Perhaps in time–'

'Mum, when I got together with Ferne, were you surprised?'

'Surprised? Not really. I sensed you were disenchanted with men.... I take it you and Ferne are finished?'

'Yeah, I was going through a bad phase with guys when we met, and there was all the stuff around Dad's death. But I did so want to be a parent.'

'There's time yet, dear. Thirty-five isn't what it used to be.'

Annie's thoughts returned to Portia and Lucy. If Lucy needed a transfusion of her own blood type, this would involve Michael. How would Portia engineer this without Vienne finding out?

'Ever wished you hadn't invited us to Brunnen?' Annie asked as they turned into the hospital grounds.

'Who could have forecast all this?' Madalena said.

Walking along the corridor to the lift, Annie thought about Johann and their parting after that misconstrued lunch. He'd kissed her cheek, hesitated, then embraced her. Before she walked away, he'd silently studied her. After leaving, she'd chided herself for her gaucheness. Perhaps he was unsure of what *she* wanted. One thing was certain: when they next met on their own, she'd have to clarify their situation.

Better to know, before they embarked on a professional relationship. If they decided to do so.

As Annie swapped her 50mm lens for a zoom, she pondered the fragility of friendships and love affairs, how easily they could unravel in difficult situations. She'd often believed Lawrence would end his relationship with Rebecca, but she'd never imagined Rebecca would call it a day. How impossible it was to know what would endure, what would disintegrate. People talked about the importance of withholding part of yourself in a relationship. They were right. Having something of your own to immerse yourself in when things went wrong was vital. She was glad now that photography had remained "hers".

A bird emerged from a nearby tree, warbled a few notes and flew off. At the sound of rustling, she raised her head to notice Lawrence feet away. Her heart sank.

'Mum said I'd find you here,' he said, lifting the lens on top of her camera bag, peering at it. 'I wanted to talk to you.'

'Again? Careful with that lens.... What did you want to

talk about? The Zurbriggen? Mum told me she asked you about running it, with me. What a joke.'

The sun had partly slipped behind a cloud, creating a beautiful effect on the lake. She wanted her brother to bugger off, leave her to her creativity.

'Yeah, yeah. Anyway, I told her running the café with you had its difficulties,' Lawrence said.

'Jessy had a stroke, you know, shortly after.'

'That's not my fault.'

'There was no excuse for your unpleasantness. I mean, the café was the highlight of her day. She was lonely. Even a brief conversation meant something. This is why I asked her opinion on new recipes. To make her feel involved.'

'Okay, okay, I'm sorry.... I *am* sorry.'

'She didn't return for three months,' Annie continued. 'And she was different, kept fingering the twisted side of her face. And she'd only come in at quiet times. Embarrassed, I'm sure.... She's in a care home now.'

Lawrence stared at his shoes.

Annie studied the sky, then the ground. The contrast in light was too great. If she based the reading on the ground, the sky would be overexposed, and if she set the light meter for the sky, the ground would be too dark. She reached into her camera case, unzipped a padded nylon bag containing a gradient filter. She rubbed the glass with a sterile cloth and slipped it over the lens.

'Anyway, so we're agreed then it wouldn't work for you and me to run the hotel.... Lawrence?'

He nodded.

She removed the filter and replaced it in its bag. Tried another one.

'How is Ferne?' Lawrence asked.

'She's with her parents. Coming to terms with what's

happened, I suppose.'

'I was angry with you, you know. About her.'

Annie adjusted the shutter speed, then stopped down the aperture. This should work. '*She* chose me, Lawrence. Not the other way round. I didn't pinch her from you.'

'Yeah, but–'

'But nothing.'

'Is she still...?'

'A lesbian? Go on. Your tongue won't shrivel up if you use the word.'

Silence.

She took several photos, moved position and took more.

This would do for now – it was nearly six o'clock. Tomorrow, after the meeting with Johann and Hilde, she'd take the boat to Flüelen and stop off here on her way back.

'You obviously haven't heard, Lawrence, but Ferne dumped me for the baby's father.... Yes, a bloke. It seems no one is capable of making a long-term commitment these days.'

'Jeez, why do people have to be so complicated? Did you ever think she and I....?'

Annie shook her head. 'We never discussed you.'

She wondered again about Johann. If their relationship did develop, would this complicate running the hotel together? And if they didn't become an item, would she constantly be hoping for more from him?

She packed away her equipment. Tomorrow, she'd bring the tripod.

Lawrence was gazing over the lake. 'I've had a crap day. I've just made a total arse of myself.'

'Why are you putting me in the role of mother confessor?'

'I don't talk to Portia or Vienne about this sort of thing

and I certainly can't tell Mum.... I've had the hots for a journalist I met at a dinner in London. Sophie Meers.'

Annie sighed. This was going to be an epic tale, and the light was constantly changing, silvery pools on the water expanding, shifting. She wanted to watch this on her own. 'You've mentioned her already. Perhaps you could summarise?'

'What? Okay, I phoned her and got someone called Nick. Sounded nerdy. When she came on the phone, I couldn't think what to say so I reminded her that she'd written her private number on the back of the business card, and that I'd assumed this meant she wanted me to get in touch. She cracked up with laughter.... I could have been selling double glazing for all she cared.'

'And the fact her partner answered the phone didn't put you off?'

'He could have been a flatmate. How was I to know she was living with someone? I racked my brain for some way to retrieve the situation, end with a shred of dignity,' Lawrence continued. 'When I hung up, they were both laughing. I could hear him in the background. Sodding prick.'

'You plonker. You have much to learn.' Nevertheless, Annie fleetingly felt a twinge of sympathy for her brother.

In a more jaunty tone, Lawrence said, 'I might phone Rebecca. Check she means what she said. After all, it could be a ploy to make me jealous, goad me into committing to her, don't you think?'

He wasn't half deluded, Annie thought. Despite the fact she'd never met Lawrence's girlfriend, she was glad Rebecca had found someone else, hopefully someone more appreciative.

'It's a beautiful evening, and I want to enjoy it. Not have to think about your idiotic behaviour.'

She waited. So did he. Finally, she resigned herself to the fact that he had no intention of leaving yet.

'There's something you need to know,' Lawrence said, as they set off along the path. 'About Dad.'

Annie listened in silence as he relayed his story. It was too much to hear at the moment. It would be a lot to absorb at any time. Poor Mum.... What an awful thing to deal with. To continue wondering about. Even though she now had Karl.

'Say something,' Lawrence urged, when he'd finished.

'I suppose you were right to tell her,' she said.

He stared at her. 'And that's it? Don't you want to shout at me about what a bastard I am?'

'I'm tired. And you already know you can be a bastard. I mean, you don't need me to drive the point home, do you?'

She was in overload. Like a plugboard with too many plugs. Surely, he must realise this? Sense when to stop?

'I expect you'll hate and despise me from now on.'

She shrugged. 'Dunno. You're my brother.'

'We are a complicated family, aren't we? This can be fodder for my crime novel.... I'm joking.... You know, at the end of the holiday, I'd like it if you and I could part on a positive note, yeah? Might this be possible?'

What he had done to Dad was sinking in. The calculated deception. Yet Lawrence had lived with his guilt for all those years. Years, no doubt, of wondering if Dad would still be alive if he hadn't stolen his money. Her brother was a prat: self-absorbed and insensitive, but he wasn't a monster.

Lawrence had read her mind. 'Maybe it's too much to ask, with the Dad situation.'

Annie touched his arm lightly. 'As I said, you're my brother.... If you do move to Paris, give me your address. I might be persuaded to visit.'

21

T wo days after Lucy's accident, Portia woke with a start. She gazed round her Luzern hotel room, with its sombre wooden furniture, taking a minute to locate herself. Today she must ask Michael to give blood to Lucy. And she'd no idea how to achieve this. How to prise him away from Vienne, who, doubtlessly, would be on high alert.

Half an hour later, she peered through the glass panel of Lucy's side room, where her daughter lay sleeping, face flushed. It was seven-thirty and she could hear the rumble of breakfast trolleys. Further along the corridor, a huddle of nurses conversed at their station, one voice more prominent. Handover time. She deliberated a moment before heading for the stairs. It was possible to catch the next train.

When she arrived at the Zurbriggen, everyone except Vienne was breakfasting in the private dining room. Despite her exhaustion, her craving for sleep, one thing dominated her mind – how to speak to Michael privately.

'How is Lucy?' Madalena asked.

'She's doing okay, but she needs another blood transfusion.'

Lawrence looked up. 'Can she manage without a spleen? I don't even know what a spleen does.'

'Never mind that now, Lawrence. Come and have something to eat, Portia,' Madalena said.

Michael pulled out a chair for Portia. 'I'm sorry to hear about the accident.'

'Let me know if there's anything I can do,' Lawrence offered.

'Sit down, Portia, and eat something,' Annie said, pouring her a coffee.

Portia slumped onto the chair, feeling her eyes fill. Sometimes it was easier to keep going when people weren't kind to you. She picked at a croissant, sipped a glass of orange juice.

Madalena rose to leave, something to discuss with Hilde, she said; she'd be back shortly. Then Michael stood, gripped Portia's shoulder and walked away. Lawrence went to check if the newspapers had arrived.

Portia turned to Annie. 'I need to ask Michael to donate blood.'

'I wondered. How will you do this?'

'No idea.'

Annie clasped her arms tightly around her waist shook her head, then exhaled deeply. 'Be careful.'

Portia left the table, hoping to catch Michael before he reached his room. At the dining room door, she collided with Vienne. They stared at each other.

Annie came over. 'Come and have breakfast, Vienne.'

Vienne allowed Annie to take her arm, then turned round to speak to Portia. 'I'm sorry about Lucy.'

'Come on,' Annie said, casting a disapproving look at Portia.

Portia waited as Annie led their sister to the table. But Vienne was pulling away now, making to leave the room. She pushed past Portia.

Portia lingered for a moment before returning to the table where Annie sat, hands clasping a cup of coffee.

'What a look, Annie.'

'You're forgetting I know how betrayal feels.'

'I'm not, but Michael convinced Vienne nothing happened between us. I have to focus on Lucy.' Portia leaned across the table. 'You haven't said anything to Vienne?'

'Of course not. But she looks awful, thinner and–'

'Nonsense, you don't lose weight in a couple of days unless you're ill.'

Annie cleared her throat. 'She has her viral thingy. And her concert.'

'It sounds as if you've changed allegiance.'

'Heavens, Portia, this isn't a war. I mean I am upset about Lucy, of course I am, but you've behaved badly. Extremely badly.'

Portia sighed. Now wasn't the time for a lecture on morals. Annie could lambast her later, once Lucy had fully recovered.

Gaston brought a jug of coffee and asked if they would like more cheese and ham. As they declined, Portia wondered how he would react if she requested a brandy.

On the Urnersee, a waft of hot air balloons drifted with deceptive aimlessness. There must be a competition underway – at least some people were having fun. She waited until the waiter had left the dining room.

'Will you help me get Michael to the hospital without Vienne knowing?'

Annie sucked in her breath. 'What specifically are you asking me to do?'

'I don't know.... Suggest you and she go somewhere together this afternoon.'

Annie looked uncertain. 'Don't you think she might be just a bit suspicious? I mean, especially as she and I don't normally do things on our own? Sorry, Portia, but I'd feel really uncomfortable being part of this.... Perhaps Madalena could do something with her?'

Portia spread apricot jam on her croissant, wishing now she'd ordered an omelette.

'And how would we explain this to Madalena?'

'Tell her the truth?'

'Annie, are you mad? It would ruin my relationship with her.'

'As you could have ruined Vienne and Michael's.'

'I'm sure she doesn't know. She would have said something when she saw me, don't you think?'

Annie sighed. 'I suppose I could suggest we help Madalena in the conservatory.'

Portia slid a flake of croissant between her fingers. She could feel the grease. 'You're not thinking. It has to be something away from here – to give Michael long enough to get to Luzern and back.'

'I'm meant to be meeting with Johann today to discuss the hotel,' Annie said.

'You can postpone that, surely? This is urgent.'

'Yeah well, perhaps Vienne and I should go climbing, stay overnight in a mountain hut. Imagine her enthusiasm.'

Annie delivered her sarcasm lightly, but her changing attitude was worrying. Portia couldn't afford to lose her support at this moment. It would be different tomorrow. It wouldn't matter if they argued tomorrow.

'Annie, please.... Couldn't you find an art gallery or museum to visit – in Zurich?'

'What if she wants Michael to come along, too?'

'He isn't into art.'

'I'll think about it,' Annie said gloomily.

'Don't take too long,' Portia said. 'I need to get him to the hospital by lunchtime.'

She finished the croissant and stood. 'I'll be in the sitting room or my bedroom. Let me know as soon as you've arranged something. And... thanks. I do appreciate this... your support.'

Portia checked her watch: nearly eleven o'clock and there'd been no sign of Michael, nor any word from Annie. Here she was, skulking, aware that Vienne might discover her any moment and challenge her. And two weeks ago, newly arrived in Brunnen, she'd waited in this same room, again dreading her sister's presence.

She thought of her status in legal circles: her reputation for persuading the most sceptical of juries; for being compassionate but dignified. If colleagues knew about her personal life, they'd view her differently. But this was a life-long burden. She'd become accustomed to hiding more than her body under the gown and wig, behind the black-framed glasses that she used to intimidate and removed to reassure.

She opened the *Tages-Anzeiger* and skimmed through it unseeingly.

Then Madalena was by her side. 'Ah, there you are, dear. What are your plans? I assume you are visiting Lucy later.'

Portia nodded.

'You look exhausted. I had hoped once you checked into your hotel in Luzern, you'd manage to catch up on sleep,' Madalena said. 'I could drive you in.'

'What are you doing today, Mum?'

'Giving Ruth and Alice a lift to the station to catch the Zurich train, shortly. Afterwards I am free.'

Finally – a solution. Mum could drive the Sowerby sisters and Vienne and Annie to Zurich. This would allow time for Michael to get to the Kinderspital and back. Vienne wouldn't question an invitation from Mum.

'Annie mentioned visiting Zurich. Why don't you drive there, drop off the Sowerbys and you and Annie could do something together? You could collect the Sowerbys later.'

'It *would* save them money on the fare,' Madalena said.

'In fact, Vienne might want to go too – Zurich has so many museums, there must be something you'd like to see.'

Madalena stared at her. 'Are you all right?'

Portia suppressed a laugh. Apart from worrying about Vienne; about Lucy recovering from surgery and being sad and bewildered about her father; about having to persuade Michael to give blood without Vienne knowing, and the deteriorating relationship with Annie... she was fine.

The bells of the nearby church struck eleven.

Madalena straightened the cushions on the sofa. 'Portia, have you contacted Elliot?'

'I'm about to.'

'Why the delay?'

She hesitated. 'Just giving him time to recover from jet lag....'

Madalena looked puzzled.

Portia took a deep breath. 'Will you speak to Vienne, then? And Annie?'

'And Michael. He might want to come with us.'

Portia felt perspiration bead her forehead. 'He's not into culture.'

'If I do this, it will be difficult to visit Lucy later. Why don't we wait until she's out of hospital, then we could all go?'

Portia studied Madalena, the lines above her mouth, the pinched look around her eyes. It was unfair to manipulate her into this trip. Lucy's accident had probably affected her mother more than she'd realised, not to mention the fire and aborted celebration. But needs must....

'It should be today,' she persisted, knowing she couldn't justify this if challenged. 'Why don't you leave Lucy's visit until tomorrow? She'll be recovering from the operation, and I'll be with her.'

Persuading people to acquiesce to her bidding was draining her limited energy. She needed to shower and change her clothes. She needed to sleep.

Madalena sat down beside her. 'Do you think Michael and Vienne are going through a difficult spell? I get the impression she is unhappy.'

Portia shrugged. 'All marriages have their rough periods. I've no idea.'

'Ah,' Madalena said. 'And have *you* sorted out your differences with Vienne?'

'Mum, this isn't the time.'

Madalena stood. 'As you wish.'

'You'll speak to Annie and Vienne, then?'

It felt like chess: anticipating, avoiding hasty moves. But Madalena was now talking about finding Vienne and Annie, informing Ruth and Alice Sowerby of the change in plan. It might work.

'Get some sleep before you return to Luzern,' Madalena said.

When Madalena left, Portia wandered over to the window. There were even more hot air balloons now hovering over the Urnersee. How lovely to be up there. Even more desirable, to be in her London office, preparing for the most difficult case.

She was nodding off when Annie came into the sitting room. 'Apparently Mum is driving the Sowerby sisters and Vienne and me to Zurich and we're going round galleries and museums. Fortunately, for you, Michael declined. The bad news is that he isn't feeling great. He was talking about going back to bed.'

Portia got to her feet. 'He can't, he mustn't. This is my only chance.'

'Then you'll have to use your considerable powers of persuasion.' Annie's voice softened. 'Anyway, we'll be leaving soon. I hope it goes okay with Lucy. Give her my love and a big hug. Tell her I'll visit tomorrow.'

From behind the sitting room curtains, Portia observed Ruth and Alice Sowerby climb into Madalena's green Renault, followed by Vienne and Annie. Watched as the car pulled out of the drive and onto the side road. Then she rushed upstairs to Vienne and Michael's room and knocked on the door.

Michael lay in bed reading. He sat bolt upright when Portia entered. 'What the hell....'

'It's okay, they've left,' she said.

'You're sure?'

He got out of bed and strode over to the window in his boxers and t-shirt. 'Sometimes Vienne forgets something.'

'They left about five minutes ago. But if it makes you feel safer, keep watch. Michael, I need you to give blood to Lucy. As soon as possible, in fact.'

He turned to face her. 'Are you being serious?'

'It's why I engineered the trip into Zurich. I needed to get you away from Vienne.'

'This was *your* doing?' he asked, as he got into bed again, pulled up the duvet.

'Will you come to the hospital with me now?'

He groaned. 'Does it have to be today? I'm pooped.... I really do feel rough. It's probably because–'

'Of course it does. It was difficult enough prising Vienne away from you. Look, I have never, never asked you to do anything before for Lucy. This is about your daughter's health.'

'You know I don't think of Lucy like that.'

Portia was aware of her voice rising. A lack of sleep and too much angst were beginning to show. 'There's no time just now for a discussion about how you relate or don't relate to her. Please...'

'What about Lawrence? He might see us.'

'He's probably at the Hotel Bergmann or gone climbing,' she said. 'I suggest we make our way independently to the station. I'll tell Hilde I'm going to Luzern. You slip out without being noticed. The side door's the safest option.'

He grinned. 'Sounds like an episode from 24. Copy that.'

'Just do it, for God's sake. There's a train at twelve-twenty.'

Her heart pounded as she awaited his response.

'I really don't feel great. It wasn't just an excuse not to traipse round galleries in Zurich with my in-laws.'

'Please, Michael,' she said, aware that tears weren't far off.

To her relief he nodded, went to the chair and put on his trousers. The intimacy of the action – as if they'd just been in bed together – provoked a blush. She wasn't attracted to him anymore, she told herself, as she detected a whiff of Vienne's perfume from the bathroom.

She returned to her bedroom, showered quickly and shoved some of her clothes and Lucy's into a bag.

The station in Brunnen was quiet, commuters long gone. On the platform, a tabby cat poked and tormented a newspaper. An elderly man blew his nose with such force that it sounded like a trumpet. Through an open window somewhere, drifted the sound of a news programme. Already Portia felt sticky in the humidity. Michael didn't offer to take her bag as they boarded the train.

'Have you planned what to tell the doctors about us?' he asked when they found seats. 'They'll expect me to visit Lucy, they'll be wondering why I haven't been there before. And Lucy will wonder who's giving blood. Have you worked out any of this?'

She shook her head. Having focused so much on obtaining his cooperation, getting him to Luzern, she hadn't considered how to present the situation. But his questions were valid. It would be ghastly if Doctor Meissner, in helpful mode, took Michael to see Lucy, believing he was her father. Or even mentioned Michael to her.

'I'll explain the situation to Doctor Meissner, ask him not to say anything to Lucy,' she said, hoping her tone sounded confident.

'You'll have to insist the information is confidential.'

'This is such a frightful situation.'

As the train pulled into Luzern, Michael turned to her.

'You haven't asked how things are with Vienne.'

'I'm assuming she believes you. But she was a bit weird with me at breakfast.'

'She hasn't said anything more. However, I can't be one hundred per cent sure I managed to reassure her.'

'All I can think about at the moment is Lucy. Surely even you can understand?'

He was silent. His detachment, his lack of emotion chilling. But she'd always been aware of his cold side.

'You don't seem upset. About anything.'

'I've run out of upsetness, Portia. It'll be a relief to return to London.'

'It'll be a relief to know Lucy's definitely going to be all right.... We'll take a taxi to the hospital.'

The taxi rank was mobbed. At the head of the line, a couple of suited middle-aged men wrangled over who was entitled to the next taxi, and there were irritable mutterings from other passengers. Michael jingled his keys while they queued, but Portia didn't dare ask him to stop. They had three hours, four perhaps. The air reeked of diesel, worsened by the heat, and the dull white of the sky oppressed her. As she was considering abandoning their wait, finding a bus, a flurry of taxis arrived and they'd reached the head of the queue.

'You'll be pleased to know I plan to stay in my hotel here for several more nights,' Portia said in the taxi. Michael didn't reply.

'Is Doctor Meissner available?' Portia asked a nurse when they reached Lucy's ward at the Kinderspital.

'He is on a ward round but he will finish soon. I will tell him you wish to speak with him.'

The relatives' room was hot and smelled of sweat and orange peel. Within minutes of sitting down, Portia felt stuck to the vinyl chair. She couldn't look at the ceiling fan, its inadequate efforts making her dizzy, and she was scared to look at Michael. He'd said nothing since they entered the hospital. What if he changed his mind about the blood test at the last minute? What if Vienne phoned him and realised from background noise that he wasn't in their room at the Zurbriggen?

Ten minutes later, Doctor Meissner arrived and bade Portia to follow him. She glanced at Michael before leaving the room. His expression was inscrutable. Aware of Michael's presence, Doctor Meissner hesitated, doubtless thinking that Michael should join them, but Portia said, 'I would like to talk to you on your own.'

'What I say must remain confidential,' she told the doctor when they were seated in his office.

He raised his eyebrows. 'Of course.'

She explained the situation about Michael and Lucy. Doctor Meissner listened.

'So, you see, Lucy mustn't find out who was here to give blood. She knows my ex-husband is not her biological father, but this is all she knows.'

'I will say nothing.'

Only then did Portia register his situation: the barely touched mug of coffee and cellophane packaged sandwich on his desk; his creased shirt and dark lines under his eyes. He must yearn for sleep as much as she did.

'I suppose you're used to dealing with complicated family situations,' she said.

Doctor Meissner stood. 'We will arrange for a sample of Herr Fotheringham's blood to be taken now.'

In the clamminess of the relatives' room, Portia nodded off, waking half an hour later to a cacophony of ambulance and police sirens. Apart from her, the room was empty. No other anxious parents. And no Michael. The Tannoy requested a doctor's presence. The announcement was repeated. She left the room, intending to find her brother-in-law.

'Frau Fontana,' a voice behind her said. It was Doctor Meissner.

'I'm looking for Mr Fotheringham.'

'Herr Fotheringham left.'

Portia frowned. 'I expected him to wait for the results. So that he'd know if he should give blood. Of course it's bound to be compatible and–'

'He requested we take a donation of blood. He gave permission for it to be used for someone else if it is not a match for your daughter.'

At least they had Michael's blood now. She felt her pulse decrease.

'We will have the results soon,' Doctor Meissner said.

Portia returned to the relatives' room. How could people work in such an adrenaline-filled environment? She took two Kalms and sat down. She'd allow herself ten minutes to regain her composure, then visit Lucy.

Two hours later, Portia awoke to the ring of her phone. It was five o'clock. Her head felt fuzzy and her neck ached from sleeping in an awkward position.

'We're back,' Annie said.

Portia calculated. Michael would probably have caught the three o'clock train to Brunnen, hopefully been safely in the Zurbriggen by four thirty. Vienne need never know he'd left the hotel. As long as he ditched his train ticket.

'Portia, can you hear me?'

'I'm just working out if Michael would be back.'

'He was in the garden when we returned.'

'Thank God. Right, I must go to Lucy – I fell asleep.'

'Give her my love. And yes, we did have a lovely trip to Zurich, thank you for asking.'

Portia switched off her phone and walked along to Lucy's ward. She could understand Annie feeling hacked off, of course, but in time they'd sort things out. The idea of relocating to Switzerland surfaced once more. A fresh start: what she and Lucy needed.

She paused outside Lucy's room. Her daughter was seated by the bedside, engrossed in a copy of *National Geographic*, headphones in, her shoulders making funky movements.

'Lucy is improving,' a nurse said. 'Once she receives more blood, she will improve further. Tomorrow you can take her out into the hospital gardens, if you wish.'

Later, as Lucy and Portia finished a game of cards, another nurse entered the room. 'Doctor Meissner wishes to speak to you, Frau Fontana.'

'I'll be right back, sweetheart,' Portia told her daughter.

She strode along to the doctor's office, a nauseous feeling permeating her. It was like receiving a jury's verdict.

When Lucy was born, on a whim Portia had phoned Michael to let him know. The impulse occurred after a difficult visit from Elliot, whose mood had plummeted several hours after the birth, as he registered the reality of the situation.

Michael had turned up at the hospital with carnations and chocolates, glanced at Lucy, and after asking Portia a few perfunctory questions, left. The visit over in five minutes, with no physical contact. Not even a tentative stroke of Lucy's cheek. Portia had heard of diehard alpha males shedding tears on seeing their newborn babies. Not

Michael. Lucy could have been a rabbit born to someone who didn't like animals, for all the emotion he displayed. Portia, an elderly client, he felt duty bound to visit, depositing the flowers and chocolates on the bedside locker.

For months, Portia had wondered if he would suddenly feel paternal and request contact with Lucy. She never considered how this might work: she hadn't needed to. There was no phone call, no letter announcing he wanted a role in Lucy's life. On balance, Portia had been relieved. It would have been impossible to conceal his link with Lucy from both Vienne and Elliot. Unthinkable to tell Lucy that her father was actually her uncle.

She now entered Doctor Meissner's office, to find him by the window, a form in his hand. His shirt was fresh and well ironed and he looked less stressed. Perhaps he'd returned home briefly to the ministering of a Swiss wife. A wholesome meal prepared for him while he showered and changed clothes. As she observed this, she marvelled at her ability to absorb these details at such a moment. As if she were dichotomous. Her barrister's training.

'Please have a seat,' he said.

Portia remained standing.

'I'm sorry to have kept you waiting for so long. We have the results of the blood test. Please, sit.'

Portia sat down. 'Is there a problem? What did the results show?'

Doctor Meissner removed his spectacles. 'The blood we took from Herr Fotheringham is not a match for your daughter.'

'And you definitely can't use my blood – you can't test it for malaria? It might be clear, it probably *is* clear.'

He leaned across the desk. 'Frau Fontana, the results

from Herr Fotheringham show that he is not the father of your daughter.'

'What? Are you sure? Could there–?'

'The tests we now perform are sophisticated. There can be no doubt of their accuracy.'

'I don't understand how this can be.'

After all those years.... She rested her head in her hands to quell the sensation of the room closing in. Struggled to think coherently. Elliot *was* Lucy's father, after all. The immaculate conception. She heard herself laugh. Not her normal laugh, though. A strangled version.

'What happens now? Should I contact my ex-husband? He's in London. Should he arrange for a blood sample to be flown over here?'

'Normally I would suggest this,' Doctor Meissner said. 'However, Lucy is making excellent progress. Her latest haemoglobin test shows that the levels have risen. I don't think it is so important now to transfuse her again. We will continue to monitor this, but she is young and healthy. She is recovering well from her surgery.'

After leaving Doctor Meissner's office, Portia wandered back to Lucy's room. Once again, she paused at the door, staring through the glass. To her relief, Lucy lay in bed, seemingly asleep. It was after eight o'clock – she could leave her daughter for the night, give herself time to absorb the information about Elliot.

When she returned to her hotel, Portia sank into the green velvet armchair and closed her eyes. Oblivious to anything but her circling thoughts, she jumped as her phone announced a text. It was from Elliot: *Can't come over, sorry*. Can't or won't? she wondered. She hesitated, then switched off her phone.

At the writing desk, she opened the leather folder and

retrieved a sheet of cream embossed notepaper. The name and address of the hotel was printed in a calligraphic font on one side; the other side featured a sepia photograph of the building. In earlier decades, no doubt, guests would have perched at this desk, writing glowing letters about their holiday in Luzern – boat trips on the lake, cable car rides. She could visualise them pausing, pen in hand, to search for a precise adjective, to check for correct spelling of a German speaking town in Switzerland. Realising she was highly likely to be the first patron ever to send this kind of letter, her face relaxed into a smile, she lifted her biro and wrote:

Dear Elliot

She clasped her hands together and bit her thumbs. Was a letter the best method? Certainly, something this important shouldn't be communicated by email, and if she phoned him the line could be bad. Alternatively, of course, she could wait until she returned home, tell him face-to-face. On the other hand, a letter would allow him time to process the news. It would be a shock, on top of which she couldn't be sure how he'd react – not initially. In time he'd be happy, free now to love Lucy as his own. Yes, even if it felt outmoded, Elliot should hear the news by letter.

She lifted her pen again and continued: *This is an extraordinary letter to be writing....*

When Portia finished, she addressed the envelope but left it open, envisaging a rewrite later when more time had elapsed. She went downstairs and out into the hotel garden. In the airless evening, the scent of honeysuckle and jasmine was particularly heady. High above, lights flickered in the distant mountains. She heard a rumble of thunder, and seconds later, sheet lightning illuminated the sky and mountains. Thunder crackled, followed by torrential rain,

but she remained outside, oblivious to her soaking clothes.
She could no longer smell the honeysuckle. There was only
darkness and light, noise and silence.

Perhaps it had taken until now for Lucy's accident to
fully register; what might have happened: a busier street, a
faster car. Perhaps, back in London again, she'd drift around
Chambers searching for someone – anyone – to talk to
about the accident. She imagined herself pausing amidst a
summing up, thinking: *I could have lost Lucy, I could have lost
my daughter.*

In her bedroom, she dried her hair with a towel and
changed into her nightie. Then she reread the letter and
nodded. It wasn't brilliant English, certainly: clumsy, repetitive. But it would do. She sealed the envelope and pressed it
against her chest.

Elliot was Lucy's father....

The following morning, Portia woke to sun streaming into
her room. It was after nine, and for the first time since
arriving in Switzerland, anxiety hadn't woken her during
the night. When she phoned the hospital, a nurse informed
her that Lucy had slept well and for breakfast had eaten two
large bowls of porridge and was complaining about not
having enough songs on her iPod. By the time Portia was
showered and dressed, she'd missed the hotel breakfast. Not
to worry. She fancied a sandwich from a stall. Then she'd
visit Lucy.

As she shoved Elliot's letter into her bag, she realised
that she and Lucy might be back in London before he read
it, but she'd still send it, by express post. While drinking a
coffee in her room, she browsed through contacts on her

phone. It took several minutes to be connected with the appropriate person, twenty minutes before she finished her call.

On a lakeside bench, while munching a sandwich, her spirits rose. Lucy would be delighted when she learned the truth, Michael would be relieved. As for Elliot, she could only hope it wasn't too late for him to love Lucy properly. The only thing which mattered now was making Lucy feel secure and loved – by both parents.

It was after lunch when Portia arrived at Lucy's room, to find it empty and the door of the en suite bathroom open. Perhaps she'd gone for an X-ray. A nurse entered the room.

'You are looking for your daughter? I will take you to her.'

'Nothing's happened, has it?'

The nurse was smiling as she led Portia to a large, bright room full of abandoned toys. At one end, a group of children clustered round an armchair, where, clad in the pink cotton hospital dressing gown, her hair spikier than ever, Lucy was reading to them in German. No heads turned when Portia and the nurse entered the room.

'She is great with the younger children,' the nurse said. 'She's a lovely girl.'

When Lucy had finished reading, and awkwardly accepted kisses from her acolytes, Portia took her out to the garden, where they lay on loungers under the shade of a mature oak tree. The city of Luzern seemed far away, the traffic a distant hum. She observed her daughter, relieved to note today's improvement: brighter eyes, movements less lethargic.

Since the previous evening, she had been wondering how to convey the news about Elliot. She didn't want to dramatise it, neither would it be appropriate to slip it into the conversation too casually.

'I've been thinking, Lucy – you and I should spend some time with Daddy when we get back to London.'

Lucy gave her a penetrating look. 'You said you couldn't tell me who my father is.'

'It *is* someone you know, darling.... It's Elliot.'

'It's okay, Mummy, you don't need to pretend anymore. I know he's not my real dad – biologically.'

'Lucy–'

'It's all right. It's all right. I've had time to think about it, here in hospital. Elliot looked after me when I was little. This makes him my real father in the important ways.'

'You're right when you say we don't need to pretend any more. But you *can* think of him as your father because he *is*. Let me explain. The hospital did a blood test which proved that Elliot is your biological father. I was wrong.'

She held her breath, waiting for Lucy to ask how they could have tested Elliot's blood in his absence. One pertinent question and her explanation would crumble. With luck, however, her daughter would switch to emotional mode, forget the logistics. Even if Lucy quizzed her in years to come: *So how did you actually find out, Mum?*

There was a long silence.

Lucy was gazing at her hands. 'So Elliot is definitely my dad, then?'

'Yes, sweetheart, he is, he definitely is.'

Portia contemplated her daughter as she continued to absorb the news. Lucy's face was turned away, and there was something about her profile, the curve of her cheekbone that reminded Portia of Elliot. She gave herself a shake.

'Does he know? Does Elliot know he's my real father?'

'I've written to tell him.'

Another extended silence, as Lucy fiddled with a paper hanky. 'Will he come back to live with us, then?'

Nearby, a workman painting window frames, raised the volume on his radio as Vertical Horizon sang *We are*. Elliot had played this when they were first married, grabbing her in one of his frequent bear hugs, shuffling them round the kitchen, ignoring her protests. She'd loved his spontaneity, his tolerance, the fact he'd tried.

She shook her head. 'No, sweetheart, that's not going to happen. Sorry.... We've moved on, but–'

'Do you still love him?'

'As a friend.'

'But if he wanted to come back, would you let him, Mummy?'

She considered. 'Oh Lucy, what a difficult question.'

Portia recalled her efforts to nudge her marriage back on course once her maternity leave had finished: taking fewer cases that necessitated travelling, arranging regular babysitters so that they could go to the cinema or exhibitions. She'd shown more interest in the buildings Elliot's firm was designing. Invited his colleagues to dinner. On a friend's advice, she'd organised special "date" nights where they stayed overnight in a spa hotel, indulged in room service and jacuzzies, where the tacit acknowledgement that this wasn't "their way" was, ironically, almost palpable. Invariably, they'd driven back to London in silence, and eventually Elliot reluctantly confessed that these weekends were too contrived. And after one particularly nasty row, that they were a waste of "bloody money".

Nevertheless, Portia had continued to try. Buying more feminine clothes. Making an effort with makeup and having her hair styled. Even considering orthodontic treatment which hitherto she'd rejected as being for overpampered

Hollywood bimbos. Unusually tuned into her behaviour, Elliot had complimented any attempts on her behalf, but sounding sad when he did, as if there was no point in appreciating her when she'd betrayed him.

Still determined to bring them closer, she reserved, when possible, enough energy for lovemaking and, restored to physical health, he hadn't rejected her. However, he withheld something and she tortured herself with the idea of him tormenting himself with images of her with another man. She never questioned his fidelity – revenge sex wasn't Elliot's style – but she knew her affair had sullied their relationship. Irreparably.

Elliot might have given up on their marriage, but he persevered with Lucy. Devising imaginative ways to help her with homework: weighing their hamsters to demonstrate open-ended maths problems; using Lego to teach her fractions. He took her to rugby matches, explaining the finer points of scrums and line-outs. She went dog mushing with him in Norway when he visited his cousin. When Portia had flu, eight-year-old Lucy accompanied Elliot to his office Christmas party, where – according to charmed colleagues – he was the most attentive of partners, plying her with food, dancing with her all evening.

The situation affected Portia too, of course. She couldn't make comments to Elliot such as, *Lucy's definitely got your nose.* Or, *Today, Lucy looked the spitting image of the photo of you on your 4th birthday.* And he never remarked on Lucy's appearance, even on the characteristics indisputably inherited from Portia. Like her indigo eyes.

She'd resigned herself to that. To the difficulties, the limitations. However, Elliot's announcement – the week after Lucy's ninth birthday – that he wanted a divorce – hit her with tidal force.

There was time now, though. Once Elliot recovered from the surprise of knowing Lucy *was* his, perhaps they could arrange some family outings, perhaps their threesomes would feel less fakey, more worthwhile.

Portia was napping in her hotel room later that day, windows open, curtains flapping in the breeze. Since leaving Lucy, she'd spent time on calls with various staff members of the Zurich office, and with Chambers, arranging for them to send references. Best of all, an interview had been mooted for the day after tomorrow. Purely a formality, they assured her. When her phone rang again, she therefore assumed it would be the Zurich office confirming the appointment time.

'Have you had the results of the blood test?' Michael asked.

'Michael... I've been wondering how to get in touch with you.'

'What's the verdict? I let them take blood – it seemed sensible, either way.'

Despite his light tone, she detected anxiety: this was a significant moment for him. Fleetingly, she flirted with the idea of withholding the information for longer, but couldn't justify doing so. Even though the fact that he'd almost certainly welcome the news, felt like a rejection of Lucy.

Which it was. And which hurt more than she would have believed.

'Your blood isn't compatible with Lucy's. You are not her father.'

'What? Really? You're certain, Portia, are the doctors certain?'

'One hundred per cent.'

The energy in his voice increased. 'Good old Elliot. This will make things much easier.'

She wanted to slap him for being so shallow. For his self-centredness. His appalling detachment where Lucy was concerned.

'And this is all you have to say?'

Michael hesitated, probably wondering why his response had engendered such anger. 'When did you find out?'

'Last night.'

'And you didn't get in touch?'

In the background, Portia heard the paddle steamer horn sounding in Brunnen – Michael must be by the lake. The harsh noise jerked her out of angry mode. Michael had a coldness to him, Elliot didn't. She must never forget this.

'Are you there?' Michael asked.

'Yes,' she said, wondering, even at this late stage, if he might say something which revealed a warmer side.

'Look, I have to go now. We're going out for dinner. Say "hi" to Lucy from Uncle Michael. Uncle Michael! Phew... Hallebloody*lu*jah.'

Portia switched off her phone. Contending with bitter thoughts about Michael's detachment, his lack of sensitivity, were ones about how awful it would be if he had been proved to be Lucy's father and Vienne eventually found out. Regardless of when. Regardless of circumstance. Such a revelation would have shattered the family, Madalena perhaps as much as Vienne herself. Michael would be aware of this and such knowledge might partly justify his jubilant reaction. But only partly.

One thing *was* clear: this episode finally signalled the end of Michael and her, fourteen years later. As clean a break as was possible. And one she'd never anticipated. She tried to identify how she felt about him now. A few moments elapsed, however, before she realised: she felt nothing.

Shortly after, she fell asleep again and when she woke, she recalled her dream. It was the middle of the night, she on her side of the bed, Elliot on his. Elliot, her semi-estranged husband. A man slowly crawling out of the trough of his depression. Unexpectedly, he'd reached for her, and she assumed he needed something: a glass of water, the window opened. Instead, he stroked her face. They made love. Hardly abandoned or passionate, but completed, so to speak. She experienced a strange double guilt the next day when meeting Michael in the hotel.

She sat up now, her body tingling. This was no dream. It was a surfacing memory. A replay. During his emergence from a dark place, she and Elliot *had* made love once. But when she discovered she was pregnant, she had assumed the baby was Michael's. That they hadn't been careful enough.

She paced the room, mulling over the events of the last few days: the horrid row, Lucy's fire, the accident and her fear. It had been a ghastly period, but with a positive ending.

How else would she have learned that Elliot was Lucy's father?

'Can you cope with any more surprises, Lucy?' Portia asked as they sat in the hospital gardens.

The scent of roses was overpowering, inducing a pleasant sleepiness.

'Something else I'll like?'

'I hope so.... Do you remember the night of the....'

Lucy rolled her eyes. 'The fire? Duh, 'course I do.... I feel awful about my behaviour. It was...'

'You asked me then if I ever considered moving back here, and I got the impression you might enjoy living in Switzerland.'

'We're going to move here, to Brunnen?'

'If you'd like to. I could work part-time for the Zurich office and we could find an apartment in Brunnen. You'd go to a day school and we'd see each other a lot more.'

A vision of a garden crept into her mind. She might not metamorphose – was there such a verb? – into a domestic goddess like Vienne or Annie. Doubtless, she'd continue to rely on her microwave too much, and be sporadic and luke-warm about housework. But she could imagine herself growing low maintenance flowers.

'Are you being serious, Mum?'

'Of course I am.'

Lucy's expression shifted to a frown. 'I won't get to see Grandma, then.'

'You can visit her in the holidays. And I think things will be different between you and Elliot – your father – now. He'll visit and you can visit.'

'And you can see me more often, because I'll be here, managing the Zurbriggen,' Annie said, appearing by their loungers. 'And if your Mum is away, you can stay in my apartment. We'll have a brilliant time, you and me.... Oh, you look so much better than the other day.'

'Annie!' Lucy said.

Annie then smiled at Portia, a real smile, one with warmth in it.

Portia clasped her daughter's hand. 'Would you like to live here?'

'I could learn to ski.'

There were all sorts of opportunities for Lucy, for both of them. But she mustn't slip into regarding Switzerland as Utopia. Doubtless there would be challenges.

'If it doesn't work out, we'll move back to London. But you have to give it a go. And one more thing – no more fires, Lucy. Promise me?'

Lucy nodded. 'I promise.'

22

While Portia and Lucy enjoyed another sunny afternoon in the hospital grounds the following afternoon, Vienne was running some errands for Madalena. About to cross the road, she noticed a new boutique. And in the window, a muted gold dress.

Her plans for a quiet evening had evaporated with Madalena's unexpected lunchtime announcement of a special family dinner for Lawrence's last night. If she were going to attend, she might as well make an effort.

She scrutinised the dress, a satiny fabric with diagonal ridges in a darker tone across the upper half, and a cowl neck.

'*Schön*. The colour is perfect,' the assistant said, as Vienne stepped out of the cubicle and studied herself in the mirrors.

She nodded. The gold complimented her hair and skin, highlighted the green of her eyes. The diagonal stripes flattered her, too. Its mid-calf length made it more flexible, formal but not overly so.

She hesitated, then pointed to her bust. 'Do you think it makes me look okay... here?'

The assistant leant forward, adjusted the shoulder. 'The detail suits you. It would not sit so neatly on someone with a large bosom.'

Vienne laughed. 'What a pleasant change.'

'There are many small breasted actresses who are considered to be beautiful *and* sexy,' the woman said.

'Really?'

'Nicole Kidman, Claire Danes. And your very British Keira Knightley. It is how a woman carries herself which makes her attractive. You have excellent posture.... Do you mind me asking, are you a dancer?'

'I almost was.... I'll take the dress, and thanks for your encouragement.'

She strolled out of the shop, gripping her shiny carrier bag. An hour and a half before dinner. Long enough for a leisurely bath before getting ready. Time, perhaps, to relax in the conservatory before the others arrived. Madalena's glasshouse was so peaceful, not too crammed with plants, nor too humid.

Absorbed in thought, she jumped at the sound of running. She turned to see Lawrence.

'Been walking?' she asked.

'Actually, I went into Luzern.'

'To visit Lucy?'

He hesitated. 'I don't like hospitals. No, I went to the transport museum. I'd planned to take her there.'

'Michael and I went by boat to Flüelen. We had a lovely walk in the forest.... Are you sorry to be leaving?'

She should have visited Lucy in hospital. Perhaps there'd be time tomorrow, after their trip to Rigi. They needn't stay long and having Michael with her would make things less awkward. She still blushed when recalling the horrid conversation with her niece.

'Talking of hospitals,' Lawrence said. 'I was surprised to see Michael coming out of the Kinderspital the other day.... I assumed you'd visit Lucy together.'

Vienne's heart pounded. 'When was this?'

'Tuesday, I think.'

The day she'd gone to Zurich with Mum and Annie, and the Sowerby sisters. The day Michael wasn't feeling well. Lawrence glanced at his watch. 'Did Annie tell you I'm thinking of moving to Paris? Time for a change.'

'Everyone's changing,' she managed to reply. Why had Michael been secretive about visiting Lucy? Why had he chosen to visit her on his own?

'Everyone needs change in their lives.... Right, this is where you and I part company,' Lawrence said. 'See you this evening, then,' and he turned off in the direction of the Hotel Bergmann.

The closer she got to the Zurbriggen, the worse Vienne felt. In her room, she dumped the carrier bag on the floor and sank onto the chair. She couldn't take much more of Michael's secretive side. It was one thing his needing space, another how he chose to spend it. She could accept that he hadn't wanted to go to Zurich, but not him pretending to feel ill so that he could visit Lucy on his own. Unless, of course, he hadn't been visiting her on his own. Had met Portia at the hospital.

Michael loved her, she knew, but she couldn't disengage from the ever-increasing niggle that perhaps it wasn't an "in love" strength of love. That perhaps he regarded her as a very close friend. With real fondness, but lacking passion. She needed more.

She removed the dress from the shiny bag, draped it

over her and laughed. How much difference could a dress make?

As she envisaged the evening ahead, the idea of dinner with even just five others felt too much to deal with. How had Michael been with her on their walk this afternoon? Had she missed any clues? She couldn't think.

She closed her eyes, imagined her heartbeat becoming regular and calm, concentrated on breathing deeply. Gradually her pulse decreased.

She now pictured herself at a grand piano on a concert hall platform, giving the Schumann her all. Hearing the tumultuous applause afterwards, experiencing the magic of having performed to her best.

In her mind's eye, she reread the fervent reviews of recent concerts. She'd lost count of the number of CDs featuring her performances; of the devotees requesting her recordings. Besides, it was she, not Michael Rezek, who'd been invited to perform the Schumann in Prague. She, who had been asked to teach at the Royal Academy of Music in London; to lecture at the *Nuova Accademia di Belle Arti di Milan*. And here she was, allowing her marriage to define her, to marginalise her professional achievements, and all because she questioned whether or not her husband loved her in the right way.

As she wandered into their private sitting room, she noticed Michael's note: *Gone down to the conservatory to be sociable! See you at dinner.* Not: S*ee you in the conservatory.*

In the bathroom mirror, she studied her sad eyes, the downturned mouth. To her surprise, a determination kicked in. Something she'd often experienced when worrying about whether she'd committed to performing a concerto that was too challenging for her or overpromised in the number of lectures she could give. She had a choice here:

allow the insecurity to devour her or resist its debilitating effect.

She bathed and washed her hair. She dabbed on green eye shadow, coated her eyelashes with mascara and added eye pencil to the straggly parts of her eyebrows. Lastly, she outlined her lips before applying a caramel gloss lipstick.

Reminding herself of situations worse than hers helped bolster her faltering determination to conquer the evening, as she slipped into her new dress. She could be ill. Michael could be ill. She could have lost her ability to play the piano. Or her nerve to perform. And equally important, even more so, Michael had assured her that he hadn't had an affair with Portia. Hope surged through her as she realised that the visit to Lucy could have been prompted by guilt, because he'd paid her so little attention in Brunnen; going on his own feeling more like being an uncle. She must remember this at dinner, if she was struggling.

Preparations almost completed, she studied herself in the mirror. The light tan she'd acquired while here made a difference and helped her confidence. A dab of perfume on her wrists and she was ready. She slid her facial muscles into a smile. An awkward movement, but perhaps this would become easier throughout the evening.

'Wow, you look terrific, lovie,' Annie said as Vienne entered the conservatory.

Madalena approached her, handed her a glass of wine. 'What a beautiful dress, dear. Come and say hallo to Karl.'

Before Vienne could reach Karl, Lawrence was by her side. 'I didn't realise I had such a glam sister. Will you wear this in Prague?'

She shook her head. 'I usually wear black.'

'Too funereal,' he said. 'Change your routine.'

She chatted her way through three courses, smiling

frequently at Madalena to reassure her. She discussed Honegger and Schoeck with Karl. Asked Annie about her plans for taking over the Zurbriggen. She responded to two calls from Charlie, managing full answers. Every time she felt her worry about Michael surface, she suppressed it, reminded herself that she'd always been prone to assuming the worst.

'You seem better this evening,' Madalena remarked at one point. 'Is the practising going well?'

'It's a lovely piano. Thanks for having it tuned. And for giving us the suite.'

Michael hardly talked, Vienne observed, his attention requiring reining in on more than one occasion by a perplexed speaker. He tugged his tie and gazed out of the window. She understood his twitchiness, of course: he knew when she was troubled, wouldn't be deceived by her façade of gaiety. Not that she was prepared to rescue him. She could have smiled at him. She didn't.

Occasionally, she retreated into herself, the surrounding conversations like distant winds; the clattering of knives and forks, tinkle of glass against plate, mimicking orchestral triangles and chimes. Once or twice, she sighted her reflection in the large mirror, surprised to see such a self-assured expression. Silently, she congratulated herself on such a stunning accomplishment, a performance worthy of a BAFTA.

'If you don't mind, I'm going upstairs to practise,' she told Madalena when they were on their second coffee.

'Don't overdo it. You look tired now,' Madalena said. 'Thanks for making the effort to join us. I appreciate it, particularly as Portia and Lucy weren't able to be here.'

As she trudged along the corridor to the stairs, Vienne wondered what would happen in the solitude of their suite, if she'd be able to work on the Schumann. The exertion of behaving normally had exacted its toll. Her facial muscles ached from their forced smiling. Fatigue had crept in.

As she reached the stairs, she came across Ruth and Alice Sowerby on their way to the bar.

'How beautiful you look this evening, doesn't she Alice?' Ruth said.

'Indeed, you do,' Alice agreed.

'I hope that Mr Fotheringham appreciates what a lovely wife he has,' Ruth added.

All Vienne could manage was a smile.

In her room, she stepped out of her pretty dress, slid a zipped plastic bag over it and hung it in the wardrobe, wondering if such care was a positive sign. Indicated an expectation of future occasions, happier times, when she might wear the dress once more. Bask in the praise it attracted. Perhaps Lawrence was right and she should abandon her concert routine of black gowns.

At the dressing table, while removing her makeup, she could taste Johann's chocolate cake, the rich biscuit and mousse mixture outlasting the coffee. Dabbing moist pads against her eyes, she commended herself again, not only for participating in the evening, but acting light and carefree.

She might not have been seated on a piano stool, with the glare of bright lights and a semi-circle of fellow musicians around her, but tonight's efforts had demanded the same energy, an equivalent amount of discipline. There might be no post-concert adrenaline high. Instead, what she had acquired was a resurgence of self-respect. She'd avoided succumbing to anxiety or self-pity.

To her surprise, Vienne heard herself humming as she moved over to the window. From here she could see the illuminated lakeside area of the Hotel Bergmann, a white jacketed waiter carrying a tray to a table. A raucous laugh drifted over the water to her. A cough. She pictured Lawrence packing his suitcase, wondered if Madalena would drive him to the airport or if he'd go by train. She remembered his comment about her glamorous appearance.

What she couldn't quite ignore, however, was that despite several opportunities, Michael hadn't commented on her dress this evening. The only person not to. But if everyone else thought she looked good, he must have, too, surely.....

She lowered herself into the armchair in their sitting room, placed her head on her hands, as the fourth movement of the Schumann coursed through her. She heard the cello's poignant question: could she be with Michael if he didn't love her enough? The violin's answer: it was up to her, what she could live with. The piano interjected, describing the theme – love, its many forms. Then the cello again, so rich, so deep, such quiet insistence: what did she want? Now the French horn was intervening – introducing a different perspective or inciting trouble?

The piano rippled along like a river hastening towards the sea: parental love, sisterly love, the love of a friend. Monogamous love, free love, possessive love. Destructive love. Love generated by fear and loneliness, by admiration and desire.

She was drowning in the piano's gathering momentum. In its tripping, climaxing notes.

The entire orchestra now pushed for an answer. A swell of strings and woodwind, brass and percussion. Her throat constricted as she tried to separate out her thoughts, her feelings, from the music.

She was not the music.

No, she was more than the music.

She sensed rather than heard Michael approaching the room, her heart thudding when he opened the door. His walk, the forward thrust of his right shoulder, conveyed fatigue. He tugged off his shoes and socks. He loosened his tie and pulled it over his head. He flung his trousers on the chair.

When he emerged from his cursory ablutions, she squeezed past him into the bathroom, splashed water on her face and brushed her teeth, joining him in bed minutes later.

They lay in bed, husband and wife of fifteen years – sixteen tomorrow. She could smell her *Agent Provocateur* fragrance. Provocateur? What irony.

'Michael, do you really love me?'

Silence, then: 'Why are you asking this now? Of course I do.'

'Not just as a friend, or a sister?'

'No, numpty. As a wife, a lover. And now could I get some sleep, please? You don't want me to be nodding off on our trip tomorrow.'

As the train chugged its way up the mountain to Rigi, a child bounced up and down on the wooden seat, despite his parents' instructions to sit quietly. Vienne smiled at him. He scowled back.

She turned to Michael. 'We used to do this as children. At least the others did. I'd be listening for the rhythm. They'd tease me.'

'Like the film....'

'*Dancer in the Dark,* yes, exactly,' she said.

The train passed meadowland, fir trees and clusters of chalets. They could hear the tinkle of cowbells from the open window; beneath them the Waldstättersee lay, grey as slate.

'Look, paragliders,' Michael pointed out. 'Perhaps I should have a go sometime.'

'It'll be strange, both my sisters living here again. And us in London. Not that I'd want to move back, despite such beautiful scenery.'

He glanced out of the window again. 'It looks like rain.'

'Not before our picnic, I hope. Would you mind closing the window. There's a draught.'

Walkers with backpacks and hiking poles embarked at Grubisbalm, followed by a chorus of *'gruezi mitenand'* as they joined their friends, segueing into an earnest consultation over maps. A checking of watches. A nodding in consensus.

Michael clasped Vienne's hand as they got off the train.

'Do you want my jacket?' he offered, when they left the station and joined the path.

She shook her head, stopped walking and perched on a boulder. Her body was trembling. 'It's *so* perfect here. And it could have been such a lovely visit home, being with the family, reminiscing about the old days.... Instead–'

He draped his arm round her. His voice was low. 'I love you, Vienne.'

She rested her head on his shoulder.

He stroked her hair. 'I can smell your perfume.'

She turned to face him. 'Michael, why did you go to Luzern on your own, the day we went to Zurich?'

'How do you know about that?' he asked, looking sheepish.

'Lawrence saw you coming out of the Kinderspital. Were you visiting Lucy... or someone else?'

'I wasn't visiting anyone. I popped in to use their loo.'

'You went all the way to Luzern to use the loo!'

'Numpty.... I suppose I might as well tell you. I went to a travel agent.'

Her pulse raced. 'Why?'

'To book a flight to Prague. To be there when you perform. You don't mind, do you? You're so independent....'

'But you could have booked the flight online. Saved yourself a journey.'

Michael hesitated. 'Okay, I might as well confess everything. I was thinking that we should do something special to celebrate our 17th anniversary. Go somewhere exotic. Rio, or the Seychelles. I wouldn't have booked anything here, of course. Better to do it in London.... But I wanted to get an idea of what was available. What do you think?'

This was the sort of comment made by other people's husbands. The sort of thing Vienne had had to tolerate hearing from friends, throughout her sixteen-year marriage. The sort of thing she'd almost resigned herself to never experiencing.

She hesitated. 'You always get angry when I mention the future.'

'People change. Anyway, I'm only talking about next year, not ten years from now!'

Michael then produced a bottle of champagne, uncorked it and poured it into two plastic glasses. He handed one to her, raised his. 'Happy anniversary, darling.'

'I was going to be so adult if you didn't remember our anniversary.'

Silence lapsed as they sipped their drinks.

'After the fire,' he said, 'when we had the horrible row–'

'I don't know what all that was about. Probably the alcohol…. If Portia and Lucy move here, I don't suppose I'll get to know Lucy, not properly. And after all my plans….'

'We'll work something out. What is most important, Vienne, is you and me. We need to work at us.'

She slipped her hand into his. The cloud was so low now they couldn't see the lake below. She was shivering, but inside she felt warm.

23

After leaving Lawrence at Zurich airport, Madalena drove to the Kinderspital in Luzern. To her pleasure, when she entered the room, a beaming Lucy was sitting by the bed.

'Guess what, Granny – I walked on my own earlier. The first time I felt dizzy and had to lie down again, but the second time I was okay. The physiotherapist held on to me at first to make sure I could manage. Then I walked down the corridor on my own.'

'The physiotherapist?'

'I've got exercises for my breathing, to make sure I don't get a lung infection.'

'I see.'

Conscious of Lucy searching her face for reassurance, Madalena retained her composed expression. At close proximity, she could see her granddaughter had lost weight, but her colour was healthy. Furthermore, her eyes sparkled. The pink striped dressing gown highlighted their indigo colour, so like Portia's. So like her own.

'You make sure you do the exercises often, young lady,' she said. 'I'll be keeping an eye on you.'

'Oh, you're so scary.'

Madalena tilted her head. '*Qui, moi?*'

Lucy laughed.

When a nurse arrived to examine Lucy's wound, Madalena stood to leave, but Lucy grabbed her hand. 'Don't go.'

Madalena watched the nurse check Lucy's stomach: its black and purple bruising, the row of stitches, the thin rubber tubes by the operation site.

Lucy groaned. 'It's a mess.'

The nurse looked at Lucy. 'Your stomach feels fine. There's no sign of infection and you can see from the yellow bits that the bruising is fading. I'll remove the tubes later. Are you in pain?'

'Not at the moment.'

'And is your arm all right?'

Lucy nodded.

The nurse studied the chart at the end of the bed. 'Let me know if this changes. Have you filled in a menu for tomorrow?'

'Not yet. I'm starving.'

The nurse smiled. 'You can eat a normal meal from then. I will bring you a menu.'

'Cool. I'm so fed up with gooey stuff.'

When the nurse left, Lucy turned to Madalena. 'I've been on a soft diet, Granny. Do you know what that is?'

Madalena shook her head, despite knowing. She would happily listen to Lucy babbling on all day. In situations like this, being a grandmother was not so far removed from being a mother. The same delight in any improvement: the removal of the nasogastric tube, Lucy's enthusiasm for food, the unaided walking, anything....

'Soup, custard, jelly and loads of porridge. Yuck. What I want is burger and chips and pepperoni pizza. And loads of chocolate.'

Madalena retrieved her notebook from her bag and scribbled down: *burger, chips, pepperoni pizza.* 'I will make sure you have these as soon as you leave hospital. Mum will be delighted to see you so much better.'

'I might be a dietitian when I grow up,' Lucy said.

'A dietitian?'

'One came to visit me. To tell me what I could eat and all that stuff. I think I'd be good at explaining things to people. 'Specially sick people.'

Soon after Portia arrived, Lucy declared she was tired and got into bed, Portia hovering.

'It's all right, Mum, I can manage. Go and talk to Granny on the balcony.'

Madalena reached for her bag. 'Perhaps I should leave now.'

Portia glanced out of the window. 'Don't go yet. We *could* sit on the balcony. It's a lovely day.'

At the far end of the hospital grounds, gardeners were cutting grass, the smell of it wafting up to them. Closer by, they could hear the twittering of birdsong.

'She'll start antibiotics in a few days' time – before she leaves hospital – and she may have to take them every day for several years, in fact, because she's at more risk of developing infections,' Portia told Madalena. '*And* she'll have to carry round a card saying she has no spleen.'

'Nevertheless, in the grand scheme of things....' Madalena said.

Easier to be rational if you were a grandmother. 'How long will Lucy be in hospital for?'

'A few more days. The stitches dissolve on their own so she won't need to have them removed.... Mum, I don't think she'll be fit to fly back for another week, so we might have to stay longer with you, if you're willing to have us. And I wouldn't blame you, not in the slightest, if you're not – after everything that's happened.'

Madalena glanced in at her sleeping granddaughter. 'It is hard being a parent.'

Portia nodded. 'After each stage you think you won't be so anxious about the next one, but you just worry about different things.'

'Portia, forgive me for interfering, but I don't think you should send Lucy to another boarding school. She needs to be with you. Don't make the mistake I made.' She waited and when it was obvious Portia wasn't going to respond, she added, 'This has been quite a visit – for everyone.'

Portia sighed. 'We've truly messed things up, Lucy and me.... I don't know what Karl must think about your family.'

Madalena smoothed back her hair. The time had come: there wouldn't be another more suitable moment. Even if she'd planned to confide in Annie first.

'Portia, there is something I wish to tell you.'

'You haven't broken off your engagement? I do hope you haven't.'

Madalena smiled, conscious of a wave of relief. No one had mentioned the subject since the evening of the fire. 'Obviously Karl isn't easily put off. No, this *is* about me, but–'

'Dear God, you're not ill, are you? Is this why you're retiring?' Portia asked. 'We've all been so focused on ourselves while we've been here.... Tell me you're not ill.'

'If you would let me speak.... This isn't about my physical health, which, as far as I know, is fine. However, as for my emotional health, as I believe it is now known, after your father died, I didn't do so well. To be more precise, I suffered a breakdown. I was in hospital for several months.' She turned to face Portia. 'I am not the strong woman who copes with everything.'

During the ensuing silence, she bit her lip, resisting the urge to reassure Portia she'd been well since then. Determined to overcome this deep-seated need to be considered indomitable.

Portia was staring at the distant chestnut tree. 'This is why you didn't want me visiting then. I'm assuming no one else knows....'

'It's not an easy thing to admit to.'

'When I saw you coming out of the psychiatric hospital–'

'I wasn't visiting Karl. I was attending a therapy session.'

'Mum, what happened? When you became ill?'

'It's hard to explain.... I simply stopped functioning. Everything seemed too difficult, like discussing menus with Johann, even washing my hair....' She stopped, remembering herself curled up on the shower floor, wondering if she had the strength to stand up and turn off the water. She forced herself now to look at Portia, bracing herself for an expression of horror, or worse still, contempt. But her daughter's eyes conveyed only concern, and this gave Madalena the courage to continue. 'One morning, I woke early and couldn't get out of bed.... My legs wouldn't work. Hilde phoned for the doctor. When he visited, he realised there was no physical cause.... I was like a computer crashing or a power cut.... if that makes sense.'

She described what happened next: the psychiatric

assessment and voluntary admission to hospital; her distorted sensations and feeling of numbness; her inability to speak, her twitching limbs; the threat of nasogastric feeding because she couldn't eat. Throughout, Portia listened in silence.

By the time Madalena finished, an hour had elapsed. Lucy was still asleep but the rumble of trolleys, the smell of meat and vegetables, heralded mealtime. Any minute now, a pink uniformed woman would arrive with a tray.

To Madalena's surprise, Portia reached for her hand. 'I'm glad you told me. And please don't take this the wrong way, and I hate to think of what you went through, but in some ways it's a relief to know you're not always strong. It's been so hard to live up to, but I wish I'd known, though – I would have insisted on coming over.'

'Thank you, dear. I intend to tell the others – in time – but–'

'Let me guess.... I was the most difficult one to tell? The intimidating barrister?'

'As I said, it is hard being a parent.'

'This we agree about,' Portia said. 'But I have news for *you*. Lucy and I have more or less decided to move here. The Zurich office has a part-time vacancy. And she will go to a day school.'

Madalena blinked. On the verge of remarrying.... Two daughters and a granddaughter in Brunnen.... How tenanted her life would become. Furthermore, Paris was considerably nearer than Skye, if Lawrence moved there.

She patted Portia's shoulder. 'If this decision has resulted from the events of the last ten days or so, then it's all been worthwhile. I would love to have you so near. But how will Elliot feel? I don't suppose there's any chance you'll get back together?'

Portia shook her head. 'I've a hunch he's met someone else. But I'll make sure he sees more of Lucy from now on. She needs him…'

Madalena drove back to Brunnen via the scenic route, stopping at a roadside stall to buy some honey. How right Doctor Fischer had been about the need to unburden. How right about most things – so far.

'Look how loose my jeans are,' Lucy said, two afternoons later. 'I wish you'd tell me where we're going.'

'Do you want help with the zip?' Portia asked

'I'm not an invalid.'

'But you only have one functioning arm.'

'Stop fussing, Mum.'

Portia studied her daughter. Perhaps her time in hospital had been beneficial, so much enforced rest. And now that she was allowed solid foods, she was eating better.

'I can walk to the car,' Lucy protested, as a nurse brought a wheelchair.

'This is your first proper outing from the hospital,' the nurse said. 'It's important to take things slowly.'

As Lucy nodded compliantly, Portia experienced a mixture of amusement and envy. There was something about the appropriate tone, the appropriate degree of gravitas.

Skills she needed to acquire – out of court.

An hour east of Luzern, at Lucy's request, they stopped at a motorway restaurant. The ever-present odour of diesel dented Portia's appetite and she ate little. By the time she'd managed half of a chicken salad, Lucy had devoured a large plate of lasagne with chips and garlic bread, drunk two cans of coke through a bendy straw, declared she was still ravenous and demolished a banana split with extra cream.

After lunch, to Portia's relief, Lucy fell asleep in the car. The closer to their destination, the more nervous she felt. What if her surprise flopped?

An hour later, Lucy woke up. 'Where are we?'

'Near Zurich.'

'Are you going to wheel me round the city?'

Portia changed gear. 'Certainly not.'

'I'm too tired to walk... I think I ate too much lunch.'

'It was that banana split wat done it, love.'

Lucy laughed. 'Seriously, Mummy, I won't be able to walk far. The physio said–'

'This isn't a sightseeing trip.'

'Are we looking at houses? I thought we were going to find somewhere in Brunnen.'

'We are,' Portia said. 'Going to find somewhere in Brunnen, I mean.'

As she left the main road and followed signs to the airport, she braced herself for more questions. But Lucy was asleep again. She woke as Portia drove into the airport car park.

'We're not flying back to London today, are we, Mum? I'm not ready to go back yet. I've arranged to read to the little kids again tomorrow. And I need to say goodbye to the nurses. And to Granny.'

'Calm down. We're not going home. I wouldn't do this without telling you first.'

'Then why are we here?'

'Be patient, darling, you'll find out very soon.'

Once she'd parked, Portia opened the car boot, retrieved the wheelchair and insisted Lucy use it. In the arrivals lounge, she scrutinised the information board, then the customs exit. Her heart raced. A medium sized man with overgrown hair and wearing baggy shorts stood there. As he noticed Portia, he waved and came over.

She tapped Lucy's shoulder. 'You have a visitor.'

Lucy glanced up from fiddling with her loom band. 'Daddy!'

Portia's eyes welled with tears as Lucy flung herself into Elliot's arms.

Later that week, Madalena leaned over the railing by the waterfront. The grassy whiff of algae was strong this afternoon. In the distance, a mist-covered Gitschen indicated imminent rain, but the boats still ferried passengers from one village to another.

As she stared at the calm, green water, there for her over the decades, she thought about her children. Each had their stories, some of which she knew and understood, some of which she might never know or understand.

Not for the first time, she marvelled at how quickly lives could diverge. Hers included. She and David had stumbled upon the Zurbriggen by chance, his decisiveness leading them along an unexpected route. Their children, it seemed, had inherited the Fontana gene.

Her gaze lingered on the ever-changing light, as she pictured their faces: Lawrence, Portia, Vienne and Annie. She recognised, too, the parallel. The lake reflected the mountains one minute, obscured them the next; sometimes revealing the whole image, sometimes only part. Similarly, her children allowed her intermittent views into their lives: clear for a while, furrowed, then clear again. And this would continue. All she could do was be there for them.

She visualised Vienne, practising hard during the count-down to Prague; Annie preparing to sell her café and cottage. She imagined Lawrence climbing the Cuillins, mulling over whether or not to move to Paris. With Portia, the detail was clearer. Madalena had seen photos of the houses her daughter was visiting today with Lucy and Elliot. This evening would bring a full report.

As for her own future, there was work to be done: a wedding to plan, a home to find. And a wonderful man to whom she could finally give the parts she'd withheld.

As St Teresa's struck five, Madalena told herself it was time to return to the Zurbriggen where Karl would shortly be arriving. She waited until the water steamer left the harbour, its large red wheels turning furiously. Their red colour reminded her she had yet to select a wine for dinner. She smiled and walked away.

THE END

Printed in Great Britain
by Amazon